ROLLING THUNDER

Books by John Varley

THE OPHIUCHI HOTLINE

THE PERSISTENCE OF VISION

PICNIC ON NEARSIDE

(*formerly titled* THE BARBIE MURDERS)

MILLENNIUM

BLUE CHAMPAGNE

STEEL BEACH

THE GOLDEN GLOBE

RED THUNDER

MAMMOTH

RED LIGHTNING

ROLLING THUNDER

THE GAEAN TRILOGY

TITAN

WIZARD

DEMON

THE JOHN VARLEY READER:

THIRTY YEARS OF SHORT FICTION

ROLLING THUNDER

John Varley

ACE BOOKS, NEW YORK

THE BERKLEY PUBLISHING GROUP
Published by the Penguin Group
Penguin Group (USA) Inc.
375 Hudson Street, New York, New York 10014, USA
Penguin Group (Canada), 90 Eglinton Avenue East, Suite 700, Toronto, Ontario M4P 2Y3, Canada
(a division of Pearson Penguin Canada Inc.)
Penguin Books Ltd., 80 Strand, London WC2R 0RL, England
Penguin Group Ireland, 25 St. Stephen's Green, Dublin 2, Ireland (a division of Penguin Books Ltd.)
Penguin Group (Australia), 250 Camberwell Road, Camberwell, Victoria 3124, Australia
(a division of Pearson Australia Group Pty. Ltd.)
Penguin Books India Pvt. Ltd., 11 Community Centre, Panchsheel Park, New Delhi—110 017, India
Penguin Group (NZ), 67 Apollo Drive, Rosedale, North Shore 0632, New Zealand
(a division of Pearson New Zealand Ltd.)
Penguin Books (South Africa) (Pty.) Ltd., 24 Sturdee Avenue, Rosebank, Johannesburg 2196, South Africa

Penguin Books Ltd., Registered Offices: 80 Strand, London WC2R 0RL, England

This is an original publication of The Berkley Publishing Group.

First edition: March 2008

Library of Congress Cataloging-in-Publication Data

Varley, John, 1947 Aug. 9–
Rolling thunder / John Varley.—1st ed.
p. cm.
ISBN 978-0-441-01563-4
1. Young women—Fiction. 2. Mars (Planet)—Fiction. 3. Space colonies—Fiction. I. Title.
PS3572.A724R65 2008
813'.54—dc22

2007046581

PRINTED IN THE UNITED STATES OF AMERICA

10 9 8 7 6 5 4 3 2 1

To Joan Litel,
Francine Glenn,
and Kerry Varley

1

★ ★ ★

ONCE UPON A time there was a Martian named Patricia Kelly Elizabeth Podkayne Strickland-Garcia-Redmond.

Whew! What a mouthful, huh?

That's me, by the way. Six-foot-two, eyes of blue.

Mom and Dad got all whimsical naming me, with the Podkayne business. It was a time of patriotism; everybody was all hot about "Mars for the Martians!" and trying to be more "Martian" than their neighbor. In my high-school graduating class alone there were three John Carters, two Dejah Thorises, a girl named Burroughs, one poor fellow saddled with Edgar Rice, and a Bradbury. The name Podkayne came from a novel from last century that I've never read. I'll get around to it one of these days, but I don't much care for science fiction.

With a name like that, what are you going to do? Everybody called me Poddy growing up. When I reached my pissed-off teenager years I insisted on Patricia, which everyone shortened to Patty. In no time at all it was Poddy again. If I called them on it, they'd just say they'd *said* Patty, and I heard it wrong, and don't blow your bubble, spacegirl.

These days I just go by Podkayne. One word, which will come in handy if I ever make it as a music star:

LT. (JG) PODKAYNE, NMR.

It looked good on the brass nameplate, sitting there on my desk. NMR: That's Navy of the Martian Republic. We're here to protect the solar system.

What I was protecting it from at the moment was one California girl named Glinda. Most of the solar system didn't really need protection from Glinda, but Mars sure did, and since Mars was my home, I took my job seriously. Well, as seriously as I could. With people like Glinda, it was a challenge.

"So, Glinda," I said. "Why do you want to emigrate to Mars?"

She thought that over for a minute. I could tell, because her brows knit fetchingly, which made a pleasant jangling sound. There was enough metal up there to open a hardware store. Finally, she formulated her response.

"Huh?" she said.

I figured it was the three-syllable word that was confusing her.

"Why do you want to leave Earth and go to Mars?"

"Oh. Well, I live to board, you know? I'm real good at it. I heard there was gigawaste snow up there on Mars. Some big mountain?"

That would be Olympus Mons, the tallest mountain in the solar system, and she was right, the snow was waste. Or wasted, or bitchin', or groovy, or cool, or the bee's knees, depending on what era's slang you were slinging.

"So you're a professional snowboarder?"

She nodded enthusiastically.

"I live to board. Like I said."

"No, I mean . . . do you make a living at boarding?" Another blank look. "Are you a boarding instructor?" There were hundreds of winter sports pros making a living on Mars; if she was really, really good, she might make it.

"I don't get it."

"Making a living," I said. "You'll need a job when you get to Mars."

Comprehension dawned, and she smiled.

"Oh, no problem. Mommy and Daddy will pay." Mommy and Daddy? She looked to be about thirty-five.

"I see. Well, Glinda, what you need to do, then, is buy a ticket to Mars. When you get there, apply for a three-month visa. It's renewable for another three months. Then you can come home to Earth."

More jangling of eyebrow hardware.

"But I don't want to come home. I want to go to Mars to stay."

"Well, that's your decision, of course, but if you just want to snowboard when you get there, it's the easiest thing in the world just to buy a ticket, make a reservation at a hotel—there are hundreds of good ones, some right on the slopes, I have a few brochures I can give you—and then if you decide you want to stay, you can make an application for citizenship at the immigration office there." And save me the paperwork, I didn't add.

"No, I want to go to Mars. I want to be a Martian."

Honey, if you stay there a thousand years, you'll never be a Martian. Hell, my father has lived there for over thirty years, and I barely consider *him* a Martian. If you get a residency permit and eventually are allowed to swear allegiance to the Republic and then have a child, *she* will be a Martian, but you never will be. Bottom line, you have to be born there. Otherwise, you'll always be an Earthie or an immigrant.

But I didn't tell her any of that.

"Okay," I said, and opened a drawer in my desk. I pulled out one of the 230-page citizenship application forms and pushed it across the desk at her. "Fill this in," I said.

"What's this?" she said, suspiciously.

"You don't have to do the whole thing right now. The essay questions can wait."

She didn't touch the paper.

"I can't read this," she said, somehow managing to entirely dismiss the idea of literacy in a few words, as though I should be ashamed for even asking. "Give me the verbal version. I prefer that."

"Then I'm sorry, Glinda, but there's no point in going any further."

"What are you talking about?"

"Mars only accepts literates for immigration."

"That's elitist!"

"Whatever." I had lost what patience I had ever had with this girl.

"No way, 'whatever.' I know my rights."

Everybody on Earth knew their rights. People in Western America knew them better than most, even though they didn't actually have as many as they thought they did.

"I'm sorry," I said. *Not!*

"I never heard such bullshit. It's in the . . . laws, and stuff. 'Nobody can't discriminate on the basis of illiteracy.' "

A double negative. "It's your constitution, not mine. This is the Martian Consulate, and we have extraterritorial status. Legally, this is Martian territory."

"I'm not leaving here until you start treating me with respect, and by God you're going to be facing such a lawsuit . . ."

"Actually, you *are* leaving," I said, and stood up. For the first time, she looked a little less than totally self-assured. She was not a tiny woman, not by Earthie standards. Say five-six, five-seven. But women my height are rare on Earth. Standing, I towered over her. It can be intimidating. I hoped she didn't know that, pound for pound, she was twice as strong as I was simply from years of snowboarding and from carrying her own mass around in the depressing gravity of Earth all her life.

She left in a huff. Maybe two huffs.

I'd been on Earth for six of their months, still had six months to go on this assignment, and I was dying from the terrible gravity, from the incredible crowds, from twits like Glinda, and from a bad case of homesickness. I was beginning to think it might be terminal. I wanted to go home.

Waaaaah! Mommy, I wanna go *home*!

Well, brace up, spacegirl. You have a job to do. It may be a stupid job and you sure didn't ask for it, but there it is. You're a Martian. Start acting like one.

I checked the clock and saw it was 3:13 P.M. Official closing time of the office was 5:00 P.M. Close enough. There was a sign on the outer door that I'd had made shortly after I arrived at my job in Western America. It said:

MARTIAN CONSULATE OF CENTRAL CALIFORNIA
THE CONSUL IS IN

I flipped the card from IN to OUT and locked the door. "Consul" was one of my many titles at the Consulate. I was also the Chief Recruitment Officer, the Artistic Liaison, the Cultural Ambassador, the Director of

Public Relations, and the resident spy. (Sssh! Don't tell anyone!) I adopted these titles when and where it suited me. In addition, I was the secretary, the interior decorator, the hostess, the cook, driver, chief pilot, laundress, dishwasher, and janitor. If the Consulate needed a mime or a clown, I could be those, too. I took the back door from my storefront office and the elevator to the Consular Residence, which was three rooms on the fifteenth and top floor of the Baker Building, Pomeroy Avenue, Pismo Beach, California, Western America.

I stripped off my fatigues—the hideous rust-and-pink baggy shirt and pants I was required to wear when on duty and best not described in too much detail lest one lose one's lunch—and applied SPF 45 sunscreen from my hairline to my toenails. Then I put on the little scraps of cellophane and dental floss Earthies require you to wear for modesty's sake, and an oversized aloha shirt that screamed with bright-colored racing cars and surfboards.

I hit Pomeroy Street and it hit me right back, with a blast of air in the high nineties. There wasn't as much of Pomeroy left to hit as there had been fifty years ago. Surf now crashed about four blocks inland of where it had at the turn of the century. This was due to what the Heartlanders called the "temporary global climate fluctuation."

The old wooden pier was sheltered by a fairly new breakwater, made from demolished buildings. There were only a few watercraft tied up in the slips. My ride, *Rosinante,* was not quite a boat and not quite a Jet Ski. She was a sort of trimaran, broad and stable. She had won my heart as soon as I saw her nested in morning-glory vines in an Arroyo Grande backyard. I boarded and kicked the old engine into life.

THE SKY WAS vast, the ocean was vast, the horizon was far, far away, much farther than it could ever be on Mars. It felt like, on a really clear day, you could see Japan. The sea was calm, long, slow rollers about three feet high, and *Rosinante* ate them up with hardly a bounce, which was why I preferred her over a conventional ski.

The sunshine was glorious! Of course, it could burn you raw, but I was covered with enough sunscreen to deflect a blowtorch, and if you spent your time thinking of what a hostile environment the Earth was becoming, you wouldn't go out at all. When I got back to Mars I'd have the only souvenir of Earth that ever impressed any Martian: a tan you just couldn't get under UV lamps.

I called up my karaoke program and flicked through the thousands of accompaniments stored there, then clicked on "Born to Be Wild," written by somebody with the delightful name of Mars Bonfire, first recorded by Steppenwolf. I fed it to *Rosinante*'s music system, and soon the sounds of heavy metal thunder were blasting out of the speakers, lead vocal by yours truly.

I followed it with "Give Me Another Reason," a Tracy Chapman hit from the thirties, then switched to Gilbert and Sullivan's "Poor Wand'ring One," from *The Pirates of Penzance*.

Taking a deep breath, I launched into Musetta's aria, *"Quando me'n vo soletta per la via,"* from *La Bohème*. It was a stretch for me. I have an extra octave available to me on top of my normal contralto, like Julie Andrews had; I can be a mezzo-soprano if I work at it, but I don't usually try it in public. Here, nobody but the great white sharks would be offended.

To cool down I swung into *"L'amour est un oiseau rebelle que nul ne peut apprivoiser,"* the famous habanera from *Carmen*. I was grinning broadly. From John Kay to Tracy, to Mabel, to Musetta, to Carmen. Quite a musical evolution for one morning.

I dropped a sea anchor and did a quick visual inspection of my hide, looking for patches of lobster red. I suppose a blonde really has no business exposing her pearly white skin to the lethal rays of Sol from a distance of only ninety million miles or so, but the sunshine was the only thing about Earth I liked. So I risked radiation burns, but carefully. I took off my big hat, and the shirt, and the bikini, and stretched out on *Rosinante*'s postage-stamp deck.

Two minutes later, my phone rang.

I said, "Accept call."

A man in Navy uniform appeared floating above the sea. The ident line below his face named him Captain J. K. Carruthers, CID, WAM, MD. That meant Commander, Immigration Division, West America Region, Martian Delegation.

"Lieutenant Strickland, how are you?"

"Fine, sir." *Until you called.*

"Ah . . . it seems your grandmother is ill."

"Grandma Kelly?" I asked. I only had one living grandmother, but I had to say something, or I felt I'd stop breathing.

"Pardon me?" He was frowning. "Oh, I see now. This says Garcia—"

"Granddaddy? What's happened to Granddaddy?"

"If you'll let me finish. Apparently it's your great-grandmother."

"Gran?" I squeaked.

"Here, I'll forward the message to you."

Dad's face replaced the captain's.

"Honey, I might as well get right to the bad news. Granny Betty is very ill. It seems to be some new variant of the autoimmune disorders, and the doctors say they can't do anything about it."

He paused, then tossed his hair back in a gesture that was very familiar to me. He looked exactly like what he was: Ray Strickland-Garcia, Ph.D., an academic, a history professor at the university, probably the foremost authority on the colonization of space. Disheveled, a bit absentminded, usually up to his eyeballs in downloads of forgotten files playing on his old-fashioned external stereo.

"They can't tell us exactly how long she might live, but it's a matter of weeks. A month at the most. She has elected to go into time suspension. She wants to see the whole family before she does this, and since you are the only one so distant right now, she insists she'll take the chance and wait until you can get here. Your grandmother has secured you a thirty-day compassionate leave, so I hope you'll lose no time."

"Of *course* I'll hurry, Dad," I said, uselessly. Even if he was still on the line, it would be quite a while before my words could have reached him on Mars. I found myself trying to twist the *Rosinante*'s accelerator even more, but she was already going flat out.

"Your mother sends her love. I . . . I love you, too. Hurry home."

I was already consulting the train schedules while I pulled *Rosinante* into her slip at the dock and hit the ground running. I ran as fast as the relentless gravity would allow, up Pomeroy toward my apartment. With the heat of the day waning, there were a few people here and there on the street, and I got a few stares. Actually, more than a few. It wasn't until I was getting into the elevator that I realized I had forgotten to put my bathing suit back on.

Earthies, you are so weird. I hope you enjoyed the show.

WHEN I BOARDED the maglev for Los Angeles a few minutes later, everyone on the train turned to stare at me. Not all at once, but as I moved down the car I created a wave of turning eyeballs. This time it wasn't because of showing too much skin, nor was it my stunning beauty, nor my height. (I lied about the six-foot-two business; I'm six-four. As for the beauty, I'm not Miss Red Planet, but the face doesn't stop clocks and the body is within acceptable parameters.) No, this time it was the uniform.

Mars is the Red Planet, right? So our flag, our spaceships, and pretty much everything else associated with government just has to be red. If you want my opinion, I'd tell you that the human eye can distinguish millions of shades, and there's no crime in using one of them that doesn't fall into the short end of the spectrum now and then.

That's not the problem. I can *wear* red, I look *good* in red, with my blond hair and fair complexion. The little red beret in particular is quite fetching on me. But whatever you call it, the uniform is *bright* and *loud*. Those are two things I prefer not to be when I go out in public on Earth.

See, a lot of Earthies don't like us very much.

So there I was in full-dress ceremonial uniform, two inches taller in my shiny black boots, a great leggy cardinal if you're being charitable, a grotesque gawky flamingo if you're not, moving down a row of people whose glances varied from freak-show interest to glaring dislike. Orders were that we were to "show the flag" when traveling. I wish whoever had written that policy was on the train with me as I tried to make myself small. Showing the flag is one thing. *Wearing* it is beyond the call of duty.

I found an empty seat and tried to lift the small bag I'd packed into the overhead rack. It didn't contain much, just stuff I'd tossed in that I couldn't do without and a couple changes of clothes. Even so, the Earth gravity defeated me on the first try. A guy in the seat in front of me jumped up to help. I had a good seven inches on him, but he tossed the bag into the rack easily, then wanted to sit beside me. I cooled him off politely. As soon as I was settled, two college guys from Cal Poly tried hitting on me, and I frosted them with a gaze I'd been working on in the mirror. It also didn't hurt when I shifted a bit to bring my sidearm more prominently into view. That was also policy: *Never appear in uniform without your weapon.* Nothing like a loaded Glock in a leather holster to put a little respect into overeager frat boys.

IT WAS THE express train, so we stopped only in Santa Barbara and Ventura and some dreadful place in the San Fernando Valley before pulling into the downtown transit center in the City of Angels.

The Transit Center is vast, and underground. I had no trouble finding the right platform, having lived most of my life without exterior reference points, but by the time I made it there I was wishing I'd swallowed my pride and taken the handicapped tram. My boots were pinching my toes, and the gravity threatened to collapse my arches.

Soon I was on the nonstop maglev to the Area 51 spaceport, and for the first time I saw some other red uniforms. I felt like a dying woman staggering out of the desert to an oasis as I joined them, two girls and a guy, all jaygees like me, and we spent the short trip exchanging Earth horror stories. When they found out I was going Up and Out . . . *going home!* . . . they tried their best to conceal their envy—after all, it was compassionate leave, someone in my family was in trouble—but couldn't quite do it. We traded horror stories about Earthies until the train pulled in at the port. Then we went our separate ways, and I never saw any of them again.

I found my way to the departure gate for the connector bus to the Martian Navy base ten miles away from the port. I was the only one waiting at the boarding gate, and when the bus came, I was the only one to board. Five minutes later I was zipping through the Nevada desert, stretched out across two hard seats. I watched a landscape roll past that most Earthies would probably call barren, desolate. Hell, I could see hundreds of yucca trees, sagebrush, a dozen kinds of cactus, even some tiny little flowers hugging the ground. A jackrabbit darted for cover as the bus cruised by. Barren? The place was a tropical rain forest, teeming with life, compared to my home planet.

Marsport 6 was just a big flat place in the desert, with half a dozen prefab metal buildings lined up along the edge. Functional, unadorned, Navy red. A Martian flag hung listlessly in the still air. Nothing moved. Nobody with any sense would be outdoors with the rattlesnakes and the tarantulas and the blistering heat. Most work around here was done at night, when the temperature sometimes dropped as low as ninety.

As the bus pulled up to the headquarters building I counted three bucket ships sitting in the distance, also painted Navy red, but not recently. They were pink and patchy, like they had a skin disease.

The bus stopped and I got out, ready to hurry into the main building, but I was stopped by a loud roar. I looked behind me and saw one of the buckets rising on a pillar of white smoke. I'd missed the last bucket of the day by five minutes.

Why do they call them bucket ships? They *looked* sort of like buckets. Just squat cylinders, wider than they were tall, with two rows of windows in a circle showing where the two decks were. A dome on top for the pilot to sit in, a metal cat's cradle underneath to hold the bubble drive. Three landing legs, nonretractable.

With the ship dwindling at the end of a long vapor trail, the only sound now was the thrumming of the big air-conditioning units sitting by the prefabs. I realized I was dripping sweat, standing out in the desert with no sunscreen and a fractured ozone layer high above me. I hurried into the main building.

The staff confirmed that there would be no more departures until

0800 hours tomorrow, when I had a chance of making the 1200 sailing of the MNS *Rodger Young*.

I asked if there were any rooms in the Motel 6 and they said take your pick, so I trudged down a hallway to the first open door, room 101. I didn't even have the strength to toss my bag on the dresser. I let it drop to the floor and collapsed on the bed. I just wanted to sleep for a few hours, but I knew there was something I had to do first.

I had three messages from Mars in my call-waiting queue. None of them were flagged red, which may sound odd given the emergency nature of my trip, but why should they be red-flagged? You don't have a conversation with people on Mars, you have a correspondence. Right then, as I was lying there, my home was 190 million miles . . . thataway. Ahead of the Earth, which was catching up. That meant that any phone call I made wouldn't arrive at home for seventeen minutes, and there could be no reply for another seventeen. Still, I felt a little guilty at not even having looked at the messages. So I clicked the first one. It was from Mom. She started right in.

"We hated to just drop this whole mess on you so suddenly, Poddy, but there really is no time to lose. Gran is very sick. The doctors think she can hold out until you get here, but it might be a close thing. So . . . I know there's no way to hurry a ship, I know you'll do all you can do to get here in time . . ."

She stopped, and took a deep breath.

"That's what the family has decided, anyway. Mostly Kelly, of course. This is for your ears only, from your mother who loves you, from me to you.

"If you don't want to come . . . don't come. When you think about it, what's the difference? She's not going to die, not now, anyway, and I suggested that they stop her and then, next time you're here, they can take her out for ten minutes or an hour or whatever she wants, and you can say what you need to say then.

"Oh, I don't know what I'm saying, this has been a surprise to me, too, and some angry things have been said. But I wanted you to know that if you'd rather not be dashing about for no good reason, I'll support you all the way. That's all I have to say. Good-bye, Poddy sweet. I love you."

Well. I found it tough to sort all that out at once.

For one thing, Mom visits an entirely different Earth than I do. I'm Mars-born. I'm tall and slender, and a simple walk in the park makes my feet hurt and my back ache. Mom still loves the Earth. She was born here, and she and Dad make a pilgrimage back every year, at first going to Florida to try and help out; later, when things deteriorated too much in the Zone, they went to California or Mexico or Rio or anyplace with a beach. They love the wind and the blue sky and the forests and . . . just about anything about the Earth except the people, who almost no one on Mars can abide. She keeps herself in shape, so after the first few days, she doesn't even mind the gravity.

So she thought she was doing me a favor by giving me an out, a reason not to abandon my long summer vacation on the world of melting ice caps.

Oh, Mom, I love you, but sometimes you haven't got a clue.

Then there were the "family discussions," and the "angry words." That would be Kelly, of course. Kelly "Don't call me Grandma!" Strickland. You may have heard of her. First president of Mars? Ring any bells?

I love Kelly, too . . . in my own way. I don't think anyone loves Kelly in quite the way they love anyone else, except Grandpa Manny.

Being the granddaughter of a former president of Mars is not quite the deal it would be if my grandma was, say, ex-president of Western America. We're small potatoes, nation-wise, except for the power thing and the Navy thing. There's not even a million of us; big-city mayors down here on Earth have more responsibility, in some ways. Of course, they don't have the means to cut off the power to Earth's billions . . .

Grandma Kelly tends to take over any situation she finds herself in, and that can include her daughter-in-law's life. They'd locked horns more than a few times.

But Mom is no wimp, and Dad backs her up one hundred percent, and if it comes to it, Grandpa Manny will have a word with Kelly, and that'll be the end of that. So I appreciated the gesture on Mom's part, but frankly, I'd have gladly abandoned my post at Pismo on a much flimsier excuse. It's not as if the ravening barbarian hordes of the Zone or the Christian Armies of the Heartland were just looking for the opportunity of Podkayne being away from her desk to establish a beachhead in the holy war against Redboy Hegemony.

I recorded a telegraphic "message-received" thing: *Doing everything possible, expect departure oh eight hundred hours, rendezvous* Rodger Young, *ETA Deimos Base such-and-such a date, over and out. PS, I love you.* Not much, I know, but a lot better than my last message: *Earth price$ are ridiculou$! $end money!*

Next message. A tough one.

She began the way she always does.

"I hate talking this way. I don't know why they don't do something about this time lag thing." Gran wasn't stupid, she knew there was nothing to be done to speed up radio signals, but she would never be comfortable with the time lag, even if she were around for another ninety years . . . which she might very well be, as I had to keep telling myself.

She still didn't look her ninety-three years. There were good effects of her almost twenty years on Mars, some of which slow the aging process. Some put you at risk for problems the human body wasn't evolved to encounter. Wrinkles form a lot slower, but you may need to have your arteries nanorooted every two years instead of every five.

Gran didn't look ancient. She looked sort of translucent, like her skin was wax and there was a candle inside her that was slowly melting her away. Her hair was thin. If I'd had to guess her age, I'd have said a young seventy.

"Poddy, dear, the first thing is, I don't want you to worry. If you want to come, then come. If you don't, then I'll understand that, too. It's not like it's that big a deal. I'll see you again. The only question is, how old will you be when I see you? When you see me again, whenever that is, I'll be just like this. A rag, a bone, and a hank of hair, but still full of enough piss and vinegar to keep me going for another week.

"I'm not in any pain. My immune system is shot to hell, they tell me, but they've cleaned me up like an old Ford getting ready for a Sunday drive, so I'm not likely to pick up any bugs. Mostly what I am is tired. Can't seem to gather any energy, even in this wimpy stuff you call gravity up here. Walking from the bed to the toilet is like going up ten flights of stairs . . . but listen to me. One thing I swore was I'd never turn into that kind of old woman who can't talk about anything but her symptoms.

"I don't know much about what this is that's fixin' to punch my ticket. I gather they didn't even have it when I was young. Poddy, I think it's just old age, and I think when they tell me they figure they can cure it eventually, they're full of shit.

"But maybe they aren't, and what's rolling the dice gonna cost me? I think the world—the one you're on—is swirling around the toilet bowl, and I don't much care whether I live to see the final flush or not. But for a chance to spend some more time with my family . . . hell, maybe for the chance to see *your* grandkids . . . I think I'll give it a shot. Maybe they'll uncork me just in time for us all to bend over and kiss our asses good-bye . . . but at least I'll have that.

"Hope you don't think I'm a silly old woman. Don't bother to call back. I'll see you when I see you. Love you, dear. Bye."

I wiped away a tear and blew my nose. I *knew* it was the wise thing to wait for some privacy to see this stuff.

So . . . heard from Mom, heard from Gran. The next message should have been from Grandma Kelly, organizing every detail of my trip from Pismo to her front door.

But it wasn't. I ticked the last blinking message light in my field of vision, and there was my favorite little brother, Mike. Also my only little brother, or sibling of any sort, but even if I had others he'd probably be my favorite. He came into my life when I was ten.

"Hey, Pod-breath," he said, getting the mandatory insult out of the way, but his heart wasn't in it. He's just learning to mask his feelings like growing little boys seem to feel they should, but he couldn't hide anything from me. Still, he soldiered on.

"Thought you were rid of me, didn't you?" he said. "Thought you'd escaped to the balmy shores of Pismo Beach. Never hear from you. Are you too busy saving Mars from the Earthie hordes? I don't know what we'd do back here at home without girls like you guarding the gateways, Pod, but I want you to know we all appreciate it."

A short silence, then a sigh.

"Enough of that. I don't know why I called you, I can't think of anything to say and you're probably real busy right now . . . but I was just feeling really sad." There was a catch in his breath, and he looked away for a moment. Ten-year-old boys want so desperately to act like grown-ups, especially if they're very, very smart.

"So hurry home. Goose those rocket jockeys and tell 'em to boost two gees all the way, okay? You've been down there long enough, you must be muscle-bound enough to take it. You probably look like Mr. Western America by now. And if you don't, you aren't working hard enough. Anyway, see you soon."

I blinked REPLY and smiled for the camera.

"Hell, peewee, I've got enough muscles in my eyebrows now to throw your flabby little ass right over Marinaris. And if I need any help I'll just ask one of the bronzed beach boys I'm bringing back with me as pets to lend a hand. Have to beat them off with a stick every time I go to the beach. I have a wonderful tan; I'm going to be the envy of every girl on Mars, just like I already am the envy of all the little Earth girls."

I paused. Did I dare depart from the kind of banter we usually exchanged? Would that just worry him more? Tell the truth, my heart hadn't been in the last bit of nonsense, but he was so far away, and he sounded like he needed me, and there wasn't a damn thing I could do about it. You can't hug with a thirty-four-minute time lag.

"You hang in there, Mike," I said. "Take care of everyone until I get there. I know you can do it. Over and out."

Then I cried for a little bit.

MY GOOGLE TELLS me that a Motel 6 was a budget chain that, when it got started, offered you a reasonably clean room for six US dollars. Navy people don't pay for the rooms, they're free, a bonus of your mandatory enlistment and just about worth the price. Our Motel 6 had tiny slivers of soap in plain wrappers, one-piece toilets that gurgled and splashed when flushed, and shower stalls barely high enough for a girl to stand erect in and narrow enough to skin your elbows when you turned around.

I took a tepid shower after first almost scorching myself when one of the handles came off in my hand. I could feel the Pismo salt and sand washing down my body and into the drain. Then I dried off, more or less, with the table napkin provided for that purpose, wound my damp hair up in a bun on top of my head, and gathered up my uniform. I took it all down to the desk and handed it to the duty officer along with a plea to have it cleaned and pressed by 0600, as it was the only dress uniform I had. He looked me up and down.

"You want some company?" he asked.

"Is this sexual harassment?"

"Just an offer. Lonely out here all night long." So I looked *him* up and down, and thought I might have been interested at another time, except for him being about ten years older than me and a career officer, but I shook my head and went back to my room.

The mattress was about the same quality as the rest of the accommodations, but then no mattress on Earth would be comfortable for me. I dragged this one onto the floor, which evened out the lumps a little, and sprawled out on it, on my back. My heels touched the floor. I moved up a little, and my head hung over the edge. They bought this stuff on Earth to save money, and it was all Earthie-sized. I got as comfortable as I could on the various gym equipment that seemed to have been stored in the ticking and figured I'd be asleep in five minutes. Hell, I was so tired I thought I could fall asleep on spikes.

And I did.

3

I WOKE WITH a bad gravity hangover. There's no way explain it to someone from Earth. I don't drink; it has nothing to do with alcohol. It's the curse of the Mars-born. We just never completely adjust to one gee. Unless I get a nap in the afternoon, take an opportunity to rest my legs and back several times a day, and spend an hour in carefully controlled exercise—swimming is about the only thing that doesn't just about kill me—I wake up the next morning with a splitting headache, feeling like I've been worked over with a length of steel pipe.

I gobbled aspirin, not that I had much hope they would help, tried to make myself presentable in the tiny bathroom, surveyed the result in the steamed mirror, and wondered how Earthies did it. If this is what six months in one gee did to a girl with good skin, nice muscle tone, to-die-for cheekbones, clear blue eyes, and okay breasts, what would I look like in ten years? My eyes were more red than blue. Were those brown bags under my eyes, or garden slugs? And could that be the beginning of . . . *jowls*?

I had to get out of this horrible place. It was crippling me!

My uniform was hanging on the door, looking brand-new. Dressed and somewhat resembling a human being, I found my way to the commissary for a triple jolt of coffee. Say what you will about the Navy, one thing they do well is coffee. Always steaming hot, never prissied up with all the additives Earthies like to contaminate it with, and strong enough to bench-press two full-grown Martians a dozen times. I could practically feel my eyelids tightening.

Breakfast is another thing the Navy does reasonably well, though I'd advise you to stay away from the eggs. I stacked pancakes and drowned them in butter and syrup and finally began to feel something approaching okay as I sopped up the last of the mess and went looking for a place to wash my face. The girl that stared back at me in the mirror looked a little less like an internee in a concentration camp, but still not the perky Podster I had grown up with. I hoped to find that girl in free fall. That's where I had left her.

"WHAT DO YOU *mean,* no bucket today?"

Okay, people can ask some pretty stupid questions when they're blindsided and frustrated. Even me. The duty officer just stared at me, as her meaning had been pretty clear. What part of N-O don't you understand, Podkayne?

I tried again.

"*Why* is there no bucket today?"

"The pilot broke his leg last night," she said. "He's still in the hospital, and I don't have anyone to spare."

"I could fly it with a broken leg. I could fly it with two broken legs."

"You're rated?"

I dug out my card and she plugged it in and scanned the information.

"Flying since you were six, huh?" I had moved up a few levels in her estimation. I don't really know why. It's not like flying a spaceship is hard, not like an airplane—which I learned to do first, by the way—but it's surprising how many Martians never bother to put in the hours you need to be certified.

"It's in my genes, I guess," I said. "My grandfather flew the first spaceship to Mars." Ordinarily I don't bring up my family history. You get tired of hearing "You're *that* Strickland-Garcia?" I hope to make my own mark on the world and not rely on my ancestors' achievements. I try to keep the lies to what is socially necessary to avoid embarrassment and friction, too, and that part about Granddad flying the *Red Thunder* was not technically true, in the strictest sense. But when the situation requires it . . .

"Well, Lieutenant, if you want to take her up, I got no problem with that."

THE FORMALITIES TOOK three minutes, and then I was outside in the smothering heat doing my walkaround.

It was a little daunting. I knew this ugly tub had been ferrying people back and forth from the desert to orbit since before I was born . . . which, come to think of it, had an upside and a downside. The bucket ships were reliable. As far as I knew, none had ever crashed except for a few incidents in horrible weather when landing struts had collapsed. The springs looked good. I checked the cradle holding the propulsion bubble for stress cracks, and eyeballed the mysterious web of titanium interrupters that would, in some way I didn't understand, release the almost unlimited energies inside the bubble in a controlled thrust. It all looked okay.

I opened inspection panels and examined the main gyro, the backup, and the backup to the backup.

That was basically it. No airfoils to test, no fuel level to check. I stood back and craned my neck up at it and didn't see any obvious cracks in the windows. My first Navy command, known only as Ferry 563, could desperately use a wash and a new paint job, but she'd get me off the ground.

I waved to my passengers waiting back at the dusty little shuttle bus. They joined me, a symphony in crimson, and I told them they could get aboard. There were four men and one woman, all outranking me according to the fruit salad on their sleeves and shoulder boards. One was a rear admiral. Suddenly this didn't seem as much fun as it had a few minutes ago. Nobody wants big brass looking over her shoulder.

There were ten seats on the lower deck and ten seats on the upper. Everybody was in the basement, and I glanced at them to be sure they were buckling up. I didn't much want to be the one to tell an admiral he had to strap in.

I made my way to the bridge and settled into the command chair, which, like the whole ship, had seen better days. One of the seams was sprung and a bit of cotton fluff peeked out. I powered up the systems and watched the indicators appear on the window in front of me as the ship performed a self-diagnosis. Oxygen tanks full. Pressurization system nominal. Radar okay. I activated the PA.

"Ah, this is . . ." I bogged down for a moment. Protocol said that, since I was flying this tub, I was the captain. The word stuck in my throat for a moment. Then I thought it over and smiled. *My first command!*

"This is the captain," I said, thankful that my voice didn't squeak. "Everybody hang on to your socks. We're outta here."

I eased the stick forward and heard the low rumble from below. A vast cloud of dust rose all around me. I moved it forward some more, and the exhaust sound grew louder. Under the ship, grains of sand would be melting into black glass. The contact lights went off for each of the landing legs, and I felt a little pressure pushing me back into my seat. All systems were go at one point two gees, and we started to climb out of the blast cloud.

One point five gees. One point seven. Two gees. I leveled the thrust out there, and settled back into the cushions.

I took my nameless ship straight up for eight miles, out of a lot of atmosphere, before vectoring the thrust to bring us into a forty-five-degree angle of pitch. Then I rotated the ship so I could look up at an ever-increasing slice of North America on my way into orbit.

To the naked eye it didn't look a lot different than it would have a century ago. The air was now cleaner. They say that at the turn of the century there could be smog from coast to coast, some days. Today was crystal clear, only a few bands of clouds here and there, much like it must have been in 1950. Back then they were only getting started on the Interstate highway system, which ended up crisscrossing the entire country with ribbons of concrete and—get this—*individually piloted vehicles*! Everybody moving at seventy miles per hour or more, rain, snow, or darkness, and no central control. The carnage was incredible. Now those routes were the basis of the electric rail system. At night they'd light up like a vast jeweled spiderweb. It's pretty. But by day you can barely see them. We were passing over the Rocky Mountains now, heading for the Great Plains. Over the bits of what once was the United States of America.

No more. The Big Wave had changed all that.

DURING THE GREAT Diaspora, when just about any country or even a wealthy group of people such as a corporation or church could build a starship, a bunch of fanatics hollowed out a small asteroid and set off for a nearby star. To this day no one knows for certain who it was, though there are three leading contenders, and each group has its advocates, so to speak. But there's always the chance that any of these three groups may one day show up, listen to the story in shock and horror, and say, "Who? *Us?*" There's no way to know, but we do know that at least two of these groups are totally innocent of atrocity.

Whoever they were, these people realized the godlike power inherent in a large ship moving at very high speed, something that a handful of alarmists had pointed out early in the bubble-drive era, but not early enough to make a difference.

Whoever they were, they'd had no regard for human life, their own or anyone else's.

Whoever they were, they took their ship, their Death Star as many people now called it, and boosted it away from the sun for many years, then boosted again to slow it down. Once stopped, they boosted again, and just kept on going, heading straight for the Earth.

They were nudging the speed of light when they got here, which made them impossible to detect; any radar echo warning of their coming would arrive only fractions of a second before the ship itself. So there was no way to stop them.

But navigation at near-light speed presented them with some difficulties of their own, and it seems there was no one aboard who was really up to the problem. Due to relativity, time had slowed to a crawl for them. They would have experienced a journey from the orbit of Pluto to Earth, for instance, in only seconds.

It was apparently too much of a problem even for the ship's computers. A single message was sent out, which was blue-shifted to the point that we almost missed it. It said, "Death to."

That was it. *Death to.*

We'll never be sure who they wished death to, though a strong case has been made that the impact point they were seeking was Washington, D.C. They came within a hair of missing the planet entirely, but close can count in things other than horseshoes. The Death Star grazed the planet, dipping into the atmosphere and then the Atlantic Ocean, before blazing off into space again in the form of superhot plasma. The collision created the largest tsunami in recorded history.

That wave killed somewhere between three and four million people. We will never have exact figures, as many were buried in mud and many more were swept out to sea. The islands of the Caribbean, the Bahamas, and the Eastern Seaboard of the United States from Florida to Cape Cod were all devastated. Among the hardest hit areas was the central Florida coast, where my great-grandmother, Betty Garcia, owned and operated the Blast-Off Motel.

She survived, and went to Mars to live with her family, and now I was going home because she was dying.

THE BIG WAVE was the biggest catastrophe other than war ever to hit humanity. It accomplished what the American Civil War had not: It shattered the Union.

Civil order in the Red Zone broke down quickly. Martial law was declared, and over several years, the country began to break apart. There was starvation and riots, and political chaos. Washington was a sewer, knee-deep in mud and rotting bodies. Competing governments were established in Chicago and in New York, which was north of the area of total devastation, and later in Los Angeles. A decade of civil wars, secessions, religious fanaticism, and sheer terrorism finally settled into the uneasy borders I could now see crawling below me on my visual political overlay.

We were just passing over the boundary of Western America, which includes the former states of California and Arizona, most of Washington and Oregon, and much of Nevada and New Mexico. Up to the north was the Free State of Idaho, a continuing war zone largely taken over by Pure White Christians. The wall the Canadians had been forced to put up was too far north for me to see. We passed quickly over the Mormon State of Deseret and soon were looking down on the vast expanse of

Heartland America, with parts of the Second Republic of Texas visible to the south.

I suppressed a shudder. There were worse postings than Western America.

There were eight splinter nations that used to form the United States of America, and three of those had an official state religion. In Heartland America it was an uncompromising form of Christianity I wouldn't wish on a dog. I didn't even like flying over the place, but it stretched from eastern Montana to the parts of Florida outside the Red Zone, and north to the Truce Line that bisected the former states of Illinois, Indiana, and Ohio.

Over the northern horizon would be East America, hugging the Great Lakes, from Minnesota to New York, reaching up to Maine and south to Maryland.

North America had been chaotic for years, and was only now mostly settled down. There had been mass migrations of whole classes of people who no longer felt welcome in their home regions, and some who were actually in grave danger. The worst was in Idaho, where thousands of people had vanished in a few bloody White Purity weeks. Elsewhere, Blues had moved to the coasts, Reds had moved to the middle, and everybody who could sneak out before the DMZ was established had fled from the Red Zone, which extended from Florida to Chesapeake Bay.

Washington was inhabited again, and north of that things were as close to back to normal as they would ever be. But to the south, up to fifty miles from the ocean that had turned from friend to mass killer in only a few hours, there was very little civilization.

Now the land was going, too. If you knew just what you were looking for, you could see it with the naked eye, in the former barrier islands now awash in seawater after half a century of global warming. Florida was a lot skinnier than it had been. The Gulf Coast towns had been crawling inland and northward for decades now as block after block, street after street, the waters advanced, and people built anew on what had been the edges of the city. New Orleans was gone.

In the Pacific, El Niño, the little boy, had become a teenager with a severe attitude problem. Melted Antarctic ice had resulted in local cooling and sinking of waters that meant the seasonal streams seldom reached where they used to. Fisheries had died out or moved, devastating the economies of western South America. Air temperatures and wind patterns had changed, resulting in an average yearly increase of up to fifteen degrees, regionally, as far north as Oregon. Pismo Beach, that furnace I'd recently escaped, used to be pleasant, or so I'm told. Now it sweltered in the summer, with even worse temperatures inland.

The parts of the Amazon rain forest that had not already been cut down withered and died when the rains didn't come.

Category 5 Atlantic hurricanes now hit the Atlantic and Gulf coasts at the rate of four or five a year. Pacific typhoons were even worse, and there were a lot more of them. Japan was hit by climatic Godzillas several times a year.

Sea level had increased twenty feet since my grandparents' day. Twenty feet wasn't much in Pismo Beach, where the land rises rapidly from the sea. But in the Ganges delta, along the Mississippi and the Amazon, and in countless floodplains around the world, the teeming populations had been relocated at great expense, and over a billion people lived in temporary camps now twenty years old and more. Much of Earth's most fertile land was now under salt water.

Then there was the tundra. Melting ice was one thing; it raised sea levels and disrupted ocean currents and weather patterns. But in Siberia and Alaska and Canada there had been millions of square miles of tundra, frozen ground. It was frozen no longer. Most of it was melted now, which sounds like a good idea, except all that tundra held billions of tons of carbon dioxide and methane.

Populations, human and animal, had shifted north and south to cooler climes. Thousands of species had gone extinct in the last decades, and many of the larger African mammals now survived only in big reserves in North America and Asia.

Poor old Planet Earth.

On the other hand, it's an ill wind indeed that blows no good. The Amazon and Indonesian and Southeast Asian rain forests are pretty much gone, but parts of the Sahara and the Australian outback are now getting forty or fifty inches of rain every year. Ultraviolet-resistant crops thrive where there was only sand a decade ago.

Who knows where it will end? I myself favor the theory that in a hundred years the equator will be a wasteland, never dropping below a hundred degrees at night, and most humans will live north and south of the tropics, including Antarctica.

Or on other planets. Why not? We're doing fine on Mars, with much harsher conditions. More people are moving to the moon. Then there are the asteroids. Even if we totally wear out the Earth—and nobody really thinks that will happen, life of some sort will adjust, just as it did after the dinosaurs died—something will survive. Maybe it will only be cockroaches, but something will survive.

Always look on the bright side, that's my philosophy. Though it's a little depressing to think of cockroaches as the bright side.

EARTHPORT THREE WAS a standard orbital environment, pretty much like the other three circling endlessly about ten thousand miles over the equator. Picture a can of creamed corn. Peel off the label and paint it Navy red. Now blow it up so the diameter at each end of the cylinder is about a thousand yards. Set it spinning at a rate that will produce .38 gees inside. Now extend pipes out each end along the spin axis and stud it with docking collars, and you have a stable long-term space environment. Navy regs don't allow personnel to stay in zero gravity for more than three months at a time, which would mean a lot of hassle moving people back and forth from Mars for R&M leaves, so we have to have access to spin gravity.

I could have let the autopilot dock us, but I wanted to test my rusty piloting skills, so I kept my hand on the stick as I eased her in. Just like riding a bicycle, they say, and they were right. It was as easy as if I'd done it only yesterday. I got a satisfying clank, flipped a few switches, and looked at a row of green lights.

"This is your captain speaking," I said, with no little satisfaction. "We have docked with Earthport Three . . . six minutes ahead of schedule. You may now unfasten your seat belts and exit the vehicle through the lock on the control deck. Please check around your seat for any items you may have forgotten you brought aboard. Thank you for choosing the Martian Navy for this flight. Please contact us again for all your Earth-to-orbit transportation needs."

I was bundling my hair into a manageable mass and wrapping an elastic band around it when my passengers came floating up through the deck and toward the airlock in the docking collar. One guy was looking a little green. An ensign looked at me and smiled, gave me the thumbs-up, but the commander didn't seem so happy, probably pissed off by my docking announcement. Probably a lifer asshole. Screw him. I didn't ask to be in this woman's Navy; I was drafted, like most everybody else. Gold braid didn't intimidate me, unless it was being worn by somebody in the chain of command over me.

SO WE'VE SPENT a little time together now. You've been with me from Pismo Beach to Earth orbit. I wouldn't say we're actually dating, but I think you know me well enough now that it's time to meet my family.

Let's don't do it at Deimos Base, though that's where a lot of them met me. You know how chaotic those scenes are, and I just hate them, don't you?

(FYI, the trip home was a total bust in terms of male companionship. The crew was too busy or paired up, at least for the duration, and as for the passengers, I never saw such a collection of total losers. It's what comes of universal conscription, we girls agreed. They have to take *everybody*.)

Let's move right on to the Utopia Planitia Time Suspension Facility.

UTOPIA IS JUST a big depression in the northern hemisphere where there's nothing really going on, like so much of Mars, only worse. There's not even a lot of craters there, just a big flat plain with a rail line running straight through it. There's a landing field that is used mostly by ambulances. Looking at the place, you'd never guess what lies beneath.

The favored euphemism for a graveyard is cemetery. A mausoleum if the remains are stored aboveground, a crypt if it's underground or in a basement. A repository for ashes, or "cremains" as they like to call them, is a columbarium. Black bubble technology is fairly new, and there still isn't consensus on what to call a place that holds humans in stopped time, but most seem to favor "vivarium."

Gran was still ambulatory and hooked up to only a small number of machines that easily fit on a cart. We went under a rather grand marble archway into the vivarium. The floor was white marble, stretching off into the distance. Overhead signs flashed slightly ahead of us, directing the GARCIA PARTY to DEPARTURE HALL #40. I thought that was a rather tacky thing to call it, then we passed other halls with names like "Until We Meet Again," "Bon Voyage!" and "Safe in the Arms of Jesus." I kid you not. I couldn't see Gran going for anything like that; the neutral #40 would appeal to her.

This farewell party was probably a challenge to Grandma Kelly, who had naturally organized it, since it's all relatively new and social standards for something like this were still in flux. What do you wear, for instance? Nothing about the party should resemble a funeral, so black is out. On the other hand, it's not exactly a luau, either. Leave the print dress with the pineapples and surfer dudes at home. It's a send-off, no question, but most honorees don't really want to go, and most of the guests are at least ambivalent about the whole thing: happy she's going to be alive, but frightened that it may, in fact, be the last time you're ever going to see her. What do you do with that? What's a proper emotional response? Mostly confusion, if the others here were feeling anything like I was.

But come with me now into Departure Hall #40, which is all abuzz with people who've come ahead, friends of the family, waiting for the guest of honor. If I don't introduce you to my family now, it'll be too late, they'll be lost in the crowd, and some of them will be drunk.

In any gathering on Mars, if she is in the room, your attention will immediately go to Kelly Strickland. I don't know what it is. You could call it charisma. Cameras love her. She is attractive, but not in a movie-star way. Her clothes are ordinary, and she's worn the same hairstyle all my life. When it started to go gray she let it, and now it's a startling silver. She's not an imposing figure, certainly not on Mars. Maybe a little bit less than average height for an Earth girl.

You could call it intensity. I've met people who can concentrate on one thing so exclusively you'd think their eyes could bore right through whatever it is they're looking at. Grandma Kelly can do it to a whole room. She can juggle a dozen tasks at the same time and not neglect anything.

Whatever it is, it was enough to get her elected first president of Mars, and she might still be president if she had wanted to serve a third term and keep running, despite a dedicated minority who hate her intensely. A lot more people wish we had her back, and every election time there is a "Draft Strickland" movement, which she always politely turns down. When Grandma Kelly is done with something, she's done. Oh, she's still political, you'd better believe it. She just concentrates on individual causes now rather than trying to lead the whole planet. I respect her tremendously, am a bit in awe of her, dislike her much of the time. But I know that if I was in trouble—*any* kind of trouble—she would lay down her life for me, right behind my own mother and father.

So I guess I love her. Sort of. It's not easy being the granddaughter of the George Washington of Mars.

She's sixty-three now, looks forty-five, and has had a life I can only envy, when I read about it. And that's what I usually have to do; she's not one for reminiscence, never dwells on the past. It's the future she's interested in, and when I say she "has had" a life, I must emphasize *thus far*. No one who knows her thinks she's going to settle down anytime soon. She was a bored little rich girl in a medium-sized town in Florida in the early twenty-first century when she met my grandfather, a poor half-white, half-Hispanic boy, and everyone assumed she was slumming. Myself, I think maybe she was. But Granddaddy Manny and his friends had a dream, and Grandma Kelly made it happen. I've never been sure if it was her dream, too, or merely the first thing that came along in her life that was worthy of her talents. For whatever reasons, they built the first ship to bring humans to Mars and return them to Earth, though Kelly almost died along the way.

What surprised a lot of people was that she stuck with Granddaddy. I love my Granddaddy Manny as much as any man in the solar system—for a while there, when I was being difficult, I loved him even more than my father—but he's not the sort of mate you'd expect for a human dynamo like Kelly.

Maybe that's his attraction. Look at him over there, on the other side of Gran Betty from Grandma Kelly, carefully holding her arm like she was a piece of delicate crystal. He's gentle, courtly, a little old-fashioned. He looks older than Kelly though they are the same age. He's balding, a little paunchy, his clothes are out of date. If you had to guess his occupation, you might say bookkeeper, or you might say hotel manager.

Bingo! That's where they met, at the famous Blast-Off Motel in Daytona Beach, now just a sad memory in the worst part of the Red Zone. According to Granddaddy Manny, it was not a roach motel, Betty never let it sink so low, but it was struggling. Manny grew up there, fatherless, and it was pretty much his life . . . and he hated it. He dreamed of being an astronaut, and through a combination of amazing pluck, luck, and sheer courage, he got to be one . . .

. . . for a few weeks. That's when he found that he and his best friend, Dak, were subject to crippling falling sickness, something that afflicts him to this day. Nothing to be ashamed of; it happens, though seldom to the Mars-born.

So he ended up in hotel management, but this time as manager of the first, and for a long time the biggest and swankiest, hotel on Mars, the Red Thunder. He was good at it. Still is, though he's largely retired now. While he was running the Red Thunder you could be assured that you would get the best, no matter what it took. And during the Martian War he performed heroically, though with little fanfare. Dad told me there were at least two hundred people, guests and employees of the hotel, who wouldn't be alive today except for Granddaddy Manny.

These days he serves on a lot of committees and doesn't seem to miss working at all. He's devoted to his two children and to his grandchildren. He was never the kind of sugar daddy who would give you anything you happened to want—and believe me, I tested him every chance I got—but if there was something you *really needed,* he would always be there with it.

That guy with the neatly trimmed beard, towering over Manny and slightly behind him, the one in the tweed jacket that might as well have COLLEGE PROFESSOR embroidered across the back . . . that's my daddykins,

Ray (don't call me Ramon) Strickland-Garcia, Ph.D. He is thirty-eight, young to be the head of the History Department at Marinaris University, but we're a young planet and a young university. Dad is the foremost expert, anywhere, on Martian history. I am the light of his life, the sun rises and sets on me, and all the planets orbit around me. And you'd better believe I took full advantage of that during my childhood. I actually *did* call him Daddykins for a while there—I read it in a book somewhere, and isn't it disgusting?—and he'd wiggle like a puppy when I did. I had him wrapped so tightly around my little finger it curled his hair.

Alas, no more. There seems to be a different set of rules after you pass eighteen, and I'm still figuring them out.

Standing next to him there, five inches shorter than his six and a half feet, is my mommykins, Evangeline Redmond. Though I *never* called her that. Mom and I have a businesslike relationship. I love her and all, and she was always there to kiss a skinned knee or console me when my heart was broken . . . but sometimes it was a bit after the fact, long after Dad had already had the first shot. That's because she's a workaholic, like Kelly. She works in the family business, which is Redmond's, the best restaurant on Mars. And believe me, in a tourist destination like Thunder City, where the clientele expects top service and food, that's saying something. The menu is French, Creole, Cajun, and what we call Martian Fusion, which is anything Mom and her parents say it is.

That's them not far away, Jim and Audrey Redmond, quiet and unobtrusive like Granddaddy Manny. Jim is checking out the long table groaning with food, which he catered, naturally. Grand-mère Audrey runs the business, Grand-père Jim rules the kitchen with an iron oven mitt, and Mom . . . well, Mom is the real reason Redmond's is the best. She's the one who created both the style and the term Martian Fusion, and the one who keeps inventing new stuff to keep the rich folks coming back. After all, there are a jillion French restaurants, several hundred just on Mars, and likewise Creole and Cajun. But where else are you going to get filet of thoat or stuffed sorak? Nowhere, that's where, because Mom trademarked both names. I'm not going to tell you what those "Barsoomian" animals really are, it's a trade secret, but if you don't have a moral objection to genetically engineered meat, try the sorak in white wine sauce. You'll never forget it.

Over there by the buffet, where he always is when the food is free, is Anthony Redmond, my uncle Tony, piling a plate. He's twenty-eight, masses around three hundred pounds, and is currently failing at his third career, having already gone bankrupt twice. He's a burden to Jim and Audrey, but it's hard to dislike him because he's so cheerful and outgoing. My advice: Let him guide you to all the most fun places in Thunder City, and even buy him drinks, but never loan him any money.

Not far from him, the handsome guy with the short military haircut, looking like the offspring of a cardinal and a peacock in his full-dress uniform, is Rear Admiral William Redmond, NMR, my uncle Bill. He's thirty, which might seem young for a proctologist (belowdecks slang for a rear admiral; get it?), but as well as being a young republic, we are a pretty nonmilitaristic one. We don't have a warrior culture to speak of. People from Earth find that surprising, as Mars and Switzerland are the only places where military service is mandatory for everyone, but the huge majority of us are only in the Navy for the one year (one Martian year: 669 Martian days, 687 Earth days, 1.88 Earth years) and spend the rest of our lives in the reserves. Lifers are rare, as the pay is bad, the chances for combat are remote if you're the kind who wants that, and the social status almost nil. But you do get to wear a bright red uniform to all formal occasions.

Uncle Bill has always been kind to me and was probably responsible for me entering my year of misery as a jg.

Standing there at his side, like the good Navy wife she is, you can see Aunt Amelia, probably the most domestic woman I know. That's not to say domestic*ated*; so far as I can tell she and Uncle Admiral Bill have a good marriage of equals. It's just that she'd have been right at home in the 1950s in Dubuque or Cedar Rapids or Charleston or someplace awful like that, reading *Betty Crocker Magazine*, dressing in calico pinafores or whatever they wore back then, and popping out babies like a gumball dispenser. Various of her sandrats, my cousins, are swarming around her and the other guests, biting at their ankles, threatening to tip over the punch bowl, tossing stuffed grape leaves and fricasseed frog legs at each other, and generally creating a blur of random activity. Some women are just born to reproduce. Amelia was a good candidate for Trans-Mars Champeen. I could never remember just how many Redmond cousins I had, possibly because at least once a year the number changed. There was one in a pram, and one in her arms, and one, as they say, in the oven.

Me, I love babies. I don't recall ever talking to a girl who didn't love babies. I don't mind the crappie nappies and the spit-up and the occasional crying jag. It's probably a hormonal thing, we're just programmed that way. Somewhere on that double-X chromosome is a gene that makes us look at a squirmy little recently postfetal human and squinch up our mouths and coo things like "Awwwww, isn't little snooky-ookums so *boooo*tiful!"

But I also love puppies and kittens, for the same reason.

Allow me a short digression on the subject of babies. As of now, I don't plan to have them. Don't look so shocked. I've got two good reasons.

One is that I've babysat most of Amelia's kids at one time or another, plus others. Spending money, what are you gonna do? I've dealt with them at all ages from a few months to early teens, and I've observed that *all* of them, at one age or another, turn into creatures that should be consigned to a zoo. Sometimes it's a stage, sometimes it seems to be permanent. With some, it's the Terrible Twos. With others it's the Frightening Fives. And don't forget the Sickening Sevens or the Nasty Nines. Girls are marginally better than boys, until they reach the Terrifying Twelves, then they're worse. Somebody once said that teenagers should be raised in a barrel and fed through the bunghole, then decanted when they're twenty. I should know; I admit it, I was a prime candidate for encooperage (I just made that up, means put into a barrel) until recently.

But that pales in comparison to the other reason to not have babies.

Part of your education on Mars is witnessing a live birth. We do it when we're fifteen. The idea is to appreciate the joy and the beauty of the event. We watch through a one-way mirror as the mother (a volunteer, naturally) sweats and screams and bleeds.

Lovely. Joyous. Beautiful.

I fainted dead away, along with two boys. How humiliating.

When I got back home me and my vagina had a serious talk. (Hey, why should that sound weird? Some boys name their penises, or so I've heard.) The conversation went something like this:

ME: But babies are so *cute*!

MS. V: Honey, you need to get a tape measure. Measure me, then measure a baby's head. Then . . . you do the math.

ME: Oh.

Not a pretty picture. In Homeland America there is an accepted church dogma called "intelligent design." I can call the whole wacky theory into question with one word: testicles. And if you need another example, tell me why a human baby should be expected to emerge from an opening that can't accommodate a lemon without discomfort.

Design, maybe, but not intelligent. If that was God's intent, then God is a dunce.

We're almost done here, then the ceremony can begin.

And we're getting to the best of what you might think an odd bunch. You're not supposed to have favorites in families, but everybody does, and Elizabeth Strickland-Garcia, M.D., is one.

She's Dad's sister, older by two years. She went with the families to the Red Zone in search of Gran and came out unscathed. Then she returned to Mars with them, in time for the war with Earth. Naturally she was a member of the Volunteer Pressure Brigade, and during the bombing she crawled into some wreckage where no one else would go, pulled out a few survivors, and then was trapped, her right hand pinned by a shift in the debris. Her suit was punctured and there was a slow leak. The pressure loss wasn't a problem; she had enough bottled air to replace the lost stuff for twenty minutes, and they got her out before that. But her heating system failed in that arm and her hand froze solid to the wrist in only ten minutes.

Well, kiss that piano-playing career good-bye, right?

Not my Aunt Elizabeth. Step one was learning to be left-handed while her stump healed. I understand that took her about three days. Step two was getting used to the prosthetic hand they gave her. State of the art for the time, pretty primitive by today's standards. Step three was medical school at Harvard. Top of her class. Internship, then time to pick a specialty. General practice, right? Maybe Ob-Gyn. Think again. Surgery.

Today she is the best nanosurgeon on Mars. Not surprising, because she practically invented the field.

Oh, yeah, and she's a damn good piano player.

That's her over there perched on a tiny chair at a big round low table in the corner where the kids are supposed to be corralled, with half a dozen youngsters watching as she does a few of her best tricks. One-handed (her "bad" hand) she could fold origami animals while her left hand pulled all sorts of crazy stuff out of thin air.

Wait a minute, wait a minute . . . who is that ravishing blonde just entering the room over there? She's about average height for a Mars-born, six-four or so, plus she's wearing three-inch heels. Her hair is up in a tight bun on top of her head, revealing her slender white neck. She's wearing a wispy golden chiffon thing that reaches about to her knees, strapless, flattering to her figure without being overly provocative. A string of matched pearls and pearl studs in her ears. Light makeup, a greenish frosting thing going on around her eyes and on her lips, very fashionable, very up-to-date.

Why . . . it's Podkayne!

Okay, I take back the "ravishing" part. That's a judgment call, and I wouldn't want to prejudice you. I try for mysterious, but seldom achieve more than a gawky, coltish, and—I hope—endearing young charm. The slightly turned-up nose always gets in the way of my attempts at sophistication. I sometimes feel I haven't quite grown into my body yet, that I'm playacting at being a grown-up woman.

I think I should have gone with the little black dress, with a longer skirt.

The hair is good, though, you can't deny that. And I have a Pismo Beach tan. As for the high heels, I hardly ever wear them and would sooner walk on hot coals than wear them on Earth, like Earth girls do, where they don't seem to mind mutilating their feet. But on Mars it's no problem. Besides, they do great things for my legs.

Suddenly, our heroine is attacked by what looks like a brown cannonball. The missile bounces almost as high as her head as it homes in on her, but instead of trying to avoid it, Podkayne opens her arms, braces herself, and catches her brother Mike in midflight. His stumpy arms embrace her and they kiss, then she lets him go.

Mike is short. About three and a half feet, and that's as tall as he's likely to get. He's what you're supposed to call a "little person." Not to mince words, which he never does, he's a dwarf. When people stare and point at him—and some still do—he delights in clomping around like Frankenstein and making an ugly face and bellowing, "Me dwarf! Me kill!" Shuts 'em right down.

You'll have a few questions, so I might as well get them out of the way.

No, he's not my biological brother . . . to which I'm supposed to add "but I love him exactly as much as if he was." I don't know; I don't have another brother to compare him to, but I never put the word adopted in front of his name, not even on the first day when Mom and Dad brought him back from Earth at age two, when I was ten. I'd already graduated from baby-doll age, but I took to him instantly like the finest toy a girl ever had, then the finest pet, then the finest friend, all in about a year's time. I took him everywhere with me, including classes, which may help account for the fact that he's almost ready to graduate from high school.

Or it could be native intelligence. Who knows? His DNA has been analyzed, of course, and aside from the autosomal dominant mutation in the fibroblast growth factor receptor gene (FGFR3), which is the cause of his achondroplasia (the most common of the over two hundred types of dwarfism), he's healthy as a horse. He's mixed race, his skin is medium brown, and his hair is kinky. There's some African in there, and some of a lot of other things. A not-atypical blend for his birthplace, which was Florida.

Mike was found by a UN patrol in the Red Zone, abandoned by the side of the road, a few weeks old, almost dead from exposure. Used to happen a lot. The UN cleaned him up, cured a few of the diseases endemic to the Zone, and put him into an orphanage in one of the "temporary" refugee camps, still jam-packed fifteen years after the Big Wave. And there he easily could have rotted, at least in mind and moral fiber, as so many have. He was a "problem" adoptee, being brown-skinned and with a disability, or at least a disfigurement. Then came Mom and Dad.

I'm not sure exactly how it happened. *She* told me the timing of *my* arrival was an accident, they had intended to wait a bit. *He* told me they'd always planned for two, and didn't want me to be old enough to be my sibling's mother when they got around to it, but Mom kept putting off the conception of Number Two. Next thing I knew they were off to Earth, shopping.

Mike has the big head and high forehead of your average achondroplast, but has avoided some of the other typical problems, like curvature of the spine and bowed legs. Most of that's due to Aunt Elizabeth, who goes exploring inside him several times a year and takes care of problems like that . . . if she can. There are limits to surgery. Not that he worries about that much. Or at least he never shows it. It can't be easy, being a little squirt in a society of giraffes, even for Chrondro the Magnificent.

"How ya doin', Chrondro the Insignificant?" I asked him.

"How's the weather up there, beanpole?" he countered.

"Ouch. You really know how to hurt a girl." I let him get the last word.

I'd come more or less directly from the Deimos shuttle, taking time only to change into my new clothes, so I hadn't had time to get up to date with Mike. And we didn't have time then, because Grandma Kelly was at the podium calling us all to order.

Madame President Kelly Strickland had addressed the Martian Assembly, which made the monkey house at the zoo seem sedate. She had faced the United Nations and shoved proposals down the throats of all the governments of Earth that, in an earlier age, could be considered acts of war. She had met with all the most powerful leaders on Earth, political and corporate, and left with their balls in her handbag. But in those cases she had the squeezer technology, and Mars's sole possession of it, to back her up, and she wasn't shy about squeezing.

Here, she had nothing. She was just Kelly. Mom, Grandma, mother-in-law, daughter-in-law . . . not a lot of power in any of those positions, not with this bunch. We were Martians, and we were Strickland-Garcia-Redmonds, and an ornerier bunch were never born. She looked the least little bit intimidated.

"Ladies and gentlemen . . . if there are any of them here . . ." But then Gran, sitting in the front row in the seat of honor, struggled to her feet and started slowly toward the podium. Kelly could keep talking, or she could help Gran get where she was going. She quickly moved to take Gran's arm while Granddaddy Manny hurried up on the other side, but she shook them both off.

"I may be slow, but I get there," she said, when she'd made it to the podium and Granddaddy had adjusted the mike. She looked so tiny, so wasted, but there was still fire in her eyes. She looked at Kelly as she took her seat beside Granddaddy.

"Kelly, I know you planned this all out. It's what you're good at, and the citizens of Mars are lucky you are. But I decided this is going to be my show." Kelly nodded, and started to clap, and we all joined in, but Gran waved us quiet.

"That's enough of that," she said. "I figure you were going to have everybody come up here one at a time and spout a lot of lies about what a wonderful person I was. Am I right?"

Kelly nodded.

"Well, bless you, sweetie. But I'm too tired for that. I think what I'll do is make a few remarks, and then get this show on the road. You first. Kelly, you are the best daughter-in-law a mom could ever have wished for. I won't lie to you, I didn't think you were going to be, what with dragging my son off to Mars and all in a leaky old ship like Tom Swift or some damn thing . . ." That got a big laugh, while Kelly pretended to be offended by the accusation.

"Okay, okay, so maybe Manny had something to do with it, too. Anyway, you two nearly killed me with worry, but the real danger was when y'all got back, and I thought my heart was going to bust with pride. And I got to say, life sure has been interesting with you around. I got to meet and shake the hands of some of the most famous and powerful people in the world . . . and nine out of ten of 'em made me wish I could wash my hand right after. I don't know how you stood it as long as you did."

Laughter, and applause. And could that be a tear leaking from the corner of Grandma Kelly's eye? It is, it is, ladies and gentlemen! Quickly wiped away, but there it was, the first liquid I'd ever seen come from that eye when she wasn't chopping onions. I felt a little moisture in my own eyes, but I cry over old country and western songs.

"So, before we go any further," Gran was saying, "where is Travis? He ought to be here for the whole silly shivaree. What were you going to do, have a grand unveiling or something?"

"Something like that," Kelly admitted.

"Well, roll his disreputable ass on out here and let's unveil the mother—oops, sorry kids. I want one more look at Peter Pan, the man who decided never to grow old *or* grow up, before I go."

That got Kelly hurrying to the doors, and soon they were opened and a white electric forklift came silently into the room with a load full of . . . nothing.

Not strictly true, of course. A black bubble looks like a hole in space. There was no way to tell it was spherical, if it was standing alone. To handle them, since they are frictionless and just about everything-else-less, you have to put them in a net. Just a tracery of strong thread; black bubbles have no mass.

The driver put the platform with the net down, and a small cap came down from the ceiling to hold the bubble in place. He cut away the netting. Gran was coming around the podium, helped again by Granddaddy. Kelly went over and whispered something into Gran's ear. Gran gave her a wicked smile.

"That's a great idea," she said. "Wish I'd thought of that. Everybody," Gran announced, smiling and gesturing, "come on over here. We've got a surprise for Travis." I hurried over close to her.

"I almost did this last time he came out of his shell," she whispered to me.

"I don't get it."

"You will. Everybody . . ." She waited until she had everyone's attention. "I want you all to stand like this." She put her hands in the air, like a holdup victim. I looked around. Everybody was standing with their hands in the air. I shrugged, held my hands up, and saw Kelly nod to the technician. He pushed a button.

The black ball vanished with no fuss at all. For Travis, one scene would be replaced by another in the blink of an eye. If things had gone well, it would be a very similar scene, here at the bubble factory. But he expected to be inside for five years. God knows Travis had enough enemies on Earth. Hell, maybe we've been invaded by superbeings from the Andromeda Galaxy and they plan to fry him and eat him for lunch, regarding the bubbles as convenient deep freezes for meat.

Anything might be awaiting him. What would you do? If you had any sense, you'd be on full alert. For Travis Broussard, that meant fully armed.

The bubble went away, and Travis landed on his feet, in a crouch . . . and looked out at several hundred people, all of them with their hands in the air.

"Don't shoot, Travis!" we all yelled. And sure enough, though he didn't have his pistol in his hand, the holster cover was unsnapped and his hand was on it, ready for a fast draw. He straightened from his semicrouch and shook his head, with a wry grin.

"Very funny, y'all," he deadpanned. He snapped the cover on his sidearm.

My "Uncle Travis" is not really my uncle. Neither is Uncle Jubal. They are of the large and cantankerous Broussard clan, but our families have been entwined for about half a century now. Jubal's invention had made the first trip to Mars possible, Travis had made it feasible and led it, but Manny and his friend Dak had had the idea to go in the first place. Travis and Jubal and the next generation, my father and mother, had fought and won the Martian War with Jubal's new invention, the black bubbles, his old one, the squeezer bubbles, and the biggest bluff in the history of warfare.

It had all been too much for Jubal. Though his inventions had provided the power to send humans to the stars and free Earth from its reliance on dwindling energy reserves, and then saved countless lives by suspending time, they had also been responsible for the Big Wave, and the Martian War had been fought over the right to control all the power Jubal had unleashed.

Actually, of course, it was human greed and madness and fanaticism that had caused those disasters, but Jubal didn't see it that way . . . and I suppose he had a point. Some of the men who built the first nuclear weapons suffered the same doubts and regrets afterward.

So just about the time I was being conceived, Jubal allowed himself to be enclosed in a black bubble, the second time he'd been in one, the second time *anyone* had been in one. He'd gone in the first time to escape from his plush prison on Earth, then had mailed himself to Dad and Mom on Phobos, which was what started the Martian War. That's right, mailed himself.

But that's all history. Read Dad's book for all the details. Uncle Jubal was still in cold storage. If he ever came out, he'd be exactly the same age, which was late fifties.

Later, Uncle Travis had become the first "skipper." There aren't many of them and probably never will be. It's an odd way to live.

There's nothing medically wrong with Travis. He is a very rich man. He and Jubal had given humanity the gift of unlimited power, which made it cheap, but it wasn't free. Taking even a tiny royalty for every kilowatt that sated humanity's vast appetite for energy made them rich beyond the dreams of Arabian princes of the twentieth century.

But Travis made a lot of enemies in his life, both by his decision to turn the squeezer technology over to the International Power Agency, and later, when he threatened to squeeze Planet Earth down to the size of a neutron if certain powerful people and corporations weren't brought to heel *right now*. A lot of applecarts were overturned, a lot of boats swamped, a lot of rice bowls broken. These were people who never forgave and never forgot. Mighty oaths were sworn, contracts were taken out. Assassination attempts began. So he invented the practice of skipping.

Jubal's bubble was to be opened in only two circumstances.

One, if it was finally safe for him to go home to his beloved bayou country in Louisiana. Given that he was the only person alive—the only one who had ever lived—who could made the squeezer machines, that didn't seem likely. Until and if someone else showed up who could do it, the powers in his brain were just too valuable.

Two . . . if he was needed. Needed "real bad," as he had put it. It was understood that "real bad" meant something on the order of an alien invasion. Some situation that only he might be able to solve in some unknowable last throw of the dice in the hope that he could pull a third miracle out of the hat that covered that special brain.

Travis had a longer list of circumstances that would bring him out of the bubble. Most importantly, he was to be released every five years. Travis had gone into his bubble for the first time when I was four. I have only vague memories of him from that time.

I was nine when he came out again, and I remember that visit clearly. I was there with a small number of family members. That's when we first started calling Uncle Travis's days of arrival "Groundhog Day." Travis would stick his head out, look around for a month to get the lay of the land and catch up on current world affairs and family events, then retreat to his burrow for five more years of winter.

Next time I was fourteen. I was appointed to be his guide, and naturally Mike, six at the time, came with me, and the two of us showed him all the new things from the last five years and filled him in on happenings on Earth in the evenings.

Now here he was again, just under a year early, looking exactly the same as he had the last time I saw him, four years earlier.

Travis wasn't slow. From the number of people there, he instantly took in that something special was going on. The date and time were posted on the wall, as they were in all these rooms, as a quick aid to orientation.

He knew that among the parameters for waking him up was the death or critical illness of a small number of people close to him, and his mind put it together quickly that this was the most likely reason he wasn't seeing the date he expected. I saw his face fall, and his eyes darted around, looking for the faces he hoped would be there.

Gran had anticipated this, and she stepped forward and smiled at him.

"I ain't dead yet, Travis, but all this fuss is for me. But since I'm the next thing *to* dead, and I'm on your list, we figured you might want to stick your furry little head out of your hole and see me one last time before I join you in the hole next door."

Travis jumped down from the small platform and tenderly took Gran in his arms. They stood that way for a while, and soon people began to clap, possibly because they were at a loss for any other way of showing their approval.

I had to get out my hankie before my mascara started to run.

THE NEXT HOUR was a bit of a blur. Gran had insisted she wanted no more tributes, no more formalities, and that if this was to be a semi-wake, it would be a semi–Irish wake, so let the singing and dancing and feasting and drinking begin.

Grandma Kelly took the demolition of all her planning in good humor and immediately began organizing the merriment along new lines. Those of us who played an instrument were pressed into service as an impromptu band. It was pretty good, though most of them were friends, rather than family. Food was consumed, and more rolled out, and the bar was open and doing a good business.

Tides of humanity shifted and eddied, as they do at these things. I hung back as much as I could, watching, nursing a Shirley Temple and smiling at all the faces, half of whom I didn't even know. I don't favor crowds, have never liked large, noisy parties. My idea of a good time is more like three or four or five good friends and just a whiff of Phobos Red to loosen me up a little.

Travis was looking more than a bit overwhelmed, a really unusual position for him. Normally, he's the most unflappable man I've ever met, and one of the most cheerful. That's from personal experience; the tales of his calm under fire are legendary. But this mob meeting him when he really wanted some peace and quiet and a few close friends to slowly start bringing him up to date was too much. I saw him being passed from person to person, a weak smile plastered on his face, and then I lost track of him.

It was ten minutes later when I turned and he turned and there we were, facing each other. He had to look up, of course, but he was used to that. I was already almost my present height when he saw me last, at the age of fourteen. His eyes widened.

"Is it . . . it can't be . . . is it *Podkayne*?"

I allowed as how it was.

He looked me over from nose to toes, and in an instant the first genuine smile of his new day broke out all over his face.

"Pod, you've . . . you've *grown*."

I could feel my face go warm. Goose bumps broke out all over my arms and icy fingers ran up and down my spine. I almost tottered off my spike heels.

Yes, I guess my secret is out. I had a crush on Travis powerful enough to squeeze a squeezer bubble.

5

★ ★ ★

I WAS NINE, and Travis was about the most exciting thing I'd ever seen.

I listened in fascination as he told his stories. I'd heard the same stories from Mom and Dad, the few times I could get them to talk about them, but neither of them was the born storyteller that Travis was. He could have me helpless with laughter one moment and breathless with fear the next, to the point that I had a few nightmares and Mom had a little talk with Travis and he apologized to me but I told him please, please don't stop, and don't worry about me, I'm a big girl and I can take it.

I sang for him. In fact, he told me I sang for him when I was four and that I put Shirley Temple to shame. I had to look her up (and have been drinking Shirley Temples ever since). When I was nine I was a lot better, since I'd been taking keyboard and voice lessons for five years by then and was something of a prodigy. I boned up on the music of his youth, about things called rap and hip-hop. It turned out he didn't like that stuff, to my considerable relief. Listen to it sometime; you'll be astonished.

Then he was gone, and I waited another five years, like a lonely maiden in a tower. It was so *incredibly* romantic! I was saving myself for him.

And one day he arrived, on a glorious white horse, to make me the happiest woman on Mars. That's how I imagined it, anyway. I wasn't invited to the opening, just adults, which should have told me something right there but didn't. I was too infatuated. Plus, I was a temperamental, obnoxious, stuck-up, sarcastic, monstrously insecure bitch at the time. I know that now, of course, but at the time I thought I was sophisticated, vastly superior to my parents and all other adults in both intellect and taste, and irresistible to the opposite sex, in spite of a troubling lack of suitors. I was a sort of antianorexic, able to look in the mirror and see not the gawky beanpole with the bad complexion who was actually there but a steamy temptress oozing hot sex beneath the pancake makeup and thick mascara. Hormones had hit me over the head like Maxwell's silver hammer, and my body had responded by growing like a weed without filling out at *all* (that came next year), and bursting out in enthusiastic acne that no treatment seemed able to do anything about. What the hormones had done to my brain doesn't even bear thinking about.

Hey, how sensibly did *you* behave during the storms of puberty?

I put all my best, clumsiest moves on Travis when he got to our home, and he rebuffed them in a gentlemanly, avuncular manner until I finally wised up, after about three days. After that I was icily polite, only because Mike was with me and he worshipped the guy. Travis never spoke down to Mike, treated him like an adult, which even at the age of six Mike could almost pass for in some ways, and that's probably the only reason I didn't strangle Travis in his sleep.

Then he abandoned me again, and I decided to become a tragic figure. I stopped eating. I vowed I'd never sing again. I thought about killing myself. (Doesn't every teenager?) I even checked out convents, but that was going a bit too far even for someone as bereft as me. Besides, the clothes sucked.

What can I say? I got over it. I put it all behind me. I grew up, I finished my primary education, I decided, like most Martians, to get my military service out of the way before college, I went to Earth . . .

. . . and now I was back, and jumpin' Jupiter! I was nine again!

At least that's what it felt like. Suddenly I felt like I couldn't take a step without tripping over myself. Travis's gaze didn't linger, he only looked at me for a few seconds, but he took it all in. He had to, he couldn't help himself. And though I no longer think of myself as a siren able to turn men into my sex slaves with no more than a sultry look, I have a more realistic body image, and I know I'm attractive though well short of being a cover girl. And I know something of the effect I have on Earthmen. With the heels I had seven inches on Travis, and looking up at women like that either scares Earth guys to death or gets them imagining the possibilities.

Travis didn't look scared.

I know what you're saying. Come *on*, spacegirl! Get real!

I mean, he was in his *sixties* when I was *born*.

On the other hand, he hasn't gotten any older. He's a good-looking sixtyish. He may very well not get *any* older, unless he stops skipping. Which is why the silly fantasy of that nine-year-old me was not *entirely* idiotic . . .

I *could* wait for him.

In forty years I'd be fifty-eight, and he'd still be sixtyish. That's not such a horrible age gap, is it? I know it sounds like a silly science-fiction story, but you have to remember, our present was at one time somebody else's science fiction. People from the turn of the century didn't even have space travel to amount to anything, for heaven's sake. They'd been to the moon six times, they had a pathetic little "space station," and their rocket ships were still blowing up all the time. How could they have imagined that by now there would be almost a million people living on Mars, and that people could be stopped in time?

Is she serious? you're asking yourself.

No. Not really. Forty years is a long time, and I know I'll have changed a lot by then if the last five years are any indicator. I'm sure I'll get over him.

Sigh.

AFTER A FEW hours, Gran caught my eye and beckoned me over. I hurried to her side.

"Tell everybody to shut up and sit down," she said. She looked tired, but there was a twinkle in her eye. I realized she'd been enduring all this rather than enjoying it, that it was all for everyone else's benefit.

"Attention everybody!" I bellowed. And believe me, after fourteen

years of voice training, I knew how to project. There was instant silence, and everybody turned in my direction. I kicked off my shoes and stood up on a chair.

"Gran has something she wants to say," I said in a more normal voice. "Please find chairs and sit down." While everybody was shuffling around, some of them none too steady, Kelly hurried over with a mike, which she handed to Gran. When everybody was settled, Gran smiled around the room from her wheelchair and slowly stood up. Kelly reached to help her, but Gran waved her off.

"I want to thank all y'all for coming," she said, in a calm, clear voice. "The food's been good, and the company's been good, and even the music's been fine." She paused. "But not good enough. Not yet. I want to ask Poddy to sing for me before I go."

Well, I hadn't been expecting it, but it wasn't a complete surprise. I get asked to sing, sometimes ahead of time, sometimes impromptu, at parties like this. After all, it's what I intend to do after I have this military foolishness out of the way. I'd even been thinking of volunteering to sing a song, and realized that the lyrics to Cole Porter's "You're the Top" had been circulating in my head for several minutes. Seemed like a nice send-off song. Of course, many people here wouldn't know a Bendel bonnet from a glass of Ovaltine or a sheet of cellophane or an Arrow collar. Well, I googled them, so *I* know.

So I put on my best Pepsodent smile (google it yourself) and started for the bandstand, but Gran beckoned me to lean down close to her. She whispered in my ear.

I was startled. Sure, it's a great song, a terrific song, but was it right for this time and place? She must have seen the doubt in my eyes because she smiled up at me and said, "Go ahead, hon. It's one of my favorites, and I think it's perfect for here."

Okay. As I walked toward the bandstand I was finding the music and the chords, and as I stepped up I told the musicians which channel I was transmitting on. They got that faraway stare when you're concentrating on the images coming up on your contact lens display, or on the nanodots attached to your cornea if you were using the latest accessing equipment. The lead guitarist nodded his head assuredly at me; he was familiar with the song, and I knew the others could fake it.

Then I jumped back down and hurried over to my father, grabbed his hand, and pulled him up beside me. This one would be a lot better with vocal harmony, and he was the best singer in the house, other than me. I told him the song we were going to sing, and he smiled.

Without further ado, we swung into "Long Time Gone," by David Crosby.

Gran was much too young for Cole Porter, though I knew she liked his music, as well as swingers like Benny Goodman and Glenn Miller. She had been a little girl during what we now call the Great Age of Rock, but during her musically formative years—and did you know that, for the huge majority of people, the music they hear when they're in their teens and twenties is what they'll listen to for the rest of their lives?—those hits of the 1960s and '70s were still getting a lot of play as "classic rock." (They *still* get a fair number of downloads, even today.) So she knew them all.

I sang the lead, but when it came to the harmonies I handled the Graham Nash part, which was a bit beyond Dad's range.

We were never going to rival the original recording, but I'm proud to say we didn't murder it.

It's been a long time comin'
It's goin' to be a long time gone
And it appears to be a long
Appears to be a long
Appears to be a long time
Such a long, long, long, long time before the dawn

While I was singing it I immediately knew it was right, and everyone else seemed to agree, too. She might be a long time gone, but there was hope for another dawn.

There was big-time applause when we were done, and I'm never one to be shy about an encore, so I looked to Gran and raised an eyebrow, and she gestured for me to go on. I sent the next song to the band, and we sang Lennon and McCartney's "A Little Help From My Friends." It went over well. Gran was laughing; her friends gave more than a little help by clapping and singing along with the chorus.

The technical crew had entered the room discreetly as I was singing, approached Gran, and one of them bent down to ask her something. She nodded, looking tired but happy, and they got her back in her chair and up on the short riser. I watched, still singing, one of the few in the room who was aware of what was going on over there. Kelly saw, and Elizabeth, and went to Gran's side.

They were about ready when I finished, and I knew I had to sing one more.

"Anybody got a keyboard?" I asked. The bass player tossed me one, and I unrolled it on a table and stood behind it. I waited for the applause to die down and the room to grow silent, then played the opening notes of Paul Simon's "Bridge Over Troubled Water."

If I say so myself, it's one of my best numbers. It's the only spiritual I know that doesn't mention any sort of God, which I knew Gran liked, because after the Big Wave she told me she lost whatever religion she had. When you're weary, you need a little help from your friends, because it's goin' to be a long time gone.

And with all due respect to Mr. Garfunkel's angelic, sweet tenor, I think I sang it that day as well as it's ever been sung. I was transported, I was somewhere else entirely, and then I came back and found myself playing the last bars and the band behind me, having slowly increased the intensity, following my lead, thundering through the last chords, filling in through the magic of synthesized sound for the full orchestra of the original . . . and then silence.

There was prolonged applause. I was dry-eyed. I never cry when I'm in the zone, no matter how deeply I get into a song. I don't get tired, either. I felt like I could have sung all night long, but I knew this was the time to stop. I made a sweeping gesture toward Gran. *You've got top billing here, Gran. The floor is yours . . .*

"Thank you, honey," she said, simply. She was holding a small box in her hand. It had a single button on it, and her thumb was on the button.

"I figure I'll be coming out of here someday," she went on. "And when I do, I'll be doing exactly what I'm doing right now, when I'm going in. So I wondered why I should be saying good-bye. Well, they tell me that in Hawaii, aloha means both hello and good-bye. So I figured that's what I'd say." She waved her hand at us, slowly.

"Aloha, y'all. Aloha, aloha, al

And instantly there was nothing there but a big black hole.

Dammit, there goes my mascara.

THE TRAIN BACK to Thunder City wasn't crowded, even with our clan and friends aboard. The drunker passengers were in the bar car, getting drunker still. A few were already sleeping it off. I had no trouble finding a seat by myself. I settled in by the window and watched the eternal cold desert flash by.

I was a roiling mixture of emotions. I was glad to be home, but sad that I'd soon be going back. I was sad to see Gran go, but there was an excellent chance that I'd see her again one day. And I was going through my usual after-performance blues, a very strange mixture of elation that I'd done well, depression that it was over, and self-doubt. Did I really have a career ahead of me as a singer? It is a brutal field, there are many, many very talented people out there, and talent is far from enough. You've got to have determination, a lot of luck, and some indefinable charisma I was far from sure I had. A good agent doesn't hurt, either.

And on top of it all, I still had quite a term to serve in the Navy before I could even really try my wings at a singing career.

Plus, there was still the question if I should try to make a living in music at all. Dad was urging me to go on to higher education first. Mom said, "Go for it. You're only young once."

I knew how to read music and I didn't intend to sing grand opera. I wasn't sure what college courses could teach me about singing that I didn't already know. But I wouldn't know that until I gave it a try, would I?

Others talked about the school of hard rocks, about paying your dues, singing for handouts in the Thunder City mall or train stations, working in little live clubs instead of looking for that big download contract.

You could always just put your stuff out there on the freemart and hope you started getting some attention. But that worked best for singer-songwriters, and I was still working on the songwriting part of the act. Just one more area of insecurity: Could I really write a killer song? I had a thick songbook already, of course; everybody's got a songbook. I knew most of them ranged from hackneyed to mediocre.

Well, give me time. I'm young.

Yeah, and how old was Bob Dylan when he wrote "Desolation Row"? Older than me, but only a little.

"Nice tan."

I looked up and saw Uncle Bill standing in the aisle.

"There's something to be said for a fractured ozone layer, Admiral," I said.

"Yeah. I always thought it was 'malignant melanoma.'" He sat beside me without being invited, which was his right both as my uncle and superior officer. And anyway, I didn't mind. It broke up my rather gloomy train of thought.

Uncle Bill is a few inches over seven feet, on the tall side even for a Mars-born. His knees touched the seat in front, even in the generous space provided by Martian transport. For a while he just watched the passing scenery with me.

"So how's Pismo Beach?" he finally said.

"I don't know how it is now, but when I left it was hot, heavy, humid, hellish. I suspect it's still pretty much the same."

"Hellish?"

"Only the Second or Third Circle. Could be worse. I hear Heartland America is Seventh Circle, sliding rapidly toward the Eighth."

"I'm not much on the geography of Hell," he said, and lapsed into silence again for a while. Then he sighed, and faced me again.

"I suppose you blame me for that posting," he said. I was surprised. I mean, I did, a little, but only in the sense that I wished he'd used more of his considerable pull in the upper reaches of the Navy, realms mysterious to most of us draftees, to get me something somewhere else. Like I said, I knew it could have been worse.

"Hate Earth, myself," he said. "Maybe I'm being unfair. I didn't see her at her best. All I remember is being left behind at Disney World while everyone else went off on a big adventure. I'm afraid I and my brother behaved rather badly."

Dad has told me about what holy terrors Uncle Tony and Uncle Bill had been when they were sandrat-sized. It was hard to imagine, looking at this dignified and sometimes even diffident man, so spiffy in his uniform, that he could have been a brat. But looking at me in my current state of adult sophistication and dignified self-assurance, you'd never have known that only a few short years ago I was an awkward, confused, sullen brat myself.

"Later, when I understood where the others had gone and what they'd gone through, I was glad to have been left behind." He was talking about the horrors immediately postwave, where my family and Travis had gone in search of Gran. To this day Dad won't talk about a lot of it, except for one story about being scared out of his wits by a tiger that had escaped from a zoo and was later shot by survivors. He makes it into a very funny story, about how close he came to crapping in his pants, and then ends it on a poignant note, the sense of loss he felt when he saw the grand, wild creature laid out preparatory to being skinned, but I know it was an important moment in his life. Of the rest of it, he says nothing at all. Mom will tell me stories of her own journey—they weren't even engaged back then, but that's when they fell in love—after she and Grand-père Redmond split from the others to find their family, which was mostly a case of wandering among refugees asking as to the whereabouts of people, just as thousands of others were doing. But of the thousands of bodies floating in the sea, of the decaying corpses in wrecked cars he had to move out of the way, of the dead children, the vacant-eyed survivors, the fighting . . . of the *stench*, my father speaks not at all.

He doesn't have to. I've read the accounts, I've seen the pictures and tapes.

"Never been back," Uncle Admiral went on. "But I want you to know, Podkayne, that if I could have spared you a tour on Earth, I would have. That's one thing that is pretty much set in stone these days. Your first half year must be spent at an Earthside post. 'Know your enemy' is the theory."

It was actually *potential* enemy—we weren't at war—but everybody knew that if more hostilities came, they would be from that degenerate, worn-out old planet, so encrusted with the hatreds of thousands of years of more or less continuous wars. The Republic of Mars got along well with everybody else.

"I got to know them pretty well," I said, thinking of little illiterate Glinda. If we ever had to fight a War on Ignorance, she could be in the front of the enemy lines, but she'd have to shoulder aside a lot of her fellow Earthies to get there.

"Well, you'll be relieved to know that your lessons are over. Seeing as you're already here, I was able to get the rest of your term on Earth waived, and a promotion to a full lieutenancy."

Suddenly the day seemed a lot brighter. I wanted to shout something, but confined myself to taking his hand and bringing it to my lips and kissing it.

"Thanks, Uncle Bill."

"That's Admiral Bill to you," he said, pulling his hand away and pretending to be stern. "And kissing superior officers is frowned on."

"Well, seeing as how we're related, I figured it wouldn't be right to go ahead with the customary blowjob."

He tried to keep a straight face, but the laughter forced itself out explosively.

"You're a pill, Podkayne, but don't ever talk like that when there are other Navy people around. They don't like jokes, and I don't need to be tailhooked."

If you haven't served your hitch yet, that's Navy slang for being accused of sexual harassment below your rank. It's rare, but it still happens. If it happened to me, I doubt I'd tailhook anybody. I'd kick him in the balls, admiral or not. We have a nut-kicking tradition in my family. My mom once planted her foot in a general's crotch so hard it lifted him right out of his boots. Or so my dad says.

"What's the deal with the promotion, though?" I asked. "Just a routine bump?"

"Well, you're still a little ways from that. But based on your recruitment record, I was able to get you a little slack there, too."

"What recruitment record? I didn't send many Earthies here."

"Practically none," he agreed. "Those few who got by you are all A-one citizen prospects. You didn't think you were sent to Hell to send the demons to Mars, did you?" He looked at me, and I expect my mouth was open in amazement, because that's what I was feeling. He laughed. "Good lord, what are they telling you these days? They don't put it in the manual, but we figure you all know that you're there to persuade marginal cases *not* to emigrate. We don't want more people, certainly not from Earth."

Well, excuse *me*! How was I to know? If they were still posting us in pairs, like they used to in Western America, maybe we'd have picked up on the straight skinny. But they dump you in an isolated wasteland all by yourself with nothing but a tutorial on how to fill out the forms.

"You haven't asked the next question yet," he said.

"What question is that?"

"About your next posting. Something became available, and I managed to slip your name into the queue. I can always pull it back out again if you don't want to go."

"Are you going to make me torture you for the information?"

"How does Europa sound?"

"Europa?" This time I couldn't restrain myself. I shouted something right at the top of my considerable range—whoopee, hallelujah, golly gee; I can't remember—and threw my arms around Admiral Bill and kissed him, hard. No tongue, he *was* a relative. Then I said the first thing that came into my head.

"When I get home, I'm burning *all* my bras."

6

★ ★ ★

FROM *PODDY'S BOOK* *of Places I'd Like to Go*:

#1) Europa:

Second and smallest of the Galilean moons of Jupiter: Io, Europa, Ganymede, and Callisto. You can see them through a small telescope from Earth; even better from Mars. The moon Europa was named after a beautiful Phoenician princess for whom the continent of Europe was named, so I'm going to be sentimental here and refer to it as "she." The poor thing was seduced or raped, depending on who's telling the story, by Zeus in the form of a white bull. Those Greek gods were real party animals, weren't they?

Diameter: 1,940 miles.

Distance from Jupiter: 417,000 miles.

Albedo: .67. That makes her the fifth most reflective body in the solar system, after Saturn's moons Enceladus at .99, Tethys at .80, Mimas at .77, and Neptune's moon Triton at .76. To give you an idea of how bright that is, Venus is .65, Jupiter is .52, Earth is .36, and Mars is .15. Albedo (since you asked) is the ratio of light coming in to light reflected back. The reason for Europa's high reflectivity is that the surface is entirely covered in water ice.

Europa is one of only six moons with an atmosphere. It's not much, but it's all oxygen. It comes from the ice evaporating and ionizing into hydrogen and oxygen. The hydrogen is too light to get retained, and blows off into space.

It's one of the densest bodies in the solar system. The list goes like this:

Earth	5.5 g/cm^3
Mercury	5.4 g/cm^3
Venus	5.2 g/cm^3
Mars	3.9 g/cm^3
Io	3.5 g/cm^3
Europa	3.01 g/cm^3

I'm not counting asteroids, so if you live on Juno, Vesta, Eunomia, Interamnia One, or other places like that which are a bit denser, I'm sorry, okay? I'm making a point here, and it has to do with surface gravity.

That high density is because the bulk of Europa and her nearest neighbor, Io, are rock with an iron core, more like terrestrial planets than any other moons in the solar system. That high density means that, in spite of its relatively small size, it has a surface gravity of .134 gee.

So if you weighed, say, 100 pounds on Earth, you will weigh 37 pounds on Mars, and only 13.4 pounds on Europa. More important to me, considering where I just came from, if your left breast weighed 5 pounds on Earth (I'm just naming a figure, not bragging), it would be a bit less than 2 pounds on Mars, and . . . well, you do the math. But *that* was the reason for my silly remark about bra-burning. With any luck, I'd never have to wear one of the damn things again.

Around the turn of the century unmanned space probes went into orbit around Jupiter and started some serious studies of the giant planet and its moons. They discovered that Io looked like a pizza and had more active volcanoes than zits on a teenager's face, but had almost no craters, because the surface was constantly being renewed by stuff upwelling from below. Some of that stuff was molten rock at 3000 degrees Fahrenheit, and some of it was lakes of boiling sulfur. Io has people living on it, but has not been extensively explored. It's a tourist destination for its great views of Jupiter, and for the excitement and danger of exploring around the volcanoes.

Ganymede, Callisto, and Europa are all ice-and-rock worlds.

Callisto is heavily cratered and tectonically dead. It's covered with an ice sheet and beneath that is a relatively thin layer of liquid water. It doesn't have a defined core.

Ganymede has an iron-and-rock core, but it has a lot more water and a very thick ice sheet covering it, which makes it much less dense than Europa. Surface gravity on Ganymede is just a hair higher than on Europa, though Ganymede is much bigger.

All three are about the same temperature on the surface—100 to 120 degrees Kelvin, say about 260 below zero, Fahrenheit—but down below the surface it's another matter. All moons are subject to tidal flexing. That means they are distorted by the pull of the primary, Jupiter in this case, and in multimoon systems, by the pull of the other moons as they pursue their different orbits. This tugging produces energy as heat.

If a Jovian moon is in real close, like Io, you get a volcanic hell. If you're way the hell and gone, like Callisto, you get a ball of slush. A little closer in, like Ganymede, you don't get so much internal heating, but it's enough for tectonic processes to work. Plates slide over each other, collide, chasms and ridges are formed. But that was all a long time ago. Many craters on Ganymede are very old, like the ones on the moon and Mars.

They told me in science classes that the situation is comparable to Venus, Earth, and Mars. Too close to the sun and you get a choking-hot planet like Venus. Too far out and you get a cold planet like Mars, where all the water has been frozen for billions of years, mostly deep under the poles. Right in the middle you get Earth, warm and comfy.

Or you could think of Goldilocks and the three bears and the porridge. Io would burn your mouth, and you'd spit out Ganymede because it was too cold. Europa would be just right.

Just right for what? Why, for life, of course. And that's just what we found when we got there. Or something very much like it. We think.

SETTING OUT FOR the Jovian system isn't quite like getting a visa and updating your immunizations and boarding a liner for a trip to Earth. If you intend to stay awhile and not just make a few orbits and snap a few pictures to show the folks back home, you need some more elaborate preparations.

Jupiter has a magnetosphere so big that, if you could light it up somehow, seen from the Earth, it would be five times the width of the full moon. There's a lot of radiation in it. Our ships and bases are well shielded, but if you planned to stay in the area of Jupiter for any length of time, it would be best to take some prophylactic measures.

Most mutations in your body aren't going to hurt anything. But there is a certain very small number of very large cells that can lead to disaster if damaged by radiation. I'm speaking of the ova, the human eggs released by the ovaries.

For a while, in the early days, just about the only females who dared to visit Jupiter were those who had passed out of the reproductive cycle and were menopausal, and women who had already had all the children they wanted or who didn't want any children at all. It was just too dangerous.

These days we had a much more elegant solution: oophorectomy. That's a fancy word for removal of the ovaries. Spaying.

It's a recent development. If you take them out and pop them into a freezer, you risk as much damage as you're trying to avoid. But then Uncle Jubal invented the black bubbles. Now you can just cut out the ovaries, bubble them, and a few years later you take them out and hook them back up to the fallopian tubes. With nanosurgery, this is about as dangerous as wart removal.

But no girl wants to spend very much time without her ovaries unless she fancies herself with a beard, singing baritone. They produce the hormones that make us the graceful, double-breasted, big-butted, almost hairless sopranos that men find irresistible, for some reason.

No worries, mate. We just replace them with vat-grown, universal-donor artificial ovaries that secrete just the right mixture of femaleness, and at the same time greatly reduce menstrual flow, cramps, and PMS. If you wonder why I didn't have this done long ago, turning "the curse" into "the mild epithet," it's simple. My periods are not cataclysmic. I seldom bite anyone when premenstrual unless they *really* have it coming.

They can do the equivalent thing with guys, too . . . but for some reason, not a lot of guys want to have it done. In fact, the ratio of sexes in high-radiation environments like Jupiter has just about reversed from what it used to be. A lot of guys don't want to have their testicles replaced with synthetic ones, even though it's impossible to tell the difference.

I've pondered that, worrying at that eternal mystery that makes life both so exciting and so frustrating. The best I can say about it is that if my gonads were hanging precariously outside my body where I had to see them every day, badly packaged and horribly vulnerable, maybe I'd be obsessed about them, too.

The other thing I can say is a lot simpler: Boys are weird.

SOMEBODY ONCE TOLD me you can sum up the solar system this way: There's the sun, there's Jupiter, and there's other stuff. You might include Saturn if you were feeling generous. Jupiter dominates the planetary system.

I can't say that it knocked my socks off as we approached it. Any good 3-D movie can give you a more awesome show than what you see from a spaceship window, and Navy ships bound for Jupiter don't have many windows, and those are small. Don't get me wrong, I'm not saying I wasn't impressed. There is a world of difference in seeing a movie and looking out a window and seeing it *right there,* but it's a feeling in your gut more than a visual spectacle.

SO ALONG ABOUT now you might be wondering how did I, Podkayne etc. etc., raw recruit, the silver bar and red globe on my shoulders about ten minutes old, get a berth to Europa? Bright, shiny, mysterious Europa, where no tourists are allowed and only scientists from the Martian Academy and a very few of the best and the brightest from other planets are welcome? And, of course, the Navy contingent to enforce the protective blockade. You probably figure it was Admiral Bill, and I wouldn't call you a liar if you said that, but that isn't the whole story.

I know, it's not fair, trading on your relations like a lot of slim-talent actors and musicians I could name who get a career because they're the son or daughter of somebody who's really good. But the fact is, a *no-talent* offspring of a big celebrity isn't going to have a very *long* career. People will stop coming once the novelty wears off. Usually, all being from a famous family with someone in a position of influence will get you is a foot in the door. After that, it's up to you. What Admiral Bill had gotten me was a chance to reaudition. I was going to Europa to be a Madam.

If you're not from Mars and if you have a dirty mind, you probably think that has something to do with prostitution. Not so. Mars has its fair share of prostitutes, mostly to service the tourist trade, and they do tour Navy bases for those poor folks who have a hard time connecting with another Navy person to fulfill their sexual needs.

No, I'm talking about the Music, Arts, and Drama Division, Martian Navy. That acronyms as MADDMN. I suppose the best way to pronounce that is Mad Damn (sometimes inverted to Damn Mad), or Madmen, and that's what the male troupers call themselves, but we ladies prefer Madams. Google USO and you'll get an idea of what I'm talking about, though the USO was volunteer entertainers visiting the troops during wartime, some of them big stars, others just singers and dancers. Martians learned a long time ago that food, water, pressure, and oxygen aren't all you need in the hostile environment of space. Put a man in a tin can with all the oatmeal, water, and oxygen he can eat, drink, and breathe, and pretty soon he'll go crazy. People need a space of their own, they need good food, many of them need contact with plants and especially animals, and most of all, they need art.

That's why everyone in a remote outpost gets a room of her own, from the admiral down to the lowest ensign. It just works better that way. Of course, the admiral has a suite and the ensign has more of a closet-type thing, but still.

That's why we allow dogs and cats and birds in faraway places. That's why there are endless organized activities for off-watch hours, from Ping-Pong tournaments to talent shows to karate matches to yoga classes. That's why we celebrate not only Christmas and Hanukkah and Eid and Arbor Day and Beethoven's Birthday, but Finnish Independence Day (December 6), Thai New Year (April 13–15), Australia Day (January 26), Brazilian *Nossa Senhora de Conceição Aparecida* Day (October 12), and Haitian Sovereignty and Thanksgiving Day (May 22). Of course, most places have a bigger to-do around Christmas than, say, Tibetan Paranirvana Day. Every day's a holiday for *somebody*, and the Navy will observe any of them if someone is interested enough and bored enough and silly enough to suggest it.

The thing is, living in a cramped environment a billion miles from civilization where your surroundings are always trying to kill you is not only dangerous, not only potentially nerve-wracking, but, more than anything, *boring*. You have to have entertainment beyond movies and recorded music. It is *necessary*. Ask any veteran.

And a talent show will get you only so far. In fact, there have been cases that can be summed up as "If I hear that fumble-fingered asshole play that lousy song on his out-of-tune guitar *one more time* . . . !" Well, it can lead to blows. Nothing can really take the place of a live stage show, whether it's *Hamlet, Showboat,* or just a jazz trio. Thus the Madams and Madmen.

Many people believe the cushiest assignment in the MADDMN is in one of the military bands, or the Navy Orchestra, which compares favorably with the Thunder City Philharmonic. Reason: They mostly stay home. All of them do tours of the outer postings, but you can view that as a road trip. Your official posting is Mars. My talents aren't suited for a large ensemble like that, and anyway, I didn't want to be posted at home. Just anywhere but Earth.

The acting troupes are always on tour and seldom see home until their enlistment is up. After all, even repertory groups don't usually have more than five or six plays rehearsed up to snuff, and you can only see *King Lear* so many times before you want a taste of something else.

VOICE IS MY main instrument, but I'm pretty good on keyboards, and competent on just about any plucked string instrument you throw at me. Guitar, lute, dulcimer, ukulele, dobro, mandolin, banjo, zither, autoharp, hurdy-gurdy, samisen . . . give me an hour to pick my way through the chord changes and refresh my memory and I won't disgrace myself on any of them, though I'm far from concert quality on all of them.

I can handle myself well on a lot of percussion instruments. I'm a demon on the castanets, maracas, triangle, hosho, lithophone, taiko, washboard, and congas.

I'm not much into wind instruments, though I play a mean harmonica, jug, kazoo, and ocarina. I can play the bagpipe, but I'm usually not asked to. Let me correct that: I'm usually asked *not* to. But of course I'm not the only one . . .

So, you may be asking yourself, with all that musical talent welling out of your pipes like ball lightning, why didn't you pass the audition the first time?

Two words: I choked. Three more: I blew it. I stunk up the place. I croaked, I basted in flop sweat, I had a panic attack so bad I could hardly breathe. For the first time since I was eight I got hit with something I could barely remember: stage fright. I didn't actually wet myself, but it was a close thing. For a while there I was sure I was going to vomit all over the stage.

It happens. But I hope it never happens again to *me*.

Clutching a remnant of pride around myself, let me point out that, bad as I was, the vote on the seven-member judging panel was four to three against me. If that's what I scored on my worst day, *ever*, I knew that if I could only get another shot, I could ace it. But you're supposed to have to wait a year before a second audition.

That's where Uncle Admiral's influence helped me. He moved me up the line. Thanks again, Admiral; I'll try to make you proud.

AS YOU APPROACH it, Europa goes from being a blazing white globe to looking more like a softball with the cover ripped off. A big ball of twine with dirt ground into some of the creases between the strings.

Europa is, in fact, the smoothest, most perfectly globular body in the solar system. The "strings" wrapping the softball are called linea, and they are cracks where the surface has fractured under a force called tidal flexing. It is subject to incredible gravitational stresses from the primary and the other three major moons, which stretches it and causes the icy crust to break and slide. Internal pressure forces salt water or slush to the surface, where it spreads out and fills in any craters that form. So we say she has a "young" surface, like Earth. Mars and Luna have old surfaces. The ice layer averages about ten miles thick . . . but that's an average, and in some places it's only two or three miles before you get to water. And in these places you will find the Europan "freckles."

That's what they called them when the first pictures came back from the Galileo spacecraft, which got there in 1995. The formal term is lenticulae . . . which is just Latin for freckles, so why be fancy? The freckles were reddish brown in color, lozenge-shaped, and they ranged from four to six miles across. It could be clearly seen that these were not impact craters but high points on the Europan surface. In the early pictures from above, they look like big rubber bands scattered across the surface, white in the middle and white around the edges.

What geological process had produced them? The best guess was they were like bubbles in a lava lamp, warmer ice working its way up through the crust.

For a long time people had wondered if this was the place in the solar system most likely to harbor life in its vast, dark oceans. The first manned ship landed in an area of the northern hemisphere between Minos and Cadmus, two of the widest, longest linea, and in the center of an area thick with freckles.

The term "freckles" didn't survive long once that ship was down. From then on, that Europan range was called the Big Rock Candy Mountains.

I COULD SEE them as we passed over the North Pole, but not for very long and not at a very good angle. In photos, they look a bit like Uluru, formerly Ayers Rock, in Australia, if it ever snowed enough there to cover the thing with a hundred feet of the white stuff. I watched them until they vanished over the horizon since I knew there was the possibility that I'd never get this close to them again. Most visitors to Europa—and there aren't many of those except Navy—never get much closer than the fifty-mile exclusion zone. As a Madam I had a better shot than most to make it to the forward research base, Clarke Centre, but I couldn't count on it.

They looked like giant jelly beans dropped from a great height and half-embedded in the ice and frosted on top.

Yummy.

One thing was quite clear to the naked eye. They were no longer the ridges with depressions in the center that had been seen on those long-ago Galileo flybys. They had grown. The largest ones were now two miles high and getting higher every day.

WE'RE USED TO temperatures on Mars that give Earthies the heebie-jeebies. On a sweltering midsummer noon it can get up to the mid-60s Fahrenheit, but watch out for those winter nights at the pole. Minus 220 is not uncommon.

The *high* temperature of the surface ice on Europa is –235. On the nightside, eclipsed by Jupiter, it can get down to –370, cold enough to freeze oxygen and nitrogen. This presents engineering problems in buildings and especially spaceports. But we Martians are good at insulation; we know how to not waste heat.

Everything has to be built up on stilts driven or melted into the ice. You have to be especially careful with landing pads. A bubble ship backing down for a landing generates terrific amounts of heat; it would melt and then boil a lot of ice, your ship would come down in it, and a few seconds after you turned off the drive you'd be frozen up to the portholes.

I don't know how the first ships to arrive on Europa managed it, but they did. People are clever that way. Slowly, the various bases were built up, each with a landing pad raised fifty or more feet above the ice and capable of supporting from one to a dozen large Navy ships.

Clarke Centre was the biggest of them all, home to a force of about twenty-five thousand people, 90 percent of them Navy personnel. It was built mostly from standard cold-planet habitat modules and, like most outposts in extremely hostile environments, grew in a more or less random fashion when more space was needed. It's a collection of domes and cylinders and shoe boxes and spheres covering almost a square mile, sometimes as much as thirty stories high. The predominant color is Navy red, but there are splashes of brighter paint here and there. It looks a little like a derelict oil refinery, preserved as a bit of cultural heritage, that I saw from a train going through Long Beach in California, a little like a junkyard, and a wee bit like a train wreck.

The ship landed lightly on a big transporter and was trundled to the arrivals area, where a rocketway attached itself to us like a lamprey, sealed tightly, and we passengers waited with our luggage while safety checks were made. Then we walked the fifty feet from ship to port, and I could feel the cold trying to suck the life out of me when I came within a foot of the wall.

Maybe it was my imagination. Surface temperature on arrival was −320. The very thin oxygen atmosphere out there would be faintly visible as a liquid dew that would boil off when the sun came up. It was still twenty-nine hours to sunrise. Europa's day is a bit over eighty-five hours, three and a half days, and it's tidally locked to Jupiter, so wherever the Big Guy is in the sky when you land at a base, that's where it's going to stay.

Clarke Centre was located near Pwyll Crater. And why so many features on Europa should be in Welsh is a question no one seems to have the answer to. It's pronounced "pool," or "poil," or "pwill," depending on who you ask, though all are acceptable because no one wants to go out on a limb and correct you, and because as far as anyone can tell, no actual Welsh speaker has ever been to Pwyll . . . and, frankly, because you seldom hear the word at all. People speak of Clarke Centre and avoid the issue entirely. I doubt you'll see *me* use the word again.

Clarke is at about 260 degrees of longitude, which puts it just into the Jupiter side of the moon. Jupiter is at the horizon, about 90 percent of it visible, and there it stays, going through phases like Earth's moon as Europa orbits around it, and is eclipsed by it. Clarke Centre and all the other bases get their coldest during eclipses.

There was none of the customs hassle you encounter practically everywhere else in the solar system when you arrive at a Navy base in a Navy ship. Even civilians don't come in for much attention, as they've already been thoroughly vetted and searched and sniffed before they ever got aboard. There was an orientation area where we checked in, were given room assignments, and were handed a few items like an events calendar, a list of base regulations and practices and customs—and every base is different that way—and even a few gifts. The base commander sent a box of chocolates. A *small* box, but hey!

I got a luggage dolly because I had a lot of stuff: one suitcase full of uniforms and two full of a *lot* of civvies—because let's face it, as a Madam nobody expected me to perform in uniform—and a bunch of my favorite musical instruments. All of it together didn't weigh more than forty pounds on Europa, but it was too bulky to carry. I quickly learned the low-gee shuffle needed to avoid banging one's head on the ceilings.

Okay, so I *did* hit my head a few times in the first hour. Everybody does.

Then I promptly got lost. Clarke Centre would baffle a gerbil in a habitrail. It's full of long corridors connecting different modules, and a surprising number of dead ends, both the physical type, as in a blank wall, and the other, as in a guard telling you this is a restricted area and you aren't rated for entry. You go up. You go down. You go over stuff and around stuff. And there you are . . . in a big shopping mall.

Okay, start over.

In the end I had to ask for directions from a passing ensign. He didn't even bother trying to spell it out but took me by the hand like a lost child and led me to my dorm—which the ensign informed me were always called "barracks" here at Clarke Centre.

The barracks contained two hundred units and a small civilian staff, including a janitor and a front desk that was manned from 6:00 A.M., base time (which was also Greenwich Earth time) to midnight. Hey, this was the twenty-first-century Martian Navy, not the British Navy of the Napoleonic Wars. We all have to serve, and we all vote, and we all like our comforts.

"Hello, Lieutenant," said the night porter, and glanced down at his desk display. "My name is William, and I guess you'd be Lieutenant Patricia Kelly Elizabeth—"

"Just Podkayne," I said. "Do we use ranks around here?"

"Not unless you insist. Junior officers only here in the Swamp. Your neighbors will be about the same rank, though of course they're all senior to you at the moment."

"Swamp?"

"It's better than Barrack 35, and Animal House was already taken. I think it's from a movie about something called the Korean War."

"Whatever. I just need a cot."

"First order of business, however, is to issue you a kayak."

Well, that's what it sounded like.

"Do a lot of white-water rafting on Europa, do you?"

He looked blank for a moment, then smiled.

"Kay-*ag*. KYAG. Short for—"

"Kiss Your Ass Good-bye. I forgot about that."

"Also known as the one-way ticket to the Big Bang, the mortician's best friend, and other epithets you'll learn when you've been at an outer-planet posting for a while." He opened a drawer in his desk with his thumbprint and took out a small box with a security seal on it, broke the seal, and unwrapped a package inside the box. And there was the KYAG.

It was a flat plastic box, two inches on a side, half an inch deep. There was a red button on one side. Also inside the package was a wrist strap and a chain.

"Put your thumb on the button," he said.

I did. A little light flashed red, then green.

"Now it will only work for you. In the last extremity, press and hold that button with your thumb for five seconds. If your thumb won't function, use any finger, or hold it to your eye; it has downloaded all your personal ID by now. If your eyes aren't working, you can put it in your blood and it will analyze your DNA. If you need it, you will very likely be bleeding."

Gruesome, gruesome. What he meant was "if your thumb has been blown off or if your eyes have been put out." The real name of the scary little device was PSU, for Personal Suspension Unit. They'd only been around about four years, and so far were only issued to people residing beyond the asteroid belt, where danger was highest. There were people who wanted to issue them to all Martians—hell, all humans—but there was still a lot of resistance. Heartlanders called them the Devil's work, but they said the same about birth-control implants.

The KYAG contained a tiny black bubble generator. This was strictly a last-resort measure, to be employed only when death was clearly imminent and unavoidable. A spurting jugular, zero pressure, falling toward a lake of liquid nitrogen . . . these were the sorts of circumstances in which the Navy allowed the use of the PSU.

So far they'd only been actually used a few times, once after an explosion in the oxygen tanks of a ship orbiting Neptune, a few times in fires in planetary habitats. That way, in the aftermath, rescue crews could go in and find the bubbles, bring them back to a hospital, and save lives. Most of the time it worked. Some of the time when the bubble was opened, the person inside was too far gone to save.

"I have to tell you some legal stuff," William said, with a sigh. "The penalty for using a PSU without demonstrable need is five years at hard labor. These are not toys. 'Demonstrable need' is usually understood to be the certainty of death within a few minutes. The example I use: If your hand has been cut off, don't use the PSU. Find a tourniquet. If your arm is off at the shoulder . . . use it.

"Misplacing your unit will cost you thirty days in the brig, loss of rank, and loss of accumulated enlistment time. In other words, you'll start all over as an ensign with your full ride still ahead of you. The Navy does *not* want these things falling into the wrong hands, and so far, none of them have. Keep it that way. You are required to have the unit on your person everywhere outside of your own room. My advice: *Wear it,* on the chain or wrist or, even better, chained to a navel ring or a nipple clip . . . or whatever else it is you females pierce. Never take it off, not in the bathtub, not to make love."

"What about losing it, as opposed to misplacing it?"

"Never happened. Oh, the penalties are severe, theoretically, as bad as setting it off without just cause. But it has a location finder in it, and the only way to turn that off is to destroy it, and the only way to do that would be to toss it into a blast furnace. These little critters are *tough,* Podkayne."

I looped the chain around my neck, not having a pierced navel or nipple or labia, if that was the word he was looking for.

"So where's my room, William?"

"Follow me, please."

I was so glad he didn't say "Walk this way," because it is *such* an old joke and he was flamboyantly effeminate, and there's no way I could have managed that sashay in a low-grav field I wasn't used to. I was seriously rocket-lagged, and behind on my sleep. My days aboard ship had been busy ones. More about that later.

We went down a corridor and passed a common room on the right that was empty this time of night. There was a big gym on the left—*not* a luxury, but a necessity, a place I'd be spending at least an hour a day to keep my muscle tone up to Mars standard. Three people were working out on the machines. We passed a sauna and a small automated 7-Eleven store where you could buy those minor items that weren't worth a trip to the PX.

Then up an elevator to the twentieth floor and a few steps around a gently curving corridor to room 2001. Hey, I'm on a space odyssey! William informed me there were ten rooms on each floor—which he called a deck. He keyed the door and had me press my palm against it, and the barracks computer memorized my print.

"We had a wire from an Admiral Redmond a few days ago," he said as he opened the door and stood aside so I could pull my baggage train inside. "He said to tell you this was his room when he was an ensign and assigned to Europa. He thought you might like it. Luckily, it was available."

I looked at his face, but it was all innocence. I had the feeling that a wire like that from an admiral would be read by William as pretty much an order, and I hoped nobody had been dumped in the hall because I was coming. You don't need that when you're the new kid on the barrack.

The first thing I saw was the cat. He had a black face and ears, blue eyes, and a cream-colored body, black legs with white socks, and a black tail. He had a *lot* of fur, a regular powder puff. He sat in Sphinx position in a comfy chair, front paws tucked under him, eyes half-open. He swiveled his head to look at me for a moment, didn't see anything interesting, and closed his eyes again.

"Oh, that's Kahlua," William said. "I thought I had sealed the cat door, though I wouldn't put it past him to pick the lock. He belongs to the previous tenant . . . sort of. I'll banish him to the hall."

"Let him stay. I imagine the owner will know where to look for him."

"I'm sure she will. Very well." William then gave me a brief tour.

My family are innkeepers from way back, and we have our own code words for amenities in rooms. This one was below a Hyatt, but far above a 6 and maybe a cut above a Holiday Inn. You could call it a suite, because there were two rooms, but you don't call quarters a suite in the Navy.

Living room with a couch and a media wall and a table and a few chairs. Kitchen nook with a two-seat bar counter, small fridge, microwave, heating surface, little pantry, and enough utensils to serve four.

You dropped your dirty dishes and trash in a chute, and clean stuff was delivered back to you in the night. The plates all had Martian Navy written around the edge in red. The usual pots and pans and gadgets.

The colors were soft and inoffensive and boring. William said I could change them if I wished but had to do my own painting.

The bedroom: just big enough for a double and a nightstand. I sat on it, stretched out on it, and it was good. Of course in .134 gee a slab of concrete would have been acceptable, so long as it was warm.

The head: much better than I expected. All the usual plumbing plus a bathtub that looked long enough for me to stretch out and soak for a while. It was five feet deep.

"Don't run it too full," William advised. "Things slosh here on Europa like you wouldn't believe."

"I'll be careful," I said. "When are inspections? Or do they surprise you?"

He looked offended. "This isn't boot camp, darling. So long as your uniform passes muster in public, no one cares how you keep your quarters, though someone might take notice if you started raising chickens. You don't even have to make your bunk."

"I probably will anyway. My family was always big on that."

"Yes, I suppose they would be. I worked for your grandfather for ten years."

I didn't know if I liked that or not, but he soon made it clear that he had loved working at the Red Thunder and thought the world of Granddaddy Manny. He mentioned meeting me when I was two or three, when he was the head concierge, and I realized he was older than he looked.

"Well, unless you have any questions . . . "

"No. Thank you, William," I said. "Should I tip you?"

He started to look offended, then saw I was kidding.

"I'll leave you to it, then," he said, and quietly vanished. I didn't even hear the door close. I thought I could learn to like William. And he was good-looking. Too bad about the sexual orientation.

THERE WAS A houseplant and a fruit basket sitting on the counter in the tiny kitchenette. I'd noticed them before, but after exploring the storage spaces (not bad, but not room enough for all my wardrobe and instruments) and doing what little wandering could be done in the little suite, I took a closer look. Apples, oranges, a mango and a guava, walnuts, almonds, black and orange jelly beans, some sort of cranberry cookies . . . and a small carved pumpkin. I checked my heads-up and, sure enough, tomorrow was Halloween back on Earth.

I opened the small envelope and took out the card, and read:

BOO!

THE STAFF AND MANAGEMENT OF THE

RED THUNDER HOTEL

WISH YOU AND YOURS A SCARY,

MERRY HALLOWEEN!!

Love, Granddaddy Manny and Kelly

Well, my heart just leaped, and I got choked up. I suddenly realized that I was way, way farther from home than I'd ever been, and though I'd not let myself think about it, I was lonely and even a little bit frightened about it all. Earth wasn't like this. I'd hated Earth, but it was crowded, warm, and homey compared to Europa. The thoughtfulness of Manny and Kelly . . . no, though Kelly was good and thoughtful and always remembered important dates, it would never have occurred to her to send me something for Halloween. And if she did, it would have been something more tasteful. This one had Granddaddy written all over it. He knew what would cheer me up.

Take it easy, kiddo. This is just another hotel room, and this is just another planet. The Stricklands and Garcias and Redmonds have always pushed outward, and even if we've been afraid, we've been there for each other. You are loved. I heard this all as distinctly as if he'd whispered it into my ear.

The plant was from Mom and Dad. Nothing fancy, just a Wandering Jew in a brass basket you could hang from the ceiling. I laughed. We're not Jewish, but I sure felt like a wanderer.

For a moment I was struck with a sense of awe at these homey touches in such a place. I'm a child of the space age—the second, *real* space age, which began after chemical rockets were made obsolete. But that age is not that old yet, and my granddaddy could remember a time when a small city on a place like Europa was barely even a pipe dream, and he was still alive to talk about it. He wasn't even that old. In less than fifty years humanity had come from one cobbled-together rocket, the old *Red Thunder*, to the point that Manny could order a basket of fresh fruit delivered to my little suite half a billion miles from my home planet. *Fresh* Europan fruit, from genetically engineered trees grown in real dirt by the environmental brigade of Clarke Centre. Just pick up the phone on Mars and order what you want, then wait an hour and a half for confirmation of the order as the transaction crawls a billion miles at the speed of light. Fruit, flowers, or a Wandering Jew.

I picked up the card stuck in the plant and opened it:

DECORATE!
Love, Mom

Perfect. Mom had been horrified at my videos of my Pismo apartment, which was much the same the day I moved out as it was the day I moved in. Mom's one of those ladies who will transform any space she lives in within twenty-four hours, or die trying. I grew up surrounded by one of the finer collections of eclectic knickknacks, batik, pottery, and Boehm porcelains on Mars, not to mention a jungle of tropical plants. Maybe that's why I never did anything to my place on Earth. Too much competition. That, and I never really wanted to see it as my home.

Maybe I'd feel different here. At least I'd be surrounded by Martians.

I'D NOTICED A long window in the living room, but it was covered by the external blast shield, like all windows in Navy bases. It was easy to forget sometimes because the Martian Navy was not like most military organizations on Earth, with all the rank and drill and privation and sometimes flat-out torture—except in the commando units, which I wanted no part of—but we *were* military, and though it had long seemed unlikely that we'd ever be called on to fight, we had to be prepared for the possibility.

There was another, smaller window in the bedroom, just beyond the bed itself. For the first time I noticed something out of place in the impersonal neatness of the place. There was a square of yellow paper stuck to the inside of the window. I put one knee on the bed and reached over for it. It was a Post-it Note, and contained a short handwritten message that must have been faxed from Mars and printed out for William to attach where instructed. It said:

Enjoy
Uncle Admiral

I reached for the window power button and Kahlua the cat jumped up on the bed and rubbed his head against my side. The shutters went up . . . and I gasped.

Let's start up close and then pan out, shall we?

At my feet was the sprawl of sparkling lights that was Clarke Centre, mostly low but with a few tall structures dotted here and there. I could count six giant geodesics with green trees inside. These would be where the stuff in my fruit basket had come from, and they doubled as city parks. There were many more long, low greenhouses with transparent roofs where truck and hydroponic gardening was done. Hence fresh flowers, fresh tomatoes, fresh eggs, and milk. The roofs of these structures bristled with lights to supplement the very weak sunshine 5 AU from Sol, only 1⁄25 of what Earth got.

Beyond that was a stretch of almost perfectly flat ice, white even at night. It was like the whole city had been set down on the surface of a giant cue ball. But not all *that* huge; the horizon was close, much closer than it would have been back home on Mars. But that was just the enchanting setting for the star of the show.

The Big Boy. Jupiter.

From Europa, Jupiter covers about twelve degrees of the sky. That may not sound like much, considering that the sky is 180 degrees across . . . but how much of the sky do you think Earth's moon covers? Most people are surprised at the answer. It's only half a degree. That means that Jupiter is twenty-four times the width of a full moon.

But the *area* Jupiter covers from Europa is the square—twenty-four times twenty-four—*or five hundred and seventy-six times* the size of Luna seen from Earth. Believe me, that is one gigantic Christmas tree ornament sitting there on the horizon.

It took my breath away. This was the view Uncle Bill had had when he was posted here, and he was sharing it with me. I couldn't imagine there was a better view in all of Clarke Centre, maybe all of Europa.

You look at Jupiter from that close, and the impression is one of immense violence. And yet I didn't feel intimidated by it, and of course I was not threatened by it. It was violence frozen in place. Time-lapse will show you just how active those storms really are, hurricanes bigger than Planet Earth and three or four times as windy. Below that swirling cloud layer, lots of hydrogen and a little helium, both in a gaseous state, gradually turning into liquid hydrogen under enormous pressure, then into metallic hydrogen—and I don't even know what that is, but the pressure has to be even greater to produce it—and finally a small rocky core.

Kahlua jumped up on the window ledge and joined me in enjoying the view. He batted at the glass with a paw and rubbed his nose against it, which is a sure sign that a cat likes something and wants to mark it so everybody knows it's his.

"Don't get snot on the window, doofus," I told him, and made a stack of pillows so I could lie back and just let the view wash over me.

I woke up a few minutes later with Kahlua standing on my chest and bumping noses with me. He was purring like a chain saw. He only weighed a few pounds here. I rolled over and spilled him onto the bed, which didn't seem to bother him at all.

I thought about getting up, getting out of my clothes, taking a shower. Then I thought about not doing it. I yawned, curled up, and felt Kahlua find a place to nestle against me. I took one long last look at Jupiter out my window, and closed my eyes.

Home? Could be.

7

I LET THE waves of applause wash over me as the lights came up on the band, took a slow bow, turned it into a curtsy that I hoped had sort of a Barbra Streisand thing going, but felt pretty sure it was more Fanny Brice, and smiled.

"Thank you ladies, gentlemen, aliens, and others," I said. "We are Podkayne and the Pod People. Tell your friends. We'll be appearing here nightly for the rest of the week before starting our triumphant world tour, by popular demand . . . and orders from Madman Central Command." This got a ripple of laugher from the mostly Navy crowd—all my crowds these days were mostly Navy.

They were still applauding, and some were standing. A few were doing double or triple flips in the air, as they sometimes do on Europa.

"Let's hear it for the Pod People," I shouted. "On winds, Joey 'Lips' Farrell. On the real imitation-wood imitation-Steinway, the genuine accept-no-substitutes Cassandra Alonzo. And sitting behind the drums, the genius of everything you can whack with a stick, Quinn the Eskimo, the *mighty Quinn*. Give it up for the hardest-working band on Europa."

More applause, rimshots, chords, a reprise of the last bars of "Memory," the showstopper we'd been ending with the last two nights. This was our torch song set: a little Billie, a little Nina Simone, Patti LuPone, Diana Krall, a touch of Wendy Dare, some Baako, and a dash of Butterfly, who I'd met once. The first set of the night had been dedicated to Ella and Barbra: "How High the Moon," "In the Still of the Night," "I'm Beginning to See the Light," "Cry Me a River," "Soon It's Gonna Rain," "Bewitched, Bothered and Bewildered," "My Man." Stuff like that. It was hard on the vocal cords, ending with the Lloyd Webber, but it was worth it; there's seldom been a crowd pleaser like that one.

Somebody threw a pair of panties on the stage. Well, it looked like I'd pleased *someone,* but not my cup of tea. I snagged them with one foot and tossed them over my shoulder to Lips. Then I waved and headed backstage. My first step took me a foot in the air and I had to try to look dignified while waiting to come down.

Almost a month on Europa, and I was still "Mars-footed," as the longtime residents put it. "Mars-headed" meant either a helmet or a bandage on the crown of your head from leaping too high too often in moments of excitement, and the end of the last set of a night that had gone very well sure qualified. I'm an applause slut, I never denied it. It's better than food, sex, or drugs (I imagine). But I had to get my legs under control. Hitting your head on the ceiling is something *Earthies* do.

"Let's hear it for Podkayne, Europa's answer to all those great chanteuses of yesteryear!" It was "Rick," owner of Rick's Café Americain, a pudgy, balding guy whose name wasn't really Rick and who did a terrible Bogart imitation and had roaming hands to boot until I showed him what a spike heel could do to an instep—he was still limping a little—in his white tux and elevator shoes. We hated each other, but the Pod People were filling his club, so we pretended we didn't. "Get back out here, Pod, take another bow, maybe you could favor these folks with another number!"

Asshole. I was done for the night, but I knew my obligations, so I returned from behind the curtain at the rear and took his offered hand—sweaty, like his forehead—did another bow, blew a few kisses, and did a vanishing act.

Pretty soon I was joined in the small dressing room by the rest of the band. Beers were cracked, instruments packed, shoes kicked off. The zipper in back of my blue satin gown was stuck, and I asked Quinn to help me with it. He did, and his hand continued down inside and cupped my bare behind. Squeezed.

I let him. A shipboard fling had turned into something a little more serious, though a long way from permanent.

That's right. I'd done the silliest thing you can do in the world of popular music. I was sleeping with the drummer.

THAT FIRST MORNING in my room at Clarke Centre I was awakened by Kahlua bumping noses, and gradually realized someone was knocking on the door. Better not be Prince Charming, I thought, realizing I was still in my wrinkled travel clothes and probably didn't smell all that good. But you don't need much energy to bounce out of bed on Europa, so I bounced, and stumbled my way to the door.

When I opened it, nobody seemed to be there.

"Trick or treat!" somebody said.

Then a hand rose into view, holding a cup of steaming coffee. I reached for it reflexively, it smelled so good, then I looked down on an elf.

That's what she looked like, anyway, in a green top and billowy pants and soft brown moccasins, blond hair in a pixie cut. Peter Pan, maybe, though the figure was far from boyish. She'd have fit neatly under my armpit. No, actually she didn't quite rise to that level. Four-foot-eleven, I later learned.

"Trick or treat in reverse, actually," she said. "I come bearing sweets and caffeine, and to check on the cat. May I come in? You don't get any coffee and donuts unless you invite me in."

I mumbled something that she must have taken for an invitation, and maybe it was, though I still wasn't awake enough to be sure. I took a sip of the coffee. It was wonderful. I mumbled something else.

"Yeah, I'm finicky about my coffee. That's from Kenya." I decided she was damn good at interpreting my mumbles.

"Hi, baby!" That wasn't addressed to me but to Kahlua, who had leaped to her shoulder—not much of a leap, actually—and was rubbing himself all over her and purring like an outboard motor. "This is Kahlua, if you haven't been introduced," the elf went on.

"Yeah, we were . . ."

"And you'd be Podkayne, the admiral's daughter, the one who stole my room from me. And I'm Karma."

"He's my . . . I'm his nie— . . . listen, I'm sorry, I didn't . . . you can have . . ."

"Don't worry about it. It was presented to me as a request, not an order, and I didn't like the room, anyway."

"What's not to like?"

"The windows. Would you mind closing them?"

I went over and hit the power button, and the big window closed tight. I looked at her and raised an eyebrow.

"Agoraphobia," she admitted. "Also a touch of acrophobia. I'm a lot happier in a room without windows, especially if it's this high up."

That was fairly common among Martians. A lot of us don't get out much.

"So how did you . . ."

"Kept the windows closed. Long as I can't see it, I'm fine. Your next question is why did I stay here for over a year, and I guess it was the cat. He comes with the unit, sort of."

"That's what William said, too. What you do mean, 'sort—' "

"Kahlua doesn't belong to anybody, like most of the pets here do. He goes where he wants, but this is his bedroom. He's the dominant male in the Swamp; all the other cats get out of his way. He came to visit last night, so that's okay. Donut?"

I took one out of the bag, took a bite, and the sugar rush finally got me feeling more or less awake.

"You're . . ."

"Short? Everybody notices that. But I'm Mars-born, just like you. Not *all* Martians live in the stratosphere."

"That's not what I—"

"Perky? I can't help it. You'll get used to it."

"Will you ever let me—"

"Finish a sentence? Probably not. I'm sort of telepathic, all my friends say so."

I thought, *you have friends?* It didn't seem likely, if she was always like this.

"I know." She sighed. "It's just nerves. I'm the shortest Martian I know, and it doesn't do much for a girl's confidence. I'll settle down presently."

"Karma . . . ?" It didn't seem worth the effort to say anything more, and I was right.

"Well, at least it's unusual. Like Podkayne. My mom is a bit of a nut, tell you the honest truth."

Right. And you're telepathic.

"You have a right to be dubious. But you'll see. Mom didn't plan on getting pregnant, but when I showed up she decided it was in the stars. Could have been worse. Just ask my brother, Fate, or my sister, Kismet."

I couldn't help myself. I laughed, and soon we both were.

"You just wait," she said. "We're going to be best friends."

I didn't think that was likely. I liked my friends to be quieter.

"You just wait," she repeated, almost . . . okay, almost like she was reading my mind. "So let's get going, time's a-wasting! Finish that coffee while I brew some more, get in the shower, change clothes . . . we've *got* to do something about this *room*. We've got to go"—dramatic pause, and she spread her arms wide—"*shopping*!"

HOW COULD YOU do it, Poddy? Don't you know better? The *drummer*? You know drummers, they're apt to spontaneously combust, die in a bizarre gardening accident, or strangle on vomit, possibly even their own vomit. That was the *point* about drummers. You never knew what they were going to do, but you could be pretty sure it wouldn't be pretty.

"Quinn," he said solemnly, when we first met, at the MADDMN compound near Pavonis Mons, back on Mars. "Just Quinn."

"First or last?" I asked.

"Just Quinn."

"Strickland," I said, just as solemnly. "Podkayne Strickland." I could have said "Podkayne, just Podkayne," since that's how I usually introduced myself, but I used ex-President Kelly's name when I wanted to impress, and somehow right from the first I wanted to impress this man.

He was cool. Just a slight widening of his eyes betrayed that he knew the name, but he wasn't about to ask if I was from *that* Strickland family.

We were all doing a rather strange mating dance at Pavonis, and it didn't have anything to do with sex. Well, of course *everything* humans do has *something* to do with sex, but that's not why we were courting each other. In *this* dance hall, sexual preference had nothing to do with it. I found myself wooing Cassandra Alonzo as passionately as I'd ever gone after any guy . . . but it was her hands I wanted, and I wanted them on the keyboards.

See, being admitted to the MADDMN was just step one. To stay there, on the pop music level, you had to assemble an act. Classically trained musicians had it easy. If you were a whiz on the violin, cello, trumpet, or clarinet, you would quickly be inducted into one of the ensembles like the military bands, drum and bugle corps, or even the symphony. But guitar whangers, drum-set pounders, jazz 'bone pickers, and contralto chantoossies usually had to unite or die . . . which in my case would mean finding myself back on the beach at Pismo.

Some groups came preformed, they'd worked together before their mandatory enlistment, but that was fairly rare. It's an axiom in the trade that pop bands have an average life of about six months before "artistic differences" tear them apart. Artistic differences usually means that all the other people in the group are behaving like assholes. Trust me, I've seen it many times. (Me? An asshole? I prefer "perfectionist," but it's *possible* some others might use a more powerful word.)

You didn't have forever to accomplish this. In fact, you had thirty days before you had to come before the auditioning board, rehearsed and ready to boogie, for a thumbs-up or a one-way ticket back to your old posting.

I had arrived at Pavonis with the intention of going solo. Me, a piano, a bar, and endless requests for "Melancholy Baby" and "Send in the Clowns" and "The Phobos Blues." I was informed within the hour that there were no openings for such an act. Come back in a year and try again. Pismo, here I come.

I was good enough to join one of the touring companies that were assembled at Pavonis. There were call sheets out for *Aida* and *The Mikado*, and I knew I could easily find work as either Amneris or Katisha (in suitable makeup). There was also *Sweeney Todd*—I'd always wanted to play Mrs. Lovett—and a new musical, something called *Work in Progress*, based on *Finnegans Wake*. I'd listened to some downloads of the

West End version, and knew I could really *own* the part of Anna Livia Plurabelle.

But these were all migratory assignments, hopping from Mercury to Sedna and all the rocks in between. I'd have to give up my Europa posting, and I wasn't about to do that. If I wanted to sing opera or Broadway, Europa had resident amateur groups I could join . . . but first I had to get to Europa, and with each passing day that was seeming harder and harder. Just getting the posting was easy. Nepotism, pure and simple. But Uncle Admiral couldn't help me when it came to the qualifying round.

IT WAS QUINN who brought us together. There were six of us at first, and we knew each other from the jams and solos we'd all attended and participated in, trying to make something work. It had been two weeks, and several bands had already formed and shipped out. The other four were Cassandra, Joey, and Jim Hartman—a fiddle player who specialized in bluegrass and zydeco, but who Quinn judged was adaptable enough for what he had in mind—and Meiko Miyazaki . . .

. . . a singer. It was obvious one of us had to die. We hated each other at first sight, and so behaved with every possible show of friendliness. I don't think any of the guys were fooled. She sang in that nasal soprano characteristic of nip-pop of the last two decades.

"Jim, who are your influences?" Quinn asked, when we were all settled around a table at the canteen with coffee and munchies.

"Well, Clifton Chenier, of course." He thought about it, his fingertips idly moving over his violin strings. "Boozoo Chavis. Buckwheat. Leftover. Rockin' Sydney. Soilent Green." Quinn nodded at each name. I knew about half of them, and it was clear nobody else there knew any of them. "Cedric Rainwater, Flatt and Scruggs, Vassar Clements, Kentucky Thunder, Yonder Mountain. Is that enough?"

"That'll do. What about you, Meiko?"

"The Usual Suspects," she said.

"No, be specific," Cassandra said.

"I am. That's a band." Meiko looked a little miffed. "They started the Okinawa pentatonic rock movement ten, fifteen years ago. Other influences . . . Happy End, Sandii and the Sunsetz, The 5.6.7.8's, Aushvitz,

Green Milk From the Planet Orange, Michelle Gun Elephant, The Termites . . ." She rambled on in that vein for a while, and all of us but Quinn were googling as fast as we could key in the names. All headbanger bands, every one of them. I never did find out for sure if Quinn knew all of those groups, but his knowledge of the music of the last century and a half was encyclopedic, so he may have.

When she was finished, Quinn turned to me.

"Podkayne? Influences?"

I didn't like the way this was going. I felt sure Quinn wanted to put together a band that would specialize in more current pop, which wasn't my strength at all. But I forged ahead, trotting out my own list of the usual suspects.

"Barbra, of course, and Ella and Billie. And—"

"Billy who?" Meiko asked. "I don't know any solo guy named Billy. Who does he sing with?"

There was a silence, which stretched out uncomfortably. Joey broke it.

"I think she means Billie Holiday," he said.

"Lady Day?" Vanessa prompted. Meiko shrugged.

"Natalie Appleton," I went on. "Sinatra . . . Frank, not Nancy. David Crosby. Anita O'Day, Baako Williams, Janis Siegel, Anita Baker, The Roches, Janis Ian, Feminem, Beyoncé, Siobhann Heidenreich, Art Garfunkel . . . is that enough?"

Meiko was looking cross-eyed, obviously scanning the information she was googling. I don't think she knew much about any of the people I had mentioned.

"Sinatra? How can this man be an influence on you? He is a baritone!"

I thought of saying "phrasing," but I wasn't sure she'd be familiar with the term.

I'm being catty here, I know it. Meiko had a narrow range and limited knowledge of those who came before her, but she was very good at what she did . . . if that was your cup of sake. Personally, I think sake tastes like warm piss.

Joey's influences: the entire Marsalis family, Benny Goodman, Coleman Hawkins, Bird, Louis Armstrong, Artie Shaw, Rolf Smedvig, Michelle Perry. And so on through Cassandra (Thelonious Sphere Monk and Dave Brubeck—interesting combination—and Glenn Gould) and Quinn (Sandy Nelson, Art Blakely, Evelyn Glennie, Willie Bobo).

So at last we were all waiting to see what Quinn had to say. And it was this:

"I'm going to say just one word to start. That word is jazz."

A pause while we all chewed that over. It was an incredibly juicy word, jazz, and one that worked fine for me.

"Miles?" Joey asked. "Bill Evans? Chick Corea? Bop?"

"A little cooler than that. Brubeck, Sinatra, scat, torch songs."

"Pop jazz?" Cassandra suggested.

"And some rock. I don't want to categorize too much. Here's the deal. We don't have to specialize too much. Pop music was in the doldrums for a long time. Rap eliminated melody, videos made it big business, downloads gave it back to the people, and the people haven't come up with anything that interests me for a long time. I don't like the formless stuff going down now; we've got melody back now, but it's nonlinear and random, and I miss the beat."

"I guess a drummer *would* miss it," I said.

"I do, too," Cassandra said.

"And me," said Jim.

"Back then they were using drum machines," Quinn said, in the tone of voice you might use to say "infected hemorrhoids." I didn't have anything to say to that. All singers have used synthesized backup at one time or another.

"Anyway," he went on, "most musicians I know feel that popular music has been in one of its periodic downswings."

Meiko looked like she was going to say something, then decided not to.

"Not all of them," Quinn acknowledged. "But a lot, and I agree with them. So there's that, and there's the well-known fact that the type of music most people will enjoy throughout their lives is *set,* sort of programmed in, by the time they're in their midtwenties."

"Exactly," said Meiko. "So take that, and add it to the fact that the bulk of Navy audiences are eighteen to twenty-one, serving out their hitches, and it seems to me we ought to be talking modern contemporary."

"Makes sense," Joey said.

"It does," Quinn said, "and that's why most everybody's doing it. But there's two things they haven't thought about, and one thing *you* all haven't thought about. One is that, on the outer-planet stations, the ratio of draftees to lifers is a lot lower. A *lot* lower. Most draftees serve dirtside, redside, or IP Patrol." That was Navy for Earth, Mars, or aboard a ship on customs patrol in the Inner Planets Naval Military Region, where the vast bulk of humanity resides: between Mercury and the asteroid belt.

"Now, I know none of you want that. So Podkayne's got a ticket to Europa, and anybody who joins in a group with her can hitch a ride."

Several eyebrows went up. He was right. None of the others had a secure posting, and they might end up in a much less interesting assignment. None of them were forgetting that they needed Madmen and Madams on the far-flung outposts of the dwarf planets, too, like Pluto, Eris, Sedna, Nanook, Tulugaak, Pukkeenegaak . . . all the way out to the edges of the Oort Cloud. These were widely considered to be hardship posts where a MADDMN troupe would spend most of its time aboard supply scows going from one long-period comet research facility to another.

My ticket to Europa. *My* ticket. I suddenly felt a lot better about things, to the point I might even consider bringing along a second singer. I could be magnanimous.

Meiko didn't look like she could be.

"So our audience ain't gonna be just people our age, that's number one," he said. He was doing a pretty good selling job. He had our complete attention. "Podkayne's got a posting to Europa. And even with our generation, musical tastes are broader than they've been in years. Our moms and dads, they grew up in a creative musical era, they look back on it with nostalgia, they want to hear that music . . . and more, because it was a time of fusion and retrospection. Influences from way back were being felt. Oldies were being dragged out of the closet and getting a lot of downloads. And it's kept up now that things are in a period of consolidation. Used to be, each generation had its own music, and the stuff that came before . . . that was squaresville, man. That's a term from a century ago. Much less so today. Now that everything, and I mean *everything*, can be ordered and downloaded, people's tastes are more eclectic. One person's music stash might have a bit of opera, a bit of ragtime, Sinatra, Foo Fighters, Sex Pistols, the Termites, the Beatles, Graham Nash, Gregorian chants, Miles Davis . . . people are at least *open* to listening to just about anything. And if you're good, *really* good, they'll come back."

"I don't see it," Meiko said.

"Maybe I do." That was Cassandra. I kept my mouth shut.

"I've done research on this, believe me," Quinn went on. "I've studied music history and the evolution of musical taste for a long time, and I can show you the data. But what you want to know is the bottom line. Can we form a group around Podkayne? Can we cover half a dozen styles but stay away from the easy, sure things that the great majority of the groups here at Pavonis are going to gig with? Can we bring this stuff to a new audience? Can we be really, *really* good at what we do?"

Meiko and I stared at each other, but neither of us said anything. Then she got up and left, without a word to any of us. The silence stretched out, and I kept my mouth shut.

"What I can't figure," Cassandra said, at last, "is what she was doing here in the first place."

Joey had been intently studying his shoes, or the floor, or something down there between his knees as he slumped in his chair. He raised his hand.

"That would be me," he admitted. "She and I . . . we've been . . . thought she might be able to fit in . . ."

"And she's really good in bed, right?" Cassandra asked.

He looked up, and his expression was so sorrowful that we all laughed, and pretty soon he did, too.

Jim said he was looking for something deeper in his musical roots, and we all wished him well, and that's how Podkayne and the Pod People was born.

And we were good. We were really, *really* good.

DESPITE ALL MY misgivings, Karma and I quickly became best friends, the Mutt and Jeff of the Swamp.

In addition to our height, we had a lot of other things in common:

Karma was tone-deaf, couldn't carry a tune in a wheelbarrow. I have perfect pitch and a four-octave vocal range.

She was one of the best dancers I've ever seen, and a gymnast and acrobat of no mean skills. She had almost made the Martian Olympic team. I am a total klutz, can't walk across a room without stumbling over my own feet.

She was a chatterbox, never at a loss for words. I am what you might call reserved unless the talk is about music.

She was instantly at home in any social situation, without inhibitions, modesty, self-doubt, or the slightest inkling of inferiority. I'm . . . reserved.

I like anchovies on my pizza, and she likes artichoke hearts. I say to-*may*-to and she says to-*maah*-to.

We both, however, love to shop.

That first day she dragged me to the mall. First stop: Bed, Bath, and *Way* Beyond. We spent a few hours arguing amiably about sheets and towels and things like that, settling on a color scheme for each room of my new home. Over lunch at Pablo's Mexican Grill—chosen because it did *not* feature a view of Jupiter and the surface—we debated the relative merits of paint and wallpaper. She favored smart paper because you could dial up any color or pattern you wanted; I told her I'd had it in my room at home on Mars, and years went by without my changing the color by a single wavelength. So we went to the hardware store and bought a few pints of eight different colors to try out.

During that day we learned a lot about each other. She was delighted but not overawed to learn who my family was.

"I've eaten a few times at your mom's restaurant. Wonderful stuff, but a bit spendy for my family. And both my parents voted for your grandmother."

She came from the middle class of Mars. Both her parents were Earth-born, naturally, the two of them managing a small ski resort on Olympus Mons.

"I could ski before I could walk," she said.

She had made one trip to Earth, when she was fifteen, a month of vacation with her family.

"I loved it!" she said. "I mean, I loved the Earth; nobody likes Earthies. But I didn't see a lot of them."

"What about the gravity?"

"Didn't bother me after the first day. We shorties deal with it better than you tall folks. We went up the Amazon, up to where there's still jungle. It was all the life! An explosion of life, everywhere I looked. We went for hikes in the jungle and I realized that everything I was seeing was alive. On Mars, everywhere you look, everything is dead."

"Sounds like maybe you should have been an Earthie."

She withered me with a look.

"Sorry, I didn't mean it as an insult."

"No, you've got a point. I've even thought about it, after my hitch is up. I thought about going to school and being an entomologist."

"What's that?"

"Somebody who studies insects."

Bugs! Oh, yuck! She was smiling at me.

"Okay, we're even. I'm an agoraphobe, but you're an entomophobe. Both very Martian things to be."

"Something I don't get," I said. "If you're afraid of open spaces, how did you manage it on Earth?"

"I don't get it, either," she admitted. "I was real worried before we went, and I didn't do too well in the cities. I didn't like to get out of the car or the train. I wanted a roof over my head! But when we got to the jungle, it just all went away. You ever been in a jungle?"

I shook my head. I guess it would be better than a walk in my underwear from Pavonis to Olympus, but not by much. A bug under every leaf . . .

"Something about it. Pretty soon I loved it."

She was an apprentice agronomist here on Europa, looking to learn all she could in the ultracontrolled environments of the hydroponic and dirt farms, orchards, and municipal parks, so that when her hitch was over she could go to Brazil and get her degree. I wished her well.

EXCERPTS FROM PODKAYNE'S JOVIAN DIARY:

Saturday, November 9

Hindu Festival of Light. Día de Caman in Peru. Cambodian National Independence Day. Dia de Virgen de la Almudena in Spain.

Rehearsing heavily for big opening at Rick's next week. Karma helped with preparations for the housewarming party. Got all the painting and most of the decorating done just in time. Made 6 of Grandfather Jim's pecan pies and gallons of Uncle Jubal's jambalaya recipe, also lots of Mom's canapés. All got snarfed down in the first hour, had to send out for cold cuts and pizza. Most of the Swamp critters showed up for at least a few minutes, plus the band and all their friends, and Karma's friends from all over Clarke Centre. People spilled out into the hallway and neighbor Chan opened the adjoining door to his apartment to take the excess; must find a way to pay him back, nice man. Sang a few songs near the end of the evening, got some people to sing along. Must find a way to discourage Karma from singing. Horrible!

Sunday, November 10

Cry of Independence in Palau. Maputo City Day in Mozambique. Militsiya Day in Russia. Potosi Festival in Bolivia. Sadie Hawkins Day in East and Western America and Second Republic of Texas.

First thought: seal door, abandon apartment, live in basement. But Quinn and Karma helped, and in an hour the place looked habitable again. And I didn't even have to do the dishes!

Thursday, November 14

Readjustment Day in Guinea Bissau and Algeria. Birthday of Hussein I in Jordan. National Day of Mourning in Germany.

I don't know if Kahlua has adopted me or if he feels he owns my apartment. Either way, he spends a lot of time here. I never wanted a cat, but he's not bad. Doesn't jump up on the counters, never pesters me for food. I know he can get a meal at any of a few dozen places in the Swamp. Spends his nights here, at the foot of the bed or sometimes snuggled up beside me. When I go out he follows, jumps up and pushes the elevator button, looks back at me smugly. He has other tricks. Once downstairs he might go with me, might not. No telling where he goes on his own, but he always finds his way back. Cats and dogs have the run of the place here except for some off-limits areas. Not like at home, no leash laws. Problem dogs get shipped out *at once*! No territory marking allowed! All are spayed or neutered, naturally. If a mouse or a rat got loose in Clarke Centre, he'd live about 5 seconds.

Quinn asked me to move in with him again. Told him NO WAY!! I like my privacy. He got a little insistent, doesn't like traveling between places. A great big half a mile! What a wimp. Q??? Quinn a mistake? Need fixing? Soon?

Monday, November 18

Flag Day in Uzbekistan. Moroccan Independence Day. National Day in Latvia and Oman. Vertieres' Day in Haiti. Mickey Mouse's Birthday, systemwide.

Rick's is dark on Mondays and Tuesdays, but Podkayne and the Pod People (3P, for short) needed the stage time, so we signed up for the free evening festival in Robinson Park. This was a longtime tradition in Clarke

Centre, beginning at 6 PM and running until midnight, every day, rain or shine. (Ha! It rains in Robinson Park every morning at 0800 and again at 1400, after lunch, for 5 minutes.) It's open mike, a mixture of pros with nothing better to do and wannabes, anybody can perform for 15 minutes, encores to be decided by a sound meter with a big red arrow. There can be 1000 people there. There can also be 20. About 500 were there that evening as we set up under the flags of Oman, Haiti, Latvia, Morocco, and Uzbekistan. We all put on our mouse ears and commenced to boogie, starting out with numbers we knew would fly and then trying out a couple we were still working on. We were well received, to the point that some of the performers who had played before came up onstage and jammed with us. It was an hour before "Major Bowes" rang the gong, and then only because 1 hour was the limit; nobody was allowed to be stage hogs.

Afterward Karma took us on a tour through the bioenvironments of Clarke Centre, hydroponic farms and old-fashioned dirt farms. Turns out you need earthworms to grow crops, and bees are still the most efficient way to pollinate flowers and some vegetables. Who knew? Plus, you get honey. They grow snails there, too. I like earthworms only slightly more than I like bees, and if I never see another snail except on my plate, drenched in butter, I'll be quite happy. But I put on a brave face as she took us through her personal jungle.

Tuesday, December 10

Constitution Day in Thailand. Foundation Day in the African Coastal Republic. Interplanetary Human Rights Day. Nobel Prize Day in Sweden. Settlers' Day in Namibia. Ganga-Bois Day in the Voudon faith.

14 shopping days left until Christmas!

(12 days to high-gee shipping deadline, Europa/Mars.)

So Quinn is seeing someone else. Question: Does that bother me? I never intended it to be a long-term relationship, I always saw it as a posting romance. Maybe that's the problem, spacegirl. Maybe he wanted something more. Well, he could have said so, couldn't he? Why won't guys talk about these things?

Trouble is, I got to caring for him a little too much. That happens, I guess, though so far, not to me. Get a grip, Podkayne. He's a *drummer*, what did you expect?

Answer to question above: Yes, it bothers me.

Wednesday, December 11

Proclamation of the Republic, Burkina Faso.

Question: Can the band survive this?

Wednesday, December 25

Tuntematon Sotilas Day in Finland. First day of Christmas.

No partridge, no pear tree from Quinn. Quinn is history. Quinn is *so* over with. We hashed it out last night, amicably, civilly, like adults. Or at least I put on my best adult face. Sometimes I have to remind myself, you're only 18, girl, and there's probably a lot you still have to learn about human relationships. That's what they say, anyway, and they also say that at your age you feel like every little setback is the end of the world. Well, I know it ain't the end of the world, but that doesn't mean it doesn't hurt. But I didn't cry, not even when he gave me that smile, the one that won me away from my common sense in the first place, and asked if I was in the mood for a farewell . . . well, you know what he said. (Drummers should be kept in cages, fed raw meat, and only let out when you desperately need a back beat.) In fact, I even kept smiling as I shook my head, but I must admit that if he'd had his drumsticks with him he'd be visiting a proctologist right now for a bit of *deep* excavation. I kept the smile in place until the door closed, and then I cried a little. Kahlua was upset, so I quit.

Bastard.

We agreed the band should stay together. Let's hope that works. We've been getting better and better, and the audiences keep coming, and growing.

The usual gifts from most of the family, some useful, some small luxuries, pretty much like the stuff I sent them, all of it ordered online, wrapped and delivered to me from stores on Europa and to them from stores on Mars, to save shipping charges. I miss the actual shopping, it all feels impersonal, but this is the first Christmas I've spent away from my family.

Different with Mike. We always try to outdo the other with gifts no one else would dare give and that most people would be shocked to see.

This time I ordered a pair of extra-extra-extralong Levi's, made for the tallest of Martians. So what did I get from him? A Victoria's Secret bra in 54-DDDD, lace-trimmed but built like two Jovian hammocks. How did he *do* that? I'm wondering if he hacked my credit or something to see what I was getting him. He sent me a picture of him wearing the jeans, the legs rolled up like huge donuts, his feet peeking out the bottom, and the waist cinched around his neck. Message: PANTS TOO SHORT, WILL EXCHANGE FOR LONGER. That arrived ten minutes after I sent him a picture of me wearing the bra with two basketballs stuffed in it. TOO TIGHT, I wrote, and it was, but just barely. Volleyballs were too small, I tried them. And that meant our messages had crossed in space and he could *not* have known what kind of picture I was sending him unless he's figured out a way to beat the speed-of-light time lag from Jupiter. Sometimes we are so close, we think so much alike, that it's almost scary.

Swamp creatures set a true feast in the commons. Karma brought a lot of greenery from the farms and we made holly wreaths and decorated no less than 4 trees, one for each corner of the room. I baked 6 pecan pies. There were turkeys and hams and a suckling pig and a goose and egg nog with brandy and mulled wine with cinnamon sticks and fruitcake from Corsicana, Texas.

The local Cooking Collective sent samples of Christmas dishes from the various cultures we Martians come from, since we haven't had time to evolve a truly Martian Christmas. If we do, it will probably involve decorating rocks.

There was bûche de Noël from France, buñuelos from Colombia, szaloncukor from Hungary, queso de bola and bibingka from the Philippines, hallaca from Venezuela, sorpotel from Goa, and Tourtière from Quebec. There was English figgy pudding, Ukrainian kutia, Lithuanian opłatek, Milanese panettone, Danish pfeffernüsse, Norwegian pinnekjøtt, Nicaraguan pio quinto, Viennese vanillekipferl, German Spritzgebäck and Stollen, Portuguese massa sovada, and Mexican omeritos.

We gorged, we wassailed (is that a verb?), which involves dipping toast in hard cider heated with sugar, ginger, nutmeg, cinnamon, and a splash of brandy. I met a lot of people, made a lot of friends. Got moderately drunk.

Then we went caroling. Yes, diary! I never tell you much about the daily work that goes on here, much of it is scientific and I know nothing about it, and I'm only a lowly Madam, but this *is* a Navy base, and watches are maintained around the clock, and at least a quarter of the personnel don't get Christmas off. So in the Navy if you *are* off duty you go around in costumes, except to the highest security areas, and sing, and bring buckets of food but no wassail.

Then it was off to the Grand Arena, our 2,000-seat basketball stadium, for the one custom that is as Martian as anything about a Martian Christmas—though we borrowed it from the Japanese!—which is the performance of the *Daiku*, or "Great Ninth," Beethoven's *Symphony Number 9 in D minor, opus 125*, the *Choral*. Most everybody attends, Christian, Jew, Muslim, atheist, what have you, because it's nonsectarian and because the "Ode to Joy" is the music we've adopted as our national anthem.

I went to the tryouts for the soloists, listened for about an hour, and in that time heard both an alto and a soprano that could sing rings around me in opera, and left without singing. I know when I'm licked. Sure enough, on performance night I was in the middle of the chorus and looking at their backs.

We hadn't had much rehearsal time, but everybody who can sing knows the Ninth. And Europa was not big enough to field a full orchestra of sufficient talent to tackle that monster, but the director found a talented person to handle every instrument and then augmented electronically. Hell, a good keyboardist can handle the whole symphony and vocode the voices, and that was what was happening that very night in thousands of smaller outposts and ships all over the System. In the very smallest places a recording had to do, but you can bet people were singing along.

We didn't butcher it.

The tradition is to run through the fourth movement as Beethoven and Schiller wrote it:

Freude, schöner Götterfunken
Tochter aus Elysium,

Wir betreten feuertrunken,
Himmlische, dein Heiligtum!

Then everybody stands and reprises the *An die Freude*:

Mars! Thy name rings out like thunder,
Best hope of humanity.
God of war, now guard of peace
We dedicate our lives to thee!

When we finished there was hardly a dry eye, including mine. And I realized something. I'd been homesick. Not as bad as on Earth, but homesick all the same. And now I wasn't. We Martians are a far-flung race. Go to Mercury, go deep into the Oort Cloud, and what do you find? Martians. We control the means of space travel, and we tend to be stingy with it; there's no other way for us to survive, and we make sure most of the ravening hordes of the home planet do their ravening Earthside. Only on Luna do Earthies outnumber Martians. Everywhere else, Earthies are limited to a strict quota . . . except for tourists, of course, but tourists aren't really human beings in any real sense, except that you can't kill them. Tourists are walking bags of liquid assets to be wrung dry and sent home poorer but happy.

In a sense, where there are Martians, there is Mars. Singing the *Daiku* showed me that. We or our ancestors came from every country on Earth. We were multicultural in a way that the American New World had often boasted of but never really was. Young though we were, almost 50% of us had been born there.

And something else. There are now children being born in the Martian colonies. On Ceres, on the Jovian moons, on Triton, and even on Pluto, there are people who have lived there a long time now, and a lot of them don't intend to go back. I don't think anyone is yet thinking of herself as Cerean or Plutonian, but that day will come, won't it? We're the oldest family on Mars, and Mom and Dad were both Earth-born. The Japanese word for them would be Issei. I'm Nisei, and I'm just entering childbearing age. But I see children four or five years of age here at Clarke Centre, and they were born *here*, on Europa. Will they want to go back to Mars, where they'll be too heavy? Will they keep up with their exercises, or simply accept that they can never go to Earth . . . or maybe even to Mars, which they have never seen and may not even have any interest in? Soon, there will be different kinds of Martians, as there used to be different kinds of Americans: Maine Yankees, Florida crackers, Texans, Sooners. Now they all live in different countries. Will Europa one day be a country on its own?

It's something I've never considered. I'll never be Europan, even if I stayed here the rest of my life. I'll always be Martian; I don't plan to settle on any of the outposts. But soon, there will be Europo-Martians, and Pluto-Martians, and Cereo-Martians, if there aren't already.

So, maybe I'm not homesick anymore because Europa feels like . . . home? Could it be home?

Well, it'll do for now.

Wednesday, January 1

Independence Day in Cameroon and Sudan. Junkanoo. St. Basil's Day.

Down in the dumps again, moody and irritated. Stayed in my room all day, missed the New Year celebrations. Don't amount to much, anyway. Though we all still operate mostly by the Earth calendar because it's convenient, Mercury gets a new year every 88 days, Mars every 686, and out here the year is 4333 Earth days. So what's the big whoop? If I'd been born here, I wouldn't even be 2 years old.

Saturday, January 11

International Thank-You Day (Thanks, everybody!). National Unity Day in the (disputed) Chinese province of Nepal. Albanian Republic Day. Sir John A. Macdonald's Birthday.

3P has been together long enough now that we figured we had a few numbers worth recording. I mean, laying down tracks and working with them, not the normal recording every band does at every concert. For the next week we plan to spend every spare moment in the studio in the hope that we can cobble up 6 presentable tracks. Most anybody with the bare minimum of talent can upload 1 or 2 tracks and make them sound reasonable, and everybody says ho-hum; 6 really sharp ones at once is considered to be the reasonable benchmark to announce that you have arrived and probably won't be going away for a while.

We started with a list of 40 we felt we could really groove on—3P's Top 40!—and whittled it down to 12, then to 8 with minimal amounts of blood being shed. After that, no one would budge, so we agreed to try all 8.

Sunday, February 2

Festa de Nossa Senhora dos Navegantes in Brazil. Swedish KyndelsmÃssodagen. Bolivian Fiesta de la Virgen de Candelaria. Groundhog Day.

We don't have a groundhog at Clarke Centre, but the sun was out, and I'd be willing to bet that if we had one, and if he stuck his head out of his burrow, he would have seen his shadow. Verdict: 6 billion more years of winter. Squirrels, gather your nuts while you can! You're going to need plenty!

We got 5 tracks down and decided we were unlikely to improve them with more tinkering. And the consensus . . . actually, it was unanimous, was that they aren't good enough yet. They lack something, and though there is a lot of language to describe music, there aren't words for some of it. It's a case of you know it when you hear it. Or more to the point, you know it when you *don't* hear it, and none of us were hearing it. That final spark that takes a piece of music from being competent to being inspired, gives it that last boost so that, even from the first bars, you know this is *it.*

I am discouraged. We know we won't be together forever; probably we only have time together as a band until the first of us gets through her mandatory enlistment—that would be Cassandra, who has just less than a year to serve. But she is also the main steadying influence on us, and she thinks we can still reach that point, and if we do, we can get back together when all of us have served our time. Well, all of us but Quinn, who has signed up for a 10-year hitch. He *likes* the Navy. Go figure.

In the meantime, practice, practice, practice.

Saturday, March 1

Yap Day in Micronesia. Heroes Day in Paraguay. Bulgarian Baba Marta. St. David's Day. International Nuclear Victims Remembrance Day. Podkayne's Birthday.

Today I am 19. Whoop-ti-do.

Actually I'm not 19, not on any calendar I know of. Actually, like Frederick in *The Pirates of Penzance*, I'm only 4 and a little bit over. A most ingenious paradox, or a stupid Earthie pain in the ass, take your pick. My actual birthday was February 29, but there wasn't one this year. I'm a leapling. Gioacchino Rossini, Jimmy Dorsey, Dinah Shore, and Aubergine were all leaplings.

Of course, if you go by Martian years, I'm 10.

The Swamp creatures gave me a party today. Mike and I exchanged gifts, too, as we always do. We don't know exactly when he was born, but it was during a leap year, and February 29 is plausible.

The best present I got, though, was not just for me, but for all the Pod People. We've been selected to make the Grand Jovian Tour, and it will occupy us for some months. The schedule hasn't been finalized yet, and we aren't in charge of it, and in fact a lot of it will remain up in the air until we actually start. You don't get a tour bus when you're in the MADDMN, you hitch rides with ships as they become available. But we will be visiting all the Galilean moons, and a lot of the littler ones. Amalthea is on the list, very close in to Jupiter. We'll be going to Ananke, Carme, and Pasiphaë. Some of them I'd never even heard of, had to look them up in an atlas. Callirrhoe, Taygete, Eukelade, and Harpalyke are not exactly household words, not even in a Martian household. (Where do they get those names?) We don't have bases on every one of the little chunks of rock that are Jupiter's 300-some satellites, but there's somebody on most of them, and the minimum staff size of a Navy base is 100, to help prevent insanity.

So I've got a lot of packing to do. We leave in a week! Bon voyage!

Monday, March 10

Commonwealth Day. San Juan de Dios in Peru. Forty Martyrs of Sebaste. Buffy the Vampire Day.

Arrive on Io. Yikes! Jupiter is huge!

Strictly speaking, humans have no business on Io. It's too radioactive. To go there you take a course of antiradiation drugs, which made me a little sick for a day.

We probably couldn't have gone to Io at all except for the bubble drive. Regular rockets couldn't have lifted enough of the heavy shielding ships require to make a safe haven for humans when the radiation really kicks up, which is every other day or so.

But scientists go there because Io is just so damn fascinating. And for the same reasons, tourists go there, too. Of all the places humans go off Earth, Io is by far the most spectacular.

For one thing, there's that amazing view of Jupiter, almost twice as big as when seen from Europa. Then there's the auroras. Io has a very thin atmosphere of sulfur dioxide, just a billionth of an atmosphere, but it's enough to create auroras that shame anything you'd see in Alaska or Antarctica. And they aren't just at the poles, they are planetwide, and continuous, 42.6 hours per day, which is also the time Io takes to circle Jupiter. Oddly, that's exactly half the length of the Europan day, and ¼ the length of a day on Ganymede. These are called Laplace-resonant orbits, or so I'm told. I learn something new every day.

Wednesday, March 12

Arbor Day, various nations. International Girl Scout Day. Independence Day in Mauritius. Moshoeshoe's Day in Lesotho. Renovation Day in Gabon. Youth Day in Zambia.

Quinn came down with old-fashioned traveler's trots the day we landed, probably exacerbated by the antirad drugs, and we had to cancel two gigs. Not a good start. But it did give the rest of us a chance to take an early look at the main thing, Jupiter and the auroras aside, that most people came to Io to see: volcanoes.

Io is the most tectonically active body in the solar system, which is one of the reasons so many scientists brave the radiation to study it. They've already learned enough about volcanic eruptions and earthquakes . . . Ioquakes? . . . to get a lot better at predicting them on Earth, where they regularly used to kill hundreds of thousands of people every year. They still kill, the geologists aren't perfect, but they're getting better, and mostly because they've been able to monitor shaky old Io continually for decades now.

That's all fine with me, but on with the show!

I'm writing in the bus on the way from the Hotel Galileo, the best of the five major tourist hotels on Io, on a short hop to Loki Patera, which is a jumble of craters that lately have been most reliable at spouting ionized gas, flowing lava, and large chunks of Io itself into space. There's always *something* spewing on Io, but the areas of the biggest spectacle change as Io's molten guts are twisted by the gravitational tugs of Jupiter, Europa, and Ganymede. The whole rock flexes and stretches.

This can make for some tooth-jarring quakes, too, which is why all human habitations there are not only underground, but mounted on big shock absorbers and springs. These structures are at least a mile beneath the surface, in caves hollowed out by bubble makers in areas that aren't tectonically active. Luckily, Io is all rock, no ice at all, because though your impression is that the whole surface is hellishly aboil, the actual temperature up there is between –300 and –100 degrees. That's mighty cold rock. You wouldn't want to touch it with your tongue!

Down at base level things are warmer, though not exactly cozy. The base is only 50 miles from the Hotel Galileo, and a train runs through a tunnel between them. The train doesn't have a schedule. Few Navy people want to visit the small tourist city, and of course no tourists at all are allowed on the base, so you just get aboard and punch a button, like an elevator. Me and Joey and Cassandra were the only people aboard for the 5-minute trip. It was my only bad moment, too. I felt confident that the engineers had built the base and the hotel to stand up to any quake that might happen, but I wasn't so sure about the tunnel.

Nothing happened, but I'm not looking forward to the trip back.

We of the MADDMN have a problem most other Navy personnel don't have. We'd already learned it on Europa. It's hard to get out and actually see the planet. Others have duties that take them to the exotic places I want to see. Our job is just to sing and dance, and base commanders can be stingy about letting Madmen deadhead, even if there's plenty of room. "What do you think you signed up for, a joyride?" one superior officer told me when I asked to take a little trip to Cilix Base on my first day off, only 100 miles from Clarke Centre. Actually, I didn't sign up for *anything*, asshole, as you well know. I was drafted, I wanted to say. My face was burning.

I didn't say it.

Luckily, the commandant on Io is more relaxed about it, so long as you take civilian transport and pay your own way.

So we did. By regulations we had to do it in full-dress uniform, which stood out in the Galileo at least as much as it did on Earth. We are the only Navy on the bus with mostly Earthies and a few Loonies, but nobody has given us any trouble. Once again, the sidearms don't hurt in that department.

The bus is a marvel of engineering. I don't know all the details, but I get the impression it's basically a hollowed-out ingot of lead. It flies, and when it gets there it lands and moves around on tank treads that can deal with the temperature differential, which can go from –300 to +500 degrees very quickly. Some kind of ceramic, I think the guide said. It's got a heavily leaded polymer dome and thick shutters that can snap shut in a few seconds if the rads get too high inside.

We're landing. Gotta go.

Thursday, March 20

Tunisian Independence Day. Legba Zaou in Haiti. Petroleum Day in Iran. International Frog Day.

If it's Thursday, this must be Amalthea.

I don't like Amalthea. It looks a lot like Phobos, and I've never been wild about that potato-shaped moon of my beloved home planet, either. I'm not sickened by free fall (or .0025 gee, the surface gravity of Amalthea, which might as well be the same thing), but I'm not like my mother, either, who is as at home in any gravity or no gravity as a fish in the sea. I'm fine with it, but I like to get a little gravity under my socks as soon as practically possible.

That's not it, anyway. It's Jupiter. It's too damn close. Somewhere between Io and Amalthea Jupiter went from being big and impressive to being just *too damn big*! Of all the Jovian Navy bases, only the one on Metis is closer, and we're not going there, I'm happy to say. I don't even like to look at it from the windows of my room here in the settlement on the edge of Pan, the biggest crater on this miserable rock. I want to do our four shows and head for Ganymede.

Catching up:

I was too busy to write after we got to Loki on Io. It was everything the tourist brochures bragged about and more. We witnessed huge boiling eruptions, with house-sized boulders flung into the air like sand grains, and great bubbling pots of lava overflowing onto the plains below. Going from such heat to such cold produced quite a show in itself, with the lava crystallizing into towering, fantastic shapes before being pushed over by pressure from behind. Every once in a while hot sand and glowing pebbles would rain down on the bus itself, which gave a nice whiff of danger, but the guide assured us we needn't worry about one of the big ones coming down on us, as their trajectories were well-known and we were a safe distance beyond them . . . and all the same we were monitoring the big ones on radar and would have plenty of time to get out of the way if one fell toward us in the low gravity. In fact, one did splash down only about half a mile away, right into the catena we were overlooking.

Then it was up and over Daedalus and Heiseh Pateras, both of which were relatively inactive at the moment, and north across a series of deep valleys and mountain ridges, and north again to the Lei-Kung Fluctus, where we landed and weaved our way through a literally hellish landscape of boiling lakes of sulfur.

Fluctus means flow terrain, and it's too rugged to drive over, but some of the flow is solidified sulfur and sulfur compounds, of which there are thousands, and those areas are fairly smooth in places. Sulfur is bright yellow, and it burns with a blue flame, but there is no oxygen on Io, so it doesn't burn there. But when hot and mixed in a slurry of other minerals, it can make a whole lot of interesting chemicals, very few of which you'd like to have in your lungs.

Io has been described as either a diseased orange or a super-duper-sized pizza. I like the pizza analogy, myself, and it's a pizza with *everything* on it, and Lei-Kung is the pizza kitchen, or maybe a whole damn pizza factory, and it has exploded many times. Every surface is draped with the quick-frozen results of those explosions, in more colors than I can describe, and to see them you drive through lakes of boiling yellow brimstone. The tourist come-ons call this region the Devil's Paintbox.

Me and Joey and Cassandra soon discovered that there were a lot of people who took that description literally. There were a dozen of them on the big bus, and as soon as we arrived at the Paintbox their leader got them down on their knees and had them shouting prayers. See, certain people, when they saw pictures of Lei-Kung Fluctus, decided they had been provided with the actual physical location of Hell. These were the Rapturists, the fruitcake sect that has taken over so much of the mid-Mississippi and lower-Appalachian regions of Heartland America. They expect Satan to begin marshaling his troops on the surface there any day now; they see it as the behind-the-lines staging area for Armageddon. Some of them had lurid pictures they pressed on us showing demons emerging from the brimstone. But mostly they prayed, which for some of them took the form of rolling in the aisles, jabbering, frothing at the mouth, and in at least one case, wetting her pants.

It was embarrassing.

I was never clear on just what they were there for, what they were praying for, since most of them were speaking in tongues and we all stayed as far away from them as possible. I was relieved to see most of the other Earthies stayed away, too. The back of the bus became, for a while, a sort of insane asylum. But were they praying to keep Satan *in* the pool of brimstone, or were they asking him to come out and fight like a demon? Did they want to rassle with him? My understanding of Armageddon and the Rapture (to the extent that they can be understood at all by a rational being) is that the outcome is preordained, the game is fixed, Jeez and the Saved are going to win, and the only real question is who is on the home team and who gets to boil in Hell.

But I didn't care enough about the answer to ask any of them. They might have told me.

Musical Update: Things went very well on Io. All our gigs were well attended, some of them were sold out, and we got a lot of compliments afterward. They danced to the dance numbers, listened to the others, and a good time was had by all.

We tried one of the potential download numbers again and Cassandra suggested a few things that pepped it up considerably. I'm not ready to say it's ready for release, but it's getting there.

Gotta go. Onstage in 10 minutes, need time to throw up.

Sunday, March 30

Pohnpei in Micronesia. Baptist Liberation Shouter Day in Trinidad and Tobago. Boganda Day, Central African Republic. Easter.

Ganymede. Maybe I'll have time to see some of it if we ever get a rest. Our fame seems to be spreading out here in the Jovian hinterlands. They've kept us very busy, adding appearances, and in the evenings we try out new material in out-of-the-way bars and clubs.

Oh, and it's Easter. What does a grown-up do for Easter? Hunt eggs? Go to church? I'm sure plenty of people did the latter, but there are no children here in the radiation belt, and the holiday pretty much went by unnoticed by the likes of me.

Monday, March 31

Mouloud (Birth of the Prophet). Cesar Chavez Day in Western America.

We've been here on Ganymede for almost 2 weeks now, and I finally had a chance to take a brief surface tour. Conclusion: Ganymede looks a lot like Europa, though not quite as smooth. Jupiter looks smaller.

And that's all I have to say about Ganymede.

Oh, I've seen plenty of Ganymede from a jumper window. We've been bouncing all over the damn place, like the silver orb in a pinball machine. Ganymede is the most populated of the Jovian moons, and the most popular tourist destination since Europa is off-limits and Io is only for the daring and the religious, and very expensive. The Navy has five major bases on Ganymede, and there are a dozen major tourist centers. Then there are the small research facilities, some of them top secret. I don't know what they could be doing that's so important out there in those lonely bases, and when we left them, we were none the wiser. Everyone was very close-mouthed. Well, *be* that way!

It's been great, in terms of the reception we're getting, and also a little wearing. We'll play all evening, then jam with whoever comes around until the wee hours, stumble into bed, then get up for a late breakfast and practice, practice . . .

It's paying off, too, I think. In our copious spare time (HAH!) we've managed to lay down 3 more tracks I wouldn't be ashamed to play for the Ghost of Judy Garland. I wouldn't say we're quite there yet, the A Train still has a few more stops to make, but Harlem is in sight.

Wednesday, April 9

Chinese Tomb Sweeping Day. Drop of Water Is a Grain of Gold Day in Turkmenistan. International Tartan Day. Mikael Agricola Day in Finland.

Today we're in . . . just a minute, I had to look, one lonely rock begins to seem just like any other . . . Pasiphaë. My Baedekeronline tells me that Pasiphaë is pronounced pa-SIFF-ay-ee, but everybody here just says pacify. I also learn that it is currently 20 million miles from Jupiter (that's ⅕ of the distance from the Earth to the sun!), travels around Jupiter in a retrograde direction every 764 days in a highly inclined orbit, which gives it a whole different perspective on the primary . . . but it's so far away who really cares? It's about 35 miles in diameter, has no gravity to speak of, and was discovered in 1908.

Population: about 4000. What they're doing out here I have very little idea. Something to do with the bow shock wave and the magnetosphere.

And that's all I have to say about Pasiphaë.

Monday, May 5

Kokumin-no-Kyujitsu in Japan. Czech Kvetnove Povstani Ceskeho Lidu. Nationale Bevrijdingsdag Liberation Day in Holland. Indian Heritage Day in Guyana. Cinco de Mayo.

Ka-ching, ka-ching! Bang, bop, pow! Pachinko! Round and round and round she goes, where she stops . . . not even she knows anymore! Yes, sir, keep your eye on the little green Ps and put your money down! Which cup are the 3Ps under?

Where am I? Somewhere in space.

If this was a video diary my tongue would be hanging out, my bloodshot eyes would be rotating like pinwheels, and my hair would be smoking.

That's how I imagine myself, anyway, though I'm glad to report that the mirror doesn't show anything except maybe a bit of darkness under my eyes.

I always used to sneer at musicians who bitched in their autobiographies about how tough life was on the road. How hard could it be, traveling around in a bus with groupies waiting for you at every concert?

Well, diary, it's a lot harder than it sounds.

I've never felt I was particularly rooted to a place. I've always wanted to travel, which is why I jumped at the Europa posting. But for the last weeks I've been longing for my own bed. Either of them. The one back home on Mars would be okay, but the one in the Swamp would be even better, and is beginning to seem a distant memory. I want Kahlua to curl up on my chest and make me sneeze. I want to look at my things, maybe move them around a little. I want to paint the walls again.

I want my nest!

Aw, stop crying about it, Podkayne. This is what you asked for, so make the most of it. Four more tracks are in the can, you're sounding better than ever. The band has come together in a way none of us could have imagined a few months ago, and the reason, I'm forced to admit, is the hothouse pressure of traveling, and playing and playing and playing night after night. We've reached the point where we play off each other effortlessly. No signals are needed, we can read each other's minds, I know what the others are going to do before they know it themselves, and when they do it, I'm *there*!

Thursday, June 19

Artigas Day in Uruguay. Algerian Righting Day. Labour Day in Trinidad and Tobago. Canadian National Public Service Day. Juneteenth in the Second Republic of Texas.

Last stop. If it wasn't, I think I'd have to kill myself.

Sinope. Not really much farther from Jupiter than Pasiphaë, in miles, and only about ⅓ smaller.

Diary, honey, compared to Sinope, Pasiphaë is the Big Apple.

If we had an agent, we'd be screaming, "Who booked us in this toilet?" But if we had an agent, she'd be steaming, too, because we *did* finish the songs we set out to do, and we *did* download them, and they *are* getting some pretty good play . . . in which case, any sensible agent would have pulled us back to the Galileans to take advantage of our newfound popularity.

Not a chance. Callisto, Ganymede, and Io are nothing but fond memories now. If the Navy sez you gotta finish your tour of the obscure gravel that makes up the outer reaches of the bazillion moons of Jupiter, well, honey, that's what you do.

But *Sinope* . . . ?

Okay, I'm being mean. The most significant thing about Sinope is not its extreme isolation. Pasiphaë is isolated, too. All you need to know about Sinope can be summed up in one number: 96. That's the population. And some of those were failing fast.

But there was a good side, I guess. Of those 96, I'd say 92 were avid fans of Podkayne and the Pod People. Our downloads had arrived ahead of us, and the Sinopeans were gaga. Of course, since the last MADDMN troupe had come through here in about 1956, they'd probably have been fans of Lawrence Welk if somebody had dug him up and put an accordion in his hands and delivered him and his ghostly Champagne Orchestra to Sinope. (You learn about some really odd acts if you study music history.)

If they'd had palm fronds, they'd have strewed them across our path from the ship. Which was a weekly milk run. Literally. We shared cabin space with butter and eggs and bread and moo juice. If they'd had donkeys, we'd have been invited to ride into the settlement on our asses.

Which were sore, as the cargo shuttles boosted at a steady 1 gee all the way, and if you think it's hard to go from Mars to 1 gee on Earth, try going from the no-grav whistlestops we'd been playing to 1 gee of acceleration. Oh, my aching back!

Every admiral in the Navy will deny it, but everyone below that rank knows this: Places like Sinope are where the hopeless fuckups are posted. The law says we all have to serve, but there are some folks who can't even manage the simplest tasks, like a recruiting post in Western America, and they are sent to monitoring outposts like Sinope, with the bare minimum of population, not much recreation, and base functions that are largely automated. It's make-work, about as important as counting the grains of sand in Saturn's rings. (There are people in the Navy that do something very like that.)

And oh, my, they killed the fatted calf, they rolled out the red carpet, they wined us and dined us, and I believe every man Jack and woman Jill attended both our concerts. We were all wondering if we'd ever get such an enthusiastic reception again as long as we lived. No telling, but I am pretty sure of one thing. It is probably the only time we'll ever sell out an entire *planet*.

* * *

By the way, diary . . . I got laid. Last performance, I could have had my pick of half a dozen acceptable prospects. Like, if I was a guy and they were girls, sort of thing, I'd have been showered in panties with phone numbers written on them. Podkayne has *groupies*! *Hurray!*

Last few numbers I started making eye contact with a guy in the front row, about my height, Mars-born (I can almost always tell), curly blond hair, slight build, and the sweetest green eyes. And long, narrow hands that looked gentle. By the last encore I felt a connection had been made, if not between our hearts, then at least between certain lower, moister parts. So I bought him a drink, and invited myself up to see his room (he was shy; please don't let him be gay!). Once there he took over, though. He was a great kisser, and the hands were all I had hoped they would be. I told him I wasn't a sexual athlete, that I preferred gentleness and slow rhythms, and then proceeded to batter him within an inch of his life. Where did *that* come from? Too much enforced abstinence, I guess. He didn't complain, and the second time was more Podkayne and less Nadia the Nymphomaniac. Still, we did about everything two humans without major fetishes can do without rubber hoses and a jar of molasses. As is my custom, dear diary, I won't go into details, preferring to relive them in total privacy, even from you. I'm sure they won't fade away, and play-by-plays are for tennis.

After the fourth and seemingly final set, not even my most ardent attentions could get his little soldier to stand at attention again, though it was fun to try. *Can you feel anything when I do this?* Flip, flop. (Actually, the GI in question was far from a PFC, though a bit short of a major general, Call him a lieutenant colonel. I don't require the top brass, don't even like them, but have to admit to a prejudice against enlisted men.)

With nothing else to do, and unable to sleep for a while—he didn't roll over and start to snore, not even after what I put him through—we talked a bit. His name was Michigan. First name, no need for last ones here, not unless we meet again. And *yes*, diary, I knew that *before* I fucked him. What do you think I am? Don't answer that, and I don't care what you think, anyway. I'm a healthy 19-year-old, almost old enough to drink liquor in Western America, and it *is* the twenty-first century.

The name was dumped on him because his parents came from Grand Rapids, in East America. I told him I liked it, which was true; people with names like Podkayne and Michigan should glory in it and give thanks we're not just another Tiffany or Brandon.

He was eager to get back home, and he was short, only 3 months to go on his mandatory hitch. He'd been posted here the whole time, with only two leaves back home, and a few furloughs to Ganymede and Callisto. He hadn't been impressed by either place.

But he was reasonably happy. He was able to be a full-time student since there was so little to do out here, carrying a full load at universities as diverse as Oxford, UCLA, and the University of Beijing. I thought about telling him that my father is an historian, but held back. Once I let something like that out he might be wanting to meet Dad, and I didn't know him well enough to invite him home. After all, I said Sinope was a post for fuckups, didn't I? I'm sure they're not *all* losers, but he might be one. As you well know, diary, I've got a tendency to pick out the loser in any group of ten decent-looking guys. Remember Quinn?

So I held back, and we exchanged numbers and said we'd look each other up when we both got back home. Only he might not be home very long, as he was planning to go to Earth to meet and take some classes from some professors in China, which reminded him, since he was still not sleepy, that he was behind on the 3 hours of exercise he had to do every day if he was to have any hope of surviving Chinese gravity in a few months, so he floated out of bed and started in on those.

I watched him for a while, naked and muscular. Gosh, I do love sweat on a man, as long as it's fresh. Makes me want to sweat, too, so I suggested an alternative exercise that would burn up almost as much as he was doing, and we could do it together, and he said if I could get the lieutenant colonel interested while he continued working out it was fine with him, and I did, without even touching either of them, just exercising the parts that guys like to look at most, which I learned to do just shortly after I attained those parts and realized their power.

And with our usual modesty we will break off the narrative here, dear diary, except to note it was the most gratifying exercise session I can recall.

Tuesday, June 24

Discovery Day in Newfoundland and Labrador. Fête Nationale in Quebec. Fisherman's Day in Zaire. Inti Raymi in Peru. Manila Day in the Philippines. Latvian and Estonian Midsummer Festival. St. Jean's Day. St. John the Baptist Day.

Home!

Yes! Europa *will* do for home, after a trip like that!

Hello, Karma! Hello, Kahlua! My, but you look pretty. Stop scratching my legs, I didn't have any choice but to abandon you.

Hello, Swamp, and all you disreputable riparian residents! I love you all!

Good-bye, Joey, Cassandra, and especially you, Quinn, I don't want to see any of your ugly faces for at least a week. Practice be damned!

The Swamp creatures love a party, and they threw a nice coming-home celebration for me. I got a bit more tiddly than I'm used to and came close to doing something I'd regret in the morning with at least three guys who'd never turned my head before. Alcohol has this amazing ability to make people more attractive. Everybody except the one who's drinking it.

There was dancing and singing—but not by me, even though I was asked several times. I was really serious about hanging it up for at least a few days. Can you overdo something you really love? Answer: Yes.

But best of all, there were two things waiting that were beyond price. The best was a message from Mike, timed to be waiting for when I got back from the tour. He said he'd been listening to a few of our tracks, and that he thought they were okay . . . "If you like old-folks music."

Good try, Mike, but I know you better than that. He had listened to them all, just as he always has, multiple times. Part of our mutual nongushing pact is that we never admit we like something the other one has done, but he's my number one fan. I know it, and he knows I know it.

The second thing was a pass during my next furlough—which starts today!—to the highly restricted base by the Big Rock Candy Mountains. I was going to get to see what very few people, even those in the Navy, ever get to see.

Yes!

9

THERE WAS A small quake as our bus neared the Alphesiboea Linea on the way to the Taliesen region of Europa. The Linea is a crack in the surface ice caused by tidal flexing as Europa is pulled this way and that by Io, Ganymede, and, most of all, by Jupiter. There's also the fact that the rocky core of Europa, way down there under the ice and the incredibly deep sea, rotates at a slightly slower rate than the ice does. The core gradually falls behind, at the rate of one complete rotation every ten thousand years. This messes with things, too.

Our driver stopped and waited it out. I gripped the armrests of my seat and made sure I was buckled in tight. The springs qnder us creaked, and the bus slued a little sideways. Then it stopped and I cautiously checked my panties: dry, thank the lord.

We had landed just shy of the Linea and would proceed on the surface from there, because strange things happened around Taliesen and it was better to be on the ground if you had to deal with them.

I'll come clean. It was right there, at the start of the journey I'd so much wanted to take, that I began to wonder what the hell I was doing here.

* * *

LENTICULAE. WHICH IS Latin for "freckles," a term I prefer. The Big Rock Candy Mountains. Europan jelly beans. They either contain life of a form so alien that we don't have much of a grip on it after twenty years of cautious study, or they are the source or focus of forces we don't yet understand and can't even detect. The best minds of Mars and Earth had studied them intensively to the extent that they could, watched them and listened to them, and we still don't know much more than when we started: They are huge, strange things happen around them, and they sing.

That they are huge is something that was known ever since the first Voyager and Galileo automated spacecraft flew by and photographed them in the 1970s and '90s.

The strange things go way back to the days of the initial ground expeditions, and include gruesome death.

The singing is a recent discovery.

THEY KNEW THE freckles were emitting very powerful radio waves in what is called ELF, for Extremely Low Frequency. This band is usually described as being from three to thirty Hertz—that's Hertz, singular, not megahertz or gigahertz!—but some of the signals coming from the freckles were even lower than that. It took a while to find that out because, after all, who's listening down that low in the electromagnetic spectrum? And once the waves were detected, they were pretty much dismissed as having no realistic use, because . . .

Well, let Admiral Autrey explain it:

"These frequencies are used by the United States Navy and others with large submarine fleets," the admiral told us. "Most radio waves won't penetrate very much water or soil. When the subs are running deep, there is no way to contact them except by ELF."

Admiral James Autrey was a thin man with an upper-class British accent and a twinkle in his blue eyes. He was tall for an Earthie, which he had to be since he was at least sixty. I was maybe two inches shorter than him.

Me and the others who made up the guest party at Taliesen Base had been shown into his office immediately upon arrival. Others in our party included Wu Zheng Han, a Martian senator, and his daughter Mei-Ling, better known as "Monet." There was Yahya Al-Wakil, a manufacturing millionaire, and his son—known as Dekko—from Ceres City, and Mandela Baruti, the ambassador from the Southern African Confederation.

Most of all there was the host of a popular talk show and his five-person crew and entourage, there to tape a show about the nonclassified aspects of the only ETL project that the public was likely to have any interest in. (Mars has its own Extraterrestrial Life, of course, but no one but exobiologists was very interested in the interstitial lichenous organisms and anaerobes that represent the last survivors of the glory days of Mars, over a billion years ago.) Europan "life" was big, mysterious, and awesome to look at . . . and still debatable, as scientists tried to come up with a definition of life that would include both Terran biota and these massive crystals.

"The problems of ELF," Admiral Autrey went on, "are twofold. First, it takes a great deal of power and a very large antenna to send a detectable signal. The U.S. Navy built one such antenna in the state of Michigan that was thirty miles long. It ate vast amounts of power, but it would transmit around the world, and deep into the oceans.

"The bigger problem is bandwidth. With ELF, it's almost nonexistent. We're used to transmission rates of trillions of bits per second. An ELF system takes several minutes to send *one* character. Extremely inefficient."

I had been surprised when I realized that the admiral himself was not only going to welcome us to his base, but actually give us the orientation lecture. Of course, we were all Important People in one way or another . . . insert modest cough here . . . but it seemed out of character. Most admirals are too self-important for stuff like that.

I had a private moment with Admiral Autrey later—a little too private—and he admitted he did it because he was bored. "Base takes care of itself, mostly," he said. "My job's mostly paperwork and riding herd on a lot of boffins with big egos. Way out of my field, frankly." At this point I gently eased his hand off my butt. Again. All hands was our Admiral Autrey, something I'd suspected during his initial talk when he'd consistently made eye contact mostly with me and the senator's daughter, who was in her early twenties and almost as pretty as me.

Actually, it was only fleeting eye contact, as a large part of his lecture was delivered directly to our breasts. And actually again, she might have been a *tad* prettier than me. But I didn't hold it against her after she looked at me, made a face, rolled her eyes, and made a jack-off motion with her fist. Amen, sister!

"So the rate is slow," the admiral went on, "but information can be transferred. And after our computers had been monitoring the ELF waves for about five years, they informed us that patterns were emerging."

"Doesn't prove anything," said the talk-show host. Oh, very well, I'll name him. It was Cosmo Wills, known to his admirers as simply "Cosmo," and to the rest of us as "that loudmouthed asshole." I considered him an irresponsible rabble-rouser—Earth-born but somehow a Martian citizen (everybody assumes money changed hands), whose political hobbyhorses all center around the Martian Republic being dissolved and becoming a part of the Greater Earth Coalition, that great jabbering society that exists mainly to pry the secret of the bubble drive out of its Martian conservators. He wants us to become just another province of Earth.

For the last three years there's been an annual referendum to revoke Cosmo's citizenship, but he's always squeaked by in spite of the votes of me and all my family. (Unfortunately, our votes count no more than anybody else's. Grandma Kelly really ought to do something about that.) (Just kidding.) As the constitution currently exists—but keep checking back, it could change!—it takes a two-thirds vote to kick someone off the planet.

Free speech? Sure, we have it. You're free to criticize our way of life all you want to . . . from someplace else.

"Of course not," said the admiral. "Patterns exist in nature independent of life. Crystals themselves are patterns."

"But what about the stuff moving around in them?" Cosmo wanted to know. "Surely that debate was ended long ago."

"A popular misconception," the admiral replied, putting the contemptuous spin on the word "popular" that the British can do so much better than anyone else. Cosmo didn't have much of a reputation for accuracy. "Things can be seen to move in the mountains. They move in patterns that, so far, have defied our attempts to assign meaning to them. Rivers move, as do glaciers. Ocean currents move in interesting patterns, but so far as we know, they are not alive."

"So you're saying you don't think they're alive?"

"I said nothing of the sort. I myself am convinced they are alive, in some way we don't yet understand. But there are cogent arguments on the other side. As you might imagine, it is the subject of a lively debate around here. Remember, not long ago the huge majority of astrophysicists subscribed to the Big Bang theory of cosmic origins. Recent discoveries concerning dark energy have cast some doubt on that scenario."

"Some people still believe the Earth is flat, too," Cosmo sneered.

"Many of them in your audience, I shouldn't wonder, Mr. Wills," the admiral said, which was one of the reasons I only moved his hand off my ass later instead of slapping him. I liked him, horndog though he was. Besides, I don't expect men to always be able to resist my endearing young charms.

"Actually, now that I think back," I piped up, "last time I was there it looked pretty flat to me." I knew that "Mr. Wills" business had riled the little idiot. He wants everyone to call him by his brand name, Cosmo. It's copyrighted.

"Maybe you should go back and research it, Cosmo," said Monet, the senator's daughter. "It might take years. Decades, even."

This dig went right over his head. I gave the girl a thumbs-up.

"What I'm interested in is a lot more serious," Cosmo said, seriously. Seriousness is also a trademark of his; he seems to have no sense of humor.

"You're speaking of the statistical anomalies," Admiral Autrey said.

"If that's what you want to call death, disability, and destruction, yes I am," Cosmo said. Even I had to admit he had a point.

YOU APPROACH TALIESEN on the ground because spaceships fall out of the sky if they try to fly there. Not all of them, of course, but we've been using flying buses on Mars and other planets for a long time now, and they're very safe.

Not around Taliesen. At first you attribute the accident rate to random chance. No connection could be found, no common failing that had caused the first four bus crashes, years ago. In each case it was the failure of a small, rather insignificant part, often a piece of electronics or programming, that led to a chain of failures that resulted in catastrophe. It all seemed so reasonable. The engineers shook their heads and chalked it up to sheer bad luck. Flights continued to Taliesen because the freckles were the most fascinating objects in the solar system, and everybody knew that whoever figured them out would be in the history books forever.

Then another three buses crashed. Finally, the engineers listened to what the actuaries had been telling them all along, one of the basic principles of life, though you won't find it in any science book.

Once is bad luck.

Twice is coincidence.

Three times is enemy action.

Seven times . . . well, nobody knew *what* was going on, but it was clear that *something* was out of the ordinary. All flights were grounded for a radius of one hundred miles, and that interdiction remains in force to this day. There were no more crashes . . .

. . . but a high percentage of buses coming and going broke down on the ground. The closer you got to the crystal mountains, the more malfunctions of all kinds happened. Often it was a part that seldom, if ever, had failed before. Computer programs developed glitches. Okay, computer programs *always* develop glitches, it's in their nature, but these were too frequent and too odd to be just chance mishaps. Enemy action? Nobody knew. Nobody knows to this day. But you have to act as if it is.

There was something else about the place, something much more disturbing. Machines were not the only things that broke down in Taliesen. People did, too.

Of the first team to actually go to one of the big crystal mountains, many years ago now, one suffered a stroke two days after arrival, and another had a heart attack the day after returning to Forward Base. Of the seven people in the first primitive exploratory mission, which lasted thirty days, five were dead within the year, all from "natural causes." The trouble was, most of them were too damn young to die of what killed them, and none had shown any warning signs, nor did they have any family history. They just dropped dead.

Again, enemy action? If so . . . of what kind? There was absolutely nothing happening around the mountains—nothing we could detect, anyway—that could account for it. No sizzling death beams, no elevated radiation levels, no theremin music and invisible Id Monster snarling and gnashing its teeth.

Nobody was about to give up exploring the Taliesen area just because of an elevated risk of death or injury. It was just too important. So what do you do? You look at the charts and minimize the risk.

Distance equaled better odds, so longer-term personnel were quartered at Taliesen Base, five miles from the nearest mountain. People could stay there for several years with only minimal increased hazard, or so the number-crunchers said.

Cryoaquanauts were at the NEMO Base, only two miles away. Stays there were limited to six months, with a three-month rotation out. NEMOs are well-known to be nuts, and would have stayed indefinitely, but such were the regs.

Last was Forward Base, one mile from the mountain, where no one was allowed to stay longer than two weeks. You planned your experiment at Clarke Centre, you hastened to Forward, did your work, and got out.

Sometimes a closer approach was authorized, but you'd better have a damn good explanation of why it was necessary, and you'd better be able to do it in twenty-four hours.

So, next question . . . what are *you* doing in Taliesen, Podkayne?

Well, a couple of reasons. I did the math (actually, I asked a computer to do it; wouldn't you?) and found that my itinerary increased my risk of death by about 0.00001 percent. It was already a bit dangerous just coming to Jupiter, and living on Europa. And come on, I'm nineteen and healthy as a bran muffin.

Then there's the fact that I wanted to go because I *could*. Simple as that. (You say you went to Europa and all you got was that lousy T-shirt?) The most interesting thing on the planet, maybe in the solar system, is Taliesen, and not many people are allowed out there. I knew the only reason I was approved for the junket was because I was the granddaughter of a former president of Mars and the niece of an admiral. Well, so be it. I wouldn't have missed it for anything.

Anyway, I had my gonads in cold storage. What's the worst that could happen?

WE STARTED OUR tour by backtracking from Taliesen Main Base to the ELF antenna, apparently the Eighth Wonder of Europa, in the opinion of the station tech who showed us around his lonely outpost . . . except the whole fifty-mile array was under the ice. We did get to see some very educational films about its construction, though.

He played us some tapes of one of the songs, speeded up about a million times, that had come from the largest Big Rock Candy Mountain, officially designated TECP-45. For Taliesen-Europa Crystalline Prominence #45.

"This is the last year of recording," he said, and the room filled with music. Each note was the same length, lasted about a second, and was in a lower register. Of course it could have been much higher and much faster, since this was a virtual sound, but the authority of the deep notes reverberated more dramatically. It lasted about a minute and a half. Our silence lasted not quite that long.

"That's *it*?" Monet, the senator's daughter, asked. "A year's worth?"

"That's it," our nursemaid confirmed.

"Well, when you get a little more, call us and we'll talk contract," Monet said.

"Could I hear it again?" I asked. The others were already wandering ahead. The tech showed me how to call up the recordings of all the TECPs, of which there were over five hundred. There were sixty-five in Taliesen, the most interesting region, and the most vocal. I downloaded them all and caught up with the group.

IN THE BUS on the way back to Taliesen Main Base I started working my way through them. Each was about four hundred notes, nonrepeating, but sometimes seeming to work variations on a theme. Each tone was discrete, there was no sliding up and down a tone scale. I queried the download and found that each note was held for 85.2 hours (3.551181041 Earth days, if you want it exactly), then the rock would stop singing for a few minutes and begin again on another note. There was no tremolo, no vibrato, no variation of any kind that anyone could find. I guess it was the equivalent of one Europan bit, or maybe byte. To no one's great surprise, 85.2 hours was the length of the Europan day and orbital period, which meant it also had a resonance with Io and Ganymede. This was truly music of the spheres, on a vast scale.

I tried listening to some of the other mountains. At first they just seemed like more variations on the same theme, but before long I began to discern a distinct voice for each TECP.

Taliesen Base listens to all the megacrystals on Europa, but concentrates its up-close work on seven of the mountains within closest range of the main base. They seldom called them TECPs; they were given more informal names. TECP-45, the largest of the seven, became Doc. TECP-40, the most active of the seven, is known as Grumpy. The least active is Sleepy. One of them is almost completely hidden by a mantle of ice and snow: Bashful. Another has the most spectacular icefalls from its summit. *Achoo! Gesundheit,* Sneezy.

No metaphor is perfect. There's nothing Happy or Dopey about the remaining two, but that's what they're called.

So there you have them, and I won't again refer to them by their acronyms.

I LISTENED TO hundreds of the songs over the next few days in my spare time.

Something about them haunted me. The songs did not use any scale that I was familiar with, and an analysis by computer agreed with me that there was no formal human system of music that employed such intervals. Since it was all one-note progressions, there was no harmony.

I did a pattern search and came up with the songs of humpback whales. It was a bit surprising to me, because these songs sounded nothing like humpbacks, but people at the base assured me that the computers had previously seen similarities. Way beyond my abilities, some mathematical algorithm, apparently.

No algorithm had yet produced any useful information.

Other, mostly atonal, works of music popped up, and I listened to them all. John Cage was there, and Stockhausen, and Xenakis, and Wyschnegradsky. Cage's piece was something with a "prepared piano," which is a piano with various foreign objects attached to the strings or the hammers or dampers. Some intriguing sounds were produced. Another work on the list was by Lennon and McCartney, "A Day in the Life."

The computer also found a mere five-note motif on a major pentatonic scale:

re - mi - do - do — (octave down) — sol

Gran would probably have known it instantly if I sang it. It was composed by John Williams and used in a movie called *Close Encounters of the Third Kind*. I watched it one night. Primitive film, and creepy, with some superadvanced alien race contacting humans for the first time. Frankly, I couldn't see the connection with the Europan crystals, beyond the obvious one that they were alien, and they sang. Maybe that's why the computer connected them, and not the content of the sounds themselves.

Shortly after that I had a thought. I called up what I was thinking of as "Doc's Tune" and played it along with Grumpy's. At last, here was harmony . . . of a sort.

Yes, most of it was musical gibberish to me, but here and there was an intriguing phrase, a harsh but interesting dissonance. Some of it was quarter-tone, and some was tritone, and a little analysis from my computer picked out chord progressions that were in 19, 22, and 72 equal temperaments.

I was sure I was also hearing the twenty-four-tone Arabic temperament. There seemed to be pentatonic Chinese intervals, too. I'd have to check that out with someone more knowledgeable about *gong, shang, jue, zhi,* and *yu,* and other Chinese modes.

There is still so much I don't know in the vast ocean of music! But one thing I was sure of: This *was* music, and there was more going on than met the ear.

WE'RE GOING TO *Forward Base! We're going to Forward Base!*

I feel like I'm four years old and Mom has just asked me if I want to go to the zoo . . . *and ride the elephant*! I hop, I skip, I jump, I glide! I got my mojo workin'! Gone put on my walkin' shoes and walk away dese Taliesen Blues!

Trouble is, you see, the bus to and from Clarke Centre only runs once a week, and after you've been here four days there's really not much left to see. So my little group of VIP tourists has been getting antsy. I haven't complained—I'm doing my best not to seem like a spoiled brat of a rich family.

But you should hear Cosmo! According to him, no one ever told him he had to hang here for seven days. According to him, he was assured he could get his work done in forty-eight hours and take a special bus to Clarke, Ganymede Central, and back to civilization: i.e., Thunder City.

According to Tina, his secretary and general factotum, she had been there when Cosmo had been told not once, but twice, exactly what the situation was.

"He just doesn't listen," she confided. "He thinks the universe exists for his benefit, and when something doesn't go his way there's always someone to blame. Usually it's me. God, I hate this job."

"Why don't you quit?" I asked her.

"Well, the money's good. I've met people who'll help me later, when I *do* leave the asshole. And you know that old joke about the guy at the circus who shovels up the shit behind the elephants. Somebody asks him why he keeps working at this nasty job, and he says, 'What, and quit show business?' "

I had time to get to know Cosmo's crew, Tina in particular, while we were waiting for our ride to Forward. There were also "Slomo," the cameraman, and Nigel, his agent, and Aldric, his dogsbody.

"Actually I was on the payroll as a gopher," he said, "but I'm not a rodent. I considered batman, which is more dignified, or drudge, which is more accurate, but I think dogsbody hits a middle ground. Any job too disgusting for the elephant-shit shoveler, that's my department."

Last but certainly not least of the minientourage—Cosmo never travels with less than five, Tina said, and viewed that few as a real hardship—was Brynne, his mistress. If her IQ matched her bra size she'd have been a Nobel Prize candidate, but she turned out to be not nearly as stupid and a lot friendlier than my prejudices had led me to expect. When their various services were not required, the four of them—minus Nigel, who was never to be seen except on the bus trips—would lie out under the sunlamps by the pool, naked, with me, Monet Wu, Dekko, and Ambassador Baruti. We would take a dip from time to time, and Tina, Monet, and I would try our best not to stare at Brynne, who had had every body mod it was possible to have and thus looked a little like an inflatable latex sex toy, though a very solid one. The best word for her was probably pneumatic, as in an inflatable tire.

Dekko and Aldric made no pretense of not staring. Staring would have been hard to conceal anyway, considering their tongues were hanging somewhere in the vicinity of their belly buttons and their eyes kept popping out and rolling around on the concrete.

Honestly, what is it about huge perky boobs, a perfect face, long shapely legs, a flat tummy . . . well, I guess I'm answering my own question, aren't I?

Brynne paid no more attention to it than a champion Afghan hound in the show ring. She shut them down effortlessly, and almost painlessly. She said right out that she would always be faithful to Cosmo, as long as he was paying the bills. She was easygoing, by her own description nonambitious, and had no complaints about the long wait other than to note it was impossible to get a good pedicure way out here, and she was getting some split ends. A body like that takes a lot of upkeep.

Of the males at poolside, only Slomo seemed unimpressed.

"He claims to be asexual," Monet told me. "He's good-looking, right? So I put a few moves on him, but there's nobody home in the libido room. Not gay, either. I suppose it takes all kinds. You think the world needs asexuals?"

"I'm just glad he's willing to do it, so I don't have to," I said.

Dekko put a few moves on me, in a perfunctory sort of way. I saw he was surprised when I turned him down. He wasn't used to that, being quite a catch with his family money and Mediterranean good looks. A nut brown, well-defined body, luxuriant curly black hair, a bit of a pouty lower lip I might like to chew on, and startling blue eyes. But there was frost behind those eyes, and a lazy sense of entitlement that turned me right off. Plus, he joined Brynne in lamenting the lack of a good pedicurist at Taliesen. I can't stand vanity in a man.

And so we passed the middle days of our great adventure.

* * *

ACTUALLY, I DID do something productive, though when I was done I wasn't quite sure what I had.

I'd listened to all the songs I had access to, some of them many times. I had a vague idea of using some passages in a song of my own. Computers hadn't been able to make any sense of the songs, but they didn't have . . . ears, in the sense of a *human* sensibility, a *musical* sensibility, to appreciate them esthetically. One of the many things a computer still can't do is tell the difference between a good song and a bad song, or a merely pleasant song. Or a *great* song. That, *I* could do. I'd never been much of a songwriter, but I'm as good at listening as anybody in music today. Frankly, I think I'm as good as Sinatra, and a heck of a lot nicer.

So I listened.

I started by playing the songs against each other, sometimes two, sometimes three. Nothing clicked. Putting three or more together just resulted in noise.

One thing a computer *can* do is sort through infinite mounds of garbage and pick out a gem . . . *if* you ask it the right question, *if* you set the right parameters. Since I didn't know what those questions or parameters were, I noodled.

You don't know noodling? It's like doodling, only without a pencil. You sit at the keyboard and you let your fingers have fun. Only this time I was using a computer.

It kept coming up with things, I kept listening to them, and rejecting them. I did that for hours, in my room or lying by the pool with my headset on.

I was drowsing off, sitting on my bed, when something began forming.

Communication. Assume they're communicating in some way. Question, answer. Statement, response. I play the theme, then I hand it over to you on the saxophone and you elaborate it. You toss it to the trumpet player. Jazz, daddy-o! Now I come in again with my new thoughts on the matter. Fusion. Be-bop. Vocalese, scat. Free funk, M-base, hard bop, modal blues.

Ella, talk to me!

Yardbird, can you hear what I'm layin' down?

I set the machine to find pairs that were offset by one day, then by two days, then three and a half days, and played them together.

Things began popping up. The third was a blend of Grumpy on one day, then Dopey in what might have been a response later, with a third, unnamed mountain known only as TECP-61 after that.

It was beautiful.

It was like nothing I'd ever heard before, though it contained elements that almost seemed familiar. For the first time, I had a line that made sense to the human ear. I can describe it, sonically, how there were heterodynes in there, weaving sinuously through the main thematic line, how a dissonance in one chord would resolve itself with stunning logic in the next, but it wouldn't mean anything. You'd have to hear it.

I was operating on instinct now. I offset the three lines half a beat each, so instead of a steady progression of quarter notes, I now had a livelier eighth-note sequence. Even better. There was still not what you'd call a discrete Western-style melody, but if you came at it from a more Eastern sensibility, you could actually sing it, though it would be challenging.

I selected thirty-two bars that seemed most interesting and unrolled my keyboard and started to jam with Grumpy, Dopey, and #61, who I took to thinking of as Jazzie, the eighth dwarf. No matter what I did to the music, it was Jazzie's theme that kept coming through.

I honestly can't say when I started singing. It just seemed to well out of me, this music, almost inaudible at first, in playback, then growing in confidence and meaning. I counterpointed, I threw in little bits that almost seemed familiar without ever actually sampling. I swooped, I soared, I crackled, I roared.

There were no words. It wasn't precisely scat, either, as my lips were hardly involved. At one time I was sustaining two notes at once, like Tuvan throat singing, something I'd failed at previously.

I was cooking.

It lasted about seven minutes, this transporting rapture, and then I knew just where to end it. I found a resolving chord from somewhere, let it hang with no visible means of support, and then I was done. I sighed, and took off the phones, and heard clapping behind me. I turned around and saw half a dozen people crowded around my open bedroom door. I felt like I was coming out of a dream, or maybe a drug trip.

"We came to see who was strangling the cat," Slomo said. Tina punched him.

"What *was* that?" she asked.

"I don't really know," I said.

"Would you do it again?"

I was certain I couldn't, not without some rehearsal, not without hearing it all again, and probably not exactly the same ever again. But hey, that's jazz.

So I played it back for them. They all came into the room, Slomo, Tina, Brynne, Dekko, Monet, the ambassador. After the first few minutes most of them were swaying in place, and I'm not sure they knew they were doing it. Tina essayed a little dance step, shook her head, and tried another. Brynne showed her something, and they played off each other for a while.

Then I played it again. And once more.

"What's it called?" Monet asked.

Hmmm. Grumpy? Dopey? Awful. But . . .

" 'Jazzie's Song,' " I said.

I DIDN'T KNOW what I had. I shipped it off to my brother Mike, and to Quinn, to see if he could do anything with it. Then I pretty much forgot it.

10

★ ★ ★

TCBP-45 (DOC) IS a faceted cliff of purest daffodil yellow, a giant lemon jujube with white frosting on top. It is three miles high, which is almost a mile taller than it was when humans first photographed it in the previous century, and half a mile higher than it was when Forward Base was established.

Europa's mountains are in clusters, not chains, each of them lozenge-shaped and steep-sided, pretty much vertical in some places.

We speak of human time and "geologic time," in which we as individuals and even as a race are the merest flickers, nanosecond ticks on the cosmic clock. Geologic time on Europa, in the mountains, anyway, is like a runaway racehorse.

Imagine a time-lapse film of the Himalayas being formed, with one frame every thousand years. At twenty-four frames/sec. it would run over thirty minutes.

There *are* such films of the growth of the Taliesen mountains, one frame every *day*, and you can *see* them grow.

Our route from Main Base took us on a winding path through five of the seven dwarfs, which come in all the primary colors and all the variations of any mineral you can imagine. Some, like Doc, seem uniform and clear as glass. Some are multicolored, or streaked with wavy lines of a different color, or contain inclusions of various sorts, some up to a mile across.

And inside them, things glow, and move.

HAPPY IS YELLOW, too, but it's more of a yellow-gold fading to bronze at the south end, and there's a big area of blue-green cabochons, "like moles, or beauty spots if you prefer, on a Chinese whore's cheek," as our driver put it. Since he himself was of Chinese ancestry, I guess that was okay. And I have to admit, it was gaudy and brassy as a whore's makeup.

Sleepy is blue all over, a vast sapphire only partially seen behind a slope of supercold cracked ice and snow. Sleepy is not as steep as some of the others, and flatter on top, so the snow clings.

Sneezy bulges at the top, a green jelly bean almost free of snow and ice. As we drove by it, a berg the size of Anchorage, Alaska, slid down the side and smashed into the ground in low-grav slow motion. When it impacted it sent a plume of snow fifty miles into the air.

Everybody *oohed* and *aahed,* and Brynne let out a fetching little squeak. Slomo crowded us all in his eagerness to capture it on camera. I couldn't be sure, but I thought he might have had an erection. Asexual, but turned on by spectacle. He'd probably cream his jeans if we were struck by an asteroid.

Larger chunks, the size of city blocks, came crashing down between us and the mountain, sending up their own flowers of white. After a while, as we were hotfooting it out of there, ice pebbles started to rain down on the top of the bus, followed by larger bits, including one that made the whole bus ring like a bell.

"Don't worry," the driver said. "This buggy is built to handle it."

I have to admit, it certainly looked like it. We only got a brief glimpse of it from the outside, but it was heavily armored, a cylinder on ceramic tracks, with walls over three feet thick layered with more armor and insulation.

There were only twenty seats in the bus, and our party, with guide, filled only twelve. But there was a separate room behind the passenger compartment and in there I could see piles of stuff held in place by cargo netting. About half of that was supplies for Forward Base, but the rest was spare parts.

"I could practically build this baby from the ground up from what I've got back there," the driver boasted when I asked him. "Just about anything that can go wrong, I got a part back there that'll fix it."

"Just about?"

He grinned at me. "Can't prepare for *everything*, now, can you?"

"So do you get breakdowns often?"

"Oh, every other trip, on average. It's the Fubar Factor." That's what the people at Taliesen called the tendency for things to go wrong in the vicinity of the dwarfs. I didn't like it because I happen to know that FUBAR stands for Fucked-Up Beyond All Repair. *Beyond all repair?*

Oh, well. I had my Swiss Army knife and a few hairpins. There's not much you can't fix with that.

FORWARD BASE WAS moveable. I'm not saying it was like a mobile home, just disconnect the water, power, and oxygen and tow it along a well-paved four-lane highway to a new campsite with a better view of the Valles Marinaris. It was on skids, and if you hooked up three gigantic tug vehicles, you could slide it to a different location at the blistering rate of about twenty hpm. That's hours per mile. The whole damn minicity, population 254, bus terminal, landing pad, dormitories, research labs, gym, two taverns, three sex workers, thirty-one dogs, eighteen cats, and Cosmo (complete with entourage), and Podkayne, et al., if they happened to be aboard. Which we were.

They don't do this often, maybe once or twice a year when something crops up they want a closer look at, so I felt lucky to see it.

Not that there was a lot to see. If Europa had snails they could have given Forward Base a run for its money. Turtles would have run rings around it.

After we de-bussed, Captain Kate Stone awaited us in full-dress uniform. She was an attractive white-haired Earth-born about my mother's age. She had what looked to be a sincere smile on her face. Well, Cosmo would soon take care of that. I shoved my way to the front and made sure I was the first out of the bus. I came to attention as well as anyone can in the low gravity, and snapped her my smartest salute.

"Lieutenant Podkayne, Music Division, reporting to base, Captain."

"At ease, Lieutenant. You're on furlough, and we're pretty informal around here. I'm a big fan of your father's books. Bit of a history buff myself. And I worked with your grandmother as a very junior aide on the naval procurement committee, some years back. I doubt she'd remember me; we spoke maybe three or four times."

"Oh, she'll remember you, ma'am," I told her. "She never forgets anybody. She'll have a file on you somewhere, probably more detailed than the Navy's."

She laughed, then totally surprised me.

"I wanted to be here to ask you if you'd be willing to entertain my troops tonight, before you leave in the morning," she said. Well, that wasn't the surprise. They sure didn't get much live entertainment here at Forward. But then she went on.

"I think I'm going to be a big fan of yours, if you keep going the way you have been. I've downloaded all your stuff so far, and I have to tell you, I just love it. So does most everyone around here. So I was wondering . . ." And she held out a glossy picture of me and the band, me out in front standing with my booted feet set far apart, in black leather with a very short skirt, looking windswept and just a wee bit dominatrix. "Would you mind signing this? For my daughter back home."

My God! *A fan!*

For a moment I was too nonplussed to say anything, then I remembered what my first voice teacher had always said about being onstage. *Remember, Poddy, smile, smile, smile!* So I flashed the old choppers and told her it would be my pleasure, and she probably had no idea just how true that was.

♥ With all my love to Jennifer ♥
Podkayne

It looked weird, lying there on the page in the pink marker the captain had given me, but I thought I could get used to it.

Then Cosmo broke in between, literally shoving his way past me, and started bitching about everything that had gone wrong—for him—on this trip. As if she had anything to do with it. He kept on in that vein for quite a while, and Captain Stone listened, more or less blank-faced. I drifted away, cringing inside, hoping none of his boorishness would rub off on the rest of us. Finally, from across the bus bay, I saw him stalk off and Tina and Aldric move in, talking rapidly.

Shoveling shit behind the elephant.

FORWARD BASE WAS moving along the south face of Grumpy to a new position three miles east of its previous location. You couldn't tell it from inside. The floor didn't rumble beneath our feet. If you set a glass of beer on the table, no ripples appeared.

We were sitting by the windows, Tina and Dekko and Ambassador Baruti and I, the windows being in Dopey's Bar, the more intimate of the two watering holes on Forward. We were looking out at Grumpy. It was a bright day outside, or as bright as it gets on Europa, so far from the sun, and would be for another twenty hours. The light hit the multifaceted walls and made them sparkle like fine rubies, or glasses of fine claret. In fact, two regions of the towering cliff faces had names reflecting those very images. A geometrically faceted area almost directly in front of us was called the Jewelry Store. If you mounted one of those stones, you'd need a ring quite a bit larger than a cricket pitch to hold it. Off to the east there was an area that undulated in sine waves; from some angles you could imagine bottles standing side by side, and thus, the Wine Cellar. There were areas that looked basaltic, and others smooth as a mirror.

Grumpy was a canvas three miles high and seven miles wide, with an irregular surface, painted by an abstract expressionist who liked red.

In fact, that was almost the only color he liked. There were traces of purple here and there, swirls and splotches, and maybe a hint of chocolate filling oozing from some mile-high cracks. Other than that, it was red . . . brick, russet, vermilion, damask, cerise, burgundy, carmine, magenta, coral, mars, crimson, fuchsia, garnet, rose, rust, maroon, scarlet, titian, cardinal, vermeil, cherry, puce . . . Red.

There were telescopes fixed to the floor along the outer wall. Here I'll have to confess something, and I hope it doesn't make me seem shallow. I can only be awed by scenery for a limited time.

Grumpy was one of the most spectacular things I'd ever seen, and certainly the most mysterious, but in the end, it's just sitting there. Most of the time, anyway, and right now it wasn't moving. It was like the to-die-for view out my window at the Swamp. Eventually it's just The View. I glance at it when I come home to see that Jupiter is still there—yup, there it is—and then I sit down and start practicing.

I felt less guilty after Cosmo wandered into the room for the first time. He stopped, looked at the amazing sight for all of seven seconds, then sniffed and went on his way. Been there, done that, didn't bother with the T-shirt. At least I was a long way from *that* degree of self-involved indifference.

Those of us who were interested and didn't have anything else to do spent about an hour exploring Grumpy's surface. If we found something interesting we'd slave all the telescopes to the one with the object of interest.

"That looks like a face to me," the ambassador said at one point. He was a solemn old guy, a career diplomat long past retirement age who had been happy to accept the job as ambassador to Mars.

My telescope swung to where his was looking. I didn't see much of anything.

"The chin is to the southwest," he said. "Then see the line of the mouth? He has a rather cruel upper lip. He looks Roman . . ."

I had it. It was very facelike. Like the "face" on Mars, which people still go to, for reasons that elude me. There's a little souvenir kiosk selling posters of the original photograph, taken back in the twentieth century, a meaningless artifact of the light.

THE SESSION THAT night at Dopey's went well. Actually, I wouldn't be bragging to say it went fabulously well. I did a set accompanying myself on the piano, to wild applause. Then I jammed with two local musicians, who were not bad.

All night long I had to keep reminding myself, *These people are starved for entertainment, Podkayne. Don't let it go to your head.*

I couldn't help it. It did. I was floating on air.

MOST OF US from the bus and quite a few residents hung around for the sunset. Even Cosmo showed up, briefly. For the next forty-two hours Forward Base would be treated to the strangest show in the solar system: the fairy lights of Taliesen.

Sunset on an airless moon isn't like it is on Mars or Earth. It's like a light switch. It's on, then it's off. Instantly it was pitch-dark, nothing visible at all except the base's perimeter lights illuminating the surrounding hundred yards of snow. Captain Stone spoke into a wrist mike, and the lights were extinguished.

It took a moment for my eyes to adjust, and then there they were. Thousands of red fireflies, some barely moving, others racing around in patternless frenzy.

Wait a minute, I've never seen real fireflies but I googled them and it seems they blink on and off. These didn't, but they waxed and waned. Some would get very bright, then fade away almost to invisibility, then come back again.

This time I felt no encroaching boredom, no urge to move on to whatever was next on the tour. I felt I could have watched them all night.

"How could anyone doubt they're alive?" Monet asked. I hadn't seen her approach in the darkness.

"I don't," Captain Stone said. "But there are other possible explanations."

"Like what?"

"Some sort of electrical phenomenon. The best candidate is piezoelectricity. It's been known for a long time, as far back as the 1820s. Crystals under stress produce a voltage. There are millions of applications in radio, sound—"

"Loudspeakers," I said. I'd heard Quinn use the term once.

"Exactly. Those mountains are under an incredible amount of gravitational stress, just like the whole moon is. The surface of the mountains certainly is rock crystal, but as for inside . . . our radar doesn't penetrate far, but we have some data that indicates the density gets less the farther you go in. Some models even predict a center filled with gas. They could very well be less dense than ice."

"Gas?" Monet said. "You mean they could be hollow?"

"I know what you're thinking. It would be easier for us to understand a form of life that lived in, even *made*, big bubbles of air. But we don't know. We don't even have a very clear idea of what the surface is made of."

"That's what I don't understand," said an irritating voice just behind me. Believe it or not, Cosmo was back. "You guys are eating up a lot of our tax dollars out here, and when I ask questions, all I get is 'We don't know.' I'm afraid that's not enough for me. Why doesn't somebody just go up and chip off some big pieces? Better yet, drill a hole in the sucker, a mile deep, and *see* what's inside."

Though I couldn't see much in the dark room, a certain heat seemed to permeate the area as Captain Stone struggled to keep her diplomatic mask in place. She knew a bad story from this guy could do her and the whole enterprise a lot of harm.

"As I'm sure you know, Mr. Wills, there are many who advocate doing just that. Never mind the danger, I'm sure we could find some volunteers for such an expedition. I would even go myself if I could convince myself that it was only a big rock out there. But what if they *are* alive? What if somebody is living in there? What would happen to them if we drilled? Maybe nothing, maybe disaster. Or what if the rocks themselves are alive? I'd think a lot more than twice before I stuck a pin in a creature that big."

I would, too, but I kept quiet. I love to listen in on a good argument. Cosmo made an impolite sound with his lips. Asshole.

"You probably know I believe that those stones out there are just that. Big stones. Junk jewelry of the gods. I did a show on it."

"I must not have caught that one."

Cosmo was oblivious to the sarcasm.

"It makes no sense that, if they're intelligent, they wouldn't have contacted us after all these years out here. What are we, anyway, chopped liver?"

I didn't get that reference at all, but for some reason I piped up.

"They're slow," I said.

It was like he couldn't believe I'd spoken, like one of the chairs had suddenly contradicted him. I, a lowly lieutenant, and he the big celebrity. Maybe he thought I was stupid. Well, maybe I was, to challenge a guy whose business was words, and whose technique was to ambush his guests, switch off their mikes when they tried to talk, and turn them into something like chopped liver.

"What does slow have to do with anything?"

"They're slow and we're small," I said. "Their songs, for all the time we've been listening to them, are still very short, by our standards. I'm wondering if they live on a different time scale than we do."

"You're saying you think they communicate with this ELF stuff?" he scoffed. I'll hand it to him, I don't think I've ever heard anybody scoff quite as well. But it was his profession.

"I don't know. Maybe. Maybe a year to us is like a second to them." Before he could scoff further, I hurried on. "Look, if those things *are* alive and intelligent, we're smaller than a louse studying a blue whale. Why would the whale notice us?"

"I'm not a louse," he said. "Human beings aren't lice."

Oh, my, have I ever been presented with a better straight line? But I let it lie.

"Say it's a flea and an elephant," I plowed on. "Maybe the elephant is aware of the flea, and maybe he isn't. But if the flea bites, he might *become* aware, and I don't think that would be to the flea's advantage."

"I agree," Monet said. "Let's don't annoy them."

Cosmo scoffed again.

"Bullshit. I say we bring in a medium artillery piece and send an experimental round into the side of that thing, see what happens. I say—"

But we never got to his next pearl of wisdom, because right then a horn started sounding and everybody started moving.

"Brace yourselves," Captain Stone said. "We're about to get a bit of rock and roll."

The lights came up and the floor began to move. Oh, my! I imagine it would have been scary enough in Martian gravity, but here, where you weighed so little, you could get thrown pretty high in the air. I grabbed on to a handrail by the windows and hung on.

While the room was shuddering side to side and up and down, I noticed with a sort of dreamy detachment some things I'd seen before but not actually taken in. For instance, all the tables were bolted to the floor, and there were benches instead of chairs, and they were also bolted down. Better to have them as something to hang on to instead of letting them become deadly flying objects.

I heard glassware rattling and looked at the bar. I saw all the bottles were secured behind a rail, like on a ship at sea. All in all there wasn't a lot that wasn't tied down in some way, other than us.

Still, you can't tie down everything. A jar of olives came bouncing toward me, was fielded by a table, and smacked out into center field. Ice fountained up from behind the bar from a cabinet that hadn't been secured properly. The bartender was scrambling to lock it down. A small amp and a mike stand bounced off the low bandstand and lodged under a bench.

The biggest part of the debris was Cosmo Wills. Naturally he had not bothered to read the stuff we were all given when we arrived at Taliesen, and had been utterly baffled when the quake started. Instead of grabbing something, he had tried to run, overdid it, and flew into the air. I saw the ceiling swat him. His head went through an acoustical tile up there, and then he tore loose and somehow managed to squirm around in the air so that he hit the floor with his head, too. He put his hands out to protect himself, which only meant that he was shoving off the floor with his arms instead of his legs when he hit, and bounced high again, and this is almost impossible to believe, but he managed to turn around in the air *again*, and hit his head into a light fixture. He held on to something this time, and hung there, howling, for the rest of the quake.

Which was a fine place for him, in my opinion. Does that make me a bad person?

IT SEEMED HE'D got his head jammed up into some wiring. It was sort of fun getting him back down.

He hung on to the acoustic tile cross bracing, kicking his feet at first, but he finally realized that wasn't making it any better. So he started shouting about how sorry we were all going to be that we'd ever been born, how he was going to sue everybody at the base for everything they owned, he was going to take the Navy apart with his bare hands. But with his head stuck up there in the sound baffles, we couldn't hear him too well.

The chief systems engineer was brought in to assess the problem. He took his time. It seemed to take even more time to find a ladder. In fact, nobody seemed to be in a big hurry about anything, and the only problem most of us were having was trying not to bust a gut laughing. Tina was doubled over, both hands over her mouth as she desperately tried to stifle her hysterical giggle, which was all too identifiable.

"I don't think he can hear you," I whispered to her. "Let it out."

This only made matters worse for her, as I'd intended. She grew so red in the face I began to worry about her. She took a deep breath, tried to steady herself, and finally collapsed in a giggling fit again.

"Can he sue the Navy?" I asked Captain Stone.

"We're lawsuit-proof, as an institution," she said, with satisfaction. "It's in the constitution. It's possible to sue individual officers for dereliction of duty, things like that, but he signed a release. He probably doesn't remember it."

I felt better. I knew that if he *could* sue, he *would* sue.

They called in more engineers. It began to seem like it was the most difficult problem they'd ever encountered. Every now and then one would have to turn away to stifle a laugh. Oh, but they were careful. Nothing they did could be seen as deliberate procrastination, nothing worse than excess caution, and who could complain about that? Nobody but Cosmo, and he did enough complaining for the whole planet.

I noticed that Slomo wasn't laughing, but he had a small smile on his face. Then I noticed something else, and sidled over to him.

"Are you getting all this?" I whispered.

"Every second of it," he said, pointing to the camera he held at his hip. "Even better, I got the whole thing, him bouncing around, banging his head. Screaming and whimpering like a child."

"I don't think he'll want to use it."

"He won't even see it. But this chip goes into my most secure file, and someday he might get a look. Call it job security. Or maybe, if I'm pissed off enough, a way to get a little respect. I might ask him to imagine how he'd like to see this on download, available to the whole world."

"My lips are sealed," I assured him, and spent the next ten minutes enjoying myself, imagining that footage on the news.

AND I LIED. I told Tina about it. And I think she told Aldric. Oops!

After they got Cosmo out of the ceiling, hardly the worse for wear except for a knot on his forehead and a broken nose that had bled freely—when he saw it he shrieked, and almost passed out—Captain Stone called up a detailed simulation of Grumpy's south face on a wallscreen. She indicated a vertical area that was about a mile wide and was represented in a different color.

"About a hundred feet," she said. "Not too bad of a shake for that amount of movement."

"That wasn't a bad shake?" I asked.

"Moderate. And now TECP-40 is a hundred feet taller." She seemed to take a certain satisfaction in that. I guess it made sense. There was so little they knew about these things that it was good to have a nice, solid fact you could measure.

"It grows faster and more often than any of them," she said. "That's why we call him Grumpy."

If that was a moderate one, I hoped to be back home before the old Grumpster got really temperamental.

11

★ ★ ★

AS IF GOD wanted to be sure we experienced the full spectrum of oddness in and around Taliesen, our bus broke down on the way home. Worse, it wasn't even the bus that would take us back to Clarke but the one ferrying us from our rockin' appearance at Forward back to Taliesen Main. Of course it sent Cosmo ballistic once again. I thought about killing him. Then I thought about putting a round from my sidearm into his left knee, then his right one, then watching him bleed. Can't prosecute me for my thoughts.

He was a real sight, with a big bandage over his nose, one eye black, his forehead still a bit swollen.

"What a fuckin' zoo!" he was shouting. "I'm going to find out who's responsible for this fucking mess, and I'm going to hang him out to dry. Driver, what the fuck are you doing down there?"

He was leaning over the hatch the driver had opened. No steam was coming out of it or anything dramatic like that, but I heard a clanking noise. The good old sledgehammer cure?

I thought about planting my boot in his butt, but the gravity was so low he'd have no trouble recovering before he fell in. That's when Senator Wu Zheng Han walked over to him and tapped him on the shoulder.

Cosmo straightened . . . and Senator Wu pinched Cosmo's broken nose between his thumb and finger, and squeezed. The sound that came out of Cosmo was halfway between a honk and an oink.

"Curb your tongue, sir," he said, reasonably. He gave another pinch—we heard another honk/oink—and let him go. Cosmo stood there, stunned.

"You have done nothing but whine and complain for this entire trip. I have tolerated it, but I will not countenance language like that around my daughter."

I looked at Monet, who rolled her eyes. I happened to know his daughter used language a lot stronger than that . . . but not around her father. And who cared what the excuse was? It was high time somebody put this asshole in his place. I only regretted I hadn't had the courage to do it myself. But the amazing thing was that the man to do it was the senator, who had been quiet as a mouse for most of the trip.

"Where the fuck do you get off—*honk!*"

"I take no pleasure in your public humiliation, sir," the senator went on. "But since the offense was a highly public one, you left me no choice. I am a man of peace, but will fight if provoked. If you demand satisfaction for this insult, I will meet with your representatives as soon as we return to Mars."

Things got very quiet. Dueling had first been proposed as a way to settle public insults in the Republic only about five years ago, and won by a narrow margin. Not with guns or swords or anything deadly, and not willy-nilly, people calling each other out just for meanness, or for some imagined insult. It had to be approved by a board of your peers, and it was closely monitored. In fact, there were so many rules and regulations and handicaps (no three-hundred-pound bruiser against a ninety-eight-pound woman) that there were only two or three duels every week. But the hassle of going through the process even to get turned down before it came to actual fisticuffs was enough to keep most people at least a teeny bit more polite.

Of course, when the blood did start to fly, it was great spectator sport. Ratings were usually high, and they'd be through the roof for a fight between a senator and Cosmo.

I could see Cosmo doing the math. Senator Wu was a tad shorter, and maybe fifteen years older. But he was known to be a practitioner of some martial art or another. So there was that. Cosmo would not relish getting his butt whipped in public. But he was also just smart enough to realize that, if it came before the board, he had no friends here. I sure as hell knew how I would testify. There was a very good chance he could be made to look like the aggressor, and a fool, which was worse, and the senator a man just offering a reasonable response to provocation.

There was also a certain look in Senator Wu's eye that I would describe as a deadly calm. So Cosmo swallowed hard.

"I apologize," he muttered, and stomped off to the back of the bus to sulk. Tina later told me that it wasn't the first time Cosmo had had to back off from a duel, and given his temperament, it certainly wouldn't be his last. Another certainty was that he would make life hell for his employees for the next few weeks.

The driver popped his head out of the hatch and looked at us, oblivious to the lovely scene he had just missed.

"Well, you want the good news or the bad news?" he asked, cheerfully.

I think we all groaned.

"Just give it to us straight, Doc, we can take it," Aldric said.

"Okay. I can move this baby, but only at about one mile per hour. The tranny's pretty much fried, except for low gear." He shook his head. "I inspected that sucker myself, just before we left. Didn't see the hairline crack." Or the fickle finger of mishap, I thought, which seemed to point directly at Taliesen most of the time.

"We'd have to wait for a part, *except*"—and here he grinned—"it's only about a mile and a half to NEMO. I'm pretty sure I can swap out a part from one of their buggies."

"So how long?" Tina asked, glancing back at Cosmo.

"Hour and a half over there. Say three hours to fix it." He grinned even wider. "Also, I got a girlfriend at NEMO, so add another . . . say an hour."

"Say two hours," I suggested, to general agreement.

NEMO STANDS FOR Navy Europa Mobile Oceanautics. We tend to forget, standing on a sheet of ice that's as deep as thirty miles in some places, that beneath it is a mineral-saturated ocean three hundred miles deep. The areas around the freckles also appear to be hot spots on the silicate rock that forms the bulk of Europa's core. Those hot spots are caused by the deep molten iron core being stirred with the gigantic runcible spoon of the tides of Jupiter, Io, and Ganymede.

For whatever reason, the ice around Taliesen is thinner than at any place on Europa, only about two miles. A mere crust, a rime, an eggshell. I'm surprised we don't all fall through like incautious skaters. That makes it the ideal site for the daredevils of NEMO, who regularly dive into an environment that may be the harshest humans have ever attempted to invade.

It was even smaller than Forward Base, dominated by the large dome that housed the submarines. When we went down the ramp in the bus bay we were met at the bottom by the base commander, Captain Glenn Scott, who seemed happy enough to see us.

Captain Scott gave us a tour of the base. NEMO was only a year old. They were doing something here that had never been done, and were still pretty new at it, according to Captain Scott. They were still learning. We ended up in the submarine bay.

"There are maybe a dozen small harbor patrol craft, based on Earth," the captain told us. "Other than that, these are the only boats in the Martian Navy."

I learned that submarines were traditionally called boats, even the underwater aircraft carriers of East and Western America, China, and the European Union. These little fish were nothing like that. They were made on Earth, which had the expertise to do it, and were about forty feet long, fat and stubby, but sleek as dolphins. They were all a Day-Glo yellow with orange stripes.

They were hanging from racks, in a row, and could be trundled out to the center of the dome, where the entrance hole was now covered with a metal cap. There were five subs, each with NEMO and a Roman numeral painted on the side, but there was no NEMO-III. The space where it would have been was empty.

"*Nautilis, Turtle, Plongeur, Kairyu,* and *Crocodil,*" he said, with proprietary pride. "The toughest little ships in the solar system. *Turtle* is mine.

Named after the first American submarine, designed by David Bushnell, 1775."

There was a name written above the empty berth: OCTOBER.

"So *October* is on a dive?" I asked.

"*October* is overdue," Captain Scott said.

"How long?" Monet asked.

"About six months now."

Well, that was a bit of a conversation stopper, considering he'd already told us that the maximum submersion time for these NEMOs was forty-eight hours. It seemed rather callous to me, too, until I realized he was dead serious.

"No ship under my command will ever be listed as 'lost' unless I see the wreckage with my own eyes," he said. "We know she's down there, we just aren't able to dive that deep. Yet. We're working on it."

And as for the crew, they had KYAGs, so there was at least a chance that they were still alive down there, encased in stopper bubbles, in suspended time. I patted the little unit attached to my own belt.

Captain Scott came up to me with a look in his eyes that I thought I recognized. And to tell you the truth, I wouldn't have been averse. He was a good-looking guy, though two inches shorter than me and balding almost to the top of his head. I liked that he didn't try for a comb-over, or even bother with transplants. That indicated confidence in his manhood, in my eyes. And he had strong arms and friendly blue eyes. Ships that pass in the night . . . I'm not opposed to that, if it's an attractive ship. I could feel my heart thumping a little faster.

"Say, Lieutenant . . ." he began.

"Podkayne, if it's not too informal."

"We're very informal around here. Podkayne, then. I was wondering . . ."

I batted my eyelashes in a way I'd practiced in the mirror since I was twelve.

"Well, since you're going to be here awhile, would you mind dropping by our canteen and favoring us with a few songs?"

I hoped my smile looked genuine. Ah, the perils of fame. No doubt the man was too overwhelmed by my star power, my charisma, to even consider me as a bed partner. Well, I shouldn't be daunted. Soon, no doubt, the situation would be reversed, and I'd have to hire a platoon of hefty guys to surround me and keep the legions of handsome young men from smothering me with their worship. Sigh.

But enough regrets. My public awaits!

"I MUST BE out of my mind to do this," Captain Scott said, gloomily.

No, we weren't in his bed, sorry to say, but the next best thing. I was sitting in the jump seat behind the pilot, Captain Scott, of the MNV *Turtle*. We were about to take a dive. A really *deep* dive.

I'm not sure exactly where I got the nerve to ask for the trip. Maybe my star power really *was* going to my head, because suddenly I knew I could convince this man to do something he knew he really shouldn't. And I did it. I told him I'd be happy to entertain his troops, if he'd give me a ride in his little motor scooter. His multimillion-dollar motor scooter.

He dithered awhile, he called up his copilot, and ten minutes later the deal was done. I did a one-hour set in the canteen, enthusiastically received, and ten minutes later we were in the big fish.

By "we" I mean myself, Slomo, Ambassador Baruti, Dekko, Captain Scott, and Dr. Nadine Land, a tiny Earthie in her midthirties, oceanographer and submersible expert on loan from the East America Navy, the woman who had taught Scott and all his other pilots everything they knew about driving these things.

The pressure was enormous down there, higher than at the bottom of the deepest ocean trench on Earth. I decided I didn't even want to know how much. These little crafts had made it halfway to the bedrock, and could go farther, but you did this sort of thing in increments. These boats were never going to reach the rock below, but the next generation might.

Captain Scott maneuvered the arm holding *Turtle* suspended in the air out over the lock leading to the water. Dr. Land was watching Scott's every move while trying not to be too obvious about it. It was clear to me that she still regarded him, and probably all the other pilots, as drivers in training.

Slomo was aboard because we all knew he'd kill the rest of us if he was denied a seat if that's what it took. No way he was going to miss filming this. Baruti and Dekko were there because of a coin toss. NEMOs seated six, absolute maximum, and were crowded at that.

I wasn't scared. Really, I wasn't. Well, maybe a bit nervous. We wouldn't be going to any great depth, just a quick pop down under the ice, and a quick look around. And forever after I could have bragging rights about having been to the most remote and hostile location humans had ever penetrated.

"Any chance of seeing a boojum?" I asked.

Captain Scott jerked his head around and stared at me.

"Where'd you hear that?"

I shrugged. "It's common knowledge at Clarke. Not even all that hard to come by in Thunder City."

He looked a little pissed off. Maybe I shouldn't have brought it up. He concentrated on his controls, and we started lowering toward the sealock.

"It's not exactly top secret, Glenn," Dr. Land pointed out. The high-pressure door was rolling away beneath us. I could see this through the lower porthole near my feet. "Why do you think we call them boojums?" she asked.

I quickly googled the word, and as I had remembered, it was from Lewis Carroll's "The Hunting of the Snark." Mom used to read me to sleep with Carroll.

"I'm presuming it's not because if you find one, you softly and suddenly vanish away," I said.

"We don't know that," she said, with a smile. "Nobody's 'found' one. We know they're out there, but only within three miles or so. We haven't tried to chase one; we don't have that kind of range yet."

"So you call them that because they're elusive?"

"We don't even know that. Hard to find, let's say."

"And you think they're alive?"

"It makes sense to me, but I'm not an exobiologist. Nobody can prove anything one way or another, yet again. One day we plan to try to chase one down."

"Nobody knows anything on this damn planet," Dekko groused. "Even the most basic things. Is it alive, isn't it alive? You'd think in all this time, somebody would know."

"Sometimes the most basic questions are the hardest ones to answer."

So, the mountains themselves, the fairy lights inside them, the boojums . . . all of them might be alive, but no one had demonstrated anything that was conclusively life as we understood it. All of them might be intelligent. Which meant, to most people, that it was simply life as we *didn't* understand it, but to most people, like Dekko—like me—that wasn't a very satisfying proposition.

We were lowered into the sealock, the cables holding us detached themselves, and the lock sealed above us. With a roar that made me jump, water under pressure began to jet into the big chamber. This was Europan water, clear as vodka, so sterile you could use it to clean wounds. I'd drunk many gallons of it, desalinated, back at Clarke. But it somehow looked alien. It was saltier than the Dead Sea, and had more minerals dissolved in it than the pools of Yellowstone. And not a trace of any of the complex chemicals we associate with life.

The doors opened below us. I strained to see between my feet. We really were crammed into a tiny pickle barrel in there, with barely room to turn around.

We started to drop. Somebody turned on the exterior lights. Outside, I could see metal walls moving upward all around us. The pipe was about a hundred feet wide, made of some bright, shiny metal, but encrusted here and there with brownish growths.

"Mineral deposits," Scott said, shining a light on a large patch of them. "We have to clean it out once a week."

The walls started moving faster, and I felt myself lifted out of my seat for a moment. Then the vertical metal tunnel ended and things got even brighter. I realized I was seeing ice. The hole we were dropping through was now about twice the width it had been. The ice had an undulant surface. In places it was white, like compacted snow, and in others it was translucent, and bright blue. Around us, at the four points of the compass, heavy cables hung, attached here and there to the surface of the ice. Every hundred yards or so we passed a quartet of what looked like oil drums with rotating yellow lights on top.

"Heaters," Dr. Land explained. "We melted our way down here at first with a big hot plate sort of thing. If we don't keep the water above a certain temperature it can freeze back again. We're like seals in the Antarctic, keeping our breathing hole open by keeping it constantly in use."

"Yeah, and it'll take us all day to go down like this," Captain Scott said. "So hold on to your valuables, I'm going to kick it into high gear."

He moved the stick forward and the ship nosed down, then he opened up the throttle. I was pressed back into my seat for a moment, then I leaned forward and to the side to get a better view.

If they ever make a movie of my life, they'll probably spend a lot of time on this part, because it's a good visual. We were speeding down a narrow tube, the details of which emerged into our lights only as we neared them. I guess we could see about a hundred yards of the ice itself, but the yellow markers of the beacons stretched out quite a bit farther than that before they vanished in the gloom. I knew we had plenty of room, moving down the center as we were, and I knew we wouldn't hit anything unless the tunnel made a turn, which it would not do. Still, the impression of headlong, reckless speed was pretty strong. I found myself gripping the armrests.

Then the whole ship rang like a gong. I felt it right down to my toes, and braced myself. Captain Scott, that rascal, leaned back toward his passengers.

"Sorry, should have warned you about that," he said, but from the smug expression on his face I was pretty sure he wasn't sorry at all. "Compression joint, compensating. We may get a few more before we reach bottom."

Then, without much warning, we shot out of the bottom of the tube and Scott pulled up on the stick. We leveled out and slowed down quite a bit. Scott angled the biggest lights on the boat to point upward. I looked up there, and gasped.

It was so beautiful!

It was the Emerald City, the Big Apple, Shangri-La, and the Mother Ship from *Close Encounters*.

And it was all upside-down.

Crystal stalactites that dwarfed the *Turtle* hung from the ice above us, bigger than the biggest Navy ship, multifaceted, transparent or translucent, in all the colors of the rainbow but dominated by red and green. We cruised slowly below and among them.

"I know every one of these rocks within about two miles of the blowhole," Scott was telling us. He pointed out some of the highlights. The Eiffel Tower, the Chrysler Building, the Taj Mahal, Ostankino, Burj Dubai, Disney Center, Trylon and Perisphere Joburg Arcology. The Lion, the Witch, the Wardrobe. The Crown Jewels, Kilimanjaro, El Capitan, the Orb and Scepter, Culinan, Bats in the Belfry. Bugs Bunny, Golden Gate, Snow White, Pancakes and Maple Syrup, FAO Quartz, Chutes and Ladders.

All upside-down.

Sometimes I could see the resemblance, sometimes it seemed a bit of a stretch, but the names were magical whether they made sense or not. The water was so clear it might as well not have been there at all and our lights seemed to go on forever, delving into the cold hearts of these fairy structures. It was all still as death until *Turtle* farted a series of big bubbles that swam like quicksilver up into the maze above us, and vanished.

"All rock, of one kind or another," Captain Scott said. "Some of that stuff looks soft as a cotton ball when you get up close, but it's hard. Like needles. Some of those edges are sharp as a razor, too."

"So you've taken samples?" Ambassador Baruti asked.

"Thousands. All perfectly normal minerals. Some of them are combinations that you won't see much of on Earth, and since the pressure is from water and not from surrounding rock, they can grow a lot bigger than what you normally see."

"What about quakes?" Dekko asked. "Are those things attached firmly?"

"Pretty well," Scott said. "But chunks have been known to break loose. If we're down here when a quake happens, we keep our eyes peeled."

"Boojum," Dr. Land said, quietly.

I immediately looked through all the windows I could see.

"Where? Where?" We were all jerking around like crazy.

"About . . . five and a half miles," Dr. Land said, dryly. "You really figured you'd be the first to see one with the naked eye?"

They passed a sonar image to our screens, and we all watched as a vague shape appeared, moving left to right, very slowly. It was tapered at both ends, fat in the middle, longer on one end. Like the Loch Ness Monster, only no visible head or flippers. There was a line of bumps down the midline of the side we could see, maybe thirty of them.

"Five miles away," I said, trying to read the scale on the screen.

"A small one," Scott said. "About half a mile long."

A small one.

"It's moving," the ambassador said. "Doesn't that indicate life to you?"

"If they moved faster, sure. But we've never observed one moving faster than the currents down here, which never exceed about five miles per hour."

"Could simply be something drifting," Dr. Land said. "Icebergs drift."

"And the currents are erratic, and chaotic, and they churn up and down as well as laterally, and there's miles and miles and miles to go down there before you reach bottom. Like I said, we're just getting started down here. There's still so much we don't know."

"Another one," Dr. Land said.

This time we didn't look around. She gave us another display, this one with the *Turtle* in the center. There were two dots out on the periphery, and the computer drew a vector to show us where they were headed and at what speed.

"Another," she said. This time she sounded a little excited.

"Is that unusual?" I asked.

"A bit. We've never seen more than three at once."

"Another," Captain Scott said, quietly. The screen display changed again, the scale shrinking until all four . . . no, there was a fifth! All five were now on the screen, and headed more or less in the same general direction. Damn. If one had been going in the opposite direction it would have been a lot more interesting, since the computer indicated they were all in the same current.

"Extend those lines," Scott said. Dr. Land must have done it, because the vectors on my screen extended. The scale shrank again, and now we could see all five lines intersected.

"They're all heading for Grumpy," Scott said.

For a moment, everything was silent.

"Is that unusual?" Dekko asked.

"I'd say so. We've never seen anything like this." He put us into an abrupt turn, away from the pod of boojums, if I may call them a pod.

"Flank speed," he said.

"Flank speed," Dr. Land acknowledged.

"Hey," Slomo protested. "They're back *that* way!"

"Sir, you will please pipe down, or I will throw you overboard."

"Can't do that, Captain," said Dr. Land. "I'd suggest throwing his *cameras* overboard."

"Hey!"

"Even better."

"I'll be quiet."

We all were, for the five minutes it took us to reach the area of the blowhole. A computer announced we were in radio range of the antenna that extended from the bottom.

"NEMO station, this is NEMO-II, returning to base. We've got some anomalous boojum activity. I'm sending the data now. I want you to prepare NEMO-VI and NEMO-I for immediate dive. Load 'em up with all the oxygen they can carry, two crew only. I want them ready for maximum range. I'm returning to base with the tour group ASAP. Please be ready to top up my tanks, as I will be going with you. Over."

"Roger that, *Turtle*. This looks real interesting."

"You said it. I intend to try to overtake. Over."

"Fine with me. I'll join you in ten minutes."

Then we were back into the tunnel, going up much faster than we went down. I kept feeling my ears ought to pop, but of course *Turtle* kept constant air pressure, like any sensible deep-sea submersible.

We only slowed near the top, and not all that much. We lurched to the surface, were weightless for a moment, and then NEMO crew were swarming over the ship, attaching cables, lifting us, and setting us down, and the doors were opening, and Captain Scott was hustling us up the ladder, out the hatch, and onto the freezing-cold deck. We tumbled down the steps. All around us was frantic activity, with *Crocodil* already being swung out, ready to be lowered into the pool. I saw two people enter the hatch of *Nautilis* and heard the hiss of air as it sealed.

"This way, this way, hurry please."

We did, and soon were back at the bus bay. Our driver, oblivious to what was going on but with a satisfied look on his face, gestured to the bus.

"All ready to go, ladies and gents. I'll have you back at Clarke in three hours."

So we all climbed in and settled down and talked to the others about what we'd seen. I was pretty sure I'd just witnessed an historic moment, but damned if I knew what it was.

And I never did find out.

12

★ ★ ★

THE LONGEST THREE-HOUR bus ride of my life started out uneventfully enough.

We were all pretty jazzed by what had happened at NEMO, all except Cosmo, who was trying to set the record for marathon sulking. We talked about it, puzzled over it, but it was clear we wouldn't learn much until we got back to Clarke and watched the news reports, if any. Research at Taliesen was still a pretty closely held affair, so there might not be much in the way of public pronouncements unless Captain Scott either established communication with a boojum, brought one back alive and hung it up in a gigantic trophy room, or lashed himself to a white one and went down, shouting, "Towards thee I roll, thou all-destroying but unconquering boojum; to the last I grapple with thee; from hell's heart I stab at thee!"

That would have to wait. When the driver said he'd have us back at Clarke in three hours, he meant a two-hour slog over the ice to the edge of the no-fly zone, then an easy hop over the frozen cue ball, and home. I curled up in the last row of seats in the back of the bus and soon was sound asleep.

* * *

I WAS AWAKENED by the tremor alarm.

"Strap in tight, folks," the driver shouted out, cheerfully. "This looks like it might be a big one. Grumpy's throwin' a hissy fit again."

I did as he asked, and waited for it. I looked out the back window, careful not to get my head too close to it so I wouldn't get banged when the tremor hit.

Then it was there, and it was a lot more than a tremor. We bounced up and down for about ten seconds, then lateral waves hit us and I was shaken like a rag doll.

"Jesus, make it stop!" Cosmo was shouting. It takes a mighty strong ego to think God or natural forces should obey your will.

After about a minute it subsided. Soon we could only hear the residual squeaking of the springs on the tracks as the bus stabilized itself. It was very quiet for a moment, quiet enough that I could hear the driver over the PA, even though he was speaking to himself, in a whisper.

"Holy shit," he said. I could see him up there, staring at his screens. Then he turned around and looked down the aisle straight at me, sitting there in the middle in the back. His eyes were round and his mouth was open.

I turned and looked. There was a red line edging over the horizon where Grumpy had been a little while ago. A towering white cloud was rising around it, fast enough that I could see the movement. Grumpy was at least twenty miles behind us, which made the clouds . . . I didn't do the math, but they must have reached up a hundred miles or more.

"Uh . . . uh . . ." The driver was consulting his screen, which was giving him emergency instructions. The overhead racks exploded, and bright yellow emergency suits rolled out. One landed in my lap.

"Declaring an emergency. Clarke Centre, this is Bus 54, declaring an emergency. Passengers . . . uh, please don your emergency pressure suits at this time." A short pause, then, "No, wait! Remove your PSU, Personal Suspension Unit, your KYAG, from your person and put it in a suit pocket, okay? Otherwise you won't be able to reach it if you need it. *Then* put on your e-suits! *Do it! Do it! Do it now!"*

I was still looking out the back window. The red line was almost invisible again, and I realized that it was because something was rising up between us and what I had to assume was Grumpy, growing again, and at an unbelievable rate.

I got out of my straps and slipped the damn KYAG box into a suit pocket, then wiggled my legs into the emergency suit while sitting down. Ahead of me, I could see legs sticking out into the aisle as others did the same. Cosmo was standing in the aisle, shouting something I couldn't hear. I squirmed my arms into the suit, shrugged it on, and yanked the zipper up. When it reached the top the suit sealed itself.

The e-suit was nothing more than a Podkayne-shaped insulated bag, a power pack, and a heater. Now, if we were hulled, if all the air leaked out, I'd at least be able to breathe for a few hours before I froze solid. I reached up and found the helmet, sealed it, then found the oxygen bottle under the seat. I snapped it in place. I looked up and saw that I was the first one finished.

"Everybody strap in!" I screamed, in a blues shout that would have made Janis Joplin proud. "Strap in! There's a really big one coming!"

I couldn't tell if I was making any difference, but I was strapping myself down as I shouted. I looked out the window to my left and saw an amazing thing. The ice was cracking as I watched. An irregular furrow opened up and a lot of snow and loose ice tumbled into it. Just as quickly, the crack closed and sprayed ice all over us. Through the supercold mist I could see the ice on the other side of the crack grind upward, ten, twenty, thirty feet. A big hunk broke off and hit the bus with a clang.

"The hell with no-fly zones," the driver said. "Preparing for takeoff, please strap in, *please strap in,* I'm boosting in thirty seconds."

With a sickening lurch, the slab of ice we were standing on, maybe the size of a city block, tilted to a thirty-degree angle, and we started sliding nose down.

"I'm boosting in ten seconds!" the driver shouted.

We were sluing sideways now, and the view out the left side was just black sky and flying chunks of ice. The driver was going to have a real problem taking off from that angle. *Straight up,* I tried to reach him, telepathically. *Straight up, and then a hard, hard,* hard *yaw to the left, nose up . . .*

We slued right again, and the ice under us tilted almost to ninety degrees. We were plunging headfirst toward a gigantic ice crusher.

"Firing!" the driver shouted. I was pressed back into my seat at about two gees. For once, I wanted more, and the driver apparently heard my plea because we accelerated even harder. He was putting more thrust into the nose than the stern, and we were evening out. Then we were leveling, then the nose was up. We climbed, and I began to think we were going to be okay.

That's when the flying iceberg hit us. It was a glancing blow, in the front. I saw the forward port-side windshield star crazily, saw the driver lifted out of his seat to smash his head on the bulkhead above him. He had been pulled right out of his straps. He had his e-suit on, but hadn't had time for the helmet, or he'd forgotten. Then I hit my own head on something, I don't know what. It rang my bell pretty hard.

I think I blacked out for a few moments. I remember seeing the huge chunk of ice spinning away from us. We were spinning, too, end over end. Three people were piled almost on top of me. In their yellow suits I couldn't be sure who they were, but the inside of one of the helmets was coated in blood.

I knew we weren't accelerating, because I could just see the front of the bus, and people and debris were piled up there, too. That meant that the tumble was what was causing the one gee or so I was feeling. The bus had become a centrifuge, still rising toward who knows where. But eventually gravity would stop us, if we weren't crushed by more flying ice, and we'd start to fall. I suspected that even if the bus and passengers survived hitting the surface, there no longer *was* much of a surface down there. What I could see out the window was a jumble, glimpsed between spinning ice cubes from just a few feet across to monsters big enough to sink the *Titanic*. It was the spring melt on a big river, a whirlpool in a giant's margarita blender. We'd be smashed to bits.

How many minutes? There might be time, as long as we kept rising.

But could I move? I was almost buried.

In addition to the three suited bodies, there was a welter of stuff you always find in a bus. Carry-on luggage, a few oxygen bottles shaken loose from beneath the seats, bottles of drinking water, even a crushed sandwich. Because of the centrifugal gravity, what had been the back of the bus was now my floor. Well, I had to try.

I levered myself up on my right elbow and reached for the back of the seat in front of me with my left hand, and pain lanced from my shoulder all the way to my fingertips. The adrenaline was wearing off, I guess, and I found that any attempt at moving my left arm gave me so much pain I almost blacked out again. I started shoving at the people in front of me with my right arm, and one of them raised its head.

"Who is that?" I shouted. I grabbed a shoulder and shook it, and the figure squirmed around and looked at me, blearily. It was Dekko. Good. He was a big, strong boy; he could help me out of this.

He put his arm under his face and lay back down, looking like he planned to take a nap. Not just now, me boyo.

"Wake up, you lazy ass!" I shouted, and punched him several times. He looked up again. One pupil was larger than the other. Concussion, I guess. Well, there wasn't time to worry about that, I needed him out of the way, and I needed his help. A little more punching and swearing got him up, on hands and knees.

"Pull this one over there," I told him, and after I repeated it several times he got the idea. The unknown person's leg was jammed under the third body, and when Dekko gave it a hard pull, there was a scream. It sounded like Tina. I saw her leg was twisted horribly. Dekko let her go.

"Don't stop!" I shouted. "Screaming is good! Screaming means she's still alive! But we don't have much time. Pull her out of there, whatever it takes!"

He did, and she screamed again, and I shuddered, and shouted, *Sorry, sorry, sorry, hon, but I've got to get to the controls!*

She stopped screaming, and I knew it wasn't because it had stopped hurting but because she had passed out. *Oh, god, Tina, I'm so sorry.*

"Now give me a hand, Dekko, I've got to get out of here."

He did, and it was my turn to scream. My left leg was jammed under the seat, and I stared in horror as I realized my knee was bending the wrong way. The pain was indescribable, worse than anything I'd ever felt, making my arm and shoulder seem insignificant.

"Can you fly, Dekko?" I gasped.

"Huh?"

"Can you . . . never mind." Even if he could, which I doubted, he was in no shape to do it. Unless someone up front was seeing to it, and I couldn't assume that, it was going to have to be me.

"Pull me out, you son of a bitch. Just fucking *yank*, okay?" I gritted my teeth as he grabbed my right arm and pulled.

Blacking out was a mercy this time, but all the pain was still there when I swam back into the light. My lower leg was flopping around, but Dekko was supporting me with my right arm over his shoulder. I got my good leg under me, standing on the unidentified third person, and stood more or less erect.

"Dek, is there a first-aid kit anywhere that you can see?"

He looked around, vaguely.

"A box with a red cross on it. I don't know if I can do this without morphine."

"Red . . ."

It was hopeless. The guy was a mental basket case, able to follow simple orders but helpless if the task required thought or discrimination. I was lucky he was still conscious. I looked out the window to my right.

Good news: We were still rising, and the longer we did that, the longer before we started falling again, and the more time I'd have to steer us out of this.

Bad news: There was another huge hunk of ice closing in on us.

"Brace yourself, Dekko!"

"Brace . . ."

I wrapped my good arm around a seat-back handle and pressed Dekko against a wall, and the iceberg hit us. It was nothing like the first impact, which was good, as this chunk was a lot larger than the first. The side of the bus kissed the ice, and there was a horrible grinding noise, and one of the windows starred, like the big window up front, and I closed my eyes.

"Mom and Dad and Mike, I love you."

Then the grinding stopped. I peeked at the window and saw it was holding. They are triple thickness, high-impact, and have a tough layer of clear supervinyl between them. I didn't hear a hiss of escaping air. The iceberg was still out there, unaltered in its course by colliding with our puny little vehicle, and we were moving slowly away again.

One more bit of good news: The friction against the berg had slowed our rotation down a bit. I figured I was standing in about three-quarter gee.

I looked up toward the front of the bus, which was now my ceiling. They say the first step is always the hardest, and this time it was literally true.

I looked down, and saw that Dekko had sat again and seemed to be asleep. Not good, with a concussion, but there was nothing I could do except get him to medical treatment as soon as possible. There had to be emergency help on the way . . .

But maybe not. If we had been hit this hard as far away as we were, it didn't look good for Forward Base, NEMO, and even Main Base. This thing could even be affecting Clarke Centre; they might be too busy to come after an SOS from us.

Maybe we were on our own.

Don't cry, Podkayne, time to be a big girl. There are still things you can do.

I reached up and grabbed one of the seat handles on the right side of the aisle, just at the limit of my reach, set my right foot on another seat, and started to pull myself up. The seat broke free of its bolts, which must have been almost severed already, and I fell back on my ass, with a seat on top of me. Pain shot through me, and suddenly I was shouting.

"Okay, Taliesen, now I'm *mad*! You think you can jinx me? Well, *fuck you*!"

I must have got a burst of adrenaline and just a moment of superhuman strength, because I tossed the seat off me like it was made of cardboard, got my good leg under me and my good hand on another seat back, and chinned myself up, screaming in pain and rage. I put my foot on a seat back and raised myself high enough to grab the next seat back. I tested it before putting my full weight on it, then pulled myself up.

The next step was easier. The closer I got to the middle of the bus, the less "weight" I would feel from the spinning. I took another step up the improvised ladder the seats provided, then another. I was into half a gee now, and the step was easier, and the next one. It seemed I could feel the difference in weight from my head to my feet, and it might even have been true.

One more step, and around a quarter of a gee. Lighter than Mars, this was going to be easy . . . until I reached the middle and had to make my way down. I put that out of my mind and lifted myself another step. I looked out the window.

Impossible to tell if we were rising or falling. I'd get a glimpse of the surface, and it seemed about as far away as it had been the last time . . . and then something vast and red hove into view. The ship went through another rotation, and I lost it, then it was there again, looming, crystalline, terrifying. I think I may have screamed.

It was Grumpy. The whole mountain, freed from the ice, could now be seen to be cylindrical in shape, with the former fairy lights now shining like laser beams instead of fireflies. We were going to be crushed; I knew it. The whole damn thing had somehow rocketed into space and now it was headed down, and I was between it and Europa.

This time I did cry, helplessly, unable to move in any direction, waiting for that final impact.

One rotation went by and no impact. Another. And another. Still no impact. I chanced a look out the window. Grumpy didn't look any closer. Could it be farther? Could the whole damn thing still be headed up, into space?

Didn't really matter, did it? Nothing I could do about it. In an emergency, you put the things you can't do anything about out of your mind and concentrate on what you *can* do, which, in this case, was continue on toward the front of the bus. So I lifted myself one more step, and a hand reached out and grabbed me by my dislocated shoulder.

Actually, by the suit that was *covering* the shoulder, but it hurt, anyway. I was almost into the zone of weightlessness at the middle of the bus, and cowering in the space between two seats, suitless, was our old friend Cosmo. During the time he could have been getting into his suit he had been running up and down the aisles, and I guess it was sheer luck that he'd been in the middle when the big impact sent everything spinning to either end. He'd managed to hold on, but his suit was twenty feet behind me, in the pile of debris and bodies I'd just left.

"It's okay," I said, through gritted teeth. "We've still got pressure. You'll be all right. Just let me go, okay?"

He didn't say anything, but with monomaniacal determination he reached out with his free hand. It took me a moment to realize what he was up to. He had hold of the zipper. He intended to peel me out of the suit and put it on himself.

Well. I promised myself right then to *never* watch his show.

His hands were shaking so much he couldn't seem to grip the zipper pull. I didn't think it would be possible for him to unzip me now that I was pressurized, but it was the thought that counted. His *intent* was to leave me naked to the elements.

So I clocked him, right on the face, right on his broken nose. It felt so good, I clocked him again, same place, ignoring the pain in my shoulder, and again, and again . . .

His grip relaxed for a moment, but he was still intent. He grabbed at me again. I was a lot better at maneuvering in very low gravity than he was, and squirmed out of the way. I reached behind me, groping for something, anything.

What I connected with was Slomo, wearing his suit, crouched in the seat across from Cosmo. He handed me what I think was a camera tripod, and I took it, and smashed it down over Cosmo's head.

He let me go, shook his head, and reached for me again. My first blow had ripped a good part of his scalp open. I smashed him again and maybe I heard bone crack. It was hard to tell. He let me go, though, and floated gently down against the back of his seat and didn't move.

Dead? Ask somebody who gives a shit.

I looked back at Slomo, trying to catch my breath. He had a camera in his hand, and another clamped to a seat top, pointing forward.

"You're *filming* this?"

"It's something to do."

"Should I hit him again? That would look good at my trial. That make you happy?"

"It'd make me very happy, but there won't be a trial, and you know it."

"I'm not giving up. Can you fly?"

"Not even by flapping my arms."

I sighed, grabbed his camera from his hands, and shoved it toward the front of the bus. It gained speed rapidly, and banged against the back of the driver's seat.

"Hey!"

"Get off your lazy ass and help me down there, and you can start filming again. Go down there on your own, I'll drop Cosmo on you, I swear to God. My left arm and my left leg are broken, so be careful or I'll rip your eyes out."

I'll give him this: Once I got him moving, he was good at improvising. He quickly found a length of yellow nylon rope in his kit bag and tied one end of it to a seat back. Then he grabbed me carefully by my good shoulder and pushed us both into the zone of weightlessness. We got turned around, feet toward the front, and he wrapped the rope around himself, under his ass and around one arm, and grabbed me with his other arm, and we lowered through increasing weight.

Along the way we saw several people strapped in, some moving, some not.

I saw Senator Wu looking grim, with one arm around his daughter, who was crying quietly. Brynne was unmistakable with those big breasts stretching the front of her e-suit. She was out cold, hanging forward from her seat straps.

Ambassador Baruti's legs were broken. A jagged point of bone had punched through one leg of his suit from the inside. There was a lot of blood around him, and he was holding a makeshift tourniquet in place. He grimaced at me and gestured to the front of the bus.

"Go, go, Podkayne! I'll be all right."

Nothing I could do, and in a few seconds Slomo's feet touched down on the pile of debris in front, and he set me down gently on my good leg.

"Clear this stuff away," I told him, and he set about it. Part of the debris was Nigel, Cosmo's agent, who I hadn't said three words to the whole trip, who was moving but groggy, and Slomo got him to help.

Pretty soon we got to the driver. His head was resting on his chest, twisted to one side, his neck obviously broken, and his forehead caved in. I swallowed back nausea as we lifted him aside and a bit of skull and brain tissue fell forward onto the control panel. I never even knew his name.

No time for tears or vomiting. I scrambled into the copilot's seat and strapped in.

"Go see what you can do for the injured," I told Slomo and Nigel, and they took off. "Try to get them to the middle of the bus. I may be slamming us around a bit."

I cleared the control panel in front of me. It was the driver's side, the port-side windshield panel, that was spiderwebbed with cracks; the one on my side was intact. I could see out, and what I saw was the churning surface of Europa, moving upward in front of me, then the horizon upside-down, then deep space, then the slowly shrinking bulk of Grumpy overhead, then blackness, then the horizon right-side up, then moving ice again. Repeat as needed, until impact.

How high was I? Still rising? At what velocity?

The control panel wasn't a lot of help. Big areas of it weren't working, and there were so many red warning lights I had a hard time sorting them out. But I saw something out the right-side window that was not very encouraging. The bus had four sets of double tracks, all steerable, one at each corner. Floating out there was the right-forward set, still attached to the bus by a few electrical cables but clearly torn away from the undercarriage. I could see hydraulic lines that had been severed. My panel told me the front-left pair were gone, too.

That wasn't a problem if I could just set us down someplace where the ground was stable. But as long as those tracks were still attached to us, any maneuvering I did was likely to set them thrashing about dangerously.

Systems status report:

Internal power: good. Pressure integrity: critical, but intact. Oxygen supply: good. Radio: malfunction. Who needs a radio, anyway? Emergency beacon: on, and sending. Tracks: right rear, okay; left rear, okay; left front, not reporting; right front, hydraulic pressure zero.

External power: stern main engine, testing, testing . . . AOK.

Bow main engine . . . not reporting.

I had a nasty feeling that the bow main engine was floating somewhere out there with the left-front track assembly. And that was not good news.

All these buses had two bubble-powered engines, mounted underneath, one in front and one in back. They enabled vertical takeoff, and could swivel in any direction. Aim them to the stern and you went forward. Aim them forward to decelerate. A child could do it, and I had, since I was twelve.

But if the front engine was gone and I applied power from the rear engine, all I'd do would be to increase the spin.

Carefully, I engaged minimum power to my remaining engine, just a whisper, as I turned the stick to the left. Slowly, the ship began to turn, through 180 degrees, until my rear engine was facing the direction of spin. The loose track out there to my right swung around and banged into the side of the bus, and I winced, but no new pressure alarms sounded. Now power up . . . slowly . . . *whang* goes the track assembly as it tries to wrap itself around the bus.

I stopped the spin in about twenty seconds. We were now falling weightlessly, along with a hell of a lot of spinning icebergs, but at least we were all heading in the same general direction, which was . . .

Down. We'd reached the top of our powerless trajectory and Europa's mild gravity was pulling us slowly back to her icy bosom. My remaining instruments were stuttering and flashing erratically, but it was clear that the surface was getting closer. We had about three minutes.

What to do, what to do?

How long had it been? It seemed an age, but I reckoned it had all happened in less than ten minutes. My knee and my shoulder were in agony, and now that I was here, now that I'd stopped the spin, I couldn't seem to think straight. I turned around.

"How's it going back there?"

"Not good," Slomo shouted back. "I've stopped Baruti's bleeding, but he's in a bad way."

"Is there anything we can do, Podkayne?" Senator Wu shouted.

"I'm open to suggestions. We really need to set down, but I've only got one engine, and if I use it I'll just set us spinning again."

"Why land?" came a faint voice.

"What's that? Tina?" She had been all the way in the back, but with the spin gravity gone she'd made her way to the front. She didn't look good, with her twisted leg and the inside of her helmet almost totally covered with blood.

"Can you boost us up again? Maybe into orbit?"

Well, jeez, why didn't I think of that? Was my brain turning to jelly? It wouldn't be easy, but landing with only the rear engine seemed impossible, and to paraphrase Sherlock Holmes, once you have eliminated the impossible, whatever is left, no matter how difficult, is what you've got to try.

"Strap in tight, everybody," I said. "I'm going to get the nose up with the attitude jets, angle the aft engine as far back as it will go, and try to nurse it into orbit without spinning again. If anybody's got a better idea, or any suggestion at all, say it now, because we've got about a minute and a half to impact."

Nobody said anything, but I could hear seat belts being buckled and tightened.

"Hang on," I said. "This ain't going to be pretty."

I eased the nose up to about a forty-five-degree angle, which gave me a view of Grumpy again, still looming but visibly farther away. It seemed clear the thing was headed out and into an orbit around Jupiter.

I eased on the power. The bus wanted to lift its tail because I couldn't angle the engine *directly* backwards. Every time it started to do that I increased the thrust from the downward attitude jets in front until the nose started to lift again. Those jets were simple chemical rockets, never intended to have much of a punch, just there for fine-tuning when you landed the bus. Their combined thrust was pitiful. I watched the acceleration gauge and the altimeter. Still falling, but the rate of fall was slowing. At this rate, it would take me five minutes to kill our downward vector and start a forward one. What was orbital velocity on Europa? Math was never my strong suit; I couldn't work it out. I had the attitude jets on full power and was glumly watching the fuel gauges sinking as the thirsty little engines burned. I set the computer to start calculating the velocity I'd need, when there was a roaring, clanging, scraping sound, a hard impact that came from the rear . . . and the power went out.

We started to spin again, and I cut off the thrusters. What the hell?

Emergency strip lighting came on in the floor. Just enough light to move around. I looked back, and saw someone at the back, looking out the rear window. He turned around, and I saw it was Slomo. His shoulders sagged.

"The loose track is back there," he said. "And I think—"

We didn't get to hear what he was thinking just then, because the spin had started everything moving again. It wasn't heavy, like before, only about a quarter gee . . . but it was too much. The driver's body hit the battered windshield in front of him, not very hard, but just hard enough. With an odd ripping sound, a hole opened under his head, and tore across the shattered surface until the whole sheet of high-impact plastic popped out. In two very chaotic seconds, everything that wasn't tied down flew out of the huge square hole in a diminishing shriek, including the driver's body, along with all of our air.

Some days you just can't catch a break, you know what I'm saying?

My suit had been loose; now it expanded. My ears popped, my knee was twisted, I screamed in pain. It became very hard to move. Those e-suits weren't designed for anything more than keeping you alive. They are just bags, and when they fill up with pressurized air they are very hard to move in.

And what was the point of moving, anyway? Slomo's voice came over the radio, sealing our fate.

"That track knocked off the rear engine," he said, quietly.

Which I already knew, as the ship drew its power from the slow release of energy from its two bubble drives.

We were now a battered, airless tin can, running on batteries, at the mercy of gravity, with as much control of our fate as a batted baseball.

So, here's my plan . . .

Well, Poddy, you really screwed that one up.

I didn't have any prayers to say, or anything like that. I figure a creator who keeps score of sins and wants to be worshipped like an insecure little boy isn't worth my time.

There was an odd *spang* sound from the back of the bus. I turned and saw a featureless black ball wedged between the seats near the back. I say wedged . . . what happened was the stopper bubble engulfed everything within a certain radius of the generator. That included parts of some seats, some of the floor, and a bit of the ceiling.

Slomo was looking at me from the middle of the bus. He had the KYAG unit in his hand, his thumb on the button, which was glowing red. He wiggled his fingers at me and smiled, and was replaced by another black bubble.

Senator Wu hugged his daughter and they became yet another. There was one all the way at the back.

I reached into my suit pocket . . .

Which was hanging open. I distinctly remembered closing the little Velcro patch, knowing how things are apt to get lost in weightlessness. It wasn't closed now, and there was no little black box inside.

Most likely location for it: a mile in front of us, and receding fast.

I glanced at the panel in front of me, still working fitfully on batteries. Fifty seconds to impact.

I started a halfhearted search of the area around me. I mean, what were the chances? Had the pocket been pulled open as Slomo and I descended to the front? Could have happened. Probably what had happened.

Forty seconds. There was a great view out the front of the bus as we swung slowly around. My, what a lot of activity in the ice down there! What a thrill ride this would be if we could move it to Pavonis Park!

Thirty seconds.

Not down there on the floor.

Twenty. Ten.

Nowhere else to look. Might as well enjoy the show.

As a virtual reality bit, it would have been a gasser. As real reality, I wouldn't recommend it.

We hit ass first, and I saw in the rearview mirror—still intact, still unbroken!—as the body of the bus collapsed like an aluminum soft drink can in Superman's fist. My chair creaked and cracked, and held on, then we slammed out full length on what looked like an ice floe, and began to slide. I hurt everywhere. Just everywhere. I was amazed I was still alive.

We were going down nose first, so I got an excellent view of what awaited me, which were giant ice cubes grinding together like molars. It ought to be quick . . . if it would just goddam happen! I was too pissed to cry. *Get it over with!*

Something slammed into my back, then slithered over my shoulder. I couldn't believe it. It was Cosmo, getting in his last licks. Even in death he wouldn't leave me alone! There was a rime of frost on him, but he hadn't had time to freeze solid yet.

Which was a damn good thing, because there it was, in his hand, what he had really been going for when he attacked me: my KYAG. One will get you ten his own was buried somewhere in his luggage.

I pried his fingers away from it and took it in my palm, and that's when the bus nosed into the grinding slush and an iceberg pinched it from my left side, squeezing the roof down like tissue paper and driving parts of it into my side and left leg.

You think you might reach a point where you're beyond pain, but you're not, you're not. At least I hadn't reached it. I was pretty sure my ribs were crushed on the left side. I wasn't going to take a breath to see . . . but then slush started flooding in all around me, rising. Cold, cold, unimaginable cold that came right through my suit.

I had to concentrate. Wouldn't it be a pisser if, after all the trouble the Hand of Fate had taken to get my KYAG to me, I fumbled it? I rotated it in the palm of my suit glove, which was now coated with ice as well as being hard to move in the first place . . . and got my thumb into position. I pressed, and the light came on, and I held.

Five one thousand.

Four one thousand.

Three one thousand.

Two one thousand.

One one thousand . . .

One one thousand . . .

Bastard wasn't working. Just my lu

ck. . . . *What the . . . ?*

Light, coming from all directions. Oh, man, fuck me, was I wrong? *Should I have been praying?* Is this that "tunnel of light," will all my loved ones rush up to—

"That's her! She's alive!"

—greet me . . . Travis? Was that Uncle Travis's voice? I couldn't see much. It was still so cold, but the slush was draining away. Ice, everything was covered with ice, and it was so bright . . .

"X-ray!"

"Done!"

"Infrared!"

"Scanning . . . done!"

I coughed, and wished I hadn't, because the pain was intolerable, and the inside of my helmet was now bright red with blood.

"Okay, put her ba

Instantly, much dimmer light. A giant metal fist moved over me, grabbed a piece of metal that had once been part of the roof of the bus, and tore it away like tissue paper. I turned my head and had just enough clear faceplate over the blood coating to see a second robot arm grab the piece of the bus that was crushing my side and rip that away, too. Which I *really* could have done without, as the pain was . . . you know, you really quickly run out of words to describe pain like that, so just try to imagine it, okay? Or don't, which would be my recommendation. Blood spewed out of me like a fountain.

I heard no voices now, but all around me was frenetic activity, moving at a pace only machines can do. The remains of the bus and my seat—and Cosmo—were peeled away, and robot arms insinuated themselves in close to me and, in seconds, cut away my suit. Needles jabbed me, and something was wrapped around my chest and tightened. I felt like a chicken being shrink-wrapped for market.

I quickly began to drift. Things kept happening, but they didn't seem very *interesting*. Is that my leg? Should it be bending that way? Oh, well.

But the pain was gone! The pain was gone! Oh, glorious day! I laughed, and coughed up more blood. Then something grabbed me under the jaw and tilted my head back and clapped something over my face, and I took a breath, and another.

And that was all it took to send me into glorious blackness.

My final thought?

Yes, sir. One *hell* of a bus ride.

13

THEY'VE MADE AMAZING advances in medicine since my great-grandmother's day (otherwise I wouldn't be here), but one thing that's pretty much the same as in the twentieth century is general anesthesia. You don't just pop out of it. It's a gradual process.

I have vague memories of nurses in isolation suits, and of doctors poking and prodding and sampling. The standard indignities. I remember wanting to pee so badly it hurt, trying to tell someone that I needed to go, finally letting loose and realizing there was a catheter in. Duh.

The first thing I remember more or less clearly is Mike. He was sitting on the bed, holding my hand, asleep sitting up. I don't know how he does that, but he does. I gave his hand a hearty squeeze, which wouldn't have crushed a bug. His eyes snapped open. My vision was a bit blurred, and I could only concentrate on one thing at a time. I couldn't even see all his face at once; it was like looking through a crazy lens.

"Podkayne!" he shouted, and started to embrace me. Then he stopped himself. "All right, my girl, no more lollygagging. I know you've been faking it. So get up, get dressed, and let's get out of here!"

"Sure," I mumbled. "Clothes . . . ?" I looked around vaguely, and when I looked back the first thing I saw were the tears streaming down his face.

"Oh, Poddy," he moaned. "I swore I wouldn't cry."

"Give us a hug, baby boy," I said, and he put his arms around me. I expected it to hurt, but it didn't. He didn't squeeze hard. After a while he drew back, snuffling.

"You look terrible," he said, wiping his nose.

"Just what a girl wants to hear. Mike, am I . . ."

"You're going to be fine, Pod. Just fine. You looked like something dragged out of a trash compactor when they brought you in, but they've got you all fixed up. That's no bullshit, the doctors tell us you'll be just as awful as you ever were in a few weeks."

"Weeks?" I yawned.

"Well, months, with rehab."

"That's nice. I think I'll sleep now." I frowned. There was something I wanted to know, but I couldn't remember what it was. Then I had it.

"What's the date?"

"December first."

Oh, good. I'd have time to get my Christmas shopping done.

And I drifted off. My last thought . . . Mike was wearing red. Mike hates red. Was my little brother in uniform? What was *that* all about?

SWIMMING BACK INTO consciousness, as from the bottom of a deep well . . .

Familiar faces. Family. Mom, Dad, Mike. Aunt Elizabeth.

"Back with us, Podkayne?" Elizabeth asked, brightly. It was her bedside manner, I guess. She was wearing goggles of some sort, and looking at a lot of machines that I imagine were telling her a lot more about my poor abused body than I'd ever want to know.

The bed was high. Mom only had to bend at the waist to put her face close to mine and kiss me. There were lines at the corners of her eyes and around her mouth that I hadn't noticed before. My mom is a beautiful woman—I must have gotten it from somewhere, right?—but she looked a lot older. I must have caused them a lot of worry. I felt all choked up inside as she kissed me again and wiped away a tear. Then Dad was there, too.

"How's my girl?"

"A little woozy."

"That's to be expected," Aunt Elizabeth said, from behind them. She had something in her hand, but kept her distance. I looked at Dad again. His face looked a lot older, too. A *lot* older, and it wasn't wrinkles. His hairline, which had been receding since I was ten, was *way* back from where it had been less than a year ago . . .

Okay. Blame the drugs.

"How long?" I asked.

Mom looked me right in the eye and didn't dissemble.

"Ten years and a bit," she said. A tear made its way down her cheek. "And we're so glad to have you back."

"Ten years . . ."

"Which means I'm older than you, now," Mike said, with a smile. But he couldn't keep it in place.

"Ten years . . ."

Aunt Elizabeth pressed something against my neck, and there was a hiss. The rising panic I'd been feeling fell away, and I sank back into welcome darkness.

Ten years.

"NO *WAY* ARE you older than me," I said.

"Way."

"Mike, I'm twenty-nine."

"Only if you go by the calendar. You know and I know that you're still nineteen. And I was twenty-one in February. Well, on March the first."

"Actually, you were five."

"Which makes you a bit less than five," he said, smugly.

We were back to normal—or as back to normal as we'd ever be, with him the same age as me—joshing each other. He was sitting in his usual place on my bed, spoon-feeding me raspberry sherbet. I had just about enough strength to lift the spoon, but not enough coordination to get it to the right spot on my face, as red blotches on my nose and cheek testified. I was on a liquid and ice-cream diet until my digestive system recovered from the trauma of many days of nanosurgery.

There was so much Mike and I couldn't really get into yet, so many things for me to sort out . . . it was going to be a time for sorting out, that was for sure.

"So you're really going to take this 'oath of secrecy' business seriously," I asked him, for the third or fourth time.

"Have to, Poddy. Gave my word. And you know 'The word of a Martian Patrol Space Commander—' "

" '—is as good as gold.' " It was a game we'd played when he was young.

There's a lot of questions you could ask when you come out of a coma—medically induced, and lasting about a month, one of the few details anyone had seen fit to give me. I hadn't asked any of them, as such; I was too woozy for the first three or four days. But I'd pieced together a few things.

Where am I?

Mars. The good old Red Thunder Hotel, the family business. I was in a small suite, with Aunt Elizabeth installed in a spare bed in the living room and in twenty-four-hour attendance. Why the hotel? Why not a hospital? No one was willing to tell me.

What happened?

I knew what happened up to the point I pulled the plug. I remembered it all quite well, every agonizing moment, including a lot I'd much rather forget. But what happened after that? No one was saying. They'd all taken the Martian Patrol Space Commander Oath.

Why not just tell me and get it over with?

Ah, at last, a question they were willing to answer.

They had a lot of experience with taking people out of time stasis. They'd tried a lot of different methods, including just answering any questions the *stasee* (new word: someone freshly out of stasis, also known more idiomatically as Rips, as in Van Winkle) asked, in the order she asked them. Usual result: confusion, anxiety, mild sedation. For instance, one question that soon arose in a long-term stasis (five years or more), especially if a familiar face wasn't there, was . . . who died?

So protocols had been developed. Only the closest relatives were allowed to see the stasee at first. Then recent history, including the macro kind (what are countries doing?), the personal kind (what are my friends and family up to?), and yes, even the popular kind (what are the hit downloads?), is doled out in bites the "reintegration counselor" thinks the stasee—oh, the hell with it, I hate that word!—the *Rip* can handle.

My RC was a tiny little Earth-born—Nigeria, I believe—named Maimuna. She explained all this to me, and listened patiently while I told her it was stupid, *Come on, Doc, I can handle it!* I realized she'd heard the same old song and dance a hundred times, then I surprised myself by realizing she might know more about this than me. So I shut up.

"We've prepared summaries of world events," she said. "They're pretty standard. We will show them to you at the rate of one per day. In a week and a half—"

"—I'll be all caught up."

She wagged a finger at me and shook her head.

"It would be a mistake to think that. You will have the information, but it will take considerably longer to integrate it. Trust me on this. Even if the ten missing years were relatively uneventful, if you were at all connected to the larger events of politics—and I know you are, not like some of the gameheads I get who couldn't name three countries on Earth or the current president of Mars—it will take some time. And one thing I can tell you, without getting into specifics, is that these ten years have not been uneventful."

"Grumpy," I said.

"That's all I can say, but of course you were there at the beginning of that event."

"A pretty big event," I ventured. But she wouldn't say any more.

So I was reduced to trying to trick snippets of information out of my little brother. He loved it, the bastard. He'd start to say something, then clap his hand over his mouth and look alarmed. But it was never anything, he was just yanking my chain.

We finished the sherbet and I longed for a cheeseburger.

"So, do you know when I get my cybers back?" I asked him.

"Same time as last time you asked me. When the reorientation is finished." He smiled. "Feeling a little Net withdrawal?"

I was, a little. You grow up with the newest corneal screens and wearing your computing and connecting equipment either as accessories or implanted somewhere around your ear, you get used to being able to answer a lot of questions with a few simple tics. Even as simple a question as "What time is it?" You look down into the corner of your vision and there's your clock, ready to tell you the time in any zone of Mars, Earth, or any other inhabited planet, plus the speed-of-light time between any two places. Or you want to know who wrote the lyric to a song, you google it, and there's a new window.

My corneas had been wiped clean as part of the nanosurgery, and I had no Net access at all for the first time I could remember.

"I can't even get a weather forecast," I complained. "I like to get the daily temperatures from Pismo Beach, so I can be happy I'm not there."

"Might tell you too much," Mike said, and grinned again. Oh, right.

"That might tell me too much about how climate change is progressing on Earth," I guessed.

"Sure. It'll all come in time, Podkayne. Just be patient."

So I was, but patient isn't something I do well. The next day they finally activated the wallscreen and showed me the first tape.

I might as well summarize. After all, for everyone else this happened a long time ago; it's old news. Everyone else had time to adjust to it day by day. But I got it 365 days at a time, and the experience is different that way, more like reading a book or watching a movie than living real life. And, I realized, that's how it would always be. There was no way of getting my ten years back.

Grow up, Podkayne. Would you rather still be at the bottom of the ocean on Europa . . . or wherever it was you spent the last ten years?

No thank you.

PODKAYNE, THE LOST DECADE: YEAR ONE

TOP STORY: Grumpy erupts. Like I had guessed, Grumpy didn't just jump, didn't just pop up and then fall back down. That big red bastard had leaped from the ice of Europa and into space. It took up an elliptical orbit around Jupiter, dipping right into the atmosphere three times, where many astronomers ended up with egg on their faces after predicting it would burn up and be swallowed like a strawberry gumdrop in a whale's belly. Instead, it seemed to thrive on the heat and friction, accelerating and finally leaving the area altogether, followed by a whole fleet of Martian Navy vessels.

Taliesen was a shambles. Forward Base and the NEMO station vanished, crushed by the waves of broken ice. Main Base sank. Only the crew at the ELF Base managed to escape with their lives. I watched some satellite video taken of the event, then had to pause it while I cried. All those people. Captain Scott, Dr. Land, Captain Stone . . .

Could they be alive? For now, they were simply listed as "overdue," like the NEMO sub *October*.

When I started the video again I was startled to see Bus 54, a shiny steel bug, crawling over the ice. Resolution was not quite good enough to see faces in the windows, but it gave me a bad turn, let me tell you. I saw the ice wave hurl us into the sky, watched us flip over and over until the camera lost us.

Clarke Centre had had time to batten down a bit, but still suffered damage. Twenty-seven people died and about a hundred were injured. Normally I would have googled a casualty list, but this was old-fashioned TV, noninteractive. I thought of all my friends there. Stupidly, I thought of Kahlua, the cat who had adopted me. Were they okay? I'd find out later, in carefully measured doses. All nonessential personnel were evacuated from Europa to Ganymede and Callisto, leaving only combat troops and scientific observers.

POLITICAL NEWS: Not worth mentioning. Some new leaders on Earth, same as the old ones. Same old hatreds brewing, some of them centuries old. Nobody got nuked, which made it a good year for the Earth.

CULTURAL NEWS: The usual celebrity divorces and custody squabbles. Blah, blah, blah. A lot of blockbuster movies I wouldn't want to see. Some people won Oscars, and most people probably had already forgotten who they were.

Oddly, there was no news of the top downloads. I called Maimuna, and she said I'd just have to trust her. She recommended I listen to oldies, which I could call up on my room memory. So I did a little of that, and drifted off to sleep.

* * *

NEXT DAY THERE was a familiar face waiting for me.

"Travis!" I shouted, and put my arms around him. He was the first one who hadn't cried when he saw me, and I was grateful for that. Enough people cry over you and you start to think of yourself as a pitiful waif.

So what did I do? I started crying again. He was so *old*! Ten years ago he'd been in his eighties in calendar years, late sixties in "body time," since he started skipping so many years. Now he looked well into his seventies. Healthy, hearty, with his usual crooked smile, but his hair was thin and his skin was mottled with age spots. He hadn't spent the last decade in stasis, that was for sure. Well, of course not, with Grumpy rampaging around the solar system. He'd want to be awake and keeping an eye on that.

"Oh, Uncle Travis, I wanted to *marry* you!" I said. No kidding, my tongue was leading a life of its own.

He raised an eyebrow and gave me a dubious look, but he didn't laugh, bless him.

"Well, I figure you'd have been too smart for that," he said. "Just ask my ex-wife."

"I had it all figured out. With you skipping years, eventually we'd be close to the same age. Now I've lost a whole decade."

"Luckiest thing that ever happened to you if it put you farther away from me."

He dried my eyes with a tissue. I felt like such a fool. Wisely, he didn't say any more about that but threw me a conversational lifesaver.

"So, what have you been up to today?"

"Let's see. This morning I climbed the south face of Olympus Mons with a four-man bobsled on my back. Oh, no, wait, what I meant was, I walked to the bathroom and back, which was harder."

He laughed, and we went on like that for a bit, keeping it light and safe. But something was fluttering around on the edge of my memory, and I eventually netted it among the random flock of butterflies that was still taking the place of coherent thoughts in my shell-shocked brain.

"I heard your voice," I said.

"That would be during the opening of your bubble."

"You were there?"

"Just an observer. We recovered six bubbles from the wreckage. After we got it all back to Mars, I turned it over to the experts and I watched as each one was opened. If it wasn't you, I had no further interest."

I thought about that. There were a few questions I had to ask, even though I was pretty sure I wouldn't get any answers yet.

"Who survived?"

"I'm not supposed to tell you that. Not yet." But he hadn't said he was forbidden, which is what everyone else had said.

"Ambassador Baruti?" I asked. There was a short pause. I glanced down at his lap, and saw his thumb was sticking up. I tried to stay as deadpan as he was.

"Come on, Travis. Senator Wu and Monet?" Thumb up.

"Slomo?" He frowned, and I realized he didn't know the nickname. Hell, I didn't know his *real* name. "The cameraman." Thumb up.

"Tina?" Thumb up.

"Brynne?" The merest shake of his head, then he patted my hand.

"No more questions about that, okay? You know I'm forbidden to tell you. And I was warned not to wear you out, so—"

"I'm not tired," I lied. "There's one more thing I think I'll go crazy if someone doesn't tell me. Why did it take so long? Ten years, Uncle Travis, my god! Were we at the bottom of the ocean? Couldn't they find us?"

"You were embedded in the ice, about a mile down," he said. "And I shouldn't have told you that, and that's all I can say. You'll know the whole story soon, so relax."

"I can't relax."

"You need a pill?" Aunt Elizabeth called out from the next room. Jeez, can't a girl get a little privacy?

"I'm fine. Travis, you're right, I am tired. But could you run me through what happened? I mean, after they got me back here to Mars and . . . and opened the bubble. It was pretty confusing."

"I'm sure it was. It's confusing enough when you've planned for it, like I do. One day they open your bubble and here's a bunch of nuts with their hands in the air, shouting, 'Don't shoot!' "

I laughed, remembering Travis arriving at Gran's stopper ceremonies.

My god, Gran! She'd been inside her bubble longer than I had . . . unless she was already out, which was something I'm sure they weren't going to tell me yet.

So Travis ran me through the procedure, which was interesting, but I fell asleep before he was through. I learned more details later.

The flashes of light were cameras, of course, taking pictures of me from all possible angles. X-rays, infrared, MRI, HGH, who-knows-what, putting together a densely detailed picture of my predicament as the slush drained out of my little sphere of catastrophe. The information gathering took less than ten seconds, then I was popped back into the bubble.

All that was fed into a computer, which made models, then technicians from robot arm programmers to medical personnel like Aunt Elizabeth came up with a plan of action. When they opened the bubble the next time everything was ready, including the painkilling injections. I remembered it all with a shudder. Then I fell asleep.

PODKAYNE, THE LOST DECADE: YEAR TWO

TOP STORY: Doc erupts!

That caught me completely by surprise. If Grumpy could do it, it of course implied that *any* of the crystal mountains could do it, but I hadn't given it a thought. But others had. The researchers still on Europa had studied the seismology surrounding all the mountains and concluded that, if any of them were going to repeat the performance, it would be Doc, and sure enough, seven months later that big yellow bastard lifted itself into space and headed for Jupiter, just like his slightly smaller brother had done. Three trips around, dipping into the atmosphere each time and speeding up instead of slowing down, as it should have, and Doc was off to the races, too. He didn't follow the exact path of Grumpy—Jupiter had moved on in its orbit—but both appeared to be headed in the general vicinity of the sun.

If more of them were going to take off, Dopey and Happy were usually mentioned as the most likely candidates, along with some that hadn't had names before.

Were people still calling them by those stupid names? Apparently so.

Early on the more sedate news organizations had tried the official acronyms and numbers, but TECP-40 just doesn't have any punch to it. People needed personification, and the names were already handy.

So someone dug around in the history books and found that the Disney people had considered no less than fifty names when creating the dwarfs, and these were applied to those TECPs that didn't have one yet, and that's what people called them. Among them were Blabby, Jumpy, Shifty, Snoopy, Awful, Biggy, Blabby, Dirty, Gabby, Gaspy, Gloomy, Hoppy, Hotsy, Jaunty, and Nifty.

What were they up to? Nobody knew anything. How did they do what they did? How did a trillion tons of crystalline matter free itself from the gravity of a small planet with no visible expenditure of energy? Vague theories were trotted out, possibly some use of the galactic magnetic field, whatever that is. Dark matter and dark energy were mentioned, darkly.

God was mentioned. God always seems to get into the game.

Bottom line: Nobody knew anything.

POLITICAL NEWS: Back to God again. The Rapturists were stirring from beneath the rocks and in all the damp, wet, moldy places of the mind and spirit in Arkansas and Alabama and Tennessee and all those other vacation wonderlands in Heartland America. They'd had some hard times after the tsunami hadn't turned out to be the clarion call to Armageddon, but true believers never die, they just annotate their beliefs and raise more true believers. Massive rallies were held all over the Heartland. The exact nature of Grumpy and Doc was debated, sometimes with thumped Bibles, sometimes with shotguns. The consensus was they were archangels coming to summon the faithful, but since the Bible apparently didn't mention Archangel Grumpy, just who *were* they? Most agreed that "Grumpy" was Gabriel. Top candidates for "Doc" were Michael, Uriel, and Zadkiel. Stay tuned to this heavenly channel for more news.

Over in the world of Islam, the Imams currently stirring up the most trouble were speaking of the "Sword of Allah." They expected Grumpy and/or Doc to wipe out all the infidels. According to them, the Big Wave was just the Big Guy getting the range on his target. Oddly enough, terror attacks were down for the year, and the one before. Lots of Muslims wanted to stick around for the show.

CULTURAL NEWS: What culture? More movies, books, art . . . and once more, no music news. I was beginning to see this as highly suspicious. Were they hiding something from me? Had people given up on music as a bad job? Was Elvis back from the dead?

MY NEXT VISITOR announced himself by leaping onto my chest and bumping my nose, *hard,* accompanied by the sound of a large vibrator.

"Kahlua!" I shouted. He just regarded me with those narrow blue eyes, bumped noses again to mark me with his scent, then curled his paws on my chest, wrapped his tail around his hind end, and seemed to drift off to sleep.

"Hi, Podkayne," came a voice from the door. Karma, who I'd seen a little more than a week ago and who hadn't seen me in ten years.

"You're looking good, Kar," I said, stroking Kahlua's fur. I noticed she was in Navy uniform. Once again, what was that all about? Do the necessary and get out, that had been Karma's philosophy.

"You mean for my age?" she said.

"Bring me up to date," I said.

"Well, you know it can only be personal details . . ."

In short: Married, to someone I'd never met. Two children, three and five. She looked tired. I guess kids will do that to you, combined with a life in the Navy. I wanted to ask her about that, but sensed that I wouldn't get any answers. So we talked about safe things.

Of which there weren't many. You know, listening to older people, I realize there are decades and then there are decades. We all know that the distance between ages nine and nineteen is immense. Granddaddy Manny once told me that the difference between age fifty and sixty is really not that much. By then you're pretty much who you're going to be. But nineteen and twenty-nine is quite a gulf. I had no idea what I'd be doing in ten years, and I found that exciting. Karma, I quickly discovered, had a pretty good idea what she would be doing—or at least what she hoped to be doing—for the next twenty or thirty. Her life had taken shape. Mine was still fluid.

I realized, with a pang, that it would be that way with *all* my friends. Good lord, what would the Pod People be like today? Who would they be jamming with, what would they be playing? I could be sure it wouldn't include poor, poor, pitiful Podkayne.

There was a story behind the cat; otherwise, we'd have had very little we could talk about or would even want to talk about.

"We rode out the quake pretty well," Karma said. "I don't think it even woke Kahlua up. Then I was busy with the rescue parties . . ." A momentary pause there, and a faraway look. But for her, the horror of that day was long ago, and there were no tears now. "Anyway, when we were being evacuated I couldn't find the damn cat. I looked everywhere, but we weren't given a lot of time. I figured he was a goner when I got aboard the ship, and when I settled down in my seat . . . there he was, rubbing against my leg and purring. I don't know how he does it."

"He's a spook," I said, and rubbed his head. He opened one eye enough to glare at me, then started that maddening thing he does of exercising his claws against my chest.

"Anyway, I brought him back to Mars, and I remembered you had an uncle who was an admiral. So I looked him up and told him about your cat. He was upset . . . we were all pretty upset at the time . . . but he took Kahlua."

"You must be a pretty old fellow by now, huh?" I told the cat. He ignored me.

"That's what I'm telling you. He's not old. Your uncle had him put in stasis, and I just got him out this morning. You probably thought he had a pretty good memory, going right up to you like that, but for him it's the same as you. For him, it's only been days since he's seen you. You can pick up with him right where you left off."

I took a great deal of comfort from that. Probably because I knew there was very little else I could pick up where I left off.

ONE GOOD THING about enforced bed rest: I had a chance to catch up on my reading. Real paper books, too, since all my cyber inputs were shut down. I finally read that book my parents stole my name from, which was called *Podkayne of Mars*.

What a horrible book! What a mean old man! He spends the whole book getting you to like this sweet little airhead, and then he does terrible things to her. Don't you hate it when an author does that? I'm not reading any more of *his* books, I promise you!

PODKAYNE, THE LOST DECADE: YEAR THREE

TOP STORY: This time it was . . . Sneezy. Formally known as TECP-12, Sneezy was a wee bit smaller than Grumpy and Doc, only about four miles long, and dominated by the color green. So now we had a yellow one and a blue one and a green one falling toward the sun, and three big holes in the Taliesen surface, already frozen quite deep, of course, and quickly filling in from landslides caused by the still-nervous crust and tidal stresses. Grumpy was getting quite close to the sun, and by the end of the year had gone within the orbit of Mercury. Navy fleets were still following it, and the others, in rotating shifts. At the rate Grumpy was going, they'd have to break off early in the new year. We have bases on Mercury and have ventured a lot closer, but Grumpy was on a course to take it too close to the primal fires for any ship we had.

I had to keep reminding myself that, not only had this all happened already, but so had the next seven years. I was beginning to get a little annoyed at that. What was the harm of just letting me know how it all came out? Obviously civilization hadn't been destroyed. Why not skip to page 500 and let me know what the situation was now?

But they stuck to their guns.

OTHER NEWS: Not worth mentioning.

THEY PUT ME on a walking machine that day, and I crept along on it for ten minutes at a pace that would have done a 110-year-old woman proud.

Why a walking machine? Why not the corridor outside my room?

Why not back and forth *within* the room? Oh, well, we don't question doctor's orders.

Aunt Elizabeth was no longer rooming with me. She checked up for about an hour that day and left me in the hands of a nurse.

Who promptly conked out on the couch.

Here was my chance! The screws were sleeping, the tunnel was complete, I'd carved a gun out of a bar of soap . . . I could be under the wire and out into the trees in five minutes, ten if I had to fight off the dogs and the odd Nazi perimeter guard . . .

Instead I settled for swinging my legs over the side of the bed and pulling my brand-new aluminum walker over with one foot and slowly, slowly putting my weight on it. I shuffled across the thick carpet. Snails would have sneered at my pace. Earthworms could have run rings around me.

I couldn't help it. I was going stir-crazy. I had to see outside.

There was a single small rectangle of window in the room, which told me I was in the old, historic part of the Red Thunder. It used to be open to the elements, hence the stingy port, from back in the days when we were still learning about pressurized environments. The old wing was now enclosed under the Mile-High Dome, but nothing had been changed. You didn't get the nice views of the dome you'd get from your open balcony in the newer parts of the hotel, but people paid premium prices to stay here. Silly, but I understood it. We don't have a lot of history on Mars, and this is about as far back as it goes.

I was winded when I got there. There was an old-fashioned blind over it, and I pulled the cord cautiously, aware of their tendency to clatter down if you didn't do it right. Then I leaned to the window to take a look outside, annoyed that my distance vision was still a bit fuzzy.

First impression: sort of dark. Second: *very* dark, and not many people around. The Mile-High is a flurry of gardens, fountains, pools, arcades, and shops, and at night like it was now under the transparent dome it should have been blazing with artificial light.

Instead, there was the bare minimum of streetlights on the paths and only a few people walking, or riding bikes or scooters. Across the small plaza outside the hotel a single vidboard showed a commercial for breakfast cereal. I looked down.

I figured I was on about the tenth or twelfth floor, out of twenty. The plaza itself was crowded with people, maybe a thousand. Hard to make them out in the semidarkness. Many of them were carrying candles, and I thought they might be singing. No sound at all came through the triple-thick Lexan. All around the people, covering the plaza from side to side, were flowers. Millions of flowers. Where they were heaped under the streetlights I could see a riot of colors. There were huge arrangements, and there were piles and piles of simple bouquets in cellophane.

Suddenly there was a commotion. Somebody was pointing, then more people, and then they were all on their feet. Some were applauding, others were waving, some were doing handsprings and backflips and other signs of unrestrained joy in .38 gee.

It looked like there was a big celebrity staying at the hotel, probably somewhere above me, judging from where people were pointing. It was frustrating. I'm no celebrity hound, but it would have been nice to know who it was. Then I remembered this was ten years later, and I might not even know the name. There'd been time for a lot of old famous faces to grow obscure, and a whole new crop of tabloid fodder to arise.

I hadn't learned much and I was tired, but it was nice to have seen something beyond these six walls. I was about to head back to bed when I noticed the scene had changed on the vidboard across the way. There was a crawl line across the bottom but I couldn't read it. It looked like a promo for a horror movie. It showed the face of a blond woman who might have been moderately attractive if she'd put on a little makeup and did something about the dark circles under her eyes. Her hair was a fright, stiff and tangled and standing up on one side like she'd slept on it. I wouldn't be caught dead going out in public like that. I watched her, waiting for something to happen.

She looked vaguely familiar.

Finally I shrugged and turned away.

Out of the corner of my eye, I saw the ugly hag on the screen shrug and turn. I turned back . . . and so did she.

I let out a shriek that levitated the sleeping nurse two feet off the couch, to bounce once on the floor and leap to her feet, groggy and frightened.

That was me.

* * *

I'M AFRAID I wasn't very nice about it. When Aunt Elizabeth arrived I told her I wanted the whole story, or I wanted a lawyer. Was I a prisoner here, or what?

It took half an hour, but finally much of the family was assembled in my room, most of them looking uneasy but none of them looking guilty. They still thought they were doing the right thing for me. I was going to disabuse them of that.

Mom and Dad and Mike were there, and all four grandparents. I'd seen them all before, separately, and though I can't say I was *used* to seeing my parents in their late forties and their parents in their early seventies, I knew it was true.

Also present was Uncle Bill, resplendent in the uniform of—yikes!—a fleet admiral. At least I guessed that's what that circle of five stars on his shoulder boards and lapels meant; I'd never seen a fleet admiral before.

Senator Wu was there with his daughter Monet. I was surprised to discover how happy I was to see them. They had been relatively uninjured in the crash, nothing more than bumps and bruises and, in Monet's case, a broken arm. So they weren't in recovery, like me, but I assumed they were still going through the reorientation process and would be in the dark as to most current events. It felt good that there were two people there who were probably as disoriented as I was, who had shared the nightmare and now the aftermath. I looked forward to putting our heads together.

But the big surprise was Quinn and Cassandra, my old Pod People. Quinn had already been five years older than the rest of us, and was looking more than ten years older now. Cassandra didn't look all that changed, but it might have been skillful makeup and maybe a touch of surgery.

I made a silent bet with myself on who would be the first to speak, and what that speech would be. Ten dollars per bet.

"Podkayne," Grandma Kelly said, making me ten dollars richer, in theory, "we understand why you're upset. Anyone would be. But we still think you should stick with the program, follow your doctor's orders."

And that made me twenty dollars richer. I noticed a few people shifting around. I wondered if a vote had been taken, and if it was unanimous. But I didn't really care.

"Grandma Kelly," I said, coming down maybe a little harder than necessary on the first word, "I'm going to be frank. I don't give a sand-rat's ass what you think. You, or all of you. I'm going to find out why I'm being held here, and what's going on outside. One way or another. Your choice here is to tell me or lock me in and tie me down."

There was a short silence, and I looked at Mom and Dad.

"So, parental units. What's it going to be?"

Mom smiled.

"What I knew it would be when I came in here. We're going to do a deal. Right, Elizabeth?"

Aunt Elizabeth didn't look happy—doctors are like that, they like to be in charge—but she nodded.

"Here it is," Mom went on. "You know from what you saw that things have changed in a big way in the ten years you've been gone. Part of that is systemwide in scope and affects all humanity."

"And involves Grumpy and Doc and Sneezy."

"Yes. The other part is personal. We're going to tell you the personal part now, and save the rest for another day."

"How about tomorrow?"

Mom looked at Dad, and then at Elizabeth, and they both nodded.

"If you want. What I can tell you right now is, you are probably the most famous person in the solar system."

I don't know what I expected, but it wasn't that. Sure, I'd figured out all those people out there were holding a candlelight vigil for me, but I thought it just had something to do with the accident, and they were just happy I'd been lucky enough to make it through alive.

Well, I *had* been the only one to do much about the emergency, me and Slomo. Maybe that was it. I was the story of the day, the chump-of-the-moment, the news footnote of the month. The Warhol Girl, entering her fifteen minutes. Maybe I was being built up as a hero. *How did it* feel, *Podkayne, when the driver's brains spattered on your face?* Oh, that should be glorious. Gag me.

It didn't feel right. None of that would make me the most famous person in the solar system, as Mom had put it.

"But what did I do?" I asked.

* * *

WHAT I DID, was "Jazzie's Song." No kidding.

I had completely forgotten that I'd shipped off the finished product to Mike, and to Quinn. Shortly after that, Grumpy exploded, and I vanished into the Europan ice.

Mike and Quinn had corresponded and became good friends. Quinn and Cassandra had fiddled with it, tweaked it here and there, but mostly left it alone. Then they went to work, copyrighting it, downloading it, promoting it.

Sometimes someone is simply at the right place and in the right time with the right product. I don't know—no one will ever know—if Jazzie would have taken off or even got much listening if it hadn't been so intimately associated with the Europan situation, if the base material hadn't come from the crystals themselves, via ELF recording and manipulation. But it was, and if I say so myself, and as proven by the reaction of the first people to hear it as I performed it live, a very nice piece of music. It was like nothing anyone had ever heard before, and it was a human interacting with the crystals, and in the prevailing nervous mood affecting all humanity, it was what they wanted to hear.

Which was great news. I was famous, and I was rich. And I "died" young, which is often a good career move, as I was saying to Elvis and John Lennon just the other day.

How rich? Very rich. "Jazzie's Song" had been the top download for *three consecutive years*. And it was all mine, less a collaboration fee for the Pod People and Mike, as my de facto manager.

All amazing, all hard to take in. And just the beginning.

There was just the one "Jazzie's Song," but there were the sides we burned on the tour, and once you've got one big hit, the public clamors for more. Quinn and Mike doled them out, and each became a hit. So the Pod People got some money, too, which made me happy. Ten years later, we were well into the point where people were trading "bootlegs" of the stuff I'd recorded before I was famous. (*Famous!* It was going to take a while to get used to that.) Like so much of that sort of ephemera, a lot of it was stuff I wouldn't have released if I was around to have any say about it, but it wasn't *awful*, and it made me a lot more money, so who's complaining?

But wait! as they say on hard-sell TV commercials. *There's more!*

Jazzie was so popular that the public wanted more of it. But there wasn't any . . . for a while, anyway. But all that ELF music was available, public domain, and anybody with a mixer and a mike could experiment with it. It wasn't long before people were making their own variations, finding stuff in there that I told myself I would have found if I hadn't been in deep freeze.

Within a year there was a whole new genre of music. For a while they called it "crystal music," but the label that stuck was . . . get ready for it . . .

Pod music.

The Big New Thing in music, not related to rock or pop or anything that came before it, really. Ten years later it was still going strong, as hard to kill as disco or rap.

And it was all my doing. I'm not getting a swelled head here, honestly I'm not. But it was *just me,* sitting on my bed waiting for something exciting to happen, mixing and discarding and listening . . . and then singing.

Ladies and gentlemen, I give you Podkayne, back from the dead!

Thank you, thank you! I am the inventor of Pod music, the Pod-o-rama, the Podster herself! I am the Princess of Mars, the Tsarina of the Sun and Moon, the Queen of the Earth, the Empress of Ice Cream!

I am the bee's kneecaps and the kitty's jam jams!

I am Champagne Charlene, I am me *and* Bobby McGee!

I am woman, hear me roar!

I am the freaking *walrus*!

And I don't have a clue what Pod music is all about.

14

★ ★ ★

SAY YOU'RE BEETHOVEN. It's 1800, you've just published your First Symphony, and you're running around Vienna trying to get the DJs to spin your piano concertos and a string quartet or two, hoping to generate a buzz in the Viennese chat rooms. Just starting to *really* learn your composing chops, in other words.

Then you take a trip to the Catskills for your health. You're walking around the forest primeval, humming this little ditty that's been running through your head, which you scribbled on a scrap of papyrus and gave to your main man, Joseph Haydn, before you left. *"Freude, schöner Götterfunken,"* then something, something, something, something. That's all you've got, just those eight quarter notes, but you know a good theme when you hear one, and you think this might get some serious downloads.

Suddenly you're struck by lightning and collapse in a stupor under the tree right next to Rip Van Winkle's. You wake up; a hundred years have gone by. (Things happened slower back then.)

There's a guy there, says his name is Gustav Mahler. *Yo, Bee, baby, we're so glad you're back.* Then he tells you that, while you were sleeping, people began to *really* take a listen to that little First Symphony of yours.

They found stuff in it even you didn't know was there. You are, in fact, the Father of the Romantic Movement in music.

In fact, people call it "Bee music" in your honor.

He's got some sides with him, and he plays some of it for you. The *Emperor* Concerto, by some Pole named Chopin. *Fidelio,* by Richard Wagner. The *Moonlight* Sonata by Franz Liszt. A *Pastoral* Symphony by Anton Bruckner. A *Choral* Symphony by Felix Mendelssohn. Plus some stuff by some crazy Russians: Tchaikovsky, Rimsky-Korsakov, Mussorgsky, Rachmaninoff.

None of it sounds familiar, except a little bit of the Mendelssohn.

Even worse, most of it doesn't make a damn bit of sense to you. These guys have taken your basic idea and run with it, and now they've elaborated it past your capacity to dig it. It might as well be Ravel, or Copland, or Bernstein, or Schoenberg.

For all your understanding of this music, you might as well be . . . well, deaf.

All resemblance between me and Beethoven stops right there, of course. He was a musical genius; I'm a damn good singer, end of story. But in my little scenario of him, and in my real life, we were both baffled, deafened, deprived of the work we might have created. There would never be enough time to catch up and resume where you left off, because the musical world had left you sleeping under an oak tree. Or a mile of Europan ice.

So I was the Godmother of Pod music. So what?

On that note, I fell into a troubled sleep. I dreamed.

I CAN'T SAY for sure when the recurring dreams began. I suspect it was while I was under the nanoknives, and sedation, but it might have been before that . . . and I know that doesn't make sense, but hear me out.

I hate it when authors describe dreams in books. It seems lazy to me. Dreams are full of symbolism, and they aren't logical or orderly. Scraps of your life are tossed into the air of your subconscious and glued together any old which-way, if you follow one theory. They might be ordered according to symbols or paradigms or archetypes or engrams, depending on who else you talk to.

I don't think anybody really knows, but we've all had them, and we know they have things in common. There's the caught-naked dream, which happens even to nudity-tolerant Martians. (There are places you go nude, and places you don't.) There's the running-in-place dream, where you're moving through molasses. There's the falling dream—so I'm told; I've never had one. Dozens or hundreds of others.

They usually involve people you know, in unlikely situations. They usually are set in places you're familiar with.

These dreams were nothing like that. They are very hard to talk about, because I don't have the verbs and nouns to describe the experience.

For one, there is a sense of no time. Not no time *passing*. No time at *all*, if that makes any sense. Maybe what it was like before the Big Bang, when everything existed as a single point and the Cosmic Stopwatch hadn't started running yet. Or inside a stopper bubble, which is the only place I can think of where we *know* time doesn't move.

You see where I'm going with this? Though there was no way to validate the notion, either *something* happened while I was in the bubble, or my subconscious *thought* something *should* have happened, and was supplying these weird dreams to fill in the blank.

Since there is no time in these dreams, nothing can be said to actually *happen*, if you can understand that. Heck, I'm the one having the dreams, and *I* don't really understand it, but let me keep trying.

I am a presence. I know who I am, but I can't say that I have an actual name. I see nothing, I hear nothing, I feel nothing. I suppose it's like being in an isolation tank, except even in a tank I'd expect to have thoughts, mental images, retinal flashes of light, the sensation of warm water on my skin. There's none of that. This doesn't disturb me, as the mere awareness of identity is enough. Perhaps it's the ultimate Zen state. I don't know. In fact, I know nothing, because . . . knowledge requires a place to put it, whether it's on a bookshelf or in electronic storage, and there is no *place* here.

See? Even the word "here" implies a place. There is no *here* here.

It is all strangely relaxing. Well, why shouldn't it be? To be *un*relaxed, you have to be engaged in something. Dealing with a problem, and there are no problems here. Stimulated, either for good or bad, and there is no source of stimulation, nothing to stimulate, no *use* for the verbs *stimulate, deal,* or *engage*. No use for *any* of the thousands of verbs I used to know, nor the thousands of nouns and modifiers. This place simply *is*, apparently outside of space and time, with no further detail available than that.

But gradually . . . and that's not right, because it implies a process, and a state of before and after, but it's the best way I can put it . . . I realize I'm not alone. I've *always* known this, because every moment is the same as any other. But there are presences here that are somehow different from my presence. I don't see them, I don't feel them, I don't hear them, but they are there. They are aware of me.

Then time begins. It's only a nanosecond, but it's the first tick of time there has ever been, anywhere (and before this there was no "anywhere" for time to exist in), and we all savor it. And now that there is time, there can be other things. So . . . in the beginning there was the Word . . .

. . . and the Word was, "Hello."

Or maybe it was God. And maybe they're the same thing.

ALL RIGHT. THE easy part is over. That's right, that had been the easy part. From now on it gets grim.

Mom, Dad, Mike, and Travis gathered in my room, where I was practicing sitting up in a comfy chair instead of in bed. Aunt Elizabeth was there, too, with her machines, probably ready to sedate me if the stuff I was about to hear was too upsetting. The agreement was that we'd dispense with the year-by-year and just tell the whole story of the seven years I was still missing.

Mike pulled a chair up in front of me and hopped onto it. This was a new Mike, to me, dead serious, no playfulness about him at all.

"We talked it over," he said, "and I asked to be sort of the moderator of this little show."

Again, a new Mike. Being what he was, he had changed very little. When I left he was smaller than a normal ten-year-old child, and he was still about the same size, so he didn't *look* any older, except around the eyes. And, of course, in body language and demeanor. He was clearly an adult, but my mind was having a devil of a time accepting that. It kept superimposing the happy-go-lucky, sweet little kid I knew over this tiny little man, and the cognitive dissonance was disconcerting.

"I suggested we find out if there are burning questions you want an answer to right now, before we get into the whole story. Some answers wouldn't make sense unless you did know the whole story, naturally, but I can only try." He lifted an eyebrow, and I got right to the first one.

"Who's dead?" I asked.

"Aside from the people on Europa, who you already know about, your uncle Anthony died two years ago."

I remembered him from the last time I saw him, at Gran's farewell party. Chubby, stuffing himself at the free buffet, a big, affable, sweet-natured failure at everything he ever tried, a man impossible to dislike unless he owed you money. Which he did, to most of the family older than me.

"How did he die?"

"He and your cousin Luther were working at a rescue mission somewhere in Africa and were killed during a refugee riot."

Luther, Luther, Luther. I could barely place the face, one of the sandrats at Gran's farewell, running around, screaming and crying, maybe about twelve. I hadn't known any of them well. Hadn't known Anthony all that well, for that matter.

Refugee riots in Africa? Obviously that was part of the bigger picture, which I had long ago figured out was not good.

"Gran?" I said.

"Still in suspension. Everyone's been far too busy to work much on the sort of medical problem she has. There's been a lot more progress on the sort of medical problem *you* had."

Meaning violent accidents, or maybe not accidents. All those Navy uniforms, Karma still in the service, the lack of lights or tourists under the Mile-High. It was sounding more and more like war.

Just for a moment, I didn't want to hear any more. *Don't bring me no bad news!* The military wife claps her hands over her ears when she sees the solemn officer approaching her house. If she doesn't hear the awful news, then it didn't happen, or she could pretend it didn't happen for a little longer. Let's rewind this tape, all the way back to before the trip to Taliesen, and let's take a different path to a different future. Like when Mom and Dad saw the first video of the Big Wave, like when people saw the Twin Towers falling in New York, like when an even earlier generation heard the news about Pearl Harbor on the radio . . . you knew that a moment had arrived that would forever divide your life between *before* it happened and *after* it happened.

For me, it hadn't happened yet. Grumpy had erupted, sure, I'd been there, I'd seen it as close as anyone had. But the aftermath hadn't arrived yet, for me, and like a little child I didn't *want* it to arrive. *Make it not happened, Mommy!* Because I knew that the flight of Grumpy and the others was one of those turning points, and I knew the news was bad. Probably very bad.

The only place you can escape history is inside a stopper bubble, and I didn't want to go back inside. Next time I was de-stasized, if ever, my *family* might not be there, and right now, they were all I had to cling to.

But I put it off just a minute longer.

"Jubal?" I asked.

"Only Travis knows that," Mike said, and looked at Travis, who spread his hands wordlessly.

"Still in stasis," he said. That surprised me. Jubal's genius had saved Mars once, and I had figured Travis would have him out and working on this problem, whatever it was.

So I sighed, and gestured to Mike.

"Let's hear it," I said, and settled back in my chair with Kahlua on my lap.

Mike stood up and started pacing.

"Grumpy circled the sun three times . . ."

. . . **AND HEADED STRAIGHT** for the Earth.

At the velocity it was moving, and with a mass of almost a trillion tons, the results would make the Big Wave seem like dropping a ball bearing into Lake Superior. The sun's gravity would slow it some, but as it approached Earth it would speed up again. Minimum impact speed of a body falling from infinite space: twenty-five thousand miles per hour.

Earth had had about two months to prepare.

It was the most massive movement of population in human history. Coastal areas were evacuated, giant refugee camps were established at higher elevations. It was summer in the northern hemisphere, so the most populous areas of the planet were at least temperate. But there were not enough tents, globally, to handle a fraction of the refugees.

Civil strife, everywhere, but worse in some places than in others. People who were already living in places like Denver and Geneva and central India and Africa and Asia were not always happy to see these hungry, homeless hordes, and often there was fighting for scarce space and food and shelter. Martial law, mass killings, starvation. Half a dozen cities vanished overnight in nuclear explosions.

Heroic examples of people working together for the common good, craven examples of people at their worst, stealing and raping and murdering.

The only people who were happy about it were the Rapturists, who had definitely settled on Gabriel, Michael, and Raphael as the real names of Grumpy, Doc, and Sneezy. They expected that Gabriel (Grumpy) would elevate them right out of their clothes and directly into Heaven, while the rest of us fought it out for the seven years of the Tribulation.

The Martian Republic was torn. Suddenly every Earthie who could afford it wanted to book passage to Mars, or anywhere else, most of which were Martian colonies. Some people who were already here wanted to go home to be with loved ones, but a lot more wanted to stay past their visas.

But what were we going to do? There weren't enough ships in the entire system to transport even a tiny fraction of the people who wanted to travel, and not a thousandth of the space that would be needed to house them when they got here.

I'm proud of my country and what we did, which was, simply, everything we could, and as fairly as possible.

People already here were allowed to stay. People who wanted to go home were allowed to do that, on ships that were pretty empty Earthbound. And at spaceports all over Earth, lotteries were conducted. We didn't intend to fill up with only rich Earthies. Anyone who could make it to a spaceport—and we had no control over that, and the carnage on the roads and in the terminals was terrible—got a chance. If you won, you got to take your family with you . . . but not your friends. The lottery forms specified immediate family only. I can only imagine the heartrending scenes; I didn't watch any of the video of that.

Ships were hot-bunked, with three people sharing each bed in eight-hour shifts. The finest luxury liners became overcrowded cattle cars, gourmet meals vanishing in favor of macaroni and rice and oatmeal.

At home, all tourism activity was suspended. Nobody was spending money on luxuries, anyway, though a lot of people wanted the casinos kept open in an eat-drink-and-be-merry spirit. No dice . . . so to speak. Soon families were sleeping on the craps tables. *Under* the craps tables, too. This came to be known as a "Martian bunk bed."

All the hotels were rapidly converted to barracks. We jammed them in there like sardines, as many as each room could take. And there were always more, as each and every passenger ship that could be pressed into service shuttled back and forth between Earth and Mars and some of the asteroid colonies at a steady one gee of boost. Many Navy ships that had even corridor space for sleeping bags were shuttling, too. We moved almost a million people in two months.

And of course it was a drop in the bucket. Billions were left behind.

There was a very strong chance that *all* those billions would die. High ground or low ground, nothing was going to save them if the impact was as hard as it was expected to be. It would be an extinction event, as bad as the one that killed the dinosaurs. The sky would blacken and stay that way for many years. The ground would open and swallow entire cities, whether coastal or mountainous.

It was going to be Hell on Earth for everybody but the Rapturists.

WHILE GOVERNMENTS AND other bodies were concerning themselves primarily with rescue operations, the military branches of these entities were not entirely inactive.

As soon as Grumpy's course became clear, two possible means of salvation presented themselves, and both of them had to be put into action as soon as possible if they were to have any effect.

Plan A: Divert it. Tall order.

Plan B: Blow it up. The idea was that smaller chunks might cause less damage, some would miss the Earth entirely, and the rest might be easier to divert.

There were voices raised, pointing out that attacking these things, in view of their incredible power, might not be a wise idea. What if we merely managed to piss them off? But most people with the capacity to do something about it decided that you could hardly be more pissed off than to aim a trillion-ton object at an inhabited planet.

I'm not a big advocate of shooting if there's *anything* else you can do, but I had to agree, retrospectively. Why not try it?

So they went with Plan B first, simply because they could do it at once and Plan A took some preparation.

One of the largest weapons in somebody's nuclear arsenal was put aboard a rocket and accelerated at a constant five hundred gees right at the heart of Grumpy, and everybody crossed their fingers.

Result: nothing. It didn't go off. The Curse of Taliesen strikes again. Probably. I mean no nuke had *ever* failed before, when used in anger.

Two days later there was no farting around. A salvo of one hundred nuclear-tipped missiles was fired. All Earth and all Mars and all the outer planets watched hopefully as they approached and began to go off.

Half of them failed, but half did detonate, and it was horribly beautiful. Tiny little pinpricks of dazzling light sparkled all around Grumpy, then expanded into perfect white spheres, and slowly faded away. Where they had been, the surface of the giant crystal glowed a lovely red.

Billions cheered.

Then the data came in. Grumpy had not deviated one foot. We could have hit it with thousands more, but what would be the point?

By then Plan A was just about ready. A dozen very large bubble engines had been constructed and loaded onto our largest cargo ships. The Martian Navy hurried them into position—if you're going to try to divert an object heading for you, the sooner you start pushing it the more course change you'll get for every erg of energy expended. They were equipped to attach themselves to one side of Grumpy and begin firing. If they could fire long enough and hard enough, it just might work.

The drone engines approached within a mile, half a mile, one hundred feet . . . and touched the surface.

And vanished. One moment they were there, the next moment they were gone. Slow-motion cameras revealed they simply sank into the surface as if it were Jell-O.

The next six went out with volunteer human pilots. By then it was iffy as to whether they'd do any good even if they worked, as Grumpy was a lot nearer the Earth now and closing fast.

But they tried. They tried . . . and now there is a statue of those four men and two women in the Plaza just outside my window.

Because they reached Grumpy, and vanished. If there were living beings inside those goddam crystals, they really *were* boojums.

So it was time for Plan C.

THE MARTIAN NAVY'S ultimate weapon is the Broussard Bubble, in both its varieties. The Republic of Mars owns all the bubble-making facilities, which is what prevented our takeover when my parents were kids and the Martian War was fought. We'd have gotten our butts kicked—we *did* get our butts kicked, with hardly a shot fired from our side; the fireworks were all from competing factions squabbling over who got to conquer us—but for Mom and Dad and Uncle Travis and Uncle Jubal going to Earth and threatening to squeeze the whole nasty planet down to the size of a pea if they didn't *cut it out*!

They did, and most Martians agree that the only reason we aren't paying taxes to some Earth country and the Earthies haven't taken the bubble technology from us is that they're still afraid of being squeezed.

There aren't many of the bubble factories because, incredible as it seems, only Uncle Jubal knows how to make them. Only Jubal *can* make them, I guess I should say. He tried to teach others how it's done because being the only human who can do it made his life intolerable, but it doesn't seem to be a knack that can be taught. So every installation that can make the machines that make the bubbles was built by Uncle Jubal.

How many of them there are is classified far above my petty rating. It's a state secret, jealously guarded, and the only non-Martian citizen who knows is Travis, who isn't a citizen of *anything*, now that the United States is fragmented.

Most of the bubble machines are on Mars. A few are closely guarded and supervised—by the Martian Navy—on Earth. But an unknown number are aboard our Black Fleet, which hovers tens of billions of miles to the north or south of the sun—no one knows which, or if it's both—like the deep-sea nuclear subs of Earth nations, perpetually combat-ready, able to deliver an object lesson or vengeance if we are attacked again.

The Republic doesn't like using these ships for anything other than a threatening presence. We don't even like them to be seen; they are based on Eris, which never gets as close to the sun as Pluto's maximum distance, and around which the Navy maintains a billion-mile spherical exclusion zone.

But this was clearly a special case. One of the black ships was called in, with the intention of surrounding Grumpy with a stopper bubble and taking it far, far away, before it could hit the Earth.

Long story short: It didn't work.

Why didn't it work? I get tired of saying this, but . . . no one knows. It's especially frustrating because no one knows why the bubble generators work *at all.* I'm not even sure if Uncle Jubal knows, since he's not able to explain it. Maybe it's just something he does with his mind, like a . . . a psychic, or something, though I don't believe in psychics or poltergeists or levitation or any of that woo-woo crap. But the fact remains, Uncle Jubal can build a bubble machine and it works. Anyone can be shown how to operate it. Someone else can build a bubble machine *exactly the same way* . . . and it just sits there. As far as I know they are the only machines ever built that can't be duplicated, that only work for one man.

Poor man. Jubal Broussard, doomed to be the goose that laid the silver egg.

This time, the bubble generator itself just sat there. They can operate from a great distance—classified, but it's many millions of miles, and may even be infinity—but no matter how far away they tried it, nothing happened. No squeezer bubbles, no stopper bubbles. Of course they tested the machines, and found they had no trouble forming either sort of bubble, even at several million miles away. But not if it was surrounding Grumpy, or any part of him. They tried it on Doc, too, with the same result.

Again, No One Knew Why. Something about the crystals made it impossible to use our weapon of last resort against them. Maybe it was their gravity drive, or electromagnetic drive, or whatever they used. Ask a physicist, if you can find one who'll talk to you about it at all. Physicists are a very pissed-off group since the invention of bubble technology. They take it personally that they can't figure it out.

So the mass evacuations continued, and everyone watched and waited.

THEN GRUMPY (OR Gabriel) began to slow down.

No one had expected it, though the crystals had demonstrated that they had a vast source of power, even if we didn't know what it was. So far, none of the crystals had done *anything* anyone expected.

It was around the moon's orbit that the deceleration began. Over the next several days the velocity dropped. Computers chewed over the data continually, figuring time of arrival—people were beginning to say that instead of the discouraging word "impact"—and total energy released if conditions remained the same. They didn't; the big rock kept slowing down, so that by the time it entered the atmosphere over the Pacific Ocean it was just moseying along . . . for an astronomical object being pulled by Earth's gravity, that is. Maybe it was going to be a gentle touchdown. Maybe aliens were going to emerge and tell us how to stop global warming, end war, stop hunger and racism and poverty and give us a really, really good recipe for chicken soup.

Maybe they were going to welcome us to the Galactic Federation. *Klaatu barada nikto*, Earthlings!

No such luck. It didn't levitate any Rapturists out of their clothes, either.

It was moving at about Mach 3 when it hit the water. Say two thousand five hundred miles per hour. Not what you'd call a soft landing, but infinitely better than the thirty-five-thousand-plus miles per hour of the first, predeceleration estimate. Impact was several hundred miles southeast of the big island of Hawaii.

The atmospheric shock wave was enough to blow down trees and break windows in Maui.

Mauna Loa is the world's largest mountain, by volume, and Mauna Kea is the tallest, though the bottom four miles or so are underwater. Mauna Kea had been inactive for millions of years, but now she and her cousin Mauna Loa and daughter Kilauea popped like red-hot pimples from the inertial mass of Grumpy settling into the seabed. What geologists call "slumps," massive landslides, came down the sides of all the volcanoes, creating tsunamis that were pretty much lost in the much bigger one created by Grumpy himself displacing about fifteen cubic miles of seawater very quickly.

All the seacoast cities of the Pacific Rim were pretty much wiped out. All the islands of Polynesia and Micronesia were scoured clean. (Almost no one was there by that time.) Australia, Indonesia, Japan, the Philippines, China. Mexico, Colombia, Ecuador, Peru, Chile. The Western America coast. The list was long.

Earthquakes shook the Mississippi Valley, India, China, Russia.

It took three days for the planet to reach a state of—more or less—equilibrium. Then the cleanup began. And the burials. No one was using the word *recovery*. The world had still not recovered from the Big Wave, twenty-five years before. No one would ever recover from Grumpy.

The operative phrase was *start over*.

Hard to call anything a silver lining in the face of such devastation, but of course there was one. It could have been *much* worse.

So the people of Earth started digging out, settling in on the high ground . . . and keeping an eye out over their shoulders to see what Doc and Sneezy were going to do.

MARS WAS FULL.

Earth governments didn't like it, but had to accept it. The door was closed for the moment. If we took one more person from Earth, she'd have to learn to breathe mighty thin air with zero oxygen in it. We were having enough trouble feeding the refugees we had. Mars had never been known as an agricultural planet.

But we were trying. Lord knows we were trying.

The months after Grumpy saw the most intensive construction human beings have ever undertaken.

On Mars, all Navy enlistments were extended indefinitely.

The economy took a terrible hit with the closure of the tourist industry, but we had power and we had food, and we simply stopped all trading with Earth and switched to a credit, moneyless economy: You work at what needs doing, or you don't get food. Computers kept track of what needed doing, and of who was doing what, and all working citizens and refugees got enough to get by on.

But tensions were high, and for the first time an armed militia was formed to quell violence, especially from the displaced, if and when it happened. Pretty soon we were calling it the Martian Army.

With squeezer technology we hollowed out vast underground bunkers in the bedrock. When they were finished they would become home—temporarily, we hoped—to the poorest of Earth's teeming, displaced millions. But not until we finished the equally extensive underground farms so we'd have something to feed them. Three hots and a cot, that was the promise, with rooms for families and all the work you can handle, then back to Earth as soon your home country got back on its feet.

Which might be never, but no one wanted to think about that yet.

On Earth, entire cities were planned, ground was broken, and the millions of homeless were put to work building them. They were all located above the high-water marks Grumpy had left, and safely away from fault zones.

Famine stalked the planet. Much of the best agricultural land was inundated with receding salt water, useless for crops. What was left was intensively cultivated with grains. Most domestic food animals were slaughtered and eaten and no one expected to raise any more in the near future. Meat animals consume more energy than they provide as food. For now, pretty much everyone but the very rich became vegetarians. There was no choice in the matter. For the duration, it was going to be rice, wheat, corn, and soybeans for breakfast, lunch, and dinner. Vegetables were a luxury, something for Sunday. Cans of Spam sold for a thousand dollars, in gold only.

In most of Africa and many other places, even rice and bread were luxuries.

And all this was done in a spirit of international and interethnic cooperation, right? It's us against the aliens, we all have to pull together, let's not worry about money and irrelevant things like that, let's put aside our old hatreds and grudges.

All you need is love. Give peace a chance. Imagine no religion.

Right?

Thanks for the nice thoughts, Mr. Lennon, but if you thought that, you're as naive about the human condition as I was.

I *wanted* that to happen, I *needed* it to happen, this was all too awful to contemplate without the normal inhumanities of man added on top like a big turd on a dog corpse squashed on the road.

And there was a lot of that, at first. Truces were declared. Many rich people gave until it hurt. There were so many volunteers to succor the displaced, the orphaned, the bereaved, that it was hard to coordinate all their efforts. The human urge to help out a downtrodden neighbor is the glue that holds civilization together, and it's very powerful.

Then it settled into the daily slog of survival and backbreaking work and always being a little hungry. Other, baser urges began to dominate. I'm all right, Jack, screw you all. Why is my nation getting the short end of the stick? Why is my city, my tribe, my clan, my family, suffering while those folks over there are doing just fine?

Countries are fragile things, as the Big Wave taught America. They can fall apart if they're hit with something big enough. Many did. Most rich countries on Earth have large ethnic minorities of one kind or another, often a lower, laboring class imported to do the work the natives were too rich to do. Resentments run deep. Other countries were cobbled together after a war, or in the aftermath of colonialism, and the mismatched groups within their borders hated each other.

Things got ugly pretty soon.

I WANTED TO quit there because I was pretty certain there was worse to come.

My world had been altered out of all recognition in just a few hours, and I'd never left my bedroom. First I was rich and famous, then a good part of Earth was devastated, millions dead. Then my home planet was transformed into a vast cattle pen—I'm sorry, but the great majority of the refugees were folks who would never have been accepted for citizenship before, having no useful skills for living on Mars—and an armed camp.

And that was only strike one. Doc and Sneezy still hadn't come up to bat.

* * *

A LITTLE LESS than a year later Doc arrived, and for the first time one of the crystal mountains did exactly as you might have expected. The only difference was that it landed in the Indian Ocean. Low-lying Bangladesh pretty much ceased to exist. More earthquakes, more volcanoes. More death and misery.

Still no Rapturists rising into the sky. By now they had decided these were not angels come to redeem the righteous but devils sent to punish mankind's many sins. They were rechristened Asmodeus, Beelzebub, and Mammon.

NEXT YEAR. SNEEZY arrived, South Atlantic. Look at a map, I'm not going to list the countries that the wave swept.

Meanwhile, back on Europa, TECP-52 took off. It had never had an informal name. Grumpy was red, Doc was yellow, Sneezy was green. TECP-52 was a brownish yellow. He was christened Dirty, after one of the dwarfs that didn't make the Disney cut. Rapturists, millennialists, and an increasing number of just plain Christians called it Wormwood.

OVER THE NEXT year three more mountains left Europa.

TECP-13, deep purple, christened Shifty. Or Azazel.

TECP-70, blue, Awful. Or Belial.

TECP-76, the smallest of the bunch, only three miles long, black as obsidian, called Jumpy. Or Leviathan.

Frankly, by that time I was getting a little tired of the cute names, myself. Leviathan beats the hell out of Jumpy, don't you think?

During the years after that, they all landed on Earth. The last one, Leviathan, landed precisely at the South Pole. Unlike the others, which lay lengthwise and half-submerged, Leviathan landed on its end. It melted the ice right down to the bedrock. Then it stood there, a dark, irregular tower about two miles high.

Like the others, it did nothing. It just sat there. You could walk up close to Leviathan, sitting in its moat of melted ice. You could pilot a boat up close to the others—though some of those who did died, of "natural" causes, and many of the boats developed engine trouble.

Then they began to sing.

Shortly after that, the weather began to change.

15

★ ★ ★

NONE OF US said anything for a while after I'd seen all the videos. It was all old news to them, but they realized it would take me a while to learn to cope with it all, if I ever did.

"Seven of them?" I finally said. "Did I count right?"

"You did," Dad said. "No one knows if any more are coming, of course, but it's been a while, and Taliesen is quiet."

"Does that . . . do you think that . . . *means* anything?"

"Maybe it means they saw *Snow White,*" Mike said, with a grin. "Numerologists are having a lot of fun with it. Seven is the number of perfection or completeness in Egyptian mythology. It's a Mersenne, a Lucas, and a Woodall prime number. It's a 'happy' number. It's the number of the Pleiades, the Shabbat, the number of Heavens and Earths in Islam, the number of deadly sins *and* virtues, sacraments, joys and sorrows of Mary, the number of the yang, the number of Lucky Gods in Japan. Also samurai, seas, continents, Ptolemaic spheres, days in the week, and rings given to the dwarf lords."

"It's the preferred number base for people missing three fingers," Travis chimed in. "The most likely number when you're throwing dice, and the number on the back of Mickey Mantle's jersey. All of which are about equally likely to have anything to do with why there are now seven Europan mountains sitting on the Earth."

It was worth a small chuckle, which was about all I was capable of at the moment.

"Any more questions?" Mike asked.

"Only about a thousand," I said. "I can find most of them out for myself, once I get online again. And that will be . . . ?"

"Tomorrow, if you wish," Aunt Elizabeth said.

"I wish." Then something else occurred to me. "Why so long?"

Several eyebrows were raised. But Mike nodded.

"Why did it take so long to dig you out of the ice," he said.

" 'Scuse me, folks," Uncle Travis said. "I've got to see a man about a spaceship." He came over and leaned down and kissed my cheek. Then he was out the door.

"What was that all about?" I wondered.

"It was Travis being modest," Dad said.

"Travis?"

"Well, you owe him," Mike said, "we all do, and that embarrasses him."

"This is *Travis* we're talking about?"

"Yeah . . . but this time . . . let's say people are feeling a little ambivalent about him at the moment."

I LOVE MY uncle Travis, but I won't argue with anyone who describes him as a loose cannon. He does what he wants to, what he thinks is best, and luckily for humanity, his instincts are good. Sometimes what is needed is somebody who is willing to cut through the bullshit.

That's why I'm not still lying frozen under the Europan ice. Travis finally said, "Enough of this shit!" The only surprise is that he waited so long. I'm not complaining, mind you. No one else had the courage to do it at all.

Here's the deal . . . After Grumpy took off, the Navy interdicted the whole of Europa. Because one of the questions that was asked very soon was, were we responsible? It was a very dangerous question, and a very political one. When Grumpy and the others began devastating Earth, it grew even more important. Did human activity stir these things up? A lot of people were dead, a planetary catastrophe was under way, and it's human nature to want to blame somebody for that. Even among Martians, tough questions were being asked. Had we been playing with fire? Prodding a sleeping giant?

Inquiries were begun. What 99 percent of the scientists concluded was simple. Examining photos that went all the way back to the very first probes of Jupiter, enhancing them with computers, comparing them to subsequent pictures taken before humans ever landed, it was clear that the "freckles" of Taliesen had been growing for a long time. Conclusion: Whatever had happened and was happening on Europa, it had not been caused by human presence.

Most Martians accepted that, but of course since we were the accused, that was to be expected. Most rational Earthies accepted it, too . . . but my conclusion is that rationality is in short supply on Earth. Maybe because most of the rational people there have already come to Mars.

Google "Europa disaster," and you'll get tens of thousands of sites that "prove" it was human meddling that caused the eruptions. Try "Europa conspiracy," and you'll get at least that many that inform you that not only are Martians responsible, but that we are in cahoots with Grumpy and company, that we *asked* them to go to Earth and wreak havoc.

The upshot of all the investigations was that the ban on landing on Europa should be extended. Just to be on the safe side. Despite the massive evidence that what had happened was the result of a process that had certainly been going on for centuries, maybe eons, before humans ever looked at Europa. Despite the fact that, so far as anyone could tell, the crystals hadn't noticed us at *all,* any more than a brontosaurus might have noticed the aphids on a fern his tail whacked a hundred feet behind him.

The interdiction made a lot of people feel safer, in a time when feelings of safety were in short supply. It displeased only a handful of people, including scientists who still hoped to learn more about the nature of the beasts and the survivors of those entombed in the various bases around Taliesen.

Not to mention Bus 54, which had a real-life celebrity aboard, plus the granddaughter of a former president of the Republic.

Years went by, and the majority of the public was adamant: Don't Fuck Around With Europa. The Navy followed the orders of its political leaders, though many if not most wanted desperately to go down and search for their missing comrades. An organization was formed, headed by—guess who?—Grandma Kelly, called MIND: Missing Is Not Dead. They didn't make a lot of progress.

Then they de-stasized Uncle Travis for the third time since Gran went into the bubble. That's right. They woke him up when Grumpy took off, naturally, as that event easily qualified as "something big," as he'd specified in his papers when he first started skipping. He stayed out of the bubble for several years that time. But there wasn't a damn thing he could do about it . . . so he skipped again, this time with instructions to take him out in only three years.

Jeez. Only my uncle Travis, huh? Planetary catastrophe wasn't interesting enough for him. But the thing was, he couldn't do anything about *anything*, he was arrayed against cosmic forces this time, not human evil, and he just couldn't stand that.

When next Groundhog Travis popped his head out of his hole, things had gone from bad to worse. Mars had become a giant refugee camp, and civil unrest among these unwanted—and, it seemed to Martians, frequently ungrateful—guests was building. They had formed their own political groups by then, hampered by the fact that they came from all over Earth, from different cultures, without a common language. One group wanted to go home . . . but Earth didn't want them; they had enough problems taking care of their own mammoth refugee problems. Another group wanted citizenship, and Martians were overwhelmingly opposed to that.

It wasn't a pretty situation. Travis looked around, said "screw this," and went back into his bubble.

Three years later he came out again.

"WHEN HE HEARD that you were still under the ice, maybe alive, maybe dead, he blew up," Dad told me that day of revelation. "Finally, here was a task worthy of his talents."

"In spite of the blockade?"

Dad grinned. "Maybe even because of it. You know Travis, he doesn't like to be told what he can't do. But your grandma helped steer him to it. She knows how to handle Travis, always has. By the time she got through with him he was so outraged I thought he'd explode. He told us he'd bring you back, whether to hug or to bury."

I made a note to myself to cut Grandma Kelly some slack the next time she got on my nerves.

"It took him most of a year to outfit his ship for the job," Dad said.

"The *Second Amendment*?"

He smiled. "Yeah, the good old *Second Amendment*."

"What does that mean, exactly? I never asked."

"The Second Amendment to the old United States Constitution was the one about the right to keep and bear arms. When the split came, East and Western America got rid of it. Heartland America still has it, but they call it the First Amendment now, since they repealed the original First."

"Probably the only thing Travis likes about the Heartlanders," Mom said, with a wink. She had what I thought was a nostalgic gleam in her eye. The *Second Amendment* was the ship she and Dad and Travis and Jubal were on when they forced the most powerful people and institutions on Earth to back down and stop their wars over Mars and bubble tech.

"Wasn't it dangerous?" I asked. "Did the Navy shoot at him?"

"We didn't think it was likely they would. We figured that if we came up dry, we'd be arrested when we got back to Mars. But if we pulled you and the others out, they wouldn't dare touch us. And we might even get up some momentum for others to go back and dig out the people at the Taliesen bases."

It had taken a moment for it to register, but I eventually heard it.

"You said 'we.' You went with Travis, Dad?"

Nobody said anything, but a lot of significant looks were exchanged. I sighed.

"Mike? You, too?"

"Guilty," he said.

"But you're in the Navy."

"Drafted, like everybody else. Grandma pulled a few strings . . . as in 'had a word with Fleet Admiral Redmond,' and got me a furlough. So nobody knows I went along, and it's probably best if you don't noise that around."

"My brother is like everyone else in the Navy," Mom said. "He wants to get those shipmates out of there, but he has to follow orders. He's hoping what happened with you will change public opinion, and he can go back with a fleet to go down and get the others. And it wouldn't be right if your brother wasn't along with the rest of us. So he turned a blind eye, and guaranteed the blockade ships wouldn't shoot. It wasn't too hard to get the captains to go along with it."

"'The rest of us?'" I said. "All right, come clean. Who all went to Europa with my crazy uncle Travis?"

"Well, there was your crazy grandma Kelly and granddaddy Manny," Dad said.

"And your crazy mom and dad," Mike added.

"And your aunt Elizabeth," Mom said, "who nobody ever called crazy. And your grand-père and grand-mère, and your aunt Amelia and all your cousins who weren't deployed elsewhere, since most of them are in the Navy or the Army now." She shrugged. "Pretty much the whole family."

"That's what families are for," Mike said, quietly.

Well, I lost it. I just plain lost it. When they had me calmed down, Mike took up the tale.

"It wasn't as hard as you might be thinking," he said. "Of course, we couldn't have done it without Travis's ship, and his money."

"Money doesn't mean anything to Travis when he has something he needs to do," Dad said.

"No, that's Uncle Travis, all right," Mike said. "But once we got past the blockade, I never felt we were in any danger."

"Did you have any malfunctions?"

"A few. But we dealt with them. Anyway, finding you was easy, with radar, since we knew where to look from the satellite photos. You were a mile down. We could count the black bubbles on the radar, so we knew it was worth going down. Then it was just a matter of melting our way down there, grappling with the wreckage, and hoisting it to the surface. We brought the whole bus back to Mars and started opening the bubbles . . . and there you have it. You were in the third one we opened."

Something told me it wasn't that simple, but it was just another saga I'd missed. I decided I'd wait and get the whole story from the family at some later date.

DURING MY SOLITARY day, a technician came in with portable machines and installed the cybers they'd removed during my treatment. Not the same stuff, naturally. Moore's Law was still working, more or less, meaning that the stuff they gave me was about thirty times better than what I'd had in terms of speed and capacity, and one-thirtieth the size of the equipment I'd had ten years before. Cheaper, too.

It used to be an all-day ordeal. They implanted various dinguses in the flesh around your ear. I got my first true cyber when I was six. It bulged a bit, but of course everybody else's did, too, so nobody cared. They fixed that in the next generation, but you still had to wear an induction charger on your head a few hours every week to keep the batteries up to speed.

The cybers I'd been wearing when I got stopped were powered by body heat, which was nice. The new stuff didn't even require an incision, just a *very* big needle (and a topical anesthetic). They jabbed it into my temporal area and injected some cyberstuff that congealed and then organized itself into the different things it needed to be: CPU, memory, transmitter, all that stuff. I'm not a cyberhead, I never tweak the stuff, couldn't even tell you what most of it is or what it does. I never jabber to others about yottabytes and zettaflops. I just maintain the firewall and continuously download the latest virus protection and leave it at that. I store important things off-site in a totally secure, hackproof facility that you have to physically go to if your data ever needs to be restored, which has happened only once in my life.

When that was done, the tech propped my eyelids open—the most uncomfortable part of the whole process—and I looked into a weird optical machine and was told to stare at the white dot. It flashed and I felt a tiny breeze against my eyes. I was stone blind for about ten seconds, and that was it. Trillions of pixels had been blasted into my corneas, reducing my visual acuity by .5 percent—so I was told—and light-gathering capacity by 1 percent. Not enough to notice.

The tech spent ten minutes calibrating everything, having me move around so the cybers could read my nervous system, generating tones in my ears and test pictures in my eyes, making sure all the plugs were plugged in and screws tightened down, ran a quick diagnostic, and voilà! I was ready to surf. The old familiar clock was down there in the southeast corner of my peripheral vision, and all the other toolbars had their icons ready to be called up into my central vision as needed.

I logged on to my server.

Hello, Podkayne. We've missed you here at Marsdotnet. You have 4,785,607 messages. Shall I sort them into text and visual?

Holy . . . I was tempted to just send them all to the garbage. Your mailbox can get pretty full in ten years. I hadn't realized how full.

But then I did a quick analysis, and of course hardly anybody was messaging me when I was frozen on Europa. Not even after I got famous because of the music. All that mail had arrived in slightly over a month, since Travis and my family rescued me. That was more than a hundred thousand messages *per day*.

Holy mother of god.

THE NEXT DAY I graduated to crutches. I put in my time on the treadmill and the stair machine and managed ten minutes of upper body exercises. I was still weak as a kitten, and starting to hurt more, rather than less. The thing about nanosurgery is, you don't look all that bad when they're done with you, no Frankenstein scars or even excessive bruising. But there's still a lot of damage on the cellular level, especially in the muscles, and the process of cleanup takes a few weeks, during which your pee smells funny and you are prone to diarrhea.

Still, I knew I had to work through the pain. I didn't take any dope, other than a few hits of some really powerful Phobos Red for attacks of nausea.

I went to the window once, this time making sure my makeup was on right and my hair was presentable. The crowd down there had actually grown. I had no idea how I was going to deal with that. I waved at them, and they went wild. Weird, and a little scary, but I smiled and waved like Little Miss Mars.

My first visitors of the day were Uncle Bill and Aunt Amelia. He looked haggard, older than his years. I'd learned that he was in charge of what they were calling the Home Fleet, which was dedicated to the defense of Mars. There were two other fleets, Inner and Outer, the first being by far the largest, since it was responsible for Earth and its environs. Those three reported only to the Admiral of the Navy and the Minister of War.

Aunt Amelia looked . . . sad. I'd expected her to look awful, the loss of a child being, according to the shrinks, the very worst thing that can happen to a person. I remembered that Luther's and Uncle Tony's deaths had been five years ago now. They'd had time to adjust, as much as you ever can to something like that.

"I have some news, and a request," the admiral said after the usual inanities.

"Name it," I said, aware of how much I owed this man.

"First the news. You've been promoted to the rank of commander, and you're going to be awarded the Navy Cross for bravery."

I must have been getting used to having stuff like that dropped on my head. I hardly broke a sweat. Commander was two full pay grades above my current rank. I'd wear three bars and a gold star. But . . .

"Navy Cross? I didn't *do* anything."

"The review board thinks differently." He held up a hand. "I had nothing to do with this, the promotion or the medal. You were nominated by Senator Wu, and the board studied the tapes, and concluded your actions were in the best traditions of the Navy."

The best traditions of the Navy. I felt my heart swell up a bit. I am not now, nor will I ever be, a "Navy" girl. And frankly, the Navy is young enough that its best traditions aren't exactly a roll of heroism comparable to the British Army or the United States Marine Corps. But it still felt good, though undeserved.

"As a commander in the MADDMN you won't be in the military chain of command," he went on. "It's a dirtside rank, but it's the equivalent of captain."

"Well, thanks, Uncle Bill."

"Like I said, don't thank me. I had nothing to do with it. Now the request." He looked embarrassed and glanced at his wife. "Normally the promotion would be just a matter of a small ceremony in an admiral's office, and the medal would be given out in the Red House by the president. There would be press, of course, but no big hype."

He was finding it difficult to go on, and suddenly it clicked for me.

"You want a big ceremony," I said.

Aunt Amelia looked grateful.

"The thing is, Podkayne, your uncle is under some scrutiny for his role in your rescue. The Navy is behind him solidly, but the—"

"The politicians want his hide," I guessed.

"That's about the size of it. Public opinion is still iffy on whether or not going to Europa was a good idea, and a majority still is against any more recovery missions. Your uncle—"

"I'll speak for myself, dear," Uncle Bill said, with a grim smile. "If I had it to do all over again, I'd do exactly what I did. But there's some question of contravention of orders, and hearings are scheduled. Your heroism and . . . frankly, your celebrity, are about all I've got going for me to get this off my back. In other circumstances I'd take the demotion quietly and do the best I could at my new job, but the woman in line to take my place as commander of the Home Fleet is . . . how can I put it . . ."

"Incompetent?" Amelia suggested. "Totally political? Earth-born, and of suspicious loyalty?"

"Well, I wouldn't go that far, but—"

I held up my hand, palm forward.

"I don't care," I said. "Whatever you need, I'm up for it. Family, right?"

They both looked relieved. Truth: I wasn't thrilled by the idea of stepping out in public just yet—all those people outside, those millions of messages, it was all a bit overwhelming. But screw that. They needed me, and I wouldn't be sitting there listening to them if Uncle Bill hadn't bent some rules to the breaking point. What else did I need to know?

SO FOUR DAYS later I ventured out of the Red Thunder for the first time.

There were half a dozen Navy guards in the hallway as I crutched my way along, and each stood at attention and saluted me as I walked past. I couldn't return their salutes, but I tried to smile and nod at everybody. It seemed an excessive honor guard, but I learned later they'd been outside all the time I'd been in residence. There was no one else on the floor, which was remarkable in refugee-crowded Thunder City. The doors at the end of the corridor were retinal-print secured. At least a dozen reporters and twice that many determined fans had been arrested in various schemes to get in and get the first interview with me, or to get my autograph, or give me flowers . . . or possibly to give me the gift Mark what's-his-name gave John Lennon.

Yes, sir, my life had changed. I now needed bodyguards. What was next? A staff? An entourage?

We went out through the kitchen, which was deserted, and the back door, where an armored and black-windowed bus was waiting for us. I was hustled inside and we took off down the street.

WE DROVE THROUGH Thunder City, preceded and trailed by police on cycles with flashing blue lights, just like an Earthie ambassador or head of state on her way to a conference. There was no traffic, which was no surprise, as vehicles like this bus were normally used only for the disabled.

It was a very different Thunder City from the one I'd left, not that long ago, and ten years ago.

There was trash. Not a lot of it, but it was a shock, anyway. All the parks had prefab dwellings in them, and little bolt-together shacks lined the malls, too. The shops that had sold luxury goods to the tourists were either shuttered or had been converted to the sale or dispensation of more ordinary merchandise.

It was a cleaner, less packed, high-tech Calcutta.

"These are the earliest refugees," Uncle Bill said, "the ones who've been here the longest. Most of them lost hope of ever going home a long time ago. Now they're losing hope of ever getting citizenship."

I saw lots of children of all colors playing, with Oriental, Polynesian, and Hispanic faces predominant. These were Grumpy's victims. They looked clean and well nourished. The adults didn't look so good. Most of them were sitting, doing not much of anything, and they had a defeated look to them.

"Many of these people were desperately poor back on Earth," Uncle

Bill said. "They didn't have jobs where they came from, and they have no qualifications for jobs on Mars. Unemployment is eighty percent. Materially, they're better off here, and they still have fragments of their cultures to cling to. Most of them have better medical care than they did where they came from. But a lot of them die, and a lot commit suicide."

What were we supposed to do? Welcome all of the Earth's teeming billions? "Give me your tired, your poor, your tempest-tossed." Your unskilled, your desperate, your illiterate, your criminal, your psychotic. Emma Lazarus never got to that part of the deal. A huge number of Earthies still lived the life of a peasant . . . and those were the *lucky* ones, who at least had land to work. Even more in Africa, Asia, and South America had *nothing*, already displaced by climate change, interminable wars, sold out by government corruption and disinterest. Some were the tenth generation of hopelessness, and some had nothing to cling to but the irrationalities of their religions, which told them to suffer in silence or to go out and slay the infidel.

In the "developed" nations things often weren't much better, having raised generations of consumers with the morals of a pit viper. We didn't ask for any of them, but here they were.

THE CEREMONY WAS held at the Sagan Auditorium, one of the places that had played prominently in my dreams when I first decided to be a famous singer. In Earth terms, think the Royal Albert or Carnegie Hall, or the Sydney Opera House, or the Dubai Theater. I sat in a chair in the wings and watched on a monitor as the house filled with a sea of red uniforms. Even many of the non-Navy guests wore red, in a patriotic spirit. There were hundreds of media reps there, and a line of beefy shore patrol between them and the stage, as they had been known to try almost anything to get to a hot interview.

Behind the stage hung the biggest Martian flag I'd ever seen.

It all got off to a rousing start with a speech by the president of Mars, a rotund little Earth-born I'd met several times over dinner at our place. He seemed a nice enough guy, and Grandma Kelly said his politics weren't completely awful. He took the opportunity to deliver a rousing speech urging his fellow Martians to stay the course, be patient, stand up for your fellow man, even if he was an ignorant Earthie. Stuff like that.

Behind him was more brass than you'd see at a John Philip Sousa concert, basically all the admirals who were not actually out with the various fleets.

I'll give him this: With the 'cast going out live, not having to worry about sound bites, he still kept it short, which is remarkable for a politician. In five minutes he was starting in on me, my "heroic" exploits, da dum da dum da dum. Behind him, the Martian flag was lifted and some tape Slomo had shot was shown. I looked away. I wasn't ready to see that stuff yet.

Finally, with a flourish . . .

"Ladies and gentlemen, I give you . . . Podkayne."

At the last minute I decided to put the crutches aside. Taking it carefully, I stepped out onto the stage and shuffled over to the podium, amid riotous applause, trying not to squint in the spotlights. I look like a prune when I squint. I made it to the president's side, and snapped off a salute. He took my hand in both of his, that officeholder's handshake that makes you want to account for your jewelry, and maybe your fingers, afterward. Then it was time to smile for the cameras.

Then the Navy Cross. I still couldn't get my mind around it. Me, Poddy the singer, the Navy Cross. The words didn't seem to belong in the same sentence. I had to lean way down for Mr. President to put the ribbon around my neck, then the sheer weight of the big gold medallion seemed to want to keep me there. But I straightened and saluted. Down there in the front row were Mom and Dad and Mike, and it took all the spine-stiffening I had in me to keep my eyes dry. There were Granddaddy Manny and Grandma Kelly, and Grand-père and Grand-mère Redmond, and aunts Amelia and Elizabeth, and half a dozen cousins. I looked for Travis, but realized he might not be welcome here. I hoped all the hoopla was doing Uncle Bill some good, politically.

Then I was presented with two velvet-lined boxes. One had my commander's bars and star in it, and the other a smaller version of the medal, suitable for pinning on one's tunic, and much more tasteful and less gaudy than the anchor and chain I was wearing.

This was the moment I'd been dreading. Part of the deal was that I wouldn't have to make a speech, but Grandma Kelly had taken me aside for a moment backstage and warned me that, when you get a politician on a stage with a hero, all bets are off. Our president might very well break the deal for the chance to get into the frame when a hero and a celebrity said her first words after returning from the dead.

"If he bushwhacks you," she whispered, "thank him, thank the Navy, thank the people of Mars, and get off."

"Thank Uncle Bill?"

"No! Don't draw attention to him. Everybody here gets the point. Keep it short, sweet, and modest." She looked up at me. "Just like you *are,* honey, except for the short part."

And damn if that weasel didn't do just as she'd suspected. I stepped up to the podium, gulped, and did exactly as she'd told me to do. Then I saluted once more and hobbled offstage to a standing ovation.

"NO INTERVIEWS! NO interviews!" someone was shouting up ahead of me. Not that it did any good. It felt like the time-honored perp walk; I had a strong impulse to cover my head with my jacket. I just felt guilty, somehow. But this *was* a ceremony, and there *had* to be a photo op, which they had limited to my route, back on crutches again, between the stage and a secure area where the bus was waiting. So I endured it.

Something was nagging at me. I thought I heard a familiar voice, rising above the babble. Who could I possibly know in this gaggle of bottom feeders?

"Podkayne! You have to speak to me!"

And there he was, about as welcome as Marley's Ghost. Cosmo, standing in the front row against the barrier, back from the dead. Well, so was I, right? But it was the first time I knew he had survived. It had seemed too unlikely that he would, but later I learned he'd only been in vacuum for about a minute and a half, not long enough to freeze solid, and not long enough for brain damage. He'd had extensive freezer burns; they'd had to replace all of his skin.

I realized he was standing on artificial legs. He was wearing short pants, so I'd be sure to notice.

I couldn't help myself. I had to go over and see what he wanted.

Which was to serve me with a subpoena. He thrust it into my hands and I took it without thinking, just an ordinary brown envelope with a government seal on it.

"You've been served, Podkayne," he spat out, and the media horde all turned toward him and began to press closer. "I'm suing you for reckless indifference causing great bodily harm. *You cut off my legs!*"

It was true. Only part of him had been close enough to me to be included when the stopper bubble formed. His legs had been left outside. It later came out that it wasn't just his legs that were outside the zone. Part of his left hip, a few inches of penis, and one testicle also had to be thrown away as spoiled meat.

"But I thought you were—"

Now he was thrusting a mike into my face.

"Do you have anything to say in your own defense?"

"But you stole—"

"Come on, come on, the world is waiting to hear. We all want to hear you justify maiming me. We all want to hear how you can explain such a thing."

The babble of the crowd was disorienting me, I guess. I couldn't seem to think straight, and I felt a little dizzy.

"Come on, Podkayne, what's your reaction?"

So I dropped one crutch and broke his nose again.

16

★ ★ ★

IT WAS A damn stupid thing to do, I admit it. Damn stupid for both of us, as it turned out, but stupider for him. Cosmo had his following, but at that time and in that place, it was dwarfed by the people who felt love and affection for dear, sweet, modest Poddy. Public reaction was overwhelmingly in my favor.

And the suit wouldn't be likely to go anywhere. Mars is not a litigious society, because we don't use the trial by jury method for civil matters. Both sides get to air their story on the Net, and the public decides. There are perils in this, but there are also checks and balances and reviews, and it works pretty well. Plus, you don't need a lawyer, and Grandma Kelly says that any system that makes less work for lawyers is always an improvement.

Cosmo was from Earth, and probably didn't understand our system all that well. He probably expected his day in court. He probably expected sympathy for his injuries, and may even have expected to sway a jury with his patented line of bullshit. I don't doubt the man would have been pleased to drop his pants in court to show his shortened weenie. We may never know, because no one's heard from him in a long time.

What he didn't count on was my guardian angel, Slomo. It never came to any sort of testimony. Slomo just sold two tapes to the *Red Planet News*, after a spirited bidding war that made him a *lot* of money.

The very next day a two-part show was being downloaded by about 99 percent of citizens. The first part was low comedy, and showed Cosmo getting bounced around by the quake, getting his head stuck in the ceiling, acting like a spoiled child and a clown.

The second part showed his actions on the bus. Martians watched in disgust as he attacked me and seemed to be trying to rip me out of my suit. Disgust turned to cold, hard outrage when, through the magic of a super-high-rez camera and macro zoom, Cosmo could be seen palming my KYAG. After that, he was doomed. After that, everybody wanted me to keep swinging that tripod until his skull was pulped.

Justice can be rapid on Mars. We don't have the death penalty, though from time to time, as in the case of a child murderer, for instance, that clause in the constitution has to be frozen by administrators until passions cool down. But the chats among the jurors—which means all citizens—suggested some highly imaginative punishments, the least drastic of which was the removal of his remaining ball, "since he obviously has never used it."

In the end it was left to me as the offended party to determine his punishment and his fine. I elected to let the people decide, and they promptly stripped him of his citizenship and *all* his money, and gave the money to me. I donated it to refugee relief charities. It was a lot of money, and that made me feel good.

The other part was more problematic. Normally, being "voted off the planet" meant banishment to Earth, but Earth wasn't taking anybody, not even celebrities. No place else would take him, so he was shipped to the nearest thing we have to a prison, which was Siberia. Actually, 1094 Siberia, a stone in the asteroid belt about ten miles in diameter. Nobody had ever settled it, so the Republic, in cooperation with some of the lustier nations on Earth who wanted an escape-proof prison for their thousands of really scary criminals, hollowed out several habitats inside and sent the worst of the worst there. Only a few Martians had ever qualified, but it was filled with some pretty rough characters from other places. When you were sent to Siberia you were given some clothes and a knife, and bid a not-so-fond adieu. Food, air, water, and sanitation were provided; other than that, you were on your own.

On the bright side, in the microgravity, Cosmo would not be needing his legs.

Like I said, no one has ever heard from him again.

WE DIDN'T GO back to my room in the Red Thunder. Most of all I wanted to go home, back to my own bedroom, with the posters of Billie and Barbra and Baako, the bust of Beethoven, my guitar and my first keyboard and my balalaika and my bandura. I wanted to see my high-school trophies and my plush Marvin the Martian and Duck Dodgers, my Magic 8-Ball and my collection of porcelain kittens. Okay, my secret shame, I collect kitschy kats, but don't tell anybody or I'll get ten thousand of them in the mail starting tomorrow.

Instead, I was driven to Pellucidar Estates, the most exclusive of the several dozen private, sequestered communities about twenty minutes away from Thunder City on a private subway. It was a bit like the Malibu Colony down the road from Pismo Beach, before it washed away, or so I'm told. Pellucidar (and yeah, I know it was the interior of the hollow Earth in the books, but Mars went through a period when we were all gaga for Edgar Rice Burroughs) is a big dome filled with about a hundred second or third homes of the superrich and/or superfamous. "Cottages" with twenty rooms, everything from the Taj Mahal to Tara to the Sheik of Araby. No kidding, one of my neighbors lived in a tent the Ringling Brothers would have envied.

I'd known I couldn't go home, at least for a while. Home was besieged by media; it was tough for Mom and Dad to come and go. They had picked this out and leased it for me, and I hadn't seen it yet. It was a modest mansion on a street of modest proportions—by Pellucidar standards, anyway. It was Spanish style, with "adobe" walls and red tiles on the roof, like a lot of the housing developments I'd seen in Pismo. I had an orange and a lemon tree growing in the small front yard, and tropical shrubs and flowers all around. There was a tall palm tree at one corner. It was a Glenn Miller house, an Andrews Sisters black-and-white era bungalow.

Mom met me at the door, along with Kahlua, who rubbed against my legs for a bit before darting outside to see who he had to do battle with to be the Pasha of Pellucidar.

"I hope you like it," Mom said. "There were only three available, and the other two were . . . well, a bit tacky."

"It's great, Mom. Perfect."

And it was. If you don't mind the irony and excess of trying to duplicate California on Mars. I was embarrassed by it, especially after driving by the aluminum hovels of the refugee families. But I needed the maximum security, and any way you looked at it, it was better than a knife and a pair of overalls in 1094 Siberia.

I was introduced to Millie, who was to be my housekeeper. She was wearing a black-and-white uniform, and the first thing I asked her to do was change into her own clothes. I felt like I was in a French farce.

The place was pretty much furnished, with Mexican blankets and pottery and folk art, bright and cheerful. There was a round entryway with a spiral staircase that led up to the bedrooms. The rooms had hand-painted beamed ceilings and mullioned windows. I glimpsed a violet-green hummingbird feeding on a red flower outside.

All my stuff had been moved. My kitties were in a fancy display case. My posters of Billie, Barbra, and Baako had been framed and hung in the main room. All my clothes had been hung by color on wooden hangers, looking forlorn and lonely in the vast walk-in closet. My shoes were arrayed on a mahogany rack, all nine pairs in an area that could have held two hundred. The dressing room and bathroom were furnished with shampoos I'd never used and makeup I'd never worn.

I figured I'd get used to it. Right now it just felt like a bigger, more luxurious hotel room.

After Mom left, I rattled around in the place for a few hours, looking into nooks and crannies. Somebody had already thought of everything. Try as I might I couldn't find anything I needed, except maybe more shoes and clothes to fill out the closet.

I called Mike.

"I hear I need a secret password to get into your new neighborhood," he said, when he answered. "And they suggest crawling the last hundred yards to your door on my hands and knees."

"Kissing my feet is optional," I said. "What are you doing tonight?" Mike was a warrant officer fourth class, a civil defense specialist based in Thunder City, and his time was not always his own.

"I thought I might take off from the dizzying whirl of my social life and come over and hold your hand. Or maybe scrub your floors and shave your legs."

"No, I have nine naked musclemen to do that. How about a little game of kickball in the rec room? You can be the ball."

"Can't turn down an offer like that. Can I bring a friend?"

A friend? Oh my, first I'd heard of that! I was going to have to stop thinking of my little brother as being ten years old.

They arrived a few hours later, in mufti. Her name was Marlee, and I was going to say she was on his arm, but she pretty much had to reach down to hold his hand. She was as tall as I was, wearing flats, and she was gorgeous, with long black hair and almond eyes and an impressive bust, dressed in a flowing apricot pantsuit. I looked her over suspiciously, since my feelings for Mike are as much maternal as sisterly, and if this bimbo was condescending to Mike in any way, if this was some sort of charity thing, a be-kind-to-dwarfs evening, she'd leave my house with cat scratches all *over* her face.

But aside from seeming a little nervous, she betrayed no signs of anything other than affection for Mike. And I eventually realized that the nervousness came from meeting *me*. So I worked hard at putting her at her ease, and soon we were old friends. In fact, the only person who didn't do herself proud that evening was me. I'm afraid that I kept imagining Mike and this girl in bed, and having to mentally kick myself in the big, stupid butt to keep from giggling. I eventually got over it. And believe me, Mike would have no trouble satisfying Marlee. I'd seen him naked many times, of course, around the house, and Mike's endowment was entirely normal, even a bit large. I knew Marlee would be impressed.

In fact, as the evening progressed, I began to wonder if I'd have to hose them down. Footsies under the table, adoring glances, that sort of thing. Good for you, Mike!

We ordered out for pizza, which was slightly less complicated than declaring a Stage Five National Alert, and the delivery boy almost dropped it when he met me at the door. I had to autograph the box top and tear it off for him. We spent the evening playing Scrabble. Marlee wiped the floor with both of us. No bimbo, this.

After three games they left, a little tipsy from the two bottles of wine we'd opened, and the door closed, and the silence of exclusive Pellucidar descended around me. My footsteps echoed like I was in a haunted house as I climbed the stairs.

I did a few laps around the bubble-filled bathtub, brushed my teeth, and climbed into the huge bed.

I cried myself to sleep. I wanted to go home.

MY SECOND VISITOR sort of made up for a lot of the shortcomings of being a virtual prisoner in paradise. There was a knock on my door, and I beat Millie to it and threw it open. Standing there, in a shapeless print dress and looking like she wanted to borrow a cup of sugar, was Baako Williams. The greatest female singer of my parents' generation, in her seventies now and more barrel-shaped than ever, smiled at me and asked if she might come in. She thrust a homemade chocolate cake into my hands and I looked over her shoulder to see if Billie Holliday and Barbra Streisand were there, too, in what I assumed was a dream. I mean, I had this lady's picture on my wall, and I'd been listening to her adoringly since I was two.

Turns out she lived a few houses down from me. She had retired the year before I started my military service, and came to Mars because the low gravity agreed with her arthritic knees.

I told her I had all her downloads, had them all memorized, while frantically signaling for Millie to brew some coffee, rustle up some snacks . . . anything to stop me from babbling.

She wanted a tour of the house, which she said she had thought about buying a few years ago when it went on the market. I wanted to *give* it to her, free. Luckily, I didn't say so.

She finally said the real reason she'd come over was because she liked my work. She was talking about the popular stuff I'd done with the Pod People before "Jazzie's Song." She said she hadn't understood Pod music at first, but was experimenting with it and even thought she might record a few things she was working on . . . and she asked, a little shyly, I thought, if I might be interested in jamming with her a little.

Does an elephant have a big nose?

So that's how I spent the second day in Pellucidar, listening to Baako's ideas about Pod music, desperately trying to convince her I understood it . . . and by the end of the day, thinking that maybe I did, a little. Midway through one song—and let me tell you, her pipes are still the finest around, retirement or not—she called up a few studio sidemen she'd known forever, an amazingly talented group of those people that only the people in the business know, and they all came over and we tossed ideas around.

It was the beginning of my first post-Grumpy friendship.

I didn't cry that night. I danced down the Yellow Brick Road in a blue gingham dress and ruby slippers, with the White Rabbit and Wendy Darling and Frodo at my side. And I wasn't *smoking* anything!

MY NEXT VISITORS called from the gate the next day. The guards wouldn't let them in. When I saw who it was, I told security it was okay . . . and they *still* wouldn't let them in. All my visitors had to be on an approved list. I decided this was a good time to try out my car. I'd never had a car before, never driven one, but I could drive a spaceship. How hard could it be?

So I got in—it's a six-seat electric dingus that I guess you'd call a golf cart, open-sided, with a canvas cover with a fringe on top—opened the garage door, put it in gear, stepped on a pedal, and nothing happened except some red lights went on in the back. Ah. Brakes. So I stepped on the other pedal and lurched backwards into a tool cabinet. Clue number one: R probably means "Reverse," not "Ride," as I had assumed. The tool cabinet was going to need some work. I looked for a gear named G, for "Go," but there wasn't one. I tried D, for "Dear me, this is harder than I thought," and away I went. Out of the garage, down the driveway, turn the wheel to the left—going up on two wheels for an exciting moment—stomped on the brake and almost went through the windshield. But now I had the hang of it. I tooled down the curving drive, and if that guy coming in the other direction wanted to play chicken, I could do it as well as him, and all that honking was uncalled-for and rude, I thought.

Let him get on the right side of the road . . . or was it the left? In California they drove on the right. Was it the same on Mars?

For some reason the ride was very noisy. There was a clattering sound coming from the back and I couldn't figure out what it was. While I was trying to troubleshoot this I sort of hit a mailbox. Okay, I demolished it. Well, it was purely ornamental, nobody sent actual paper mail anymore. I made a note to see about getting a new one, though. I didn't want to piss off my new neighbors.

I rounded another curve and there was the gate, and the guardhouse, and I thought I should start thinking about slowing down. No reverse thrusters, so I looked down for the brake, then looked up. Oops! The guards were diving out of the way. I stepped on the brake and came to a halt pretty much where they'd been. No harm done.

I got out, and the car started rolling backwards. Well, what was *that* all about? One of the guards managed to stop it. Should I have thrown out an anchor, or something?

My guests were waiting inside the guardhouse. No handcuffs or drawn guns, mercifully, but they had a sort of hangdog look of prisoners. They were Tina, Slomo, Quinn, and Cassandra.

I spent a few moments straightening out the guards, giving them a piece of my mind. I said I didn't care what their rules were, my rules were that my guest list was and would remain a work in progress. I had the instinctive feeling that if I didn't put my foot down early and strongly, they could easily come to think of themselves as my jailers rather than my protectors. Baako later told me I'd done exactly the right thing.

So I signed for the prisoners and took them out to the car. They were showing a strange reluctance to get in. Slomo walked around the back and squatted down. He yanked on something and came up with a big piece of fiberglass that had formerly been my back bumper. Attached to it was a bright orange electrical cord, and wrapped around that was a red metal toolbox, open and empty.

"Maybe you'd let me drive, Podkayne," he said. "You're probably still feeling weak."

"Oh, I'm fine," I said, getting into the driver's seat. "I'm getting the hang of this, now that I've got the pedals figured out." They got in, a bit reluctantly. I looked behind me, stepped on the go pedal, and crunched into the corner of the guardhouse.

I SAT IN sullen silence as Slomo drove us at a ridiculously low speed back to my house. It was slow because of the little signs that said 15 that were posted along the way, which meant the speed limit was fifteen miles per hour. How was I to know? It was *ridiculously* slow because Tina was walking along beside us, gathering up wrenches, hammers, levels, and saws that had spilled out of the toolbox. Nobody said anything as we drove by the wrecked mailbox.

"I'm truly sorry," I told Cassandra.

"It's okay," she said. "It's not broken." She examined the bloody towel one of the guards had given her. She held a clean corner of the towel to her nose and it came away clean. "I think the bleeding's stopped."

Slomo's shoulders were shaking.

"If anybody laughs, I'm going to kill them," I said.

"Just a momentary chill in the air," he said, without looking back. He coughed loudly, then again. It was Tina who broke first. She plain doubled over, like she was in pain, and then went to her knees, howling. Which broke Slomo's will, and he started giggling, too, and then Cassandra did, which started her nose bleeding again.

I glowered at them, which just made them laugh all the harder. Okay, so I couldn't drive a goddam golf cart. I'd almost—*almost!*—flown that crippled bus to safety.

"If that parking brake hadn't been on," Slomo said, "you'd have gone right *through* that guard shack!"

"I'll bet those guards are going to put in for hazard pay!"

Ha, ha, another county heard from. You want to make something of it?

***"CASTILLO ENCANTADO?"* SLOMO** asked, as he eased us into the driveway.

"What are you talking about?"

"The name of your place," he said, pointing. Sure enough, there was a small sign swinging from a wrought-iron stand. I hadn't noticed it when I arrived the first time.

"My house has a name?"

"All houses in Pellucidar do," Tina said, proving she knew more about my new neighborhood than I did. "No street numbers here."

"What's it mean?" I asked.

"Enchanted castle, I think," said Cassandra.

"Or haunted castle. Seen any ghosts?"

"Yuck. I hate that."

"So come up with a new one."

We tossed that around for a bit, and the best we came up with was Pod's Pad. It would do until something better came along.

Kahlua came bounding up, ready to repel invaders if necessary, sniffed shoes, then started rubbing against his old friends. I bent over to scratch his head, and that's apparently when I passed out.

I WOKE UP stretched out on my couch with a damp cloth being held to my forehead. A doctor was checking my pulse. I started to sit up, but he pushed me back down, gently. I couldn't figure out what the problem was, though I couldn't remember how I got there. But I felt fine.

"I'd like to take her in and run some tests on her," the doctor announced.

"Hey! I'm right here. You can talk to me. What happened?"

"You passed out. This gentleman carried you inside and called for me."

"How long ago was this?"

"Fifteen minutes."

That was pretty fast response time. Turns out Pellucidar has a complete emergency room and doctors on call twenty-four/seven. Another fringe benefit of the rich and famous.

"But I feel fine." It was true. I felt rested, and stronger than I had even this morning. In fact, I felt like I'd had a full night's sleep.

What I wasn't ready to tell anyone yet was that I'd gone to that strange place I'd begun to think of as the inside of the bubble.

EACH TIME I returned there, I had a stronger sense of location.

How often had I returned? It was hard to say. During my recovery I slept a lot, as surgery patients do. I estimated I had it about twice a week, something like that. This was the first time I'd had it during my waking hours, and it seemed to have knocked me out. I was told that I'd been unconscious for just about ten minutes, that I hadn't seemed in any distress, that I'd been breathing deeply and had a faint smile on my face.

Whatever had happened, it clearly was not an epileptic seizure. People who have those are disoriented when they come out, and I felt fresh as a daisy. I was ready to rassle alligators. I was hungry.

The doctor had me hold out my arms and touch my nose with my fingertips, and I nailed it. He had me walk a straight line, heel to toe. There were a dozen little tests like that, and I aced them all. At last he shrugged.

"There are many kinds of seizures," he said. "I'm going to have to put it down to a plain old-fashioned fainting spell, caused by blood leaving your head when you tried to stand up. Even though your blood pressure is fine. And I'd recommend you get those other tests done, let us take a look at your brain."

I knew something he didn't know, which was that I'd gone to that place that isn't a place. I wanted to keep that for myself.

AFTER THE EXCITEMENT settled down I sent Millie to the kitchen to fix snacks and drinks for everybody. We talked of old times for a while. Music with Cassandra and Quinn, the bus trip with Tina and Slomo. It felt good to have them there. Tina and Slomo and I were a small group of expatriates living in a foreign country, our old country being the previous decade.

Quinn and Cassandra were links to my musical past. They'd moved on, making money off the tracks we'd burned before "Jazzie's Song," and moving in and out of groups exploring and expanding Pod music. If anyone was going to help me get hip to it, it was these two.

Turned out they weren't there just to rehash old times, though. Tina soon got to the point, and she was direct about it.

"I'd like to talk to you about your career," she said.

"Career?" I hadn't spent much time thinking about that.

"If you want to keep on singing, you have some choices to make."

I guess it was obvious I wasn't going to be playing piano bars and coffeehouses if I was going to perform in public.

"What's your point?" I asked.

"Simple. You need management, and I'm applying for the job."

She didn't try to sell me on it; she sat back in her chair and let me think it over. What became clear to me pretty soon was that I wasn't even prepared to set foot outside Pellucidar. I wouldn't know how to go about it. All those people outside my hotel room, the endless stories I'd seen in all the news media, that monstrous queue of messages waiting for me to delete or answer . . .

"Will you screen my messages and answer my fan mail?"

"Of course. That's part of the job."

"Then you're hired."

THERE WAS A lot more to it than that, of course, but that's how it began, with a handshake. She would hire a top public-relations person, and a staff to sort through the messages. She would book my first post-Europa concerts.

"That will be tricky, since you're still in the Navy," she said. "But I've talked to some people in the Madmen, strictly informally, and they all feel that the Navy won't interfere with a reasonable number of private gigs because it's good for the Navy. There's talk of a big tour, a morale builder, mostly to Earth. If that's what they want, that's what you'll do, of course. But you'd own all the rights to recordings of those tours. The Navy is barred by law from profiting on artistic creations or performances by personnel."

"A tour of Earth?" I said. "Do I have to?"

"Legally, yes. Practically, you're too big for them to really push around, and if you put your foot down they'd probably never ask. But it would be a mistake. For one thing, nobody can count on getting out of the armed forces these days. They can extend your enlistment indefinitely. For another thing . . . hell, they *need* it, Podkayne. Morale is very low in the Earth-based forces. It would be the patriotic thing to do, and frankly, if they ask you to go and you don't do it, I'd have to resign."

"Oh, don't worry, I'll go where they send me," I said. "I'll go where I'm needed. I just don't have to like it."

"Nobody does. But we do what we have to."

There were lots more details to iron out, but most of them I could answer quickly: You handle that. That's what I'm paying you for. The matter of pay was easy, too. She named a salary that seemed reasonable to me, and she'd have the option of taking that or a percentage of what we made, as an incentive.

Then she and Slomo took off, and Quinn and Cassandra got together in the room I'd set aside for my instruments and other equipment. We played around with some ideas, and Quinn made up a list and called some contractors to have the room converted into a real studio. They said they could have it all done in twenty-four hours.

By the time they left I was beginning to feel more engaged with this brave new world than I had since I woke up. I had a direction, even if it was still rather nebulous. I had people who wanted to help me, and I was going to have an actual career, not merely empty celebrity that felt, somehow, posthumous.

I was excited, and went to bed feeling good about myself.

THE NEXT MORNING I was in the kitchen, scanning the day's news over coffee and warm croissants from the Pellucidar bakery—delivered fresh from the oven!—when I sprayed, gasped, and almost choked on a mouthful. There it was, a headline in *Scandals*, Thunder City's most scurrilous drudgeloid:

POD DRIVING DRUNK?
PASSENGER INJURED IN PELLUCIDAR CRASH!

Horror-stricken, I ticked on the VIDEO button and saw myself look over my shoulder and crunch into the corner of the guardhouse. Cassandra was thrown forward and hit her face on the dashboard and started streaming blood. Then I saw it from another angle. And then another, in slow motion.

I didn't bother reading the story. I called Tina at once.

"Hi, Podkayne," her small image answered in a corner of my vision. I dragged the window front and center, took a deep breath, and screamed.

"Help!"

"Don't worry, we've been on it for an hour already."

"But I wasn't drinking!"

"And it's too late for breath or blood tests. But *don't worry,* hon. I handled *much* worse than this when I worked for Cosmo. You wouldn't believe the scrapes I had to get him out of. This is *nothing*. You gonna be okay?"

"I guess. But how can they *lie* like that? I think we ought to sue them."

"Part of the job description. And suing is a bad idea, over something this minor."

"Minor."

"That's right, minor. Believe me, in a few hours everyone on Mars will be back on your side. In fact, nobody ever even left your side, even if the story had been true. You have a vast store of sympathy out there, Pod."

"I don't want sympathy. I want the truth."

"Which is what we're getting out there, as I speak. The problem, my dear, is what I pointed out yesterday. You haven't made a public statement, you haven't made an appearance. The media are getting *desperate,* Poddy. We have to get you out there. Just a few interviews. And most of all, a concert. People want to see you. If they don't see you pretty soon, not even the walls of Pellucidar can protect you. As you've just seen. Gotta go now, dear. Keep watching."

I did, though I was dreading it. My croissants went cold, and so did the coffee.

But pretty soon there was Quinn, being interviewed by a more reputable news source. He came over very well. He was laughing, not as hard as he had in the car the previous day, but it was clear that it was all a joke to him.

"She wasn't drunk," he said. "She was completely sober. She just doesn't drive very well." To prove it, there was security cam footage of my garage door opening, and the crunch as I backed up, then pulled out, trailing the toolbox. More cams showed me hitting the mailbox, and tools falling out. I heard a stifled giggle, turned, and saw Millie. She'd piggybacked on my news window, so we were both watching an imaginary screen hovering over the kitchen table.

"I'm sorry, ma'am," she said. "But it's funny."

"I told you not to call me ma'am," I said, sourly. "Is it really all that funny?"

"Forgive me, but look at it again, and imagine it's not you."

I did, and she was right. Okay, lighten up, Podkayne. You looked like a fool. Deal with it. And while you're at it, get someone to fix up that damn car and *sell* it. It's not so far to walk to the gate.

WE DIDN'T SUE, but we got a retraction and a written apology. *Scandals* knew it had crossed a line. That issue sold very well, but the negative response was so intense it frightened the editors, and a huge number of advertisers canceled, as well as 10 percent of their subscribers. I almost put them out of business, which made me feel very good.

So where did the original video come from? Obviously it was an inside job, and the management of Pellucidar did their best to find out. The men at the gate swore they didn't do it, and I believed them. But there were unseen people in the security department, people who monitored all the cameras. It must have been one of them who did the capture and succumbed to a bribe from *Scandals*. But they never found him.

THE NEXT DAY I traveled into town to visit Podkayne, Inc.

That's not what they called it. We'd settled on the name Kahlua Management, with Tina as manager and only one client. Then there was the Official Podkayne Fan Club, which took care of the grunt work like sorting and answering mail and sending out "autographed" pictures.

We occupied two floors of a big office building downtown. It was a bustle of activity when I arrived. There were twenty people in cubicles just handling the mail. I went from booth to booth shaking hands, many of which were cold and sweaty. Nervous, I realized, sort of like I'd been when Baako arrived at my door. What an odd feeling. I wondered if I'd ever get used to it.

There was a public-relations department, an art department busy making posters for teenagers to put on their walls. There was a media-relations department, scheduling interviews. I lost track of it all. I found I now had thirty-seven people working for me.

I wasn't just a celebrity now. I was a commodity.

17

★ ★ ★

THUS BEGAN THE Podkayne Road Show. First order of business: A total makeover, from hair to shoes.

This wasn't as dreadful or extreme as it sounds. I don't know many girls who don't enjoy being fussed over at a salon, getting a pedicure, trying on new clothes. But the funny thing was, after it was all done, I didn't look all *that* different.

"We're not out to change you," Tina said. "The goal is to enhance what you've already got. We'll stay with clean, cute, girl next door. But we have to do something about that *hair*. And the clothes . . ."

After two days of intensive work, the hair was trimmed a bit, treated with something that made it look an even lighter, glossier shade of gold than it already was, with a few subtle streaks and a bit of a wave. I liked it.

My closet no longer looked so deserted. Practically all my old stuff was gone. Now I had dozens of outfits from the best designers on Luna and Mars. Suddenly, I had fifty pairs of shoes.

I learned more about makeup in those forty-eight hours than I'd picked up in my previous nineteen years. I could even do some of it myself, for day-to-day purposes. For appearances in public, there were three people working on my face and hair.

When the makeover was done I liked the result. When Mike saw me the first time, for once he didn't have an affectionate insult ready; he just stared. Marlee looked me up and down with narrowed eyes, and slowly nodded, then smiled.

"Excellent. Brings out all your strong points, hides the weak ones."

I wanted to ask her what the weak ones were, but didn't, because as far as I could see she didn't have any weak points at all.

Even Mom and Dad approved, which was a big relief, as they had been dubious, afraid Tina was going to tart me up in some ridiculous avant-garde rags. Grandma Kelly had much the same reaction as Marlee: a cold appraisal, then a satisfied nod.

I felt reborn, for the second time.

WE STARTED MY emergence into the public sphere with interviews.

We completely ignored the cesspools of the drudges and went only with the most high-class people. Tina was always at my side, just out of camera range. The agreements were strict, and in writing. Questions were submitted beforehand, and Tina and I rejected anything we didn't feel comfortable with. The camera and the operator—Slomo—were ours, so we kept the originals, no outtakes mysteriously turning up on the Net afterward. And we got something nobody *ever* got: Final cut. Those were the terms. Your interviewer showed up at our studio, asked softball questions, and edited it right there, on our equipment.

They hated it, of course, but journalism, especially celebrity journalism, had long ago sunk past the point where independence was something worth the fight. Nobody refused our conditions.

And after all, what did it really matter? I wasn't part of the government, making public policy. I wasn't a businesswoman caught with her hand in the till. I was just a singer, with an interesting story to tell.

Actually, they got off lucky, in my humble opinion. Lots of A-list stars—still hard to think of myself on that list—charged big bucks for interviews, and the ladies and gentlemen of the press paid gladly. We did it for free. And we didn't have anything to cover up; there were no scandals to dig out, unless you want to call a little spot of nepotism by Uncle

Bill getting my Europa posting a scandal. But that never came up. Frankly, if it had, I'd have cheerfully admitted it.

No, the only even vaguely controversial questions I faced were about Cosmo, and my "drunk" drive through Pellucidar, and I didn't even dodge them. With Cosmo, I admitted I'd never liked him, but suggested the tapes spoke for themselves.

As for Ms. Poddy's Wild Ride, I had practiced looking shame-faced—it didn't take much practice—and admitted I'd gotten in over my head. Then the interviewer would show the tape, and we'd both laugh.

"Good work, Pod," Tina said, after the first time we tried it. "It humanizes you, makes people like you. We've all felt like fools from time to time."

"Yeah, but not usually for an audience of billions."

Even Kahlua got into the act. During one interview at Pod's Pad, he climbed up into my lap and started purring so loud the sound engineer had to adjust his levels. You should have seen the guy who was interviewing me . . . can't recall his name, they all sort of look the same. You'd have thought he'd just broken the story of the first Grumpy eruption. *Podkayne has a cat!* It was the headline of the day. The next day, pet shops from Luna to Pluto reported a surge in cat sales. Birman cats in particular commanded a premium. Throughout the System, male Birmans were introduced by breeders (the only ones authorized to have fertile cats, in most countries) to female Birmans and encouraged to crank out kittens ASAP, if you please. Four months later every girl who could afford one had a black-faced kitten on her shoulder.

If I'd had any idea, I'd have kept Kahlua's existence a secret. But the . . . ah, the cat was out of the bag. I hoped they all went to good homes.

I ONLY DID five interviews, and I limited my public appearances to three per week. I didn't want to be seen with politicians, business leaders, entertainment-industry moguls. I turned them all down flat, or I could have been eating rubber chicken six times a day and listening to pitches for endorsements, lines of clothing, action figures, and movie deals in all the time between.

"None of that," I told Tina early on. "I'm not an actress, I'm not going to be a brand name, and I've already met all the politicians I want to meet."

"Fine," she said. "That's what I was going to advise, anyway. I'm not here to make you famous, you're already that, and I'm not here to make you rich, ditto. Believe it or not, after all those years with Cosmo, I just want to do something for art, and maybe for some good causes. What do you think of that?"

I thought it sounded damn good. So my first public outing was a visit to a hospital treating wounded Navy people. The facility was locked down, no pimparazzi allowed, just me and Slomo and my two bodyguards, who knew how to keep discreetly in the background.

Public relations? I guess so, but it was from the heart. I didn't even try not to cry. There's a time for crying. I talked to dozens of them: maimed, gassed, irradiated, some of them incurably blind, missing limbs.

I sang for them, and I was awful, but they didn't seem to care.

I was still getting up to speed on the situation, hadn't realized the Martian presence on Earth was going so badly, but from the stories I heard, I knew I had to learn more. I began to see why there was growing sentiment here at home to pull the troops out and let Earth go to hell on its own terms. The mission had begun as humanitarian, but we couldn't help everybody, and there were those on Earth who still blamed us for Grumpy and friends. And there were those who just plain resented our presence, had resented it for more than two decades now, and resented even our help.

I'd have to talk it over with Mike and see what he thought.

That same week I visited my old school, good old Burroughs High (go Fighting Soraks!), and the next week the music department at Marinaris U. I was warmly received at both places, and each time the day was proclaimed Podkayne Day. If I visited City Hall or the Senate, they'd proclaim it Podkayne Day, too. Enough!

At each place I went it was just me, Tina, and Slomo, plus a certain number of police to keep the other media away. (I visited a police station early on, signed autographs for everybody, and they were solidly on my side. Another bit of PR magic from Tina that I never would have thought of.) We arrived and departed like thieves in the night, usually managing to fool the pooparazzi.

* * *

TINA SUGGESTED IT would be diplomatic to throw a housewarming party and meet some of the neighbors. It sounded okay to me, especially since I didn't have to do the planning except for choosing the guests. Mom's catering company brought the food, and I didn't go overboard on it with expensive and hard-to-get meats and such. I knew a lot of these people would expect it, but screw them. I couldn't eat like that, in good conscience, when children were starving on Earth. The menu was strictly vegetarian.

The guest list was another matter. I was shocked to see how many famous and rich people from Earth were now living on Mars in places like Pellucidar and other guarded enclaves. The image of rats deserting a sinking ship came to mind, but I knew that was unfair. I'm sure my own family, if we'd been Earthies, would have fled what looked like the possible destruction of the Earth and the troubles afterward.

Tina estimated the house and small yard could comfortably hold about a hundred people, with a bandstand set up in back. So I took the list of about a thousand names—and you'd recognize pretty much *all* of them—and started drawing lines through them. Some of the people I crossed off I'd have given almost anything to just say hello to a year (eleven years) ago. The only names I wasn't familiar with were people who'd become known while I was in stasis.

I started by inviting Mom and Dad and Mike and Marlee, and the grandparents. Uncle Bill sent his regrets, saying it was best for him to stay away, for political reasons.

I got it down to one hundred, showed the list to Tina, and asked about a few people she hadn't put down. She assured me that, if they were on Mars, they would come. The final cut was heavily into music people, with a few movie stars and a handful of people I admired for other reasons. She chuckled while she read it.

"What's the matter? Don't you approve?"

"Oh, honey, that's entirely up to you. But there will be little joy in celebrityville tonight. Yea, verily I say unto you, there will be weeping and wailing and the gnashing of teeth. Epic fits will be thrown, crockery will be smashed, agents will be fired. You still haven't completely grasped just how in demand you are, sweetness. This is the party of the decade. The party of the century. Everybody who is anybody *must* be here, and if you're not here, then you're second-tier at best. Some of these people have egos wider than Marinaris, and this will not sit well."

"Maybe we should forget about the whole thing. I don't want to make people angry at me."

"Poddy, every time you see anyone from now on, you're going to make a thousand people jealous. Nothing you can do about it. As for angry . . . don't let it worry you. They can't afford to be angry at you. They'll just keep sending invitations asking you over for drinks and a chat—we're getting about a thousand per day—and angle all the harder to be on the guest list next time you appear in a group setting."

I knew a little about that. I'm glad I answered the door when Baako came over, but after that I let Millie do the greeting . . . and deliver the line: "Miss Podkayne regrets she's unable to lunch today." (Thank you, Cole Porter.) As long as I snubbed everyone equally, I figured, the social damage would be minimal. And if I invited in even a tenth of the people who came calling, I'd *never* get any work done.

Every day I seemed to discover a new peril of being famous.

THE PARTY WAS a success, but not quite as I had intended it.

These people were too smart and savvy to jostle and gawk and gush, so I was able to spend a bit of time with everyone. I saw Dad in an intense discussion of history with an actor who I hadn't suspected would even know what Nazi Germany was. Dad told me later that the man was a lot smarter than his screen persona. Mom was trading recipes with the lead soprano from the Thunder City Opera. Mike was charming, and he worked the room on a pair of two-foot stilt shoes, which he sometimes wears at social occasions so people won't have to bend or squat down to hear him, which he hates.

I was dazzled at first, I'll admit it, but less so as the afternoon wore on. The thing about famous people is that there is an initial shock, a sensory dislocation to meeting in the flesh a face that you recognize as well as your own family. He or she doesn't look quite real at first. Then after you've talked for a while, a personality starts to emerge, and most of the time it's nothing like you had expected. Sometimes that's good, like the history-buff actor, but often it's sad. Behind the mask is often a desperately insecure, childish, shy, or just plain boring human being, with all the faults we all are heir to.

After a few hours, and a few drinks, I began to feel uncomfortable. I couldn't put my finger on it, but I kept chewing it over. I watched them, chattering away. And I began to pick out certain people. Not all of them, but quite a few who didn't seem quite right. It was like they weren't comfortable just being who they were, whatever that might be. It was like they were wearing masks, costumes, doing a cold reading for a part. Constantly auditioning. Their smiles didn't look genuine. It was like they'd become a parody of themselves. Often it was the actors, but some of the musicians were the same way.

While I was pondering thoughts like this Tina came up beside me and we both surveyed the crowd.

"I think it's going well, don't you?" she asked.

"Sure," I said, without a lot of enthusiasm.

"Well, take a good look at the men, Podkayne. There's a few here not much older than you are, and there's a good chance that one of them will be your future husband."

I couldn't have been more shocked if she'd slapped me with a raw fish.

"What would make you say . . . I mean, what the hell do you mean?"

"You hired me to manage you, and part of that job, I think, is to tell you the truth. Sometimes it's a hard truth. You are very famous, honey. From now on it's going to be hard to meet people. By that I mean 'ordinary' people, excuse the expression. You can't marry a fan or an admirer, that never works out. If you go clubbing or just walking the streets, you'll be mobbed. So where are you going to meet people? Unless you've got a high-school sweetheart you haven't told me about, or a friend from 'before,' the people you meet from now on will fall into a few narrow categories. Employees, business associates, and other famous people who have to be protected from an admiring public."

"There's other musicians," I said, a trifle desperately.

"Yes, that's been known to work. But he'd better be a star in his own right. Most guys have a problem with a wife who's famous. They'll call him Mr. Podkayne."

I felt sick. Being famous was supposed to be a good thing. So far, it had been a growing series of restrictions. Tina patted my shoulder.

"Don't fret it. Maybe you'll get lucky. You're young, you have a lot of time. You can date, you can wait, you can do anything at all. The world is your oyster."

I don't like oysters all that much. I felt a little sick.

That's when I caught a reflection in a mirror hanging on the wall. It was a strange girl in a strange dress that didn't seem to suit her. She looked awkward, standing there with a drink in her hand. It was me, of course.

"Excuse me," I said to Tina, and hurried upstairs to my bedroom.

I locked the door and went into the bathroom. I stripped off the dress and got a jar of cold cream. I removed all the makeup I was wearing and put it back on the way I always had. Just a bit of pale lipstick and a slash of color around the eyes.

In my closet I found an old dress I'd always liked and hadn't sent off for auction. Sentimental reasons, I guess. I put it on and went to the mirror again. I liked what I saw. I felt comfortable in my skin again.

I left the hair alone. I liked the new hair.

I went back downstairs.

There was a lull in the conversations as everyone checked me out. Was it an incredible faux pas to change clothes in the middle of a party? Ask somebody who cares.

I had a much better time after that. I did notice a few of the women eyeing my clothes with expressions that might have been disdainful. Again, I didn't care.

After a while Tina edged up to me again.

"You have every right to fire me," she said.

"What? Are you crazy?"

"I was wrong and you were right. You hired me to be right, all the time."

"Don't be silly. What are you talking about?"

"I was wrong to try to change you. This is better, this is you. I won't try to mold you again."

"Okay, but it was fun while it lasted. I just couldn't keep it up."

She leaned in closer to my ear.

"I'll tell you something. Tomorrow, the next day, half a dozen of these women will be wearing outfits that look a lot like what you're wearing. Trust me on this."

We laughed, and I figured she was kidding.

She wasn't, and she was right.

I GOT RID of almost all the new clothes and shopped for what pleased me. Confession: I kept the shoes. Throw out perfectly good shoes? Get real.

ALL THIS PREPARATION was really in aid of The Concerts. I knew I was going to have to perform in public again, and I had the worst case of stage fright I've ever had, and I wasn't even onstage.

There were going to be five concerts. As soon as they were announced, the orders started coming in. Soon there were a hundred thousand people standing in an electronic line for the two-thousand-seat auditorium. More than ninety-eight thousand people were going to come up empty.

When I saw the ticket prices I screamed. I told Tina we should charge less than that. She said that a lot of them were going to be scalped, anyway, for prices five to ten times what we were charging. I didn't know what to say, except to suggest that there should be a random drawing. She said that would be unfair to those who had been alert enough to get their orders in fast.

Something just didn't feel right about making that much money for five nights' work. Would I have felt differently if I'd grown up poor? My nuclear family was always comfortable, and some of my family qualifies as being rich. But I was rich now, and didn't feel the need to get richer, especially considering what was happening on Earth.

Mike came up with the solution. We established the Podkayne Foundation, and I donated my share of the gate for all the concerts. I felt better.

IT ALL WENT well. The Pod People had been augmented with six more sidemen, all the very best, and we rehearsed for two weeks. We worked up a few new numbers, but would be relying mostly on my "posthumous" hits in a more traditional vein, mostly because I was still very insecure with Pod music. I just didn't feel it in my soul yet, and was wondering if I ever would.

Baako broke her retirement to sing a duet with me. We had an excellent opening act. All in all, I should have been happier about it than I was. The audiences were totally uncritical, and the critics were mostly kind, except for a few who pointed out—correctly—that I had nothing new to say. Even they were nice about my performances of the old stuff, which I felt could have been a *lot* better.

And then it was done, my recuperation period was at an end, and the Navy took over my life again. They promptly sent me and the band to Earth for a "Goodwill Tour." I never in my wildest nightmares thought I'd be eager to go to Earth, but to tell the truth, it felt a little like an escape. I was itching to go.

18

★ ★ ★

SO WERE THE last several months a Cinderella story, or what?

I said it felt like an escape to leave, but the prison was really velvet-lined. Let's not bitch and moan. Believe me, I had a very good idea of just how lucky I'd been.

But Cinderella turns into a pumpkin, or breaks her glass slippers and cuts her feet to ribbons, or something like that. I can't remember, but I know it wasn't pretty.

I had avoided the worst of the pumpkin carving, though there were still a lot of people who wanted a piece of me. None of my closetful of new shoes were made of glass, though there was one sexy plexi see-through number with two-inch heels . . .

Never mind. Here the story takes a sharp turn toward Dante's *Inferno*. A descent straight into Hell. But only as an observer, like Dante. And I didn't even make it anywhere near the Ninth Circle.

THE SHIP THAT took me and my crew to Earth was the *Guardian of Peace*, and it didn't bear much resemblance to any Navy ship I'd ever seen ten years ago. It was classed a cruiser, and we traveled with an escort of three destroyers, all built five years ago: *Utopia*, *Elysium*, and

Isidis. Those smaller ships were purpose-built to be deadly, armed to the teeth with everything short of bubble generators. Before Grumpy, the Navy hadn't been designed for ground combat, and we were still catching up. Most of our ships had been like the *Guardian,* intended to carry troops and smaller, more agile defending vehicles. Any hostilities, it had been assumed, would happen in space.

But now most Navy activities happened on the ground, on Earth, and the natives could be very hostile. So the *Guardian* was ugly, retrofitted with slapdash armor welded all over her once-lovely hull. It would stop small-arms fire, 50-caliber machine-gun rounds, grenades, and suffer only minimal damage from small ground-to-air missiles. Anything incoming bigger than that, in the air or on the ground, was supposed to be handled by her destroyer escort.

It made her heavy. Added weight was not a big problem with a bubble drive; you just increased the thrust and she could be as fleet as she ever was, but not nearly so nimble. The old bitch's skin (and I'm not being disrespectful, that's what the crew called her, with affection) was heavier than her frame had been designed for. When maneuvering, or on landing and takeoff, she creaked and groaned and popped like an arthritic knee joint and often sprung a small leak or two. This didn't alarm the crew, so I didn't let it worry me. Much.

We orbited for a while at ten thousand miles, and I spent some time at a port looking down on the Earth.

Spotted around the globe in all the oceans there were now permanent storms concealing the interlopers from Europa. The storms were as small—small!—as a thousand miles across, to as big as fifteen hundred miles. Wind speeds near the centers frequently reached three hundred miles per hour.

They'd begun to form when Leviathan arrived. You couldn't help thinking that the obsidian monolith was acting as a coordinator for all this activity. They had been sitting there for almost two years now, each with a Europan crystal mountain at the center.

God, how I hated them.

The seven megastorms spun off lesser hurricanes at the rate of several per month, and most of those rated Category 3. Many were Category 5, with sustained winds of over 150 miles per hour. Those daughter storms themselves spawned tornadoes and, of course, brought torrential rains with them.

The storms were lifting prodigious amounts of water into the atmosphere, to the point that on most of my orbits I only got glimpses of land through the clouds. So much water was rising in the heat sources around the crystals that sea levels, rising for more than fifty years, had receded to levels not seen since the second decade of this century. Much of Florida was emerging from its watery grave. Not that it did anybody any good. Florida had been hit again by the tsunamis generated by the crystals landing in the Atlantic, and now endured hurricane hits at the rate of one every three months. There was no longer a "hurricane season." They could arrive anytime.

We passed over Africa. The countries bordering the Mediterranean were unaffected by the waves, but no place was immune to the storms and rains. Crops often drowned in the fields. The Sahara was speckled with new lakes. Everything to the south of the former desert was no-man's-land, ungoverned, lawless, starving, or dead. No one went there anymore, not even the United Nations relief agencies, not even Martians trying to keep the peace. Bleeding Africa was widely seen to be terminal.

Arabia and the Middle East. With one of the ship's excellent telescopes I could pick out the ghost cities and palaces of the old Emirates and the House of Saud. Down there were palaces vast and luxurious almost beyond imagination, looted and empty now, abandoned since the years when oil suddenly became almost valueless. Down there were three of the ten highest skyscrapers on Earth, man-made islands, all being slowly buried in the wind-whipped sand, now turning to mud in the monsoons that had begun falling, bringing more rain to the area in a week than it usually saw in a decade.

I didn't train the telescope to the north even once. Too many melted-glass, radioactive scars, too many weeping sores on the planet from Cairo to New Delhi.

India. Mumbai and Calcutta, flattened and now washing away. Indonesia, with its remaining population trying to scratch out a living at the higher elevations. The Indian Ocean was brown with topsoil.

Down south, Australia, one of the least affected places on Earth. The shifting ocean currents and wind patterns and storms had largely spared it. The outback was getting enough rain to grow crops. For the first year the Aussies gave away a lot of food. Now, with the unpredictable winds, hailstorms, and deluges, there was no telling if a harvest would be bountiful or nonexistent, and they had sealed themselves off and were trying to be self-sufficient, with their navy patrolling the Timor Sea, the Arafura Sea, the Torres Strait, and the Coral Sea, turning back refugee boats from Southeast Asia, sinking those that kept coming. Not that there were many boats left after the waves, but human ingenuity can always make new ones.

The vast blue Pacific. The Philippines devastated, all the tiny islands and atolls scattered across Polynesia and Melanesia and Micronesia all empty. Bare, uninhabited.

South America . . . I had no Virgil to guide me, only the Net, which was erratic on Earth these days. The Andes created a sheltering wall from the storms that swept the Pacific, and the Amazon Basin, which had been drying out, was green again.

Europe was drowning in rain.

Some of the Rapturists were finally reinterpreting their Bibles. Maybe they *weren't* going to be swept bodily into Heaven, but this sure as Jesus looked like *some* sort of Apocalypse. I couldn't argue with them about that.

ALL THE SPACE on the *Guardian* that wasn't taken up with living quarters and our portable stage and things like that was full of food. Mostly it was rice and flour, vegetable oil, corn meal, soy protein. But there were some luxuries like frozen vegetables and canned fruit, and most of all, candy. The Navy had found that there was no morale raiser for a hungry band of refugees quite as good as candy. We had tons of the tooth-rotting stuff. On Earth, sugar was now more valuable than gold.

It was all grown in the vast, relatively new hydroponic farms deep underground on Mars, Deimos, Phobos, and some asteroids. I hadn't visited them, but I took a virtual tour, and was astonished. They stretched for miles, lit by bubble-generated electricity. With a bubble generator you could do some serious tunneling in bedrock at incredible speed. Just squeeze the rock down to little silver globes. It was warmer down there, too—some of the farms were as deep as ten miles. There was a huge labor force of refugees, most of them eager for something to do. It wasn't enough to feed a fraction of the Earth's remaining population, but it fed Martians and refugees on Mars, with enough left over that every ship that left for Earth did so stuffed to the scuppers with the surplus.

I was glad we had the food, because the only other thing we had to offer was . . . me. And I figured that if I was on an enforced twelve-hundred-calorie-per-day diet, I'd choose a sweet or even a soyburger every time.

I was wrong. We were a smash everywhere we went.

We'd land, set up our defensive perimeters with the destroyers arrayed around the *Guardian*, and sweep into town like the circus train. If they had a big arena we'd set up in there. If they didn't, we'd set up our covered stage and do the show outside. About half the time, it rained, but we didn't cancel any shows because of that. The people were used to rain. I'd look out at a sea of yellow slickers. If there was a big storm, we sometimes had to postpone, but we never canceled, we just waited for it to blow over.

I was safe and warm and dry behind my huge plexi bulletproof shield, which was also used to project special effects. I would stand there in my glitzy outfit, bathed in light, backed up by my band and towers of speakers, and look out over people huddling in the wind and rain, and listen to them roar their approval of my silly little songs. And I'd think, *What am I doing here?* Look at all those people in the rain and the wind and the mud, and they're loving every minute. What must their lives be like *outside* this little island of glamour? In what way was this *better*?

I googled some of the songs of the Great Depression. For every "Brother, Can You Spare a Dime" there were ten like "Life is Just a Bowl of Cherries," "We're in the Money," or "Let's Have Another Cup of Coffee." Total fantasies, and I guess that's what you need when your life is grim. So we gave them all the fantasy I could dish out, and ended each concert with "Jazzie's Song." They were on their feet every time.

Meanwhile, I retired to my dressing room for a stiff drink. Maybe two.

WE ALWAYS MADE time to visit the children in the refugee camps. I would arrive with a sack bulging with candy, and I'd talk to them and to their parents. A lot of them didn't look so good, though no one was starving in the places I visited. Not that plenty of people weren't starving; it just wasn't safe to go there. Many of the children looked far too old. Hollow-eyed. They'd seen too much, lost too much. All of Earth was now a war zone, and we were losing, and nobody had the smallest idea of what to do about it.

After these visits I'd retire to my dressing room for a stiff drink. Maybe three.

WE PLAYED CHICAGO, and we played Katmandu. We played Geneva, and we played Alice Springs. We played Denver, Paris, Moscow, Yakutsk, Vientiane, Lucknow, Poona, Chongqing, Brazilia, Mexico City, Quito, La Paz, Manchester, Bloemfontein, Pretoria, Luxor, Las Vegas, Dallas, Budapest, Berlin, Bucharest, and Belgrade.

And a lot of other places. We were on the road for six months.

What was it like? Pretty much all the same.

You're kidding, right? I hear you say. Just how is Katmandu like Manchester? Well, in the sense that I usually couldn't see much through the rain in my armored limo, and in the sense that, everywhere I went, what I mostly saw was the inside of concert venues and the ubiquitous, sprawling refugee housing where the people fleeing the coasts now lived. There are probably Buddhist temples somewhere in Katmandu, but I never saw them. I'm sure there's something distinctive about Manchester, too, but it was all a blur seen through a tinted window to me.

What was that like? In a word: ugly. Back when Grumpy was approaching, people evacuated coastlines and lived in tents, or simply out in the open when the tents ran out. Later they built temporary shelters from whatever was at hand, varying with the wealth of the country, mostly fiberglass (rich countries), plywood (medium-sized countries), and scrap wood, corrugated tin, and cardboard (everybody else). Years later, before the arrival of Leviathan and the beginning of the wind and rain, many people were still living in these "temporary" quarters, in their own shit. Then the storms began and blew the houses away, like the first two little pigs. People began replacing their homes with ones made of stone, brick, or concrete, whatever was available locally, like the third little pig.

The developed nations started building sturdier shelter much earlier, and when the weather hit, most people were living in poured concrete boxes that had the sole virtue of being quick and cheap to build. They were on the outskirts of every place I visited, with absolutely nothing to distinguish one project from another except the smells of food cooking and the various types of cultural squalor. It produced a sense of disorientation in me that lasted for the whole trip.

I HAD A new wardrobe that Tina helped me pick out, this time suitable for the new and only slightly improved Podkayne. I'd had to buy a lot of bras, which I'd thought I'd never have to do again. They ranged in design from spiderweb to cantilever bridge to armored gun turret, depending on the outfit. I tried on a girdle and shouted *too much*! I'd do like the Earth girls and just let my ass go wherever it wanted to go. Which was south.

I had fifty pairs of shoes and not one of them was comfortable in one gee. They'd all been fine at home. My feet hurt all the time, even bare, but never more than by the end of a concert spent (mostly) standing up.

Gripe, gripe, gripe. I know, I know. It could have been worse. Worse was all around me, everywhere I went. That's why I was needing a drink or four to get to sleep at night.

But something else was happening. I was still having my . . . fainting spells, episodes, dreams. I got away with covering them up for a while, because I wasn't socializing except to rehearse and to eat meals in the ship's mess. Later, I even started bringing my food back to my cabin, and still later asking to have it delivered, the one instance of "diva" behavior I will cop to. Nobody seemed to have a problem with it. I just didn't want to be around people. Everyone respected it, wrote it off to moodiness. We "artists" are allowed to be moody, even difficult; everybody understands.

Then in the middle of one concert—and I honestly can't recall where we were—I passed out onstage.

It was apparently pandemonium. I, of course, don't recall it. As usual, all I recall is that space that wasn't space, and time that wasn't time, and the awareness of presences all around me in directions I could not understand. There were many thousands of them, disembodied, not speaking but making their presence known in some way. Angels? Spirits of the dead? Souls in limbo? I had no idea. These spirits didn't talk, other than to make me aware of their presence. And if I had to guess, I had the feeling that they were as clueless as I was as to where they were and what they were doing there.

As always, I came out of it peacefully in ten minutes, to find I was backstage with a battalion of medical teams hovering over me, debating what to do. *Whew,* just in time, I figured, before somebody decided to do exploratory surgery! I sat up, to general shock and dismay, and was pushed down again and urged to be quiet. I sat up again and tossed off the blanket that had been wrapped around me.

"I'm fine," I said.

"I think you should take it easy," the ship's doctor said.

"I know what I'm doing, Doc, trust me. Now, I've got a show to finish." It was one of my finer moments, I have to say. I probably should have put on a brave face, staggered just a little, maybe held the back of my hand to my brow tragically, because it was obvious from the expressions all around me that everyone present thought they were witnessing a great moment in musical entertainment, as the exhausted but scrappy Podkayne refused to let a little thing like a possible stroke get in her way. *The show must go on!* Nobody ever told me exactly *why* it must go on . . . but I did feel it. Those people out there had come for a show, and I'd give them one.

But the joke was that I really *did* feel fine. Better than before I passed out, which was always the case with these episodes.

Afterward, back in the ship, Tina knocked on my door. I knew what was coming, and had decided it was time to come clean.

"Podkayne, we've got to talk."

"You're right."

"I've seen it before, I should have stayed closer to you, should have been a better friend."

"What's that?"

"The drinking, Pod. It's time to admit you have a problem."

I laughed, then stopped quickly when I saw the look on her face. I reached over and touched her hand.

"I'm sorry, I can see how you'd think that. I do drink at night, sometimes too much. But I never, never, *never* drink during the day, and certainly not before a performance."

"Then what . . ." She suddenly looked stricken. "Oh, my God. What is it, Podkayne? How bad is it?"

I shrugged. "Nobody knows, but the doctor I saw wasn't alarmed. It's just fainting spells, Tina, and I get them from time to time since the accident. And I'll see the surgeon about it today."

I did, and he examined me and pronounced me fit as a Fender. Then he sent me to the ship's shrink, and we talked for a while.

"Stress," she decided. "Nothing to be alarmed about, as such, but the source of the stress should be addressed."

"That's easy. It's a killing schedule. I could use a rest."

"Yes, that's a problem," she said. "I see a lot of it with troops on the ground, and, of course, there's nothing I can do. I have some pills that might help. But they might affect your performance."

"No thanks."

Sometimes the episodes came at night, and no one but me noticed. Sometimes they came during the day, and I'd fall over like I'd been hit with a hammer, and be perfectly okay ten minutes later. What's *that* all about?

I did my best to reconstruct the days since they'd started happening. It wasn't easy, and there were big gaps when I simply couldn't remember. But I fed all the data into the computer and the clever little rascal noticed a pattern at once. It even gave me a little graph to ponder.

The fainting spells with associated altered state of consciousness were coming three and a half days apart. That figure seemed oddly familiar.

So I did a little experiment. I knew to the second when the last one had happened. I had the concert tape, with a counter down in one corner. I made sure to be in my room with a video on me when three and a half days had passed. And sure enough, I conked out. There they were again, the floating points of light/not-light in the space/no-space and time/no-time. I sensed a feeling I can only describe as warmth from one of them. There were others, somehow far away and yet contiguous with all the rest of us, and they seemed to be angry spirits. (I don't know what other term to use.)

I came to on my back, on my bunk, feeling terrific, and backed the video up. Saw myself slump with a goofy grin on my face. Noted the time. Handed it to the computer to analyze. 85 hours, 13 minutes, 42.4 seconds. Or . . . 306,822.04 seconds. Or . . . 3.55118 Earth days.

I already knew, but I checked the orbital and rotational period of Europa. 3.55118 Earth days.

What was *that* all about?

I GOT THE music in me. I got the music in me. I got the music in me.

Did writing "Jazzie's Song" have anything to do with it? Each note of the Europan crystals' song was exactly 3.55118 Earth days long. But Jazzie had been compressed, sampled, digitized, altered. Still, was it possible that some process had happened in my brain during that odd state I recalled so vividly when I was writing the song? Something that attuned me to their cosmic rhythms?

Search me. I'll ask my Magic 8-Ball.

But deep questions like that aside, the information enabled me to solve a problem, which was passing out onstage, or in front of my friends. I knew when the next one was going to happen, and could make sure to be safely in my cabin or my dressing room for the ten minutes I'd be incapacitated. It could be my little secret until the madness of the tour was over.

THEN, AFTER SIX long months, it *was* over. Canceled.

The news didn't completely take us by surprise. We'd been following the debate back home about giving up the whole Earth rescue mission as a bad job. Or maybe not so much that, as an admission that we'd done all we could, and further "peacekeeping" and "humanitarian aid" wasn't having enough effect to justify the lives being lost and the drain on everything Martian.

I've mentioned before that the Martian Constitution is open source, meaning anybody can amend it. Earthies think we're crazy, but Earthies love their incredibly complex laws and, in spite of what they claim, their lawyers. And open source doesn't mean some weenie can insert a codicil to the effect that it's illegal to be Billy Smith because he's a nimrod. There's open, and then there's open. Junk and idiocy is sorted and deleted in minutes, and the poster can be fined (after open discussion and majority agreement), and is banned from the franchise for varying periods, up to and including life for the most determined putzes.

Changes to the sidewalk-spitting regulations can take as little as a week to be ratified. Changes to murder law have to resist challenges for six months. Debates on national policy require a year, a 60 percent majority, and ratification by the Senate.

The pullout debate had been going on for five years, slowly building momentum as dead and wounded Martian citizens came back from Earth. The faction wanting a withdrawal had finally carried the day, and there was no shilly-shallying about implementing it. I'd been so distracted that I didn't even know where my family stood on the issue. Not that we're monolithic in that respect, but as soon as the evacuation order came I sent off a message to Grandma Kelly asking her opinion.

"Come home, Poddy," she said, simply, about an hour later. "You've done a lot of good, but there's nothing more you or anybody else can do. Your uncle Travis wants to see you as soon as you arrive. Says it's urgent."

And what was *that* all about?

WE WERE AMONG the first ships to get back home. There was no big hoopla, no flag-waving and no bands playing. No ceremonies at all. We weren't returning in triumph, and we weren't returning in disgrace. We were just returning, and we were tired.

Much of the family met me at the Thunder City Port and took me out for dinner at Mom's place. I tucked into the finest vegetarian meal I'd ever had, at least a thousand times better than anything I'd had on board ship.

Between the salad and the main course, Uncle Bill handed me an envelope. I opened it, and was staring at a sheet of thick vellum, embossed with a lot of important-looking seals. It was my discharge papers. I felt a sudden rush of elation, tinged with just a little sadness.

"Thanks, Uncle Bill, you've come through again."

"No thanks necessary, Commander. We're downsizing now that we're pulling out. Technically your mandatory service was over years ago. It runs by the calendar, not by your internal time. Anyway, now we're demobilizing most of the people whose mandatory enlistment was extended for the crisis."

I gave him a big kiss, anyway.

"What about you, Mike?" I asked.

He shrugged. "I still have some time to go. And I may go career. The Navy's treated me well, and I'm doing important work, and I like it. I'm still thinking it over."

Over dessert, Grandma Kelly beckoned me to the ladies' room, rather mysteriously, I thought. I joined her; that age-old female excuse of needing to "powder my nose." As usual, she got right to the point.

"Poddy, are you feeling tired? Because I told Travis if you needed a night of rest, or even two, that you damn well deserved—"

"I'm fine, Grandma. I'll see Uncle Travis."

"Maybe you should stop calling him Uncle Travis, dear. You're old enough. He isn't really your uncle, and neither is Jubal. Family, sure, but not blood."

"Okay. What the heck is this about, Grandma?"

She grimaced. "He won't tell me. All he'll say is he needs to see you and take you somewhere. I've held him off, but you know how Travis can be. I asked him specifically, 'Are you about to involve my granddaughter in an adventure, Travis?' Because the last one he involved my son in nearly got him killed."

The way I heard it, Grandma was involved in that one, if only at the beginning. Not being there at the end was what had really grated on her. But I stayed silent.

"Maybe I'm just getting old," she said, "but I've found as the years go by that adventures are highly overrated. A little adventure can go a long way."

"Amen to that."

"Of course, you've been on quite an adventure of your own, and paid a heavier price than I ever did." She reached out and squeezed my arm. "Just tell the son of a bitch—and I use the term with all possible affection—that if he allows you to get so much as a hangnail, he's going to have to deal with me, and I'll be armed to the teeth."

I told her I'd pass it along.

Travis was waiting for me outside, with an armored limo. I questioned him on the way to wherever we were going, but didn't get any satisfactory answers.

We were whisked away in a private car on the high-speed maglev rail to Argyre Planitia, about forty-five minutes away. From there we transferred to a local line, slightly slower, but again we were the only people on the car.

I wasn't sure where we were when we got off, but Travis took me to a Mercedes rover and we got in and passed through the lock and out onto a paved road.

Two hours later we were on a dirt road bulldozed through a rocky plain, then a track that led down into a canyon.

"Very mysterious, Travis. This place we're going. Does it have a name?"

"I call it my Fortress of Solitude," he said, and grinned at me. I googled the term and was presented with a lot of images from old comic books.

"Where's your blue suit and cape?"

"I'm working undercover."

"Well, I'm pissed. You could just have just picked me up and flown me here."

WE WERE ALMOST to the South Pole when we entered a tunnel through a camouflaged barrier door. Stranger and stranger.

We drove some miles as overhead lights came on in front of us and went off behind us. Every mile or so, airtight doors got out of our way and slammed shut behind us. I knew without being told that if our vehicle hadn't been sending out the right encrypted and scrambled signals that the doors wouldn't open and, knowing Travis, that there might be some nasty surprises to any intruder.

By now I was getting a pretty good idea of who we were going to meet. It was exciting, and a little scary.

Finally we pulled into a garage bay and I followed Travis to another security door, which opened and closed behind us. We were in what turned out to be an apartment, large and quite nice except for the location, which would be a long commute to just about anywhere.

"Must be hard to find a maid willing to come out here," I said.

"Robots. Plus, I'm hardly ever here."

He unlocked a door with an actual key, not something you see every day. Beyond was what I'd expected to see: An eight-foot black sphere being held in place with a net.

"I guess you know who's in there," he said.

I nodded. My mouth was dry.

"All right. Now you're wondering why I brought you here. I'm not going to tell you yet. I have my reasons, but trust me, there's nothing to be afraid of. There's plenty of things to be mystified by, but that's another story. I'm going to ask you for one thing. Don't say anything when he comes out. He's on powerful medication. He'll be groggy. Can I count on you?"

I nodded again. And without further ado, Travis walked to a desk and pressed a button on its top. Instantly and without sound or fury, the bubble vanished. Inside, sitting in a chair, was Jubal Broussard.

"—d is with thee. Blessed art thou among women, and . . ."

He started twisting his head around in all directions, but not with a lot of urgency. It was clear he was doped up.

"Everything's okay, Jubal," Travis said in a soothing voice. "Nothing to worry about. Everything's okay, nothing to fear." He helped Jubal to his feet.

Once that was accomplished, Jubal looked around the room and his eyes settled on me. At once he grinned broadly. And he said this:

"Podkayne!"

I DIDN'T PASS out, though I felt faint. Vaporish, as my Victorian forebears might have put it. I found a chair and sat down. Travis helped Jubal to a chair, too.

"So . . . you've had him out," I tried. "You had him out of stasis, and you told him about me and other family members? Showed them pictures?" Because when Jubal had first been put into a bubble for the long haul, I hadn't been born.

Travis was shaking his head.

"When Grumpy landed I took him out, against my better judgment. The deal was, Jubal was to stay inside until I could take him to a better world. A world he could deal with without being afraid all the time. The bayous of Louisiana, specifically, or Florida. Somewhere that people wouldn't bother him, or try to kidnap him for the knowledge in his head."

"Louisiana," said Jubal, dreamily.

He looked different from the pictures I'd seen. And I'm one of the few people who have ever seen a picture of him. The number one frustration to the media all over the system is that no pictures of Jubal exist. Probably the most important living human, and no one knows what he looks like. Over the years Travis and my family have carefully dropped hints here and there, and composites have been drawn, which are usually used in videos about him. They bear a suspicious resemblance to the standard picture of Jesus Christ, though with white hair.

But Jubal is in our family albums, on our computers, under slightly more tight security than the Martian national treasury. We don't have a lot of snapshots of him, but I'd looked at them all many times, and they show a fellow with slightly chubby cheeks and usually a big smile, with a long white beard and bushy white hair. A lot more Santa Claus than Jesus. He's barrel-chested with powerful arms, and he's about a foot shorter than I am.

Jubal had changed. The hair had been trimmed short and combed in a conservative style, and the beard had been trimmed down to less than an inch. It changed the shape of his face. Now you could see that he had a strong chin, and freed from the hair that was always drooping into his eyes, a high forehead was revealed. It was a good face, and not one I would have expected to be under all that hair.

I said he was stocky, but I didn't see any fat under the old-fashioned polo shirt he was wearing. He was in tennis shorts and shoes, and his legs were almost hairless.

All in all, not a bad-looking dude, for an old guy.

"Everybody was saying, 'Where's Jubal?' " Travis was saying. "When the bubble generators didn't work on the crystals, lots of people thought only Jubal could figure out how to fix them, or think up something else to stop what was going on. I got a lot of pressure, and I finally decided to talk to him. Hell, maybe he *could* do something. How was I to know? If I woke him up later and found out he could have done something . . . anyway, I did wake him up. And the first thing he said was . . ."

"Podkayne," Jubal said, and looked at me and gave me a sloppy grin.

"He said, 'Where's Podkayne?' " Travis elaborated.

"But you'd never awakened him before? I mean, after I was born, you never brought him up to date—"

"No. I hadn't. This is the second time. I showed him no pictures, before or after he asked for you. I didn't tell him you were . . ." We both glanced at Jubal, who seemed blissed out. "You know."

"Did he . . . uh, Uncle . . . I mean, Travis, I don't like talking about this with him sitting right there."

"I don't think he can hear much."

"I can hear, me," Jubal mumbled. What he really said was more like "Ah kin hear, me," but I'm not going to attempt to reproduce his accent, other than a few words. It seems condescending, somehow. Just assume that when I quote him as saying *this, that, there,* and *those,* he's really saying *dis, dat, dere,* and *dose. I* is always pronounced *ah*. You'll get the hang of it.

"Sure, but you're not really processing, are you, Jubal?"

"Not processing," Jubal agreed.

"It doesn't matter. He knows all this. I got him out of the bubble, gave him a day to come out of the drugs, sleep it off, get comfortable, and then I walked him through the situation, what had happened, what was likely to happen next. Naturally, that isn't what he wanted to hear. All he wanted was for me to tell him he could go back to the bayous and not be bothered."

"Not be bothered," Jubal agreed.

"I told him that if he couldn't think of something, there might not be any bayous to go back to, ever. That got his attention. So he thought about it."

"And he didn't . . ."

"He didn't. Jubal is amazing, Podkayne, but he's not a wizard, and he's not a god. He had no magic spell, and he doesn't know how to bring down some sort of plague on Grumpy and his pals. He worked on it for a month, and told me he had no idea as to how they made the bubble generators not work; he didn't have a clue."

"Not a clue, me," Jubal agreed. He was flying so high I'm sure he'd have agreed if we said we were both blue monkeys and he was Queen of the May.

"But about once a day he asked for you. By name. He didn't know who you were, just your name . . . and what he said was the 'feel' of you. I didn't know what he was talking about. Still don't. I told him you were Ray and Evangeline's daughter, and that made him very happy, but that you were currently on Europa and couldn't come see him for a while, and that made him sad.

"Eventually we both gave up. We weren't getting anywhere, and Jubal was miserable, as usual. So he took his medicine and got back in the cage, and here we are."

"Here we are." Jubal giggled, and sort of mooned his eyes at me.

"Last thing he said to me, before he started his Hail Mary, was that you'd be waiting for him here the next time I got him out of stasis. Which, when I think about it, was either a damn good way of making sure I *brought* you here, or clairvoyance. For now, I'll go with number one, but I'm not as sure as I used to be."

"I guess not."

"Do you have any thoughts on the matter?"

"No," I lied. He raised one eyebrow and I think he didn't believe me, but he didn't press it. Which was good, because I wasn't ready to talk about it.

"Okay. Meantime, I think it's beddy-bye time for your uncle Jubal." He got to his feet. He was right. Jubal's chin was resting on his chest. We got him to his feet and supported him to a door that led to a bedroom. There were pictures of the Louisiana Bayou country all over three walls, and the fourth was a video of a swamp. I heard a sound, and watched an alligator slip into the water. It all looked hideous to me, but I guess home is where you grew up.

We peeled off his shirt and got him down to his skivvies—which had little bottles of Tabasco sauce printed on them—and took off his shoes and socks. What a chest the man had, and a tummy flat as a washboard that looked like it could stop cannonballs. He was almost hairless up there, too, except a little around the nipples and navel.

I peeled back the covers and Travis guided him and laid him out and

I covered him to the neck. As I was about to straighten up, one of his hands darted out and seized my wrist. It was gentle, but I felt he could snap my bones like dry spaghetti if he wanted to. But I felt no threat, and leaned back down.

"Podkayne," he whispered. "We have to go back to the no-place place."

"What did he say?"

"I'm not sure," I lied again. I gave Jubal a big smile, and kissed him on the forehead. He smelled of licorice and cinnamon. "Sleep now, Jubal." And he did.

So what was *that* all . . .

But this time, I had an inkling.

the heart to do it. And it wasn't like I had any more pressing business at the moment. Later, I stayed because . . . but we'll get to that.

After the first two days Travis took off on some mysterious errand. I remember that from his visits when I was a child. We'd do things as a family, then he'd have to go somewhere on his ship, to handle some business he couldn't talk about. Of course, he was always taking care of business of one sort or another, a billionaire's day is seldom empty, but most of it could be done on the phone. No one knew what he was up to, but he'd return after a few weeks, spend some more time with us, then maybe take off again for a few weeks or maybe go back into his black bubble.

I didn't really mind. Jubal was good company, and for some reason, he seemed to adore me. It was puppy love, which Travis told me was probably all Jubal was capable of, but that was okay, too.

He taught me to sing Cajun and zydeco style. Zydeco is like Cajun, often with the same instrumentation, but is dominated by a back beat like rock. It may come from the French word *haricot,* which means beans. Traditional Cajun can be a one-step, a Cajun jitterbug, or a waltz. Jubal played the button squeeze box and I learned some tunes on the fiddle, and we augmented with karaoke washtub and drums. Jubal had a strong baritone voice and a good ear. I picked up some French, which Jubal assured me would be almost incomprehensible to somebody from Paris. Every evening we had us a regular *fais-do-do*. We played everything from *"Les Haricots Sont Pas Salés"* and *"Jolie Blonde"* to "Diggy Liggy Lo" and "Iko Iko." When we weren't playing we listened to recordings of Boozoo Chavis, Clifton Chenier, Amédé Ardoin, Shirley Ray Bergeron, BeauSoleil, and Buckwheat Zydeco. I went to sleep every night hearing the music and trying to see how some elements of it could fit into my sound.

But that was just for fun. There was something else we had to talk about, and we both knew it, but I was waiting for Jubal to bring it up and he didn't seem to be in a hurry. I decided to wait him out.

The moment arrived when he asked me to sing some of my own material. So I pulled up the karaoke versions of our Pod People recordings and did the vocal parts live for him while he prepared the ingredients for what he called "the best jambalaya in Lafayette, Louisiana." He seemed to be enjoying the songs, but his foot wasn't tapping and his body wasn't swaying to the music. Well, most of it isn't foot-tapping music.

Then I started into "Jazzie's Song," and he stopped chopping okra and turned to face me. I almost stopped, but he motioned for me to go on. His concentration was complete, and after a few minutes he closed his eyes. Jazzie isn't stomping music, either, though you can dance to it in several unlikely time signatures; but he was absolutely still as he listened.

When I finished, he said, "That's the song." *Dat de song.*

"What do you mean, Jubal?"

"Sing it again, *ma jolie blonde*."

So I did. You're never supposed to sing the same song exactly the same way twice, unless you learned it by rote, and I added a few little touches here and there, and found that he smiled every time I did it, no matter how minor the variation.

"Even better," he said, when I was done. "I don't axe for it again, right now, no, but could you might do it again for me, in the later time?"

"Anything you want, Jubal," I said, and that seemed to be it for a while. I joined him at the counter and peeled shrimp.

Jubal and Travis's kitchen was unique. It had to be the only one anywhere that took advantage of bubble technology for such a mundane task as food storage. There was no freezer, and only a small refrigerator. In their place was a giant pantry with racks and racks, each about three feet across, stacked with black bubbles. Each shelf was labeled with what was inside the bubble. That's where the fresh okra had come from, and the shrimp, and the rice, which had come out still steaming and fresh after twenty years. I hoped Mom could see this someday. She so hates having to throw out so much fresh produce at the end of the day because it's slightly wilted, not up to her high standards, and having to buy more the next morning.

We sat down and dined on fresh delicacies that very few Earthies or Martians had been able to taste for a long time. I didn't think Jubal realized it, and I wasn't about to tell him. Jubal would feel guilty.

Myself, I managed to keep my guilt in check and devoured two heaping bowls, pausing only to wipe the sweat off my forehead and toss some ice water down my burning gullet. Jubal liked his hot peppers, but so did I.

"YOU BEEN TO the no-place place," Jubal said. It wasn't a question.

"I didn't have a name for it," I said. "But that will do."

"In you dreams, or in you wakin'?"

"Both."

I told him about my fainting spells, which came as a surprise to him. Jubal had been subject to petit mal seizures, sometimes called absence seizures, since his father beat him in the head with a board studded with nails. He would black out now and then, from a few seconds to a few minutes. With him, it was most often a fugue state. Most of the time he didn't even fall down; he might just sit there staring into space and uncommunicative, or even sort of sleepwalk. It was so much a part of his life that no one was likely to notice if they came in any sort of pattern, not even him.

He was immediately fascinated by the periodicity of my episodes.

"When the nex' one be?"

It had been something I'd worried about, and had been preparing to tell him, anyway, so it wouldn't come as a shock—though I'd thought about locking myself in the guest bedroom. The fact was, my next one was due in about an hour.

When he heard that, Jubal went into a frenzy of excitement. He led me into his laboratory, which didn't look at all like Dr. Frankenstein's, but was mostly a lot of workbenches, metalworking tools, and bins of what looked like junk salvaged from some very old electronics. I looked around while he rummaged on shelves and in drawers, raising a cloud of dust wherever he went. He hadn't used the place since Travis last woke him, some years before, and it hadn't been cleaned in a longer time than that. Jubal didn't trust the cleaning robots to put everything back where it belonged.

When Jubal had gathered all the stuff he needed and turned it all on and tested it, he sat me down in what looked suspiciously like an old dentist's chair and began attaching stuff to me.

"Okay, I'll talk!" I said, as he fitted a headband. "I'll tell you anything you want, just don't pull out any more fingernails. I just got a manicure."

He looked confused for a moment—he did that a lot when people spoke to him, since the main thing he lost from his father's rude psychosurgery was language skills—then he smiled and giggled.

"You jokin' wit' me, yes," he said.

"Well, I sure hope so."

"Nuttin' to worry about, *cher*. All this stuff just to listen." He flipped various switches, looking more like a mad scientist than he had before, probably because of the excited gleam in his eye. Everybody knows Jubal is a genius; they tend to visualize him sitting around thinking. We forget that he is and always has been an experimenter. He makes stuff, and he likes to explore.

While I waited, I watched quite a show on a big old flatscreen he rolled into place. There were a dozen views of my face. There was a regular video camera. There was something that showed what I assumed was my brain. There was a long electronic bar graph above it, measuring activity like the meters on a soundboard. There was a much more complex 3-D, rotating, color-coded representation of my entire head that was being sliced and diced at different angles. It made me uncomfortable to look at it. All those bones, all those muscles, tongue, tonsils, sinus cavities . . . who wants to see that?

I settled instead on one that showed my face surrounded by multicolored flames, sort of like solar prominences. Or maybe a hairdo like the Bride of Frankenstein with a Tesla coil shoved up her ass.

"What's that?" I asked.

"Curly aura. Curlin' aura. I can't think of the word, me."

I found it. (Two minutes till blackout.) The word was Kirlian, and the description of it read like a lot of bushwa to me. Actually, it read like bullshit, but I knew Jubal was offended by bad language, and I was practicing.

"Mostly bushwa, I think," he said, and I laughed. "But I been lookin' into it, me, and ain't figgered out just *what* it is."

"So what are you looking for?" (One minute to blackout.)

"Lookin' for a connection, me."

"To the no-place place?"

"That's it. See, Podkayne, that music you sing, and the things I feels when I'm in that bubble . . . uh-oh, here we go. You skeered?"

I wasn't skeered; I'd been through it too many times before. But I was a little nervous about all the machines. I shook my head.

Then I woke up to see Jubal leaning over me. He was holding one of my eyelids open, shining a light and peering in as if gazing down a deep well.

I felt great, as always.

"I'm back," I said. He straightened up. "Didn't you used to be partially bald?" I don't know where that came from. Giddiness? His hand went to the front of his head.

"Almost to the top my head, me," he admitted. "Then I use some stuff, you rub it on, I got hair again." He looked away, embarrassed. Why are so many men afraid to admit they can be as vain as women?

"Looks good," I said, sitting up, starting to remove all the hardware.

"It thicker, too. Used to be blow-away." He ran his fingers through his hair in an absent sort of way, then smiled.

Good lord, was he flirting with me?

"Looks good on you, the way you've trimmed it. And the beard, too." Better question: *Good lord, was* I *flirting with* him*?* "Why'd you do it?"

"Got tired of lookin' like Santy Clause, I guess." We both laughed. "Lost me some weight, too, when I was in prison on that island, and on Mars, later on." The island was in the Falklands, where he'd been isolated for his own protection for many years. "Mostly it because I didn't eat much anymore, me. But I always got my exercise."

Granddaddy Manny said Jubal used to work out his frustrations with hours of rowing, which accounted for his huge arms.

"I hear you used to almost live on donuts, sometimes."

"Krispy Kremes," he said. "Bad fo' me, I know that. But they made me feel better, so I et 'em. Hadn't had one in . . . what de date? I forget, me."

I told him what year it was. It didn't seem like an odd question anymore.

"Thirty years."

"Calendar time."

"Right, right. Less than a year, Jubal time. Wish I had me one now."

So we trooped into the pantry and found the black ball marked Krispy Kreme and opened it. I was instantly hit by the amazing aroma of warm donuts. We each grabbed one and closed the bubble again, so they'd be fresh out of the cooker next time we opened it, tomorrow night . . . or thirty years from now.

We finished, licked our fingers, and eyed each other.

"Just this once," I said, and we scrambled, jostling each other on the way to the pantry, giggling like kids.

THAT EVENING HE blackened some catfish for me. When he opened the catfish bubble there were dozens of honking big ones, and they were still flopping around! Can't get much fresher than that.

He cut off their heads and skinned them and filleted them. At least I assumed he did all that. As he was cutting the first one I abandoned ship. I'm not used to being quite that intimate with my food. It was great stuff, served with fresh corn bread made from scratch and something called dirty rice.

I finally got him to start talking while we were doing the dishes. And yes, we did them by hand. It was a low-tech kitchen, no microwave or blender or other power appliance (though there was a waffle iron, and Jubal made yummy waffles), just a stove with burners and an oven, and lots of hand utensils. Jubal *liked* washing dishes, liked chopping stuff by hand. Well, Mom was the same way, except the dishes part.

At last we sat down in the living room, groaning from full stomachs, and for once Jubal got right to the point.

"Podkayne, you been to the no-place place," he said again.

"I've been somewhere, Jubal, in my dreams or visions, or whatever you want to call them. What I've been figuring is, my head must have got whacked when I was tumbling around in that bus, and some of my neurons aren't firing like they used to."

Travis and I had taken him through a mild version of the bus crash. It upset him, but then lots of things do. Jubal is too sensitive for his own good; ultraempathetic, he *hurts* when other people hurt.

"That's what I used to figger, too. I always getting these little bads, these petit mals, the doctors call 'em. And wit' me, it was probly true. But I don't think that's what happen to you, no."

"Is this really important, Jubal?"

"I think it is, me."

"Tell me why."

He took a deep breath and looked off into space. As I said, Jubal is terrible with words. When he has complex thoughts to express he tries to string them together in his head first in some sort of logical order, then put them into the damaged word-processing part of his brain. Which sometimes works, and sometimes doesn't. Now, he took a deep breath.

"I think it all connected, me. The no-place place, and the place I go to when I makin' the bubble machines, and the big ol' rocks droppin' in from . . . from . . ."

"Europa," I said. Until Jubal's pronounced a word a half dozen times—even if he mangles it—he can't file it in those rusty file cabinets he uses for word memory.

"Ropa. E-you-ropa."

"Europa."

"You-ropa. That cold moon a Jupiter, Europa. Those things, they got a holt on you mind some whichaway, and mebbe on me, too."

"I figured. But they don't seem to be doing anything to me. I mean, I don't have any urges to help them destroy the Earth, or anything."

"It ain't like that. It . . . a window. I don't think they even see us; we too small and quick for 'em. But I think they live in that no-place place. They own it, like we own this . . . this continumum." *Continuum.*

"So where does that leave us?"

"Probly nowhere."

"You can't use what you know to . . . I don't know . . . stop them?"

He shook his head, sadly.

"First, I don't hardly know nothing. I got little kiddy toys like the squeezer and the stopper, me. I sorta understand 'em, but I can't 'splain 'em to nobody else, no."

Kiddy toys. To Jubal, I guess they were.

"What do you mean when you said 'quick'?"

"They thoughts is slow," he said. "That music you make, it be their thoughts, in their minds, and you have to goose it up to even hear it at all. Computer, it use bytes, little hunks of info'mation. Whizzin' around in that computer brain like nobody's bidness. We slower than that, but we hummingbirds compare to them. Time they finish a thought, why your children and they children and *they's* children born and died. I don't think we'll ever track their 'tention, me. We just too quick, and I don't 'speck they really lookin', and might not care if they *did* look."

"Is there any way that can work to our advantage?"

"I don't see how, me. Mebbe so, but I ain't seen it yet."

OVER THE NEXT few days I got the benefit of Jubal's thinking about the crystals, the bubbles, and a lot of other things, much of it way over my head. There's no point in using Jubal's words, or not many of them, anyway, as they were often confusing and took me a while to decode. So let me summarize, going all the way back to that year of Manny, Kelly, and the *Red Thunder* . . .

"That first day, when I was 'splainin' to Manny, your granddaddy, 'bout how the squeezer work . . . I dint know what I was talkin' about."

He said he had " 'splained" the squeezer in terms of superstrings, and six dimensions, and "twists in space." But he'd had years to do more study while interned in the Falklands, and he'd decided he was looking at it from a too-parochial way. He disproved string theory—whatever that is—to his own satisfaction, and even published some of his results, which was rare for him, so "everybody wouldn't go harin' off down the wrong gator trail."

The real model, he said, contained ten dimensions. He tried to explain it to me, and lost me at the fifth, or maybe, on a good day, the sixth.

So he got to wondering how, if his theoretical model had been so inaccurate, he had still managed to make the bubble machine.

He could remember the moment vividly, he said.

"I was lookin' at a new circuit chip. It was a two nanny-meter thing, so eensy-weensy it was apt to melt from your eyetracks on it. I do that to relax sometimes when my brain hurts. I 'magine I'm an electron just a-racin' around tru them logic gates and stuff. Sometimes I can see a way to make it better, me. Put in an overpass here and there, or tunnel some electrons tru the quantum expressway. I ain't tellin' it right."

Right or wrong, he lost me several exits back. The cyberpatrol had pulled me over for insufficient IQ points in the fast lane, and flashing my baby blues at them wasn't doing me a damn bit of good.

By whatever roundabout route, one day Jubal found himself in possession of what he called a "singularity." He couldn't describe it to me, no matter how hard he tried. He said he could describe the process, but he'd tried it many times before with people who could do the math, and they'd gotten nowhere. So he didn't try . . . for now. I didn't know what he meant by that, but he was on a roll, so I let him pass over it.

"In a few weeks I figgered out how to poke that thing here and there in a bunch of dimensions, and it would do tricks. The bes' one was makin' these little silver bubbles that I could make bigger or littler by goosin' it here and there. And I built me a thing, held the singularity safe as could be."

That would be the original bubble maker, which he'd cobbled together from scraps in his laboratory in Florida. The outside of it was just several electronic remote controls, like they used to use with old television sets. He used them because they had buttons and knobs that he could wire for his own purposes, but the insides didn't contain anything the manufacturers had put in there. He must have had at least a vague idea that he was playing with fire, even with that first one, because he made it such that if you opened it up, the singularity went away.

"I was playin' with the quantums," he said. "It was like that German cat. Dingley's cat. Only it was rigged. Wit' the singularity, I could stack the deck, see? I could change the odds by givin' it a bowl of milk here and a kick in the butt there."

Googling . . . okay, Schrödinger's cat. I remember we talked about it in one of my science classes, which we called Physics for Dummies. It was a famous thought experiment to demonstrate some principle of quantum mechanics. I wasn't clear if it meant that quantum effects *do* scale up to the "real world," or that they don't. If you understand all this, please consult a physics site for more info; the rest of you dunces, come along with me and we'll try to get out of this alive.

There was a lot more about quantum stuff, which I have a hard time understanding when it's being explained by a professional, with good audiovisuals. Confession: C-student in Physics for Dummies. You wanna make something of it? And it doesn't really matter, anyway, in a practical sense, except to another scientist. What we were about to get into might as well have been voodoo. In science, you're supposed to be able to replicate an experiment, right? That's basic. A machine should work for everybody, and not only if you "hold your mouth right," as Jubal put it. There should be no crossing of one's fingers involved, no incantations to the spirit of Schrödinger or Max Planck or anybody else. You shouldn't have to be hypnotized to make it work.

But that's exactly what Jubal did, eventually. Hypnotize me. Finally I'd had enough of trying to understand it all. I didn't see what difference it made, anyway.

"Jubal, let's just admit I'm a dumb bunny and you tell me what you're trying to get at?"

He smiled tenderly, and reached out without thinking and patted my knee. Then he hastily withdrew his hand and blushed like a teenager.

"Okay. You no dumb bunny, you, but I know you ain't got the math. What I want, I want tell you what the no-place place is like fo' me, and see do you reckanize it."

And that's what he did.

"I BEEN IN the bubble t'ree times, me. First it was to get away from that island. Then I went in again for a long time. Long *real* time. That first time I noticed the . . . the . . . I called 'em the points of light, but they wasn't really points, and they wasn't really lights. I'm messing this up . . ."

"No, I was there, Jubal, I know what you're talking about. No time, no place, no eyes or ears or any other senses I know, but *something*."

"Yeah, I can't do no better than that, either, me. Something. I thought about it a lot that first time Travis took me outta the bubble. I hyp . . . hyp . . ."

"Hypnotized?"

"That's it. They hipenized me lots on that island. I learned how to do it my ownself. I hipenized myself, and I tried to bring it all back. And it all slippery, but I got some pieces of it, 'cause I used to thinkin' 'bout multidimensimul geometry. And the first words outta my mouth, I said, 'Where's Podkayne?' "

"That's amazing," I said.

He smiled. "Me, too, *cher*. 'Cause I didn't have no idea why I said it, me."

"You're kidding."

He grinned. "Nope. It just pop out. And then I got a picture of a real, real pretty girl, who was smiling at me and I think she was singin' a song, and . . ." He stopped himself and blushed furiously. "I didn't mean nothing . . ."

"Sure you did," I said, grinning back at him. "Jubal, believe this: No girl has ever been insulted when a guy calls her pretty. So long as he means it."

He was so flustered it took him a few minutes to get back on track. It was enough time for me to ask a few questions of my own. *What are you up to, Podkayne?* Are you deliberately needling him? You've never been a tease. You like a guy, you come out and tell him so. Well, I liked Jubal plenty, but he was so insecure about himself I felt I had to walk on eggs. And as for the whole sexuality angle . . . I felt sure he had next to no experience at it. Maybe his sexuality had been one of the things destroyed when his brains were scrambled by Crazy Daddy. Dancing the Cajun Jitterbug with me was probably as far in that direction as he could go.

So Podkayne, stop teasing him. *Lay off, girl!*

"Anyways," he said, after a while, "I thought about it, and I hipenized my ownself, like I learned to do, and tried to get back to that no-place place."

"Did you?"

"I got back some memories, me. See if you reckanize any of this."

HE WAS IN the place I've found so hard to describe, and given his verbal limitations, Jubal found even harder. But he groped his way through it.

Since there was no time, no space, no location, no sensory input that was familiar to either of us, all I can do is use euphemisms to describe the experience. When I say he, or we, "felt" something, accept that it wasn't feeling something in any way you or I or Jubal had ever experienced before. When I say something seemed "distant," I realize that in no-space nothing can be distant from anything else. Yet there was a "feeling" of distance.

Got it? I didn't think so. Take heart from the fact that if you're confused, you're in the same boat with me and Jubal. Or with me, anyway.

After a while in his trance state Jubal came to perceive, to feel, other presences around him. There were thousands of them. Most were clustered in a group not far away. Later, thinking about it, Jubal concluded that these presences, these abstractions of consciousness, were in the Utopia Planitia Time Suspension Facility, where Gran is. He "felt" that he could read their minds . . . but they were almost as blank as fetuses in the womb. Yet he could sense emotions in them.

He could sense more "points of light" much, much farther away. They seemed to be in three groups, which was odd, considering there was no possibility of numbering anything in no-space, which wasn't a geometrical point, and wasn't a mathematical infinity. But the number three came to him after the trance. He could guess what those points were. They were the trapped souls on the three black ships he had helped Travis trap in big black bubbles.

"I felt guilty 'bout that, me," Jubal said. "Always will."

"They were bad people, Jubal. They would have killed Mom and Dad and Travis and you."

"I know that, me. And I could feel something . . . not right about 'em. In the trance. Don't make no difference. I still feel bad."

What are you going to do with somebody that decent? I searched my conscience for any feelings of guilt about what I'd allowed to happen to Cosmo—because I'm pretty sure that if I'd shown mercy, the Martian people would have let him off. I didn't feel a thing. Does that make me a bad person? So be it. But it didn't stop me from recognizing a truly good man when I found one.

Jubal felt presences even farther away than that. Could they be the people who left on starships before I was born and still hadn't returned? It was possible. But there were others, even farther away.

"Thousands of light-years," he said, and I don't know where he came up with the figure, but I was willing to believe him. If it was right, then it could hardly have been human beings he was sensing. Other races, living around other stars?

Impossible to answer.

There was another cluster of points of light. His trance state brought it back to Jubal that he'd been aware of them at some point before Travis woke him up the first time, shortly after Grumpy lifted off. He tried to remember if he had been aware of them appearing, but that was such a slippery concept he couldn't get a handle on it. If there is no time, how could he be aware of a time when those points of light weren't there, and a time when they were?

But some information had been transferred in some way, because he knew my name, and he knew my face. Travis showed him my picture in an array of other girls who looked something like me, and he picked me right out. Travis told him who I was, and Jubal wanted to see me, and Travis told him that I wasn't available, that I was off-planet. He didn't mention that I was buried under a mile of ice.

"I knew it, though," Jubal said. "I knew you wasn't on Mars, and I knew you was in a bubble." He shrugged. "Travis tries to proteck me. He knows I gets the jimmy-jams real easy."

He said it sort of forlornly, and I wasn't sure if it was because he regretted the fact that he was so easily upset or the fact that Travis protected him so thoroughly. Note to self: Think that one over, later. Everybody had a tendency to treat Jubal like a child because he was—let's face it—so childlike in so many ways. Everybody in my family older than me had a history with Jubal, and their stories always mentioned how immature he was, emotionally, socially, everything but intellectually. I was seeing him fresh, without any preconceptions—or if I had any, I was quite willing to throw them out. Jubal was seeming to be a much more complex individual than I'd been led to believe.

"Those points was you and the others, on Europa," Jubal said. "And how you *shined*! All of y'all, in a way, but you most of all."

"You recalled this after you came out of the trance the second time? After you met me, down here in the Fortress?"

"Yessum. That first day, I went to bed all druggy, and I put myself under, and I knew those points of light were different. They was magnificated."

"Magnified?"

"That, too. But I come to feel that we was touching, me and you. In that no-place place. The others, they was shinier than most, but you was just a-blazin'!"

He went silent, recalling that moment. I thought it over.

"So . . . what does it mean?"

"I'm tryin' to figger it out, me. Befo', I didn't make no contact with nobody, no. Knew they was there, me, but that was all. And I didn't contact any of them others what was trapped with you, not a one. But they was mixed up with this other thing, which I think, mebbe, is them crystal things. And what with you passin' out and all ever time Europa makes a trip around Jupiter . . . it muss all conneck some whichaway."

"You think on it, Jubal, that's what you're good at."

"I think them crystal things live in that no-place place. And you bein' so close to them, and all, I think they connected to you, and you still tangle up with 'em."

"Tangled?"

"It's a quantum thing. A particle can be tangle with another particle, don't matter how far apart they are, they influence each other."

"That sounds spooky."

"That's what Einstein said, too. 'Spooky action at a distance,' he said. But it's the real deal, no doubt about it."

So what did this mean to me? I wanted to know. He shrugged.

"Mebbe it jus' means you gonna pass out ever t'ree and a haff days. But I been wondering if you might be the onliest one who ever has contacted them critters."

"But I didn't contact anyone! Anything?"

"That song of yours."

" 'Jazzie's Song'? That was just me fiddling around with—"

He was shaking his head. "It be the music of the spears, *cher*. I think it may have some of that no-place place in it, if we study on it. I don't know nothin' bout music, me, 'cept a few old Cajun stomps. But I know this is different."

"But Jubal . . . what are you saying? . . . you think they're trying to contact me? Us? Humans?" I sure as hell didn't need this. But he was shaking his head.

"I don't think they even notice us, *cher*. But you done listened in to 'em, and some whichaway that got you tangle with 'em."

Long silence. Deep sigh, from me.

"So what does it mean?"

"Like I done said, mebbe nothin'. I thought and I thought and thought about it, the first time Travis woke me up, and I don't have no idea a tall how to do anything about them things. All I know is, you the onliest one ever touched 'em some way, and something about that touching tuned you in to 'em, and made it doable for you to reach out to me or me to reach out to you, in the no-place place."

And that was it, for that day. I had plenty to sleep on, and I wasn't happy with any of it.

I'D NEVER BEEN hypnotized before, but Jubal was good at it. It wasn't what I'd expected. I didn't get all goofy, and I was fully awake and aware, but some things seemed different. My head seemed clearer. If he'd asked me to walk around flapping my arms and clucking like a chicken, would I have done it? I don't know, maybe I would have, to humor him (and I later learned that that's what hypnotic subjects often thought they were doing), but he didn't ask. I don't think I was under all that deep, at least the first time.

He kept the first session short and asked me to imagine myself back in the no-place place. We didn't get very far. My recollections of the dreams and episodes, if there was any difference, were still hazy.

The second time I figured it didn't work, because I fell asleep there on the couch. I don't mean your standard psychiatrist's couch; this was just your normal soft-leather overstuffed sofa where Jubal and I often sat together in the evenings watching classic movies, since most of the HD3D stuff made in the last fifty years was too much of a sensory overload for him. But when I woke up, Jubal seemed happy, and told me I'd been in a deeper trance. I looked at him suspiciously.

"You didn't make me do anything stupid, did you?"

He didn't seem to understand at first.

"You know. Parlor tricks. I saw a stage hypnotist once. He had people acting crazy, and stuff."

He looked shocked.

"*Cher,* I would never . . . oh, my, no, Podkayne, *ma cher* . . . maybe I oughta should set up a camera, something, and then you could—"

I put my hand on his, which always cut off the awkward flow of words, the few times I'd done it. We didn't touch much. Jubal didn't touch *anybody* very much, including Travis. I wondered if he confused touching with pain, given his terrible childhood.

"I trust you, Jubal," I said.

"I jus' don't want you to think I'd do anything . . . I mean, I wouldn't take any . . . I wouldn't touch . . ." His tongue finally was completely knotted, and I patted his hand and then withdrew mine. I thought the fact that he said he'd never touch me meant that he'd been *thinking* about it. I knew with absolute certainty that he never would, but the idea that such thoughts entered his mind was intriguing. Somewhere in that lost little boy, that incredibly damaged and abused child, was a man, with all that implied.

THE BEST SESSION of all was the next time I was due for an episode. We both thought it would be interesting if I was in a trance state when it hit. Would it apply some sort of double whammy to my perceptions? I was game to try it.

But I began to think we'd started too late. Thirty minutes before I was due to keel over, Jubal was still patiently droning at me and I was still trying to make my mind a blank, but I was too nervous about it. Losing consciousness is never a lot of fun, even if you know you're going to feel great when you wake up. It's too deathlike, not at all like sleep. So I was resisting, unconsciously.

So when I woke up, refreshed and feeling very hungry for some reason, I shrugged and sighed.

"Didn't work, huh?"

He smiled at me.

"You was deep as you ever been, ten minutes before the time, you," he said. "What was it like?"

I thought about it.

"I wish I could tell you something spectacular . . . but I didn't notice anything different. It's all still so vague; it's like trying to grab smoke."

He looked disappointed, but then he brightened.

"Sleep on it, *cher*. It's dreamland, the no-place place. And I get mos' of my best ideas when I'm asleep."

SO THAT'S WHAT I did. And I woke up in the middle of the night with music playing in my head. Blasting in my head, filling me with a sense of urgency I hadn't felt since that crazy time—trancelike, I realized, now that I had something to compare it to—when Jazzie first came to me.

I stumbled out of bed in my nightgown and made my way to the main room, where my recording equipment was. No keyboard, no guitar, not even a kazoo.

"Somet'ing wrong, *cher*?" Jubal was standing there in his pajamas. They had little cartoon alligators on them.

"I need a keyboard, Jubal." Lord, Podkayne, you sound like a junkie.

"A . . ."

"Keyboard." I mimed playing one, and I was so far in the zone I could actually hear the chords I was hitting, on the bare wood of the table in front of me.

Jubal asked no more questions but ran toward his laboratory. Meanwhile I was hunting feverishly for a pencil and paper. Music can be such an evanescent thing, it can be here one minute and gone the next unless you write it down or record it. Right now this stuff existed only in my head, which wasn't a very good storage medium.

I had my head in my hands, trying to keep the musical string in my mind, a haunting theme that I just knew, when I pulled on that string, would let loose a torrent of sounds that would flow through me . . . and then Jubal unceremoniously grabbed me by the upper arm and pulled me toward the kitchen. I followed, and he sat me down at the big, high oak preparation table and brought up a barstool and sat me down on it. He had a keyboard in his hand, and when he unrolled it dust flew.

"Gee, Jubal, you've got a bit of *everything* in there, don't you?"

"Hush, chile. I be back." And he was off again. I started experimenting with just the tiny little built-in speaker. Squeaker, really, but it was all I needed. Next time I looked up, Jubal was hooking up a small speaker and amp, and my minicorder. He interrupted me only once, to spray the keyboard with some cleaning stuff and wipe it up and down with a dishrag. Arpeggios!

I began.

Eight hours later I had "Jazzie's Return."

I shipped it off to Tina, Mike, and Quinn, and then Jubal led me to my bedroom and tucked me in, and I slept for twelve hours.

IN THE MORNING, it was as if it had never happened. Was it my music, or was I just channeling something from those goddam crystals. I asked Jubal about it over breakfast.

"Don't know, *cher*. But if it was channelin', they didn't do it tru me, 'cause I ain't got a creative note in my head. It was you done the work."

"Yeah, but did they do something to me?"

"I don't think so. I think you just somehow tuned in to whatever it is they talk about, and you made your own thing out of it."

"So what are they talking about, Jubal? I keep getting the feeling you know more than you're telling."

He shook his head.

"You got the wrong idea, *cher*. I don't know nothing more than you do."

"But you have some ideas?"

He thought about it for a while.

"I ain't saying I know anything, me. I ain't even sayin' what they doin' is talkin', the way we know it. I don't think they intelligent, not the way we measure it. I think they just *is*, like a animal is. They don't got no plans, they ain't doing nothing *to* us, not on purpose like. They just like big ol' boar hogs wallowin' in our oceans. It's what they *do*."

"I don't get it."

"Always when we think about meetin' aliens, we figger we gonna talk to 'em. Mebbe we fight 'em, but that's juss talkin' wit' you fists. We never figgered they wouldn't even notice us.

"Say they's some sort of gas critters livin' in the middle a the sun. A billion degrees down in there. They ain't chemical, they's nucular, that's how they live. How we ever gonna talk to 'em? But say they like to come to the surface now and again. Cool off, mebbe, or they like to mate up there in the thin gas. Or mebbe they just playin', jumpin' around like porpoises or otters. And we see 'em, and we call 'em solar provid . . . solar . . ."

"Prominences."

"What you said. When what they is, is solar dolphins. And they kick up a heck of a racket, oh, my! Radiation all over the place. Northern lights, and satellites gettin' burned out, and radios all fouled up. You think them gas critters know what they're causin', ninety million miles away? If they knew, you think they'd care what's happenin' on a little freezin' cold speck o' mud and salt water?"

"I guess not."

"I think these crystals, they like that. And I think they done it befo'."

I thought about that.

"You're kidding, right?"

"Not kiddin'."

"When, Jubal?"

" 'Bout sixty million years ago."

Hoo, boy.

IT WAS ACTUALLY around sixty-five million years ago, and you may have heard of it. Little thing called the Cretaceous-Tertiary Extinction? Dinosaurs dying in a rain of flaming meteors? Ring a bell?

At least that's been the prevalent theory—collision with an asteroid, though there're some who still hold out for other causes.

Jubal had done some work on his own. He showed me a graph.

"They's six major skinkshuns the fossil people tell us," he said. "Mebbe seven, if you count the one we're in the middle of now."

"You mean Grumpy and the others?"

"No, *cher*, the one been goin' on for quite a while. Call it the . . ." He didn't even try, but pointed at the word, which was *Holocene*. The ongoing extinctions caused by environmental changes brought about by man. Pollution, global warming, habitat loss, you know the drill.

Here's what the chart showed:

65 million years ago	Cretaceous-Tertiary Extinction
----	
200 million years ago	Triassic-Jurassic Extinction
250 million years ago	Permian-Triassic Extinction
----	
360 million years ago	Devonian-Carboniferous Extinction
440 million years ago	Ordovician-Silurian Extinction
490 million years ago	Cambrian-Ordovician Extinction

" 'Cept for them two gaps," Jubal said, "they's been a big dustup ever fifty to eighty million years. And if you look at the graph, you can see little bumps there, about halfway through them gaps. It looks per . . . periodical to me."

"You think this has happened before."

"Six times, at least. Mebbe more, 'cause before that there wasn't a lot of critters around that left fossils."

"But the gaps . . ."

He shrugged. "Like I said, you can see a bit of a rise in each of 'em. Mebbe the conditions wasn't quite so bad them times. Or mebbe they flat didn't come. Mebbe they didn't need to, those cycles."

"You're talking about life cycles."

"Yessum. The critters we know, certain time a the year they come into . . . well, they get so's they want to . . ."

"Come into heat. Breed."

"Yessum." His face was a little pinkish. "Ever critter has its own way a goin' about it. Some cicadas, they stay underground seventeen years, then they come out to mate. They around a few days, lay they eggs, and die."

"You think the crystals are mating?"

"Could be sumpin like that. Could be sumpin else we won't never understand. Whatever they doin', they doin' it on a big scale, because they be big. Say they makin' a nestin' place, gonna have little kids and bring 'em up. They's changin' stuff around, makin' the environment better."

"Terraforming," I whispered.

"Well, *un*terraformin', you wanna get technical. When they done, Earth might be a lot more like Europa. Planetary engineering, in a hurry."

Terraforming is the fairly wacky idea of turning a planet that's not really suitable for human habitation into one that is. It's engineering on a giant scale, and some of the ideas would boggle your mind. And that's about all it had been up to now: boonboggled. There were a few pilot plants on Mars that dumped oxygen into the atmosphere at the rate of thousands of tons per day. And one day they might give us a marginally breathable atmosphere, say about like the top of Mount Everest in the winter. Last estimate I saw: about ten thousand years. Nobody's built a new one since before I was born.

Jubal looked at me solemnly.

"These little spikes in the graph. They don't look like much. Looks like somethin' hit hard, and then went away quick. And I guess that's right, when you look at the whole big picture. But they's quick, and they's *quick*. These things live on a different time scale than we do. Fact is, these skinkshuns lasted for thousands a years, and it was a different world every time, after. Looks like we might of got out just in time, us."

BY "GOT OUT," Jubal meant that humanity had established itself on other worlds, pretty much independent of Mother Earth. Unless the crystals had designs on Mars and Luna, the species would probably survive.

But would we survive on Earth?

Certainly not in the numbers we had attained before this started; in fact, our population was already significantly reduced. But I didn't see why a lot of people couldn't survive underground, burrowing into the rock, no matter how harsh things got.

After all, that's one of the ways we live on Mars. Would Earth end up with a harsher environment than Mars? Not if this extinction went like the previous ones. The dinosaurs died off, but remember that a certain number of species survived every one of the mass extinctions. Then they evolved to fill the niches left behind by the ones that couldn't adapt.

I guess it was possible that one of the surviving species would adapt to fill the gap left by bipedal big-brained apes.

THE NEXT DAY Jubal said he wanted to play a game. It turned out to be a lot more game than he bargained for . . . but I'm getting ahead of myself.

"Somethin' been bothering me since way back yonder in Florida, with your grand-père and grand-mère, when they built that ship and flew it to Mars. When I made that first bubble machine. Ever since then, people, they been gettin' mad at me 'cause I can't 'splain how I done it. So I wanted to try it wit' you."

I couldn't have been more floored if he'd asked me to come up with the Grand Unification Theory Einstein couldn't figure out, or read Chinese.

"*Me?* Jubal, that's crazy. I got a D in calculus, and I can't even recall how I managed that. I have to take off my shoes to count to twenty."

"It ain't math . . . at least, math behind it, but it only be part of it."

"Nobel Prize winners couldn't follow you, and you expect me—"

"We got somethin' special, you and me," he said, raising his voice just a trifle, which for Jubal was like grabbing me by the shoulders and shaking. I shut up and listened.

"We was both in the no-place place at the same time . . . in this universe, anyway. Now, the *math* says no information kin be exchanged if no time has passed, but me, I got a lots of information. Your face, your name . . . even a feelin' that I knew you." He looked down, then up at me from the corner of his eye. We were sitting side by side on the couch, facing a lot of weird-looking junk he'd brought in from his lab. I didn't know what was making him uncomfortable, but I kept silent. He'd get to it.

"I felt like . . . if I met you, I'd like you. Like I was in ykur head."

"Jubal, you like pretty much everybody, don't you?"

He shook his head.

"I don't *not* like many people, 'less they done somethin' awful to me or mine. Mos' people, I don't think about 'em one way or t'other."

"I think we're all like that, except the most evil people."

"I think you right. So I ain't all that different from anybody else." He seemed to take comfort in that thought. The crown of eccentric genius sat as heavily on his head as the burden of brain-damaged, language-challenged idiot savant weighed upon his back.

"The onliest way I can 'splain how the data, the information . . . the *feelin's* got transferred from you to me is that we got tangled."

"Entangled? Like the quantum stuff you were talking about?"

"Something like that."

"Jubal, I told you that stuff is way over—"

"You don't *have* to understand it, *cher*. All you have to do is feel it."

"Okay. Feeling I can do. I got a Ph.D. in feeling."

He grinned. "That's funny. I like that. A Ph.D. in feeling. Wish more folks had one, it would save us all a passel a trouble." He got serious again.

"Anyways, all I wants to do is try a little spearmint. It just be a game, really. I want you to look at some stuff, and see what you see."

"Okay, I can do that, too. I'm real good at seeing what I see."

He got up and did some things to the equipment he'd brought in. Hooked up the thingamabob to the whatchamacallit, checked to see the doohickey was synchronized with the absquatulator. Made sure the mimsies were borogroving frabjously.

"First time I made me a bubble generator, I was studyin' on this new . . ." He paused, his brow furrowed, and he said, carefully, "heuristic"—he breathed a sigh of relief—"chip. It was somethin' different, and I'd made me some changes to it, see what it could do. I used to do that sometimes, to relax."

Some folks put their feet up in front of the TV with a cold brew. Jubal stares at microscopic computer chips. Takes all kinds.

"I got a little drowsy, me, and I went all . . . sort of cross-eyed. And all at once it all tumbled right into place, and I was lookin' at this thing I'd made, me. And it weren't like anything else I ever seen, no."

"The singularity, right?"

"That's what I called it, but I ain't sure that's what it be. It's a twist in space, and I was skeered of it, tell you the truth. But I figgered out how to handle it."

"And all this has . . . what to do with me?"

"It be the mind that make 'em, Podkayne. And you and me, we had our minds tangled. So I was wonderin' if mebbe you could make 'em, too."

Oh, brother. Sounded pretty wacky to me. But what the hell. What did I have to lose? I settled into the couch and Jubal brought up an image on the big screen that was part of his equipment. It was a real mess, ultrathin lines intersecting with tiny dots, curving things that looked like tubes. I couldn't make any sense of it."

"This was an early heuristic chip," he said. "Them dark things are nanotubes, made out of strands of carbon molecules, and the dots are buckyballs, little geo . . ."

"Geodesic?"

"What you said. Named after Bucky Fuller. This was the first chip that tried to work like the human brain, with lots a connections, instead of a bunch a transistors. A silicon chip, once you make it you can't mess around with it or it just stop workin'. These new chips, you can fiddle around with 'em."

I knew a tiny, tiny bit about this stuff. I knew it was the basis for all modern computers, and the stuff implanted in my head was decades more advanced than this picture. Which didn't help me a bit because the picture meant nothing to me.

"What I want you to do, *cher*, is not so much look *at* it, as look *tru* it." He looked at me with raised eyebrows.

"Can you give me a little more help?"

"You know them pitchers, they look all screwy, little bits and pieces a stuff, and you look at 'em and you don't see nothin', then . . . you see somethin'?"

Googling . . .

"Stereograms." I pulled one up out of memory and attempted to link it to Jubal's implants . . . and recalled, for the third or fourth time, that he didn't have any. Jubal had " 'splained" that he "didn't like to be cut on, no." No point in telling him the surgery was about as intrusive as having your ears pierced; he didn't like needles, either. So I tossed the image to the computer in his jackleg setup, and it came up on the screen.

"Yeah, that's what I'm talking about, me!"

It was a random pattern of multicolored dots.

"You stare at it for a while, kind of walleyed, and somethin'll pop out at you."

I'd seen them before, had no idea how they worked, but I knew how to do it. I stared, and let my eyes relax, and there it was, a leaping dolphin with colored spots all over it. It stood out maybe six inches from the background dots.

"You see it?"

"I see it."

"Now, try the same thing with the other one."

So I did. I stared and stared, and nothing happened.

"Do *you* see anything?" I finally asked.

"Not yet." So we stared some more. After a good while, Jubal sighed, and did something with his machines.

"Let's try with the new one," he said, and another image appeared on the screen. This was even denser than the first. I sort of recognized it from pictures of modern cyberstuff, the liquid kind that crammed impossible amounts of circuitry into something the size of a pea.

"Now, could I put you in a light trance?"

"Have at it."

I went under easily now, and recognized that semidetached state where things were just a little more vivid, just a little sharper than normal consciousness. Colors were intense, but sounds were muffled, except for Jubal's voice.

I tried to let my mind go blank, as Jubal requested. When I felt it was as blank as it could get without a lobotomy, I focused on the pattern . . . then tried not to focus.

And what can I say? I don't know how to describe what turned out to be almost an hour of staring, except to say that I stared. I don't think I even blinked much.

A few times I felt like I was starting to slip into something. If you've ever looked at a stereogram, you know the frustrating feeling of being *right on the edge* of seeing something, of feeling that the image is trying to come out, that that incredible soft, wet calculating machine behind your eyeballs is working furiously to decode the image the stereogram is trying to send you, but it remains as elusive as a will-o'-the-wisp. (What is a will-o'-the-wisp, anyway? Googling . . . ah. Swamp gas.)

Then the balloon popped. No, make that a soap bubble because it wasn't startling; just one moment I was deeply into the picture, and the next moment I wasn't.

I found myself sitting very close to Jubal. Our hips were touching. We were both leaning forward, and our heads were inclined toward each other. My right arm, apparently leading a life of its own, was draped over his shoulders. I felt the solid muscle beneath his shirt, beneath his skin, and I inhaled the scent of him.

I guess the bubble popped for Jubal, too, because he shook his head just a little bit, and then turned to look at me, his eyes slowly swimming into focus.

I leaned forward and kissed him, gently, on the lips. Then I moved back, waiting.

Time really is relative. A couple seconds can stretch out almost eternally, as you realize that this moment could change your life forever. The rest of the world went away, and I stared into his eyes, looked at his lips, gently smoothed his hair. It all depended on him.

He moved forward, just an inch. That was all I needed. I moved against him, pressing my lips to his. He closed his eyes and let it happen. I opened my mouth, and put my other arm around him. His hand came up, tentatively, and brushed ever so gently over my hair. I took the hand and pressed it to my cheek, and he finally began to kiss me back.

I moved his hand down to my breast, and when he squeezed it I felt something explode inside me. I heard moaning, and realized it was me. My skin felt flushed and moist. It was suddenly too hot in the room. I pulled back for just a moment and tore my blouse off and put his hand back where it had been.

Never breaking the kiss for more than a second, I got his pants down and mine off, and I straddled him.

What followed was about as close to rape as a woman could do to a man. But of course to be raped you have to be unwilling, and he was not unwilling. He was just shy and tentative. His hands touched, but barely skimmed over me. I broke the kiss and whispered in his ear.

"I won't break, Jubal, *cher*."

Be careful what you wish for. He hugged me, and I thought a rib was going to crack. He squeezed my butt and I knew I'd have bruises, but I didn't care. He arched upward and almost threw both of us over the back of the couch, but I clung like a cowgirl on a bucking bronco.

Then he cried out, and again, and again. It had all lasted about two minutes, and I had been on the edge, and I hadn't made it over, but I didn't care about that, either. Because now I was deathly afraid. *What on Earth possessed you, Podkayne?* This was a badly damaged man, uneasy with his own emotions. How would he react to this, now that it was over?

Over temporarily, if I had anything to say about it.

I gently eased away from him and looked down at his face. Tears were leaking from his eyes. *Oh, god, what have I done?*

"What's the matter, *cher*?" I whispered.

"I'm sorry," he said.

"Sorry? Sorry for what?"

"I don't know nothin' about this, me. About . . . sex. But I know it ain't supposed to be that quick."

I stopped myself from laughing and spent the next little while kissing away his tears, loving the saltiness of him.

"Honey, I'm guessing it's been a long time for you," I said.

"It been forever."

I took his face in my hands and stared at him.

"This was your first time?" He nodded. "Oh, Jubal, *cher*, that's so wonderful!" I hugged his face between my breasts, then let him go and grinned down at him.

"It is?"

"Of course it is. I'm so proud of us."

"I didn't do much, me. I know it's s'posed to be different than that."

"Well, I'll let you in on a little secret," I said, getting up and kicking off my shoes, which was all I was wearing. "If you don't get it right the first time, there's always the next time." I squatted down and removed his shoes and socks, then pulled his pants off. I stood and held out my hand. He took it, and I pulled him to his feet.

Then I led him to the bedroom.

YOU COULD PUT it down to sheer horniness and I wouldn't blame you. That wasn't what it was, but still, the last time I got laid was back on Europa, over a year ago—or ten years ago, calendar time. No time for a relationship during the Earth tour, and no inclination, and nobody I liked well enough. But a girl *does* need it, that's well-known, or she's liable to get grouchy. I'd been feeling mighty grouchy for a long time.

He's old enough to be your grandfather! I hear you say. Yeah? You wanna make something of it, punk?

But you have a point, I know. The man was born in 1980, for heaven's sake. That meant he was pushing ninety, *hard*. But you can't count those many years in the bubble. Clock time, he was fifty-seven.

Ouch. I know. I know. I know there were a million practical reasons why this whole thing was a very bad idea. But love knows no practicality. Ask Romeo and Juliet.

Okay, bad example.

The fact is, all those practical considerations vanished every time I looked into his eyes and saw the joy there.

Oh, cher, *all those wasted years . . .*

* * *

I ACTUALLY SAID something like that to him, later that amazing day. We were both sprawled across the wreckage of my big bed, eyeing each other warily from time to time, like two exhausted boxers wondering if the other guy could possibly last another round.

"What waste, *cher*?"

"Well, all those years without making love. It just seems like a waste."

"I real shy, Poddy."

"I know that. But still."

He patted my thigh. "Better late than never. And if I'd been making love all this time, I mighta fallen in love too early, and got married, and had to settle for second best without ever knowin' it. There's a time for everythin', *cher*."

THAT NIGHT, WITH Jubal snoring gently against my breast, I had a hard time getting to sleep. I was trying to sort out my feelings.

Had I been aware that he was falling in love with me? Yes. Jubal was transparent as a pane of glass, he couldn't hide his emotions, and I could see it in his eyes. I knew it was more than simple lust, too, because I've seen that before. I'm not runway model material, but I'm not bad-looking, and any girl learns to recognize that look in a boy's eye about the time she starts to develop into a woman.

Had I been aware that I was falling in love with him? Tougher question. I'd never been in love before; do you always recognize it instantly, or is that just storybook stuff? I'd dated about a dozen guys in school, for different lengths of time. Some I had sex with, some I didn't, but they all came up lacking in the end. Either there was something about him I didn't like, or there was just no spark there. It didn't bother me, I wasn't in a hurry, I had career plans and figured it would happen when it happened. Look at Mom and Dad, thrown together by catastrophes; they might never have met without the Big Wave and the Martian War. Mom told me it was an immediate attraction she felt with Dad, but that the love part grew gradually until suddenly it was just there. So I grew up not expecting to get struck unexpectedly by the thunderbolt of love, impaled on Cupid's arrow, or hit over the head by Maxwell's silver hammer.

And that's how it had been, a gradual building of affection, turning slowly to thoughts of love*making,* as distinct from love . . . and then out of the blue . . . *the thunderbolt*! I could still feel it, churning around pleasantly down there in my belly. Was that right? Shouldn't I be feeling it in my heart? The fact was, though my heart had been thumping like a kettledrum, the real feeling, the physical ache, had been some inches below that. And I'd felt it before, when a boy put his hands on me, here, and there, and someplace else. That had been lust, pure and simple. Was this?

No. That had been there, the sexual part of it, the trembling, the flushing, the suddenly slipperiness, the instant hardness of the little girl in the pink boat, but there had been something else along with it.

A bursting. A flowering.

I thought again about that moment. The instant decision, not made consciously but springing directly from either my belly or my heart, take your pick, to make the first move. Did I figure I'd be jumping his bones about ten seconds later? No, honestly, I didn't. But I had known deep down that the rest of my life hung in the balance in the next few seconds. If he didn't respond, if he didn't make the *second* move, then that would be it, very likely for all time. I had never kissed a man before without knowing if the very idea of sexuality would terrify him, without knowing if he *had* any sexuality.

One inch. He moved forward one inch. It was all he was capable of, and it was the equivalent of a hundred-yard dash for a normal man. I had some inkling of the walls he had built against human intimacy, how deeply he had believed that this was an experience that would be forever denied him. Jubal was the most loving man I'd ever met, and there were plenty of people who loved him back, so he wasn't deprived that way. But the love between a man and a woman . . . he knew that just wasn't going to happen. He told me as much, later that day, in bed.

You sure know how to pick 'em, Podkayne.

Oh, shut up, you bitch subconscious, or I'll toss you in a barrel and nail it shut.

But she had a point. Was there ever, in heaven or Earth, a worse mismatch? Let's add it up, shall we?

In the debit column, right up at the top you have to put the age thing. "The age thing," . . . *hah!* He was almost three times my age. If he lived to be one hundred, I'd be sixty. He'd be a wreck, most likely, and I'd still have a lot of life to get through without him. More likely, by the time I was sixty he'd be dead.

There was the intelligence thing. When people were making lists of the great men of physics, it usually went like this: Isaac Newton, Albert Einstein, Stephen Hawking, Jubal Broussard. Not necessarily in that order. I was a B student in science, a C student in math. On a good day.

There was the emotional thing. I see myself as a pretty grounded person, even after all the upsets in my life recently, what with nearly being crushed to death by an alien creature and then being rebuilt practically from scratch, losing ten years of human history, and having megacelebrity dropped on me like a gold-plated elephant turd. None of it had made me timorous, or big-headed, or really done much to change the Poddy I was proud to be, in spite of my occasional faults . . . though I know I'd be the worst judge of that. But it was nothing compared to what had befallen Jubal at a tender age, before he was formed as an adult. Brain damage is probably the worst thing that can happen to you. At least, it was the thing I feared the most. Jubal had heroically adapted to it, but it hadn't left him unmarked. It never does, according to the reading I'd done on the subject, and all our high-tech medicine still can't do a damn thing about it. Jubal was prone to mysterious sulks, to withdrawal and depression, to bouts of despair.

He didn't like new things, didn't like meeting new people, and would be happiest as a semihermit in a mosquito-infested swamp I could hardly imagine inhabiting, hunting alligators and eating possums and raccoons. Me, I'm a city girl; I love the great indoors. I'm slightly agoraphobic, I fear bugs of any kind, and I'm not really comfortable around animals except dogs and cats. Jubal was going to be a high-maintenance companion, and I wondered where we could live that would make us both happy.

Then there was the stature thing. Jubal was . . . there's not an easy way to put this for a six-foot-four girl . . . *short.*

Okay, I know it's silly, and it's sure not a deal-breaker, but I just thought I'd mention it in the debit column. We looked at ourselves in the mirror standing side by side and had giggling fits. He was five-four in his bare feet. We were the very picture of Mutt and Jeff, except I had bigger boobs than Mutt. He was a fireplug, I was a willow. He was wide and I was narrow. Well, that's what the Y chromosome is all about, isn't it? So we can tell one sex from the other? Only usually the guy is taller.

Okay, on to the pluses. Were there any? You bet.

About the age business . . . in some ways I was older than he was. He was never childish, but frequently childlike, in the best possible way. He had not a lick of an old man's cynicism, ossified opinions, petrified imagination, envy of youth, or even regret for things not done. He knew who he was and was comfortable with it, and he had the sense of wonder and exploration of a twelve-year-old combined with an IQ that might reach into four digits for all I knew.

Intelligence? While I'm average, at best, in the hard stuff, my verbal skills have always rated in the 99th percentile. And I had no problem with not being able to keep up with his mighty brain, because I wasn't even interested in trying. I intended to follow his mind wherever it led us. We fit together like yin and yang, strengths matching weaknesses. I could even help him express himself. Besides, I'd always preferred smart guys, and with Jubal I'd hit the jackpot.

Emotions? I could sense a tidal change in his behavior even that first day, and I thought it would get better. I could see him emerging from his hard shell, working at his shyness—with me, at least. I liked it that his emotions were right out on the surface, that he had no hidden agendas. With Jubal, what you saw was what you got, and I liked what I saw. How many people do you know who are like that? I couldn't think of another.

Short? The hell with that. I liked leaning down to kiss him.

As for where we could possibly live . . . that was going to be a problem, but there would be a solution, I knew there would.

So put it all on a balance, and how does it add up, logically? Well, I'd call it a draw, with the scales tipping slightly toward "Run like hell!"—mostly because of the age difference. I could see I was going to have a problem selling that one to some people. But I'm an adult, and I'm stubborn, and if anybody couldn't accept us they could just go to hell.

But none of that really mattered, because there was nothing logical about it. Cupid had planted his cherubic pink butt on the other side of the scale, and the needle had swung *hard* in the other direction, and was now reading "Go for it, Podkayne!"

WE HAD AMAZING days there alone at the Fortress.

We didn't spend the *entire* time in the sack, but it was a close thing. Jubal was eager as a puppy dog, and an amazingly fast learner. He was game for anything, and his delight at some of the things I showed him was a joy to behold. He quickly learned to prolong our mutual pleasure, and when he brought me off—frequently!—he was as proud as if he had invented the wheel, or fire, or the squeezer machine. Prouder.

We watched old movies. He taught me to cook. He brushed my hair and painted my toenails. I taught him poker—which he was terrible at, there was very little bluff in Jubal—and he taught me pinochle. We didn't even try chess. I knew he'd be twenty moves ahead of me. We showered together and we bathed together. We took the elevator to the surface and made a snowman out of dry ice. He lapped milk out of my belly button, when I could stop giggling enough so it didn't slosh out. I did his beard to make him a little more Ernie, and styled his hair to make him a little more Lennie. We read books to each other. Jubal could read just fine, never stumbled over a word, though he mispronounced many. He just usually couldn't find the word he was looking for when speaking. We played nonviolent video games. One day, we painted each other like circus clowns, head to toe. The lovemaking was particularly good that night. What was *that* all about?

So, basically, this is the scene, if this were a movie, where there would be a montage of us cavorting around doing silly things and laughing a lot to some sort of rollicking music, sharing secret smiles, a little bit of slow motion. Which is what we did, except the slo-mo part. But enough of that.

We worked out together in the well-equipped gym. Jubal could bench-press me all day long without breaking a sweat, but went back to barbells because I wasn't heavy enough. We rowed together through a video environment of some of the world's scenic rivers: the Mekong, the Nile, the Orinoco, the Columbia. It was all kind of sad, knowing most of these scenes were outdated, the estuaries inundated and virtually flushed out from giant waves, but it was better than just sweating on the rowing machines.

Every day we spent an hour with me in a trance, staring at different things Jubal thought might nudge my mind into the impossible frame of reference where one could make a "twist in space," as he put it, and create a Broussard Singularity. I asked him to make one, so I would know it was possible, but he refused, saying he didn't want to influence me. I knew the whole thing was crazy, but I kept quiet. He had this conviction that because we had been entangled (something I didn't understand or even fully accept), I could become the second human capable of doing it.

What the hell. It only cost me an hour a day, and the sessions were relaxing. You can't play pinochle all day long. Or screw.

THERE WAS ONE subject I knew I'd have to talk over with Jubal, but I kept putting it off, and that was religion. His father had been some kind of backwoods messiah preacher, his church some weird combination of Catholicism, snake-handling, and penance through pain, the mortification of self and others. Jubal and his siblings had been the most frequent others.

He could not tolerate obscenity or profanity, and I had to watch my mouth when I was around him.

When he came out of the bubble he had been reciting the Hail Mary, so I assumed he was devout in some way. If he wanted me to go to church with him, I'd do it, though I suspected I'd feel hypocritical kneeling and praying. And I'd have to draw the line at handling snakes.

But finally I took the bull by the horns, or the snake by the tail, and just asked him what church he went to.

"Church?" he asked.

"You know, what is your religious faith? If we're going to be together we'll . . . we'll have to work that out, some way."

"I ain't got no church, me."

"But you believe in God, right?"

He eyed me suspiciously. "Do you, *cher*?"

Honesty is the best policy, or so I've been told. I hoped it was true.

"I can't say I do or I don't," I said. "I don't think there's any scientific evidence for a God, but I don't know enough about the universe to say one way or the other." There. Was that sufficiently weasel-worded?

"Well, I knows plenty about the universe," he said, "and I'm wit' you, honey. One thing, I'm real sure that if there's a creator, he ain't some bearded ol' thunderclappin' bullyboy wit' a bloody shirt and a bad temper."

"But I thought you believed in the Bible."

He laughed, then quickly got serious.

"When you was a chile, Poddy, did you ever have a gris-gris to keep the boogeymens away?"

I had to google for a second, but then I knew what he was talking about.

"For a while there I remember checking under my bed and in the closet to see if there were any monsters in there," I said. "But I don't think I had any spells to keep them away."

"Too bad. They can be a comfort. The words theirselves, I mean, not any real power they have, which they don't. When I was little, I used to say the Hail Mary and the 'Our father, who are in Heaven,' and the Twenty-third Psalm, 'Yeah, though I walk through the valley of the shadow of Daddy . . .' That's how I said it, *cher*. Hopin' we wouldn't need to do any repentin' that night."

"Oh, Jubal my darling . . ." Has anybody ever found the limits of man's inhumanity to man? To a man's own son? He put his arms around me and hugged me gently.

"There, there, Poddy. It all over now. But when I'm scared—and I'm scared a lot, I know it ain't manly, but I can't he'p it . . . I say them words. I take comfort from 'em, me."

I sniffled for a while, and he continued to console me. Not manly? I should have been consoling *him*, not the other way around.

"You probly wonderin' 'bout them words, too," he said.

"Words?"

"What they call 'four-letter words.' Some of 'em a lot longer than that."

"Swearwords."

"That another name for 'em." He sighed. "I know words is just words. But I got me a conditional *re*-flect."

"Conditioned reflex?"

"What you said. My daddy, if we young 'uns'd say a cussword, he'd whup us something awful. He had a long list of 'em. He didn't even like us to say"—short pause—"darn. Said it was just the same as . . . damn." He swallowed hard.

"If we didn't say them words often enough, he'd say 'em for us, and whup us while he was sayin' 'em. I done some studyin' on it, Poddy. Say you take a little puppy, and every day you beat him, all the while a-hollerin' 'Bullfrog!' *Bullfrog, bullfrog, bullfrog! Whup, whup, whup!*" As he said this he pounded the couch we were sitting on.

"Pretty soon you don't have to hit him, you just holler 'Bullfrog!' and that puppy'll whimper and cry and pee hisself."

"Jubal, that's so awful."

"It is, ain't it. Poor little puppy." And I knew he was thinking about that imaginary little puppy, not "hisself."

"That's what happened to me, *cher*. I hear them words, and my bowels clench up, and my heart goes to poundin', and I break out all sweaty. Sometimes I get plumb sick and I urp up my food."

I squeezed his hand.

"Jubal . . . you know they have ways of deconditioning reflexes like that."

"They do?"

"Honest to . . . honest Injun. They can help with phobias, too. You're not the only one. I freak out when I see a bug, and I don't like open spaces much unless I'm wearing my pressure suit. That last one's pretty mild, but believe me, if a spider crawled on me, I'd . . . oh, Jubal, just thinking about it makes my skin crawl."

"Really? I don't mind spiders, me." He was thinking it over, and I thought he was drawing just a bit of confidence at the thought that a "normal" person like me had irrational fears, too. "I might like to look into that, one a these days. I don't think I'd ever say them words, but it sure would be nice if I could hear 'em wit'out gettin' all trembly inside."

THEN ONE DAY, Travis walked in on us.

No, not "in the act," but maybe it was the next worst thing.

Jubal and I were sitting side by side on the couch, watching *West Side*

Story. Damn good music and dancing, by the way. I jumped up, smiling, and hurried over to him, intending to give him a big hug . . . but was stopped cold by the look of shock on his face. For a second I couldn't figure out what was the matter. Then I did.

Oh, *please*, Travis!

Jubal was so involved in the movie that he hadn't noticed Travis's arrival at first. Now he looked up and got the big, goofy grin he always got when he saw his favorite cousin. He started to get up.

"Podkayne," Travis said, "could I speak to you in private for a moment?" He grabbed me by the upper arm, quite roughly, and started pulling me toward the kitchen. There wasn't much I could do about it. He was much stronger than I was.

We burst through the swinging door and Travis whirled us around, standing with his back to the door. Then he hissed:

"What the fuck do you think you're doing?"

"Get your hand off me, Travis."

He looked pained, maybe even a little apologetic, and let me go. I steamed for a moment, glaring at him. Nobody manhandles me that way.

"What are you talking about?" I whispered. I couldn't think of much that would upset Jubal more than an argument between me and Travis.

"What am I *talking* about? Get some *clothes* on, Podkayne. You're stark naked!"

"I will not," I said. "Don't saddle me with your stupid Earthie morality, Travis. At home, sometimes my family wears clothes, and sometimes we don't."

"This isn't your home."

He had me there, but I was stung. When Travis had showed up when I was a child, I'd always felt that our home was his home. He'd seen me running around naked until I was four, then again when I was nine, and when I was fourteen. He'd never seemed bothered by it. I knew what the difference here was, of course, and it was Jubal, and I know I probably should have kept my mouth shut, but it had to come out sooner or later.

So I said, "Besides, Jubal likes seeing me this way. It makes him happy."

"Jesus Christ, Podkayne, are you fucking him?"

I slapped him so hard I'm surprised I didn't take skin off his face. He pretty much ignored it.

"So you *are* fucking him."

I slapped him again. This one finally seemed to get his attention.

"As you so gently put it," I growled, "yes, I am fucking him. Or to put it more accurately, he's fucking me, and doing a damn good job of it."

He turned so red I thought he was going to hit me. Instead, he turned his face away and spoke softly.

"Jesus Christ, Podkayne, listen to me, do you have any idea what this—"

"No, you listen to me, Travis. I know you love him, and I know you protect him, but I want you to ask yourself this. How long has it been since you've given him a chance to . . . to be something beyond what he's always been?"

"You don't have any idea what you're saying."

I did, though, because Jubal had confided in me, one night when it was dark in the bedroom, just a single candle, and he was on the verge of sleep . . . one of those times when you can confide things deeper than you've ever revealed before. He told me that sometimes Travis made him feel a little too protected. This was a bit like the Pope saying maybe God was a little too nosy and bossy and interfered too much. The sort of thing you might need a good stiff drink for, before and after. And he didn't come out and say it in so many words, I had to decode it, because every other sentence was about how much Travis loved him and how much he loved Travis. All true. But one thing I've learned is that love can be the dirtiest of all those four-letter words that scare Jubal so much. When it turns to possessiveness. Love can morph into something ingrown, infected, and ugly. That kind of love can smother at best, and kill at worst.

But I knew I couldn't tell Travis any of that, at least not then. It would betray Jubal's confidence. No, I knew that I would have to count on Jubal to stand up to what might be his greatest fear: losing Travis. The rest of my life hung in the balance.

"Now," I said, as calmly as I was able. "I want you to splash some cold water on your cheek and try to get rid of those red marks. We don't want to upset him. And I'm going to smile, and take you back into the living room, and you and Jubal are going to sit down and visit a spell. He may have some things to say to you."

He looked at me oddly. I could practically read his mind. This wasn't the cheerful little Poddy who'd had a crush on him, not the Podkayne he was used to. I felt in control . . . of him, anyway. And I could read the beginnings of doubt in his eyes. I knew he would do what I told him to do.

If only I could feel more sure Jubal could stand up to him. Travis is a very forceful personality. Was he fair? Would he listen?

We went back into the living room, where Jubal was looking nervous, wringing his hands with a half smile on his face. He knew something was up, and he probably had a pretty good idea what it was. I made myself smile, and I hoped Travis was doing the same.

"If you boys will pardon me," I said, "I think I'll go powder my nose, and you guys can catch up on the news." I went off down the hall, made it to my bedroom door, closed and locked it behind me, then sprinted to the bathroom and lost my breakfast into the toilet. Damn good andouille and cheese omelet, too. What a shame, eggs being as rare as they were these days.

I washed out my mouth and cleaned myself up, then did a few deep-breathing exercises while staring at myself in the mirror. I guess the course of true love never did run smooth, but this was taking a toll. I looked old. What would Jubal do?

I showered and shampooed my hair. I spent an hour on makeup, starting over twice. From the closet I chose a modest white-ribbed turtleneck and a gray skirt, and plain black flats. I wanted to look as grown-up as possible. I draped a heavy gold chain around my neck, with my Navy Cross hanging from it, and chose a pair of earrings that matched.

I went to the bedroom door. I rested my forehead against it for a moment, then took a deep breath and went back to the living room.

Jubal and Travis were standing at the end of the couch, hugging fiercely, Travis slapping Jubal on the back. I waited, my heart in my throat.

Finally, Travis noticed me and beckoned me over with one hand. As I was walking toward them, Travis broke the embrace and turned toward me. Tears were streaming down his face. He held out his arms, and I came into them. I had to bend down a little as he spoke in my ear.

"Bless you, Poddy, bless you," he whispered. "I've never seen him happier."

Well, my heart didn't have anyplace to leap to, being in my throat already, but it did some really fancy gymnastic moves in there and for a minute I wondered if I'd choke. But it tripped a release valve and turned on the waterworks. Travis took my hand and placed it in Jubal's, gave our clasped hands a pat as I wondered if Jubal was going to crush my fingers, and then he drew back to admire us.

"So," he said. "Y'all ready to set a date?"

JUBAL DIDN'T DARE appear in public at all, even to the extent of coming to Thunder City under heavy security and secrecy. It was just too dangerous. There were too many powerful people with long memories who would like to examine the goose that laid the silver bubbles, and wouldn't mind if he died in the process. And it was better if I stayed away, too, what with the clamor building over "Jazzie's Return."

Oh, yes. While Jubal and I were canoodling, Mike and Tina and Quinn had done a little fiddling with my latest effort, put it out there, and it had immediately shot to the top of the charts. There was clamoring for at least another concert, more if possible, and Tina told me that if I wanted to do a systemwide tour, it was mine for the asking. But she didn't pressure me in any way, and when I told her that I wouldn't be ready for anything like that for quite some time, she seemed to understand. Maybe a year from now, she suggested, and I let her think I was agreeable to that. In fact, at the moment at least, I'd rather have died than even *think* about going on tour again.

Besides, now I had Jubal.

Was "Jazzie's Return" really that good? I didn't know. I liked it, and it seemed to have something new to say in this still-rather-mysterious (to me, anyway) new genre of Pod music. But I also realized that my celebrity had reached such heights after the Earth tour that I could have recorded "Ninety-nine Bottles of Beer on the Wall" on a Jews' harp and it would have shot to the top, too. That happens, and an artist should be aware of it. I woke up to it when I realized I was getting the same huge amount of applause on nights when I was clicking like a Geiger counter as on nights when I was about as sharp as the butt end of a bassoon.

The audience begins to adore you for your reputation, as much as anything. You can do no wrong. My best career move at this point would be to die. Then every snippet I'd ever recorded, outtakes, bootlegs, do-overs, could be marketed as "The Lost Podkayne Sessions."

What an artist needs most at this point in her career is somebody honest enough to tell her when she stinks.

Anyway, because of that, when Travis issued his invitation a few days after coming back to the Fortress of Sillitude (sorry, Solitude), it was for the "family" to come to him rather than us going back to town.

Travis has two families, and they had always been more or less separate. That's because his biological family, the Broussard clan, were mostly on Earth, and his adoptive family, the Stricklands, Garcias, and Redmonds, were all on Mars. But that changed after Grumpy, and most of the Broussards were now either Martian citizens or residents. Only a few diehards were still holding out Earthside.

Everybody got an invitation, and it took two buses to bring them all out to the Fortress. It was chaos for a while there, with me being introduced to dozens of Broussards I'd never met before, since practically all of them had arrived on Mars while I was sleeping on Europa. Jubal was in heaven. Though he doesn't do well in crowds, this crowd consisted of practically all the people in the universe that he cared about. He and I had spent the whole day cooking a massive smörgåsbord, or as Jubal put it, "He'p yourself style." Now he had become quite the social butterfly, and half his conversations were in bayou French, which I gathered he was a lot better at than at English. I resolved to learn it as quickly as possible.

My parents were there, and both sets of grandparents, and Uncle Bill and Aunt Amelia and some of their brood, and Mike and Marlee (still together, my fingers crossed), and Tina and Quinn. Somebody had brought a guitar and somebody else had brought a squeeze box, and I tried my hand at the washtub bass, and soon there was stompin' and dancin' and feastin' fit to beat the Mardi Gras. *Laissez les bons temps rouler!*

After about an hour Grandma Kelly took me by the arm, gently, and without a word led me down the hall to my bedroom and closed the door behind us. Mom was there, looking worried. She faced me and put her hands on my shoulders.

"I'm not going to be judgmental, baby," she said. "But please tell me. What's going on with you and Jubal?"

Well, it was a lot better than "Are you fucking him?"

"Is it that obvious?"

"It might have taken me a bit longer if I only had you to look at, but not a lot longer."

"The way Jubal looks at you . . ." Grandma Kelly sighed. "The man always was a bit of a puppy dog. If he was a basset hound, he'd be tripping over his own ears."

"So what have you done, Poddy?" Mom asked.

"I've fallen in love with him, Mom."

They both looked at me like I was maybe a piece of furniture they were thinking about buying, both of them leaning toward no.

"Have you thought this over?" Mom asked.

"How much thinking can you do when you're in love, Mom?"

"There's that," she said, with a sigh.

"The serious answer is, yes, I have. I know it's not going to be easy. And you probably think I'm stupid, him being so much older . . ." I didn't know where to go from there.

"Not stupid. You've never been stupid, Poddy. In fact, sometimes I've wondered if you were being too analytical for your own good. Some of those boys in high school were . . . never mind that. Kelly?"

Grandma Kelly moved into position. What was this, good cop, bad cop?

"Does Travis know about this? He does? What did he say?"

"He was against it. I had to slap him around."

Grandma didn't smile back at me.

"Was?"

"Then he talked to Jubal." That seemed to stop her for a moment. "He doesn't own Jubal, Grandma. And Jubal stood up to him, for once."

They looked at each other, and Grandma gestured to Mom, like *"She's your daughter, you've got the floor."*

Mom was silent for a while, then nodded.

"It's not just the age, Poddy. It's almost like he's a relative. Hush! I know he's not, by blood anyway. He's an old friend of the family." Did she step a little hard on the word *old*?

"But he's only a little older than you now, Mom. And he's younger than Grandma. I mean, when they met, he was older, but now he's . . ." Something was tickling at my brain. *Ah, but I was so much older then . . .*

"What Evangeline is saying," Grandma put in, "is that . . . well, we all know he wouldn't hurt you. He's not capable of it. He's the sweetest man I have ever known. I admit, I never thought of him as lover material . . ." She shook her head. "What I'm saying, if *you* hurt *him*, I will slap you *so* hard . . ."

"You'll have to get in line, Kelly," Mom said.

"I'd never hurt him," I swore. "And his sweetness is one of the reasons I fell in love with him."

"Well, all right, then." Mom hugged me, and Grandma got into the act, and it was another of those three-way lovefests. I'll admit, it didn't touch me as deeply as with Jubal and Travis, my eyes remained dry—I mean, where did they get off, giving me the third degree?—but I knew it was because they loved me, and loved Jubal, and didn't want either of us to get hurt.

But still. Nosy. I hope I never get that way . . . but I probably will. The nosy gene was all around me.

Grandma pulled back a little and looked at me, narrow-eyed.

"'One of the reasons'?" she asked. "Tell me more, just between us girls."

I mimed zipping my lips. "Personal, Grandma. I'll never tell." She shrugged, and started to turn away. "But he *is* hung like a stallion, and fucks like a bunny rabbit."

Two seconds of shocked silence—gotcha!—and then we all three started laughing so loud that Dad knocked on the door and stuck his head in for a second. He took in the scene and wisely decided it was none of his business.

"MY REASON FOR bringing y'all out here—and I *do* have one, other than drinking . . ."

You'd never know it to look at us. We are not, by and large, a hard-drinking family, though the various Broussards were demonstrating both a larger capacity and a better ability to hold it than the rest of us.

Jubal never has more than one beer, and Travis, an alcoholic, drinks coffee or ginger ale. But a lot of people were feeling no pain.

"What I'm offering is a Mystery Tour. Any of you who are interested can board my ship, the *Second Amendment,* in one week's time—to get your affairs in order—and take off on a ten-day, all-expenses-paid junket to a mystery destination that I guarantee you'll find interesting."

"Getting your affairs in order sounds ominous, Travis," one of the Broussards said. They knew him as well as the rest of us did. There was general laughter. Travis held up his hands, palms out.

"I guarantee this is safe as a trip to the store. What I meant, you may need to line things up so you can get time off from your jobs."

"So what are we going to see?" somebody asked.

"That's why it's called a Mystery Tour."

There were more questions, a lot of them, but Travis wouldn't be budged. I caught Grandma Kelly's eye, and she leaned over and whispered in my ear.

"Same old Travis. He loves to be in control, and he loves surprises."

"Do you have any idea what he's up to?"

"Not a clue. How about Jubal? He know anything?"

"Well, if Travis told him something in confidence, he wouldn't tell anyone, not even me. But I don't think he knows." Which wouldn't stop me from grilling him about it, tonight, in bed. We ladies have our methods.

When the party broke up I didn't have any sense of who would be going and who wouldn't. Some were obviously interested, and some were dubious, and a few just couldn't get away. I approached Jubal as he was kissing a cousin good-bye.

"Will you go with me, *cher*?" he asked.

"Whither thou goest," I told him, secretly relieved that I wouldn't have to cajole him into it. Jubal hates travel, but I wouldn't have missed this for anything.

A WEEK LATER, most of the people who had been at the party boarded the *Second Amendment*. It was a huge ship; everybody got a private cabin. We cruised for four days, accelerating for half, turning around and decelerating for half. Mars quickly got smaller, but the best clue was that the sun got smaller, too. That meant we weren't going to Earth. And the turnaround time meant we weren't going to Jupiter.

That left the asteroid belt, and there were way too many of those for me to estimate which one might be our destination.

We never lacked for things to do, and we ate like kings, dining on stuff most of us had seldom had since the crisis began, all taken from a bubble pantry like the one in the Fortress.

But basically, not a lot happens on an ocean voyage or a space voyage. We had poker tournaments and I lost a few bucks. We worked out. Kelly appointed herself cruise director and organized lots of fun stuff to keep us all occupied.

The rest of my biological family had a little time to adjust to me and Jubal as an established fact. Dad was the hardest sell, but the more he observed us, the easier he got with the idea. Granddaddy Manny was fine with it from the beginning.

Mike was suspicious as hell. Jubal was a legend to him, like to so many other people, and he went around frowning at the thought of his big sister—his former big sister, now that he was as old as I was—involved with this geezer. Then one day he came up and apologized for being a jerk. It was a little like he was reading prepared lines, and later Marlee confided to me that she'd had to "slap him around a little." Figuratively, of course. After that, he and Jubal hit it off famously.

There was really only one thing of note that happened on the trip out. One night, as we were getting ready for bed, Jubal suddenly dropped to one knee and took my hand. He seemed upset, and I couldn't imagine what the problem was.

He stuttered around it for a moment, then inadvertently slipped into French. He stopped himself and finally managed to choke it out.

"Podkayne, will you marry me?"

I had to work very hard to stifle a laugh, which would have been one of sheer relief, because I knew it could be misinterpreted.

I looked at him down there, looking desperately up at me, and then I got down on my knees and took both his hands.

"I love you, Jubal. Of course I'll marry you."

Once more, there was the rib thing as he hugged me and kissed me. I'd have to train him to be more careful, but just then I didn't mind at all. What's a cracked rib or two at a moment like that?

Then Jubal leaped to his feet and went to the bedroom door, flinging it open. Travis was standing there, looking almost as nervous as Jubal, which meant he hadn't been eavesdropping.

"She say yes!" he shouted. Jeez, Jubal, wake up the whole ship, why don't you?

And about an hour later I was walking down the aisle . . .

TRUTH: I HAD never imagined a ceremony. When it happened, I'd assumed we'd hop a train down to City Hall and fill out a civil contract. Jubal had confessed he wasn't religious, and I sure wasn't, and I wasn't one of those girls who'd dreamed about a big wedding and designed her gown when she was eight.

But Jubal wanted a ceremony, and I had no objections.

Travis had had a week to set it up, "Just in case you said yes," he later told me. Nobody else knew except Mom, who had to be in on it because she provided the wedding dress, which had been hers when she married Dad. A few alterations, and it fit me like a glove. It was white, and floor-length. I couldn't believe what I saw when I looked in the mirror. *Why, Poddy, you're glowing!*

Travis must have bought some sort of wedding-in-a-box, because he had everything. There was no "aisle" on the *Second Amendment,* so he brought along some church pews and cleared out the biggest room and set them up to make one. There were tons of flowers all around the room. Later, there was a simply monstrous cake. There was the "Bridal

Chorus" from Wagner's *Lohengrin*. I wouldn't have been surprised if Travis had popped a flower girl out of one of his bubbles to strew rose petals in my path.

Jubal was resplendent in a black-and-white tux. Granddaddy Manny was his best man because Travis, in his capacity as captain, had to perform the service. Admiral Bill was in full-dress uniform. I had Broussard bridesmaids whose names I couldn't even remember. Grandma Kelly was Matron of Honor. I had a corsage to toss.

Dad walked me down the aisle to where Jubal was standing . . . on a box! I almost burst out giggling, but by a supreme effort of will maintained my dignity. In place of an altar there was a table draped in the Martian flag, so it was clear this was a civil ceremony. Jubal had written the vows himself, with help from Travis and others, and mercifully they hadn't put together one of those awful, sappy, breathless, embarrassing ego trips I'd seen at other secular weddings. Basically they'd just taken the traditional vows and stripped out the religious stuff. If Travis had asked me to "love, honor, and obey" I had brought a (borrowed) pencil to rewrite the contract, but it was "love, honor, and cherish." Nobody's going to obey in my marriage; we'll talk things out like civilized people, and then I'll get Jubal to do what I want him to do.

The dress was old, the veil was new, and the flowers were violets. Close enough for jazz.

When Manny handed the ring to Jubal I practically fainted, and had to interrupt the proceedings just for a moment.

"Jubal, that rock is enormous!" I whispered. "It's as big as the Hope Diamond."

"It *is* the Hope Diamond," Travis whispered, and shrugged when I gaped at him. "When the United States went bankrupt after the Big Wave, I picked up some bargains at the Smithsonian disaster sale. Had it remounted, in case I ever found the right girl." Fat chance. Travis had had many girlfriends in the course of a long and colorful life, and they always dumped him.

"The stone don't matter," Jubal said. "Only the love matters. With this ring, I thee wed."

And that was about it. We didn't do a recessional, just started partying right there. Dad was crying, Mom was misty-eyed. Travis lit a cigar, shocking a few people, then passed out more. Luckily, the ship's air system sucked the illegal poison away almost instantly.

Pretty silly, huh? Only the best day of my life.

IF IT HAD a name, I never heard it. More likely it just had one of those generic asteroid names like 22 Kalliope, or a number and the name of the discoverer, or just a number. People still tend to think of the asteroid belt as choked with rocks, but the fact is it's so diffuse you can blast right through it with barely a care. Total mass of the belt is about 4 percent of Luna. Just the biggest four—Ceres, Vesta, Pallas, and Hygiea—are over 50 percent of the mass of the whole belt.

Ceres is the only one big enough to be round. All the others are lumpy in one way or another. The mostly common way to describe these rocks, of which there are over three million half a mile or more in size, is "potato-shaped." This one was a big Idaho spud, a rough ellipsoid seven miles long on one axis, about four, maybe five miles in the other, with a few lumps and a few shallow craters.

The only thing a little odd about it as we approached was that it seemed to be rotating around its long axis. No reason why it shouldn't, but just eyeballing it, the spin seemed to be *exactly* along that axis, like somebody had aligned it that way.

Which is exactly what Travis had done, of course. Was he taking us to a bigger and better Fortress of Solitude?

We were all gathered in the main room, watching the approach on a big screen because we were decelerating, ass backwards to our target. The ship was in autodocking mode, no pilot necessary. We were getting nearer quickly and would soon go into free fall. I was holding Jubal's hand tightly. He hates free fall. He had been weaning himself off of his tranquilizing medication—he'd been drug-free for the wedding—but had taken an extra dose today.

"But you my best trank, Poddy," he had said, and he was proving true to his word, so far, with hardly a shiver as we neared the moment of main engine cutoff.

"Are you ready to spill the beans, Travis?" Kelly asked.

"Soon, soon," Travis assured her.

I was focusing on something I'd spotted on the side of the big potato.

Something white and far too regular to be a natural feature. It looked like writing, and it had rotated into view several times as we neared it.

"Travis, could you give us a better view of that white patch?" I asked.

"Sure thing."

The camera zoomed in, and I tilted my head to read the letters, which must have been a quarter of a mile high. Because of the unevenness of the surface, they were slightly askew, like the famous Hollywood sign, now long gone.

It said ROLLING THUNDER.

Well, it was rolling, all right, but naturally it was doing it in the total, eerie silence of space. I timed the rotation—I was beginning to have some idea of what this thing was—and gave the number to Jubal and asked him to work out what the centrifugal "gravity" would be inside it, if it was hollowed out, as I suspected.

"Have to know how much is hollow, *cher*," he said. "Futher out you get from the axis, the more gravity you get."

"It's two-thirds of a gee," Travis said.

"Then you got a hollow in there about . . . two miles wide," Jubal said.

"Exactly two miles," Travis said, sounding a little annoyed. He liked his surprises. "I hope you all have been keeping up with your exercises. You're going to weigh a little less than twice what you do on Mars." We'd been boosting at half a gee, which isn't unpleasant. Two Mars gees would actually be three-quarters of an Earth gravity. Two-thirds Earth gees would be heavier than I like, but not nearly as onerous as Pismo Beach.

Nobody said much as the main engines cut off. Jubal was holding my hand tightly, barf bag in the other hand. He looked a little green for a few minutes, but came through it okay. Then there were little pushes and shoves as the ship's computer eased us into a vast docking bay and pressure doors closed behind us. A passenger tube extended itself and locked on to us, and Travis led the way out. I tugged Jubal along like a toy balloon.

Travis led us down a few corridors and into a big chamber with seats in concentric circles. He instructed us to strap in, and when we did, the room started to move.

We gradually built up weight, and not in a pleasant way. Something seemed to be pulling me to one side. I realized it was the . . . googling . . . Coriolis force. We were going down, but also in a circle. Even I, with what I thought of as good space legs, felt a little queasy. Jubal quietly filled the barf bag, looked sheepishly at me, and patted my knee.

"I be okay now."

We were soon at the bottom of the elevator shaft. I started to get up, and fell back in my seat. Whew! Point six six gees took a little getting used to. Jubal gave me his hand and hoisted me to my feet.

The elevator doors yawned wide, and we were in a semicircular tunnel about fifty feet wide and twenty-five feet high. The floor was flat, the ceiling arched over us. And right before us was . . . a choo-choo train.

I'm not using the word lightly. It looked like it had been assembled by a child with no sense of history at all. Up front was a simply massive black locomotive, with polished chrome work, pipes running all over the place, and wheels as tall as I am. There were painted highlights of red and orange. Every surface gleamed.

"Is that a steam engine, Travis?" Granddaddy Manny asked.

"Used to be. Southern Pacific Number 4449. Runs on bubble power now. This is more of the stuff I picked up at the United States disaster sale. Cheap."

Hooked behind it was a long silver observation car with a glass bubble on top. It was clearly from another era. After that was an even older car, made mostly of wood. And at the end was . . . what else? A cheerful little red caboose.

I looked down the tracks behind the train and saw that the rails split and entered a larger area, where I could see other cars. Travis had always liked to collect things. After he became a multibillionaire, his toys just got larger. I had a feeling we were standing inside the largest toy of all.

Travis produced a train conductor's hat from somewhere and put it on his head, then ushered everyone into the passenger car. Up ahead, I could see a man leaning out of the cab of the locomotive. I wondered who he might be.

When we were all seated under the dome, the train blew its whistle and slowly pulled forward. We passed under hanging strip lights, and then through a pressure door. I could see it close behind us. In a quarter mile or so, another set of doors opened. We passed through three sets of doors, then through the last one, which took us into the interior of the *Rolling Thunder*.

I knew places like this existed, though there weren't many of them and this may have been the largest. I had never been inside one. No stereo hi-rez video can even begin to prepare you for it.

"Six miles long," Travis was saying. "Two miles in diameter. Six and a quarter miles around the cylinder, thirty-seven and a half square miles of land area. That's twenty-four thousand acres, almost ten thousand hectares. Volume is twenty cubic miles of air."

Picture being inside a cylinder six miles long and two miles in diameter. It's rotating around the central axis fast enough to produce .66 gee, but there is no sense of spinning. Wherever you are, down is directly below you, though you can see the ground curving gently upward in two directions; call them east and west. Look due north and south along the spin axis, the ground is flat right in front of you, but curves upward at the sides until it meets overhead. That is, I know it *did* meet, but I couldn't see it because a long light source ran right down the center of the cylinder, where it was weightless. I guess that was what was going to pass for the sun in here.

The ends of the cylinder were rounded, like a tank for holding high-pressure gas, like propane or maybe liquid oxygen. That was because this giant cavern was made by squeezer machines taking big round bites out of the surrounding rock and compressing it down to whatever size you wanted it to be. You could dig out this entire space in an afternoon.

Filling it with stuff would be another matter.

It took me a while to notice, because at first we were all gawking at how the ground curved up, around, and over, but from time to time we passed groups of people working. The engineer would toot his whistle, and the work crews would look up and wave to us. Some were driving bulldozers and other heavy equipment. Some were building structures out of metal, stone, or wood. I saw one group stringing barbed-wire fences, and another herding cattle, if you can believe it. I saw goats and sheep, I saw ducks swimming in a pond. We passed through a "forest" where all the trees were about ten feet tall, tied to stakes. For a while a dog ran alongside the train, barking happily.

But mostly it was the people I noticed. They were about equally divided between men and women, and there were even a few children. One woman carried a baby on her back, papoose style.

Who were these people?

THE TRAIN FOLLOWED a corkscrew path. Looking ahead, it seemed like you were about to take a ride on a roller coaster, but when you got there, of course, it was perfectly level. We went over bridges that crossed dry streambeds with rocks at the bottom. We clattered over switch points where other tracks crossed our line. There were grade crossings where various vehicles waited for us to pass.

The land we traveled through was oddly formed. Every quarter mile to half mile we ran along a low trestle that took us up to a ridge, from fifty to maybe a hundred feet high, where the land *seemed* to begin to slope gently down again. It was hard to be sure because being inside the giant cylinder distorted my perceptions. But I could see that the interior was lined by these ridges, sort of like the ribs of a really huge whale. They curved away on each side and met overhead, a series of rings, one after the other, stretching from one end of the cylinder to the other. I thought it might be some sort of artifact of the squeezing process, as successive bites were taken out of the solid rock and metal. Turns out it was something different. I'll get to that later.

We went through two villages, and I could see more up the sides and overhead. They were completely different, architecturally. I recognized the styles, since Martian architecture, at least in the tourist places, was modeled on various Earth fantasies; many of the casinos and hotels were themed to one region or another, but nicely Disneyfied. The first village was Merrie Olde England, with half-timbered homes and shops with thatched roofs, a few horse-drawn vehicles, and a partially completed stone church. All around the church were more stones, carefully numbered, and some tall stained-glass windows, and masons were putting more stones in place as we watched. It looked like Travis had bought an entire village and took it apart, for reassembly here.

The second village was Japanese. Paper walls, enclosed gardens, a Shinto temple, cherry trees.

In the distance I could see what looked like a riverside town built on stilts on the edge of a dry riverbed. The houses had corrugated tin roofs. Cajun? South American? Indonesian? I couldn't tell without a closer look.

After a while we pulled into a station that might have been built in the early part of the twentieth century. It was made of wood planks, painted yellow with white trim. Travis told us this was our destination, and we all got out and gawked some more. The curving effect was even more impressive—and disorienting—when you were standing outside. And there was another funny thing that made it even worse. The station platform was not quite level. I had thought the train listed a little to the right, too, but I couldn't be sure. Now the tilt was obvious. Everyone around me seemed to be standing at a slight angle, as if bending into wind. It probably wasn't more than five degrees, and it was always toward the back of the cylinder, against the direction we had been traveling.

"Come this way, friends," Travis said. "And watch your step. Until you get your ship legs, this tilt can trip you up."

I was already feeling too heavy, and the tilt didn't help. Jubal didn't appear to like it much, either. I held his hand and we made our way behind Travis.

We crossed a cobblestone street and entered Anytown, U.S.A.

That's just what I called it, but it wasn't, not really. It wasn't a California town, nor would it have fit well in Heartland America. I did a search and match, and found this was a darn good replica of a New England town. Vermont, maybe, or New Hampshire.

Travis led us along a street filled with the sounds of nail guns and power saws and the sweet smell of sawdust and the sharper smell of paint. People waved to us as we passed, but no one joined us.

We emerged onto a green town square. There was a finished white church with a tall steeple, a hulking granite bank, two-story buildings still being erected. The square was edged by towering trees that must have been dug up entire and transplanted. I thought they might be maples, though all I knew for sure is they weren't pines. That's about the extent of my knowledge of trees.

There was a cannon, probably from the American Civil War, and a flagpole with an American flag hanging limp. In the center was a bandstand draped with red, white, and blue bunting, and sitting there were two dozen men and women in bright blue coats with gold braid and white pants and shoes. The conductor on his podium tapped his music stand, and the band started playing "The Stars and Stripes Forever."

I leaned over to Jubal.

"Pinch me, darling. I think I'm dreaming."

"Me, too, *cher*."

"You didn't know anything about this?"

"Not a drop, me."

There were chairs, and we found seats. The band finished, and we applauded, and then Travis marched up onto the bandstand. He spread his arms wide.

"So . . . what do you think?"

Nobody had anything to say. He grinned.

"I know y'all probably think this is all pretty extravagant, maybe even silly."

"You're a mind reader, Travis," Grandma Kelly said, to general laughter, including Travis's.

"Well, we have a little time before y'all can start exploring. There's going to be a picnic here in about an hour. So relax, and I'll tell you a story.

TRAVIS HAD STARTED work on *Rolling Thunder* about twenty-five years ago. It didn't have a name then, and no real purpose. Travis just had more money than he knew what to do with, even after all the charities he contributed to. And he was getting damn tired of being one of the most hated men alive. No matter how many good works he did, no matter how much food and medicine he donated to poor countries, he was and always would be the man who had threatened to squeeze Planet Earth down to the size of a bowling ball.

Oh, he had his supporters. Most Martians loved him, and he could move freely there. But on Earth the ones who hated him most were the most powerful. They were the ones who had waged the war on Mars with the intent of stealing bubble technology, and were largely still anonymous since no one had ever stepped forward to claim responsibility for the two opposed waves of black military ships that had attacked us. These men owned the media and paid the wages of the people who formed public opinion, and Travis never stood a chance against them.

"I guess most of you realize that this was meant to be a starship," he said. "It's patterned on the larger ones that were built in the years after we first went to Mars, when space travel became cheap and easy and not limited by weight. They built about a hundred of these things, but this one is about twice as large as the biggest one. And they set out for the stars."

"And never came back," somebody pointed out.

"Yeah, and that's always been a problem for me."

No kidding. It was a big problem for anybody who thought about the Great Diaspora, possibly the biggest fizzle in human history. Of all those ships only one, the Death Star, had returned, and it had never reached the stars. It just went out far enough that it could be traveling at nearly light speed, then it crashed into the Earth, causing the Big Wave.

Where were those ships? Not all of them planned to return, but several had carried smaller ships, manned or unmanned, whose purpose was to come back and report on what they'd found. None had done so. What had they found? Something so horrible that return was impossible, or something so wonderful that they didn't care to return? Most people assumed it was the first, and no starships had departed for a long time now.

"Like I said, at first it was just something to do. I figured I could live in this place in peace, inviting only friends to share it. I thought Jubal might be happy here, too. Or if I got disgusted enough with the human condition, I could just fly off into the great black yonder."

Progress was slow at first. The actual hollowing-out took only a week or so, but the rest was detail work. But there was no hurry. Travis hired workers, supervisors, scientists, bought cargo ships, went shopping on Earth for things like locomotives, churches, the Hope Diamond, livestock, forests, several cubic miles of Mississippi delta mud, exemplars of plant and animal species. Anything the ecologists said he'd need to keep the biome healthy and functioning, and anything that caught his fancy. Then he went into a black bubble and popped out every five years to check on the progress.

And I'd thought he came out to visit me. Well, not really, but it was my girlish fantasy. Now I knew where he disappeared during those times he spent out of the bubble.

Then came Grumpy and his destructive companions, and things took on a new urgency and gave him a whole new outlook.

"What you're looking at now, my friends, it my solution to the problem of the Europan crystals."

There was a momentary silence.

"So," somebody said, "you plan to trap 'em in here, Travis?" There was general laughter.

"Would if I could, nephew. I'd blow 'em all to hell and gone if I could, but that's been tried. I'd shrink 'em down to the size of a BB, but that didn't work, either."

"So what you gonna do?"

"Run like hell."

Long silence.

"When you said 'solution,' I was hoping you had figured out a way to kill the damn things," Dad said. "I was hoping you'd figured out a way to fight them."

"Believe me, Ray, I tried. Jubal tried. We saved the world once, you and I and Evangeline and Jubal—mostly you, it was your idea, and Jubal, it was his brains. But I am sorry to admit that I only seem to have one world-saving in me. I can't do it over and over; I'm not Superman."

"You live in the Fortress of Solitude," I pointed out, which got a laugh. I was bursting with pride about what he'd said about Mom and Dad. How many girls had parents who faced up to the most powerful people on Earth . . . and won?

"This ship is now a lifeboat," he said. "An escape capsule. Believe me, my friends, it hurts me, physically. I can feel it like a pain in my gut, what these things are doing to my beloved home planet. *And they're not even fighting us!* Jubal thinks they're just doing what comes naturally to them, and we happen to be in the way. Every bone in my body wants to stand and fight them . . . and every ounce of my brain tells me . . . well, I get an image in my mind when I think about fighting them. Two dung beetles in the path of an elephant's foot. The foot is on the way down. And one beetle says to the other one, 'Okay, here's my plan . . . ' "

There was no laughter. We all knew too well that he was right.

"We have fought them with everything we have. When you're losing that badly, the only sane thing you can do is retreat and regroup."

"Travis," Grandma Kelly said, "so far they've only hit the Earth. We're still doing okay on Mars. Why run?"

He winced at that word but nodded.

"I'm not saying all humans are going to die from this. Not even on Earth, maybe. But it's going to get a lot worse before it gets better. Frankly, I'm surprised Mars hasn't been attacked yet. Y'all did the right thing, sheltering as many as you did, but it's not nearly enough."

"What do they expect of us?" somebody asked.

"Miracles. Everything. You're doing well back on Mars—relatively speaking—and they're dying by the millions. People don't think logically in a situation like that. Somebody's going to make a move on you, and you're probably going to have to call in your own black ships to deal with it. It won't be pretty, and a lot of innocent people will die along with the guilty. I don't have any solution to that, either, but I don't want to stick around to see it."

Travis sighed and spread his hands to indicate the vast interior.

"I've done what I could. This place will be ready to move in about a year, less if we hurry, but I've just about run out of money. I don't give a damn about that, but I'd hate to take off with less than we need.

"What I'm offering y'all—and a bunch of others you haven't met yet—is passage on the good ship *Rolling Thunder* . . . to the stars."

There was a long silence. I looked at Jubal, and we made a decision wordlessly, just by me raising my eyebrows and Jubal nodding.

"Travis," I said. "I've got money."

ONCE UPON A time there was a Martian named Patricia Kelly Elizabeth Podkayne Strickland-Garcia-Redmond-Broussard.

Singer. Songwriter. Ex-Navy. Ex-celebrity. And now, ex-Martian.

Jubal and I and most of my friends and relatives are now citizens of the galaxy.

TRAVIS WAS RIGHT, the last year wasn't pretty.

Nobody knew if the new Martian immigration policy started the war, or if it had been coming anyway. Shortly after we got back from the *Rolling Thunder,* the government and the electorate made an offer to the people still on Earth—still a billion or two—that some thought was more than fair and some thought was an outrage. Mars would now take anybody, absolutely anybody . . . but they had to be in a black bubble.

The same offer was made to the huge majority already living as refugees on Mars. Go into a bubble, or go back home. We can't feed and house you all.

The remaining immigration offices on Earth were immediately swamped with volunteers. These were what I viewed as the rational ones, who had thought it out, weighed the alternatives, looked at their starving children, and understood that this was the only chance at survival.

Things were much worse on Earth now, and the situation was deteriorating. *Average* winds in most places now exceeded sixty miles per hour, with many places suffering even worse. Rainfall was nearly constant. The only crops surviving were those being grown in the vast underground farms tunneled into bedrock, and it wasn't enough to feed a tenth of the population. Stored food was almost gone. The people already living underground were fighting the ones remaining on the surface, as it became clear there was not going to be enough room for everyone.

To many people like that, trapped on the surface with the winds never-ending, their children dying of starvation, the chance of going into a black bubble with a full belly (they got a week's free room and board and medical attention before going in) didn't look so bad.

Then there were the irrationals. Some had been crazy all their lives, for religious reasons; others had been driven mad by the rain and wind and lack of food. Many viewed it as black magic, Satan's work, against the will of Allah, you name it. Rumors flew wildly, the main one being that it was plain and simple murder. The black bubbles would kill you, or if they didn't, the Martians had no intention of ever letting anyone out again.

I must say, that last accusation may have been closer to the truth than anyone wanted to admit. I don't believe for a moment that Martians intended to encapsulate the refugees forever . . . but I understood that, once they were inside, they were a problem solved, and it might be a long, long time before anyone got around to solving the secondary problem of what to do with them. I didn't know what to think of their chances. But I do know that, if we could convince the doomed people to cooperate, we could store the entire population of Earth in an amazingly small volume. A human doesn't take up much space if you don't have to feed him and can stack him like a weightless cannonball.

The immigration officers had a volunteer Martian go into a bubble, stay an hour, and emerge unharmed to demonstrate that the bubbles did not kill.

That worked with the rationals, but didn't do a thing for the others.

You can't reason with a conspiracy theorist, especially a hungry and desperate one. There were riots, pitched battles, offices stormed and burned. Still, millions were encapsulated and shipped off to Mars.

The same thing happened on Mars itself, on a smaller scale. The riots were quickly contained, though Thunder City became an armed camp, ugly and militarized. But in the end, only a few elected to return to Earth.

THE ATTACK CAME two months after we returned to Mars. I'm lucky to be alive. My whole family is lucky to be alive.

Ships from Earth streaked for Mars at high acceleration. This time we weren't caught napping, though.

The Inner Fleet fought a larger Earth fleet equipped with nuclear rockets that accelerated at thousands of gees. Naval battles used to be fought side to side, blasting away with cannons. By the 1940s the great battleships and aircraft carriers never even came in sight of each other, but compared to the Battle of 20 Million Miles those World War Two ships were practically rubbing the paint off each other.

The battle was fought over five days. Though outnumbered, our Navy had weapons of our own in the form of bubble missiles. These were a lot cheaper than nukes, and thus we had a lot more of them. They were simply bubbles containing several thousand tons of rock squeezed down to the size of a grapefruit, and were actually a lot more powerful than nukes. We used them at a frightening rate, but there were a lot of targets, and they were moving fast.

We destroyed their entire invasion fleet, but some missiles got through. The Home Fleet fought a desperate last-ditch battle against these and got most of them. This was a battle we could have actually seen in the sky, except we were all hunkered down as deep as we could get, watching on TV.

Four missiles made it through. Three were diverted to a greater or lesser degree. Two landed harmlessly in the outback, harming no one. One hit three miles from Thunder City and rocked us pretty good. There were blowouts, and 1,439 people died.

One hit Deimos Base. It cracked off a large chunk, and the devastation inside was enormous. Over 2,000 Navy personnel lost their lives.

One of them was my uncle, Fleet Admiral William Redmond. He died at his post, directing the combat operations.

We buried him with full military honors, his closed casket draped with the Martian flag and his posthumous Medal of Valor. Inside with what was left of him was my Navy Cross. I didn't want it anymore.

All hail Admiral Redmond! All hail the Martian Navy!

OUR VENGEANCE WAS not swift, but it was terrible.

It took a while for our own Black Fleet to descend like nightmare bats on the solar system from their distant orbits. They existed as a deterrent, like the massed nuclear weapons that nations stockpiled after 1945, and the promise was implicit: You fuck with us, and we will destroy you. The crews of the Black Fleet were carefully chosen, and thought to be reliable if punishment had to be meted out. That punishment could include the squeezing of entire cities, but *not,* contrary to what the powers on Earth were told, the squeezing of the entire planet. We would not destroy the planet . . . but we'd do almost anything up to that point. That threat had held the Earth powers in line for a long time, but no more.

As in the previous wars, it was far from clear who had attacked us. No declaration of war had been made; no one had announced who they were before they started shooting. That made it easier to deny responsibility if things went bad.

The political situation on Earth was far too complex for me to follow, but the military situation was fairly simple. Very few military ships were landing or taking off from Earth. The winds were usually so strong that going through the atmosphere was extremely hazardous to all forms of aviation. The Martian Navy had lost several ships over the past year.

The generals on Earth had solved the problem several years earlier, when the climatic trend became clear. They based their fleets in orbit, mostly at the Lunar Lagrange points, ahead of and behind the moon's orbit. I'm sure these huge bases had formal names, but everybody called them "battlestars." There were five of them, all run by a Byzantine consortia of nations and corporations and individual power brokers—many of whom were more powerful than nations. Alliances shifted constantly.

It proved impossible to determine which battlestar or combination of them had launched the attack, and they all stood together, neither admitting anything nor ratting out any of the others.

So we destroyed them all.

An announcement was made:

Your bases and all your ships are about to be destroyed. You have one hour to evacuate. All lifeboats leaving your ships and bases will be spared; all armed ships leaving your bases will be destroyed. Your one hour begins now.

Lifeboats began leaving in thirty minutes.

Two of the battlestars decided to fight it out. As soon as the first ship undocked, the bases and ships were surrounded by thousand-mile bubbles and compressed. Sixty minutes later, the three remaining bases asked for and were given one additional hour to evacuate. Then those empty bases were compressed, too.

The five squeezer bubbles were taken to high-Earth orbit, about ten thousand miles, and detonated where everyone on Earth could see it, and the Black Fleet returned to its hiding place.

In two hours, the nations and institutions of Earth went from being the most powerful force in space to being totally unarmed. From that moment, Earth became irrelevant to solar-system politics, a beggar planet.

Do I regret the lives lost on those battlestars whose commanders decided to fight? You bet I do. A lot of the people who died were certainly grunts like I had recently been, just serving out their terms of enlistment.

But if you want sympathy, go to the families of those civilians killed in the bombing of Thunder City. I'm fresh out.

LONG BEFORE THESE events, while I was still sleeping under the ice, something else was going on, quietly, under the radar. On Earth, on Luna, on Mars, everywhere, Travis's agents were hiring.

"How did you keep it secret?" I asked him, once.

"Nothing secret about it. We just didn't take out ads on the Net. It was mostly word of mouth. I let it be known I was building a ship and that I was looking for crew and passengers."

They didn't have to be rocket scientists—though some were—and they didn't have to be ecologists, though he attracted plenty of them, too. Grumpy's arrival had given Travis a sense of urgency concerning the *Rolling Thunder.* At that point no one had any idea if the crystals were going only to Earth, or if they'd hit Mars, Luna . . . everywhere. Having a ticket on the first ship out of the system, or maybe the only lifeboat leaving the *Titanic,* looked pretty attractive to a lot of folks.

There were conditions.

You worked for nothing but your food and lodging, and a ticket out of Dodge. Those few who had a problem with that were simply not taken on. Travis's agents recruited carpenters, masons, steelworkers, anyone with a skill to help build the ship. Travis already knew that even his billions might not cover everything he needed in a project this size.

You didn't have to be blue-collar, an artisan, a farmer, or a scientist. Travis recruited artists of all sorts, scholars, historians, librarians.

But there was one other condition. You had to be prepared to spend part or all of the voyage in a black bubble.

The capacity of *Rolling Thunder* to support life in its huge centrifugal terrarium was not unlimited. In fact, the ecologists told him there was a population cap that could *not* be exceeded, *ever,* or the whole thing might collapse. That number was a lot smaller than Travis would have liked.

"When we get to wherever we're going," he told me, "some Earth-like planet, the more people we have, the better our chances of survival are. I'd like to hit the beach with a hundred thousand, *minimum.* Twice that would be better. Maybe more. One thing I've got, though, is room."

That's when he took us down to the catacombs.

NOTHING DANK OR gloomy about these underground caverns. What we saw was a series of tunnels about a hundred feet in diameter, encased in insulation but still quite chilly. There was no need to heat them much, and cold seeped in from the surrounding rock. We were given warm clothing and taken on a tour, riding on railed vehicles equipped with grappling devices. The temperature was just above freezing.

The tunnels were arrow-straight, lit by overhead strips, and so long they seemed to reach to the geometrical vanishing point. All along each side of us were standard warehouse racks in all sizes from shoe box to Dumpster or even larger. They were not at all heavy-duty, because they didn't have to be. All they supported were black bubbles. Thousands and thousands of black bubbles in nets to hold them in place.

Each net and each rack was clearly labeled with a description and a bar code.

"Once you've made the bubble, there's no way of telling what's inside," Travis was saying, as we rolled swiftly by this fantastic . . . warehouse? Library? Attic? A little of all those, I guess. He stopped beside a row of some of the larger bubbles. One of them said: "Elephant, African, Male, about twenty years old," and a lot of other information.

"From now on I'm calling you Noah," Grandma Kelly said.

"Noah was a piker," Travis said. "Two by two isn't enough for genetic diversity. I've got dozens."

"Why elephants?" Dad asked.

"Why not? They're extinct in the wild now, and nobody on Earth is going to have the time or resources to care for captive ones. Do I think we'll *need* elephants where we're going? I doubt it. But they cost me nothing. Nothing to transport since they have no mass, nothing to feed since they're frozen in time. When we get where we're going, there may already be something like elephants filling that ecological niche. We may never open these bubbles. But I don't like a world without elephants. I think it's a poorer world. *All* the big mammals on Earth will soon be extinct. I'm saving everything I can."

"Sounds good to me," Mom said.

"I've got little blue poison-dart frogs. I've got rats and snakes and dragonflies. I've even got mosquitoes, because, who knows, maybe they're necessary for the ecology in here. We're playing a lot of this by ear."

"I hope we don't need skeeters," someone said.

"Me, too."

We didn't go all the way down that tunnel. There was a cross tunnel with a curving floor, and we took it to the next storage tunnel to the west.

"Books," Travis said. "Some are cataloged, some are just what could be salvaged, tossed into big bins and then put in bubbles. They won't deteriorate."

He took us to bigger tunnels that held boats, aircraft, land vehicles, all in bubbles. Zero maintenance, zero dry rot, zero deterioration of any kind.

The last tunnel we visited—though there were many more—contained people. There were already a lot of them in there, but there were endless empty slots.

Everyone was quiet as we rolled down the tunnel. It was silly, of course. These people were alive, or at least potentially alive. But the atmosphere was that of a mausoleum, and respectful quiet seemed to be called for.

Travis stopped the vehicle and we all got out and browsed. You could shop for people here. Need somebody who could work in decorative ceramic tiles? Just enter the job description and three names and locations pop up. Can't remember where you left your son, Skipper? Enter his name, and the machines retrieve the proper bubble for you. It was all a little creepy, especially when I thought of myself sleeping in one of them for a decade, but it was the best solution to a bad problem, and I'd have to get used to it. It was going to be a big part of my life for some time to come.

I wandered, reading the labels. So many names, so many occupations, and yet such anonymity.

Tranh Van Minh. Age 35. Occupation, rice farmer.

"Peasant, really," Travis said, from behind me. "But that sounds condescending."

"You know him?"

"Never met the dude. But here." He called up the bar code, and I saw a picture of a small, smiling man. There was a picture of his wife and his three children. Then there was an extensive written biography.

"I ask them all to write about themselves," Travis said, quietly. "A biography, as long as they'd like to write it. And hopes, dreams, stuff like that. Poetry. Anything."

"He wrote this?"

"And his family. We only accept literate people."

"In English?"

"That doesn't hurt, but it's not necessary. We want to bring as many languages with us as possible, and keep them in use. But English will be the working language."

We were still quiet as we climbed back aboard, and not much was said as Travis took us to the inner surface, boarded us on the train, and we rolled back to the ship.

Everyone had a big decision to make.

THERE CAME A time when all the decisions had been made.

All the preparations had been made. All the people we were interested in taking were loaded aboard, peacefully, timelessly sleeping. Everything that we could afford had been bought and stored away.

Travis was broke. I was broke. Neither of us cared. I was glad to be shut of the money, to tell you the truth. There had been far more of it than I could ever have used, my tastes being fairly simple.

I did one last tour, going only to Martian locations, saying good-bye to the planet of my birth. It was no secret that I was leaving. There was no resentment, no hard feelings. Most of the people in the audience were related to someone or knew someone who was going with us. I donated all the proceeds to Earth rescue operations. Soon, no ships would be going to Earth at all. They would have to fend for themselves.

So there came a time . . .

WE WERE ALL assembled on the village green, of the village that still had no name. None of them did, they were just Village 1 or Village 20; there hadn't been time for frivolities. Places were going to be named by the people who lived in them after we made sure the place wasn't going to fall apart. They were mostly in suspended storage now. The asteroid that had become *Rolling Thunder* was sturdy rock, through and through, but acceleration was going to stress it.

No bands played, though there was food and drink. It was not a festive occasion. You might have expected Travis to be excited, pumped by the culmination of this long project, but he was gloomy, almost despondent. For once, it was Jubal who had to try to cheer him up, not the other way around.

"We're leaving with our tails between our legs," he moaned at one point. Travis hates to lose, and he hates to run.

"No, *cher,* no. We doing the smart thing. We seen how dangerous a place can get, practically overnight. We need to be other places, too."

Travis knew he was right, logically—hell, he was the one who started this thing in the first place. But logic doesn't always mesh with emotion. Some part of Travis really did think he *was* Superman, or at least he ought to be, or the combination of his daring and Jubal's brains should be. And Superman never ran from a fight. He never gave up. He never lost.

And he lived in a comic book.

There was the traditional countdown. Though it was hardly necessary, I saw people bracing themselves as the clock neared zero. I realized I was doing the same thing. Travis was sitting at a control console, and we were all watching from a drone camera about a mile away, focused on the stern of *Rolling Thunder.* At zero, the scene lit up. Eight fantastically bright lights in a circle around the axis of rotation, balanced around the center of mass, began to shove the huge rock. These were the bubble engines, powered by the unimaginably compressed rock excavated from the asteroid. There was enough energy in those bubbles and the many others aboard to keep firing for ten thousand years. Total mass/energy conversion is a frightening thing, if you do the math with the good old $E=mc^2$. Nuclear bombs only release a small fraction of the energy in matter. Bubbles convert it *all,* but luckily for us, they could do it a little at a time.

We felt nothing at first. You don't want to hit a big rock like *Rolling Thunder* with a croquet mallet; you want to ease it forward. But gradually we began to feel a shift beneath our feet. The rock was still rotating, of course, providing two-thirds of a gee, and it always would rotate. But now we were getting another thrust vector. The ground that had formerly had a slight slope to it now became level.

"Point oh five gees," Travis announced. "One-twentieth of a gravity. It may take us a while, but we'll get there."

By "there," he meant near-light speed. Jubal explained it to me, how it doesn't really matter how fast you accelerate, as long as you can do it forever. It just keeps building and building and building; why be in a hurry? If we boosted at one gee, we'd have to have decks perpendicular to the axis of thrust. This way, we got all our serious "gravity" from the spin, and a little extra at right angles from the thrust.

Once you reached a big fraction of light speed—you could never actually reach it, according to relativity, and confirmed to me by my genius husband—it hardly mattered how far you were going, unless you were planning on coming back. Time would slow down relative to the rest of the universe, and the miles would just race by. A thousand-light-year trip wouldn't take much longer than a ten-light-year trip. Of course, there would be a lot of changes if you went back to Earth . . .

There were thousands of strain gauges throughout the rock beneath us, and soon the computers reported that all was well. No cracking, hardly any bending. They estimated that we could pile on ten times the acceleration and still have a nice safety margin.

I'd asked Travis at one point why he had decided on two-thirds gee for the centrifugal gravity.

"I don't want to get there with a bunch of weak-legged Martians," he said, and grinned when I scowled at him. "I know you'd prefer Martian gravity, but we have no idea what our new planet will mass. It might be a bit more than one gee—but not a lot, I don't want us all to get hernias—or it might be less, in which case we'll all be the stronger for it."

Which made sense, but I didn't have to like it. I'd been thinking about getting another bra—I'm sure Travis has some somewhere, probably the low-cut, push-up kind—but Jubal doesn't think it's necessary. I'll defer to his judgment, for now.

When Travis was sure the multiple computers had the situation well in hand—as if they had needed his guidance at all—he moved to another console, which controlled all the interior machinery. Again, computers would handle it, but they needed him to push a button first.

"Here we go, folks," he said. "Let's hope this works."

I didn't see what could go wrong. It was just pumps, and they were brand-new and thoroughly tested, though quite large. They were Martian-made, and we Martians know a lot about pumps.

We all looked to the "north," which was the bow of the big ship. Mountains had been sculpted all around the hollow hemisphere at that end, a ring of mountains where pine trees grew. Some of the mountains were half a mile high, and would make for good hiking. The higher you went, the lighter you'd get! Now water began to gush from some of them, and flow down their sides, slowly at first, then faster as it moved into regions of higher gravity. By the time the streams reached the surface, they were going over waterfalls, sections of white water, deep pools. We'd be putting trout in there.

Over a few hours the method behind the system of cliffs built into the floor became apparent. There were depressions where lakes formed, then the stream would dash or trickle over the low cliffs and into a new environment. There were three rivers moving slowly south, filling in low areas as they went. We'd have to name them soon. There was going to be a *lot* of naming going on. We watched them brim over, getting closer and closer to us, and we all walked a short distance to where a wooden mill had been built over a dry creek bed paved with natural rock. Inside the millhouse was a real grinding stone, and outside was a big wheel. We would make flour there. Travis figured we all needed to learn "rural skills," though I'd believe he was willing to lend a hand at tasks like that when I saw it.

The water came flowing down, and soon the streambed became a burbling brook, and the big wheel began to turn. Something about it made my city girl's heart swell. I felt Jubal hug my waist, and I knew he felt it, too. My eyes teared up, then I was applauding, along with everybody else.

We were under way.

***ROLLING THUNDER* IS** a living, breathing organism. Each day I'm struck by its incredible beauty, not just around me, not just in the distance, but overhead!

There were forests. There were "mountains." Quiet streams and rushing rivers. I quite liked it. Jubal and I had picked out a home in the little tin-roof town built out on stilts in a marshy area where bullfrogs the size of house cats filled the evening with their song.

Every few days Kahlua would bring in a brightly colored songbird and lay it solemnly at my feet. Yuck! But I guess it's the thought that counts. There were no mice, no rats. We had them in storage—never know what you might need!—but I hoped they remained in the category of mosquitoes: Got 'em, don't want to use 'em.

We did have June bugs and other insects deemed essential to the ecology. I was slowly getting to the point where I didn't freak out every time one landed on me. Jubal even had me handling one for a short time.

Everybody was calling the town Jubalville, over Jubal's protests. He wanted to call it New Lafayette.

We're getting to know our neighbors, who are either unimpressed by Jubal's great brain and my notoriety, or are damn good at acting that way. Which is fine with me. Baako lives two doors down from us. The other night we had a crawfish boil. Baako and I sang *"Allon à Lafayette"* and other numbers appropriate to the setting. I've learned about a hundred words of Cajun French and can almost make a sentence.

As the central light pole dims—our equivalent of nightfall—I can still see tractors halfway up the slope tilling soil for corn planting. A little to the south is an orchard, with both full-grown trees, brought here intact and transplanted, and seedlings. Apparently I'm going to learn to farm. I'm going to be a farmer in the sky. A singing farmer, but a farmer nonetheless. Not what I had set out to be, but life takes some strange twists. I've found I enjoy tending our little patch of garden out back. I'll enjoy it even more if I conquer my horror of earthworms. You should taste my tomatoes. To die for!

SINCE IT *IS* a living, breathing organism, *Rolling Thunder* is subject to both the joys and sorrows of the human condition. To everything there is a season. A time to plant and a time to uproot. A time to mourn and a time to dance. A time to weep and a time to laugh. A time to die, a time to be born.

Turn, turn, turn.

A TIME TO die . . .

We woke Gran Betty on Mars before most of the family settled down in the ship. We gave her a condensed version of the horrors of the last ten years, but she was no fool. She understood how bad it really was. When told *Rolling Thunder* would depart in a few weeks, she asked to be put back in the bubble and then awakened again when we got moving. When she came out again she surprised us all.

"I'm not going in again," she said, to the assembled family of which she was the matriarch.

"But Mama . . ." Granddaddy Manny said.

"Hush, son. They didn't figure out how to cure what I've got in ten years, right? And Travis, be honest with me. How much advanced medical research is going to be happening in this big old rock?"

"Well, Elizabeth is aboard, and—"

"I said be honest, you old bastard."

"Practically none," he admitted.

"I thought so. Y'all are going to be too busy making a living, and that's as it should be. I think I've already lived my allotted time. That's what it feels like, anyway. I don't want to wake up in a few hundred years to find all y'all are my age or dead. I'm going to let nature take its course."

And that's what she did. She died a week later, sitting in a rocking chair on my front porch, Manny and Kelly at her side, a lot of heroin coursing through her veins and a fat joint handy in an ashtray. Letting nature take its course didn't mean you had to die in agony.

Her last words to us were spoken with a smile as she looked up at the bountiful land arching over her head. With the last of her strength, she lifted her hand to it.

"Look at this, children," she whispered. "Not bad for a little girl from Florida. I was born before men walked on the moon, and I've gone from running a cheap motel to traveling on a starship. I wish I could get there with you."

"You'll be there with us, Mama," Manny said.

"In spirit. In spirit. I'm so happy."

An hour later she was gone. It was the second time I ever saw Grandma Kelly cry.

A TIME TO be born . . .

Four months into the journey, Marlee gave birth to a perfect little boy. I guess all fathers are proud, but Mike seemed ready to explode with pride. He makes light of his short stature, and I tease him mercilessly about it because I know that's the way he wants it, but I know it hurts. It would hurt on Earth, and it's worse on Mars, where I'm considered only slightly tall for my sex. Being a father was important to him.

I'm sitting on my front porch, alone, babysitting. Mike and Marlee are off somewhere learning about pruning fruit trees, I think, then they plan to have dinner together in a restaurant that just opened up a few miles from here. I look after little William once a week so they can have some time alone, baby-rearing being a sometimes stressful job. I don't mind.

William is three months old, gurgling at me, his tiny brown hand gripping my finger tightly.

I'm a little distracted, wondering when is the best time to tell Jubal I'm pregnant.

Oh, yeah, I know what I said before. But I never really ruled out having babies, did I? Jubal and I had never talked about it, but we didn't have to. There was just something about Jubal that told me it would be the best news he'd ever received. So I wasn't worried about that, not a bit.

I'd had another girl-to-girl talk with my vagina.

ME: Yeah, I know Marlee opted for that "natural childbirth" nonsense. Never saw so much sweating and hollering in my life. And the blood!

MS. V: Yeah, and what about *me*?

ME: All you have to do is handle the fertilization part, and I *know* you like that.

MS.V: Well, sure, but . . .

ME: No buts. They can cut it out. Doesn't even leave a scar anymore.

MS. V: Now you're talking! Let's get fertilizing!

So I stopped taking my birth control, and my reinstalled ovaries did their egg-dropping thing, and Jubal's little wigglers did their thing with their usual enthusiasm. And here I am, three months gone, puking every other morning, just almost, sort of, beginning to show, and looking at myself in the mirror every morning to see if I have that fabled motherly glow. No sign of it yet. Aunt Elizabeth is the only one who knows so far, and she says everything is looking very good, and that's after about a hundred tests.

So, now, when to tell Jubal? See, he's sleeping . . .

NOTHING IS EVER going to entirely solve the age problem between us, if problem it be, which I don't concede. But life aboard *Rolling Thunder* is going to be different, *very* different in a lot of ways. Consider black bubble hibernation.

The star we're headed for doesn't really have a name, just a catalog number. I don't know how Travis's panel of astronomers chose it, except that the giant telescopes on Luna confirm there's a planet circling it at about the right distance from the star, and it definitely has water and oxygen. I am not going to name the star because Travis asked us all never to do that. He's worried someone might still come after Jubal, and I can't say he's wrong. So, we're not currently aimed at that star; we're going to change course a bit as soon as we're comfortably out of the range of telescopes.

But the trip is going to take about forty years. That's ship's time; I don't know how much time will pass back home, but it will be a lot more.

There are some people aboard who would be perfectly happy to spend that entire time awake and working. Maybe they'll be allowed to; that hasn't been worked out yet. But most of us will be spending greater or lesser amounts of time in hibernation. No one will be spending *all* their time in a bubble. Part of the signing agreement is that everyone gets a little time outside, though with the last, relatively unskilled ones rounded up more or less to provide strong backs, a population base, and genetic diversity when we land, that time will be short, a few weeks here and there to stretch their legs, as it were.

Others—skilled workers, administrators, engineers, and "friends of the captain," which means my family and Travis's friends—will be out for longer periods. We friends will be able to choose what we want to do. I know, unfair, but it's his boat and he gets to make the rules. Travis is the Supreme Captain of *Rolling Thunder*, and though we are forming a civilian government (with Grandma Kelly in the thick of it), his word is the final law. That's always the way it's worked on ships, and I wouldn't change it.

Jubal and I don't plan to spend the next forty years awake. He'd likely be dead before we ever reached the new star.

We had tentatively worked out a schedule for the first few years, though. I was going to stay awake, and he would sleep three weeks out of every four. I'd be gaining ground on him, age-wise, at a ratio of four to one. I'd never catch him, but this plan would mean he would be gone for three weeks—which I knew I could handle—and then I'd have him for a week. He'd have me all the time, by his clock. At some point we'd both go into hibernation for five or ten years, then reassess when we came out.

The baby was going to disrupt that plan, but that was okay. I expected to stay awake until I gave birth, then Jubal and I would talk it over. My preference would be to stay awake another four or five years, and I fully expected Jubal would want to do the same, so the child could grow up with both of us. Then we could all three hibernate for a while, and decide how much time to stay awake until we got to our destination. I was thinking we should give the child enough awake time—with both of us, of course—so that he or she (don't know yet, and don't care) would be almost grown when we arrived. Say fourteen or fifteen waking years, out of forty ship's years.

I know it sounds weird. Everything about black bubbles is weird, and that's only part of it.

With the majority of the people aboard spending a lot of time in suspension, we were all going to get slightly out of synch, except for "friends," who would be able to choose to hibernate in a group and thus remain about the same age, relative to each other. Our family had already talked about it, and had some tentative plans. Again, the baby might throw that a little out of whack, but we'll figure it out.

For most people the dislocation could be a bit more severe. Everybody was going to be going by two clocks: internal time and calendar time. (Don't even *think* about back-in-the-solar-system time, you'll make my head hurt.) Of course, we're not going to separate families temporally, but you might not always be awake at the same time as all your friends.

Our hope was that the little interior world of *Rolling Thunder* wasn't going to be too exciting. Excitement we didn't need, because it almost always meant trouble. We were hoping for bucolic, even boring, at least in comparison to the last decade. We were hoping that the biggest events would be more in the nature of gossip. Who's going with whom, who just had a baby, who got married, who died. How Farmer John's pigs broke into Farmer Fran's rose garden and rooted it up. What went on at the square dance, the town meeting, the football game, whose prize heifer won the blue ribbon at the Rolling Fair. Nice rural stuff that had kept rural folk satisfied for thousands of years. That way, bringing the newly awakened up to speed wouldn't be lengthy or too traumatic. Just hand them a big file of newspapers and let them read for a while.

But I could imagine conversations in the coming years.

"Were you awake when . . ."

"I've been sleeping the last six years . . ."

"I'm twenty-five internal years, forty-one calendar . . ."

"What year were you born, and how old are you?"

It was likely to be confusing, but I thought we'd adjust.

Travis seemed confident that we would. He was still awake, but soon he planned to go on a fifty-one-weeks-off, one-week-on schedule. He had three subcommanders who he trusted who would take care of ship's business while he slept. Then he'd wake up and get brought up to date, do a stem-to-stern inspection, savor being lord of all he surveyed, then go back into a bubble.

Sounded like a good plan to me. Most of us couldn't take Travis for more than a week at a time, anyway.

THERE WAS A possibility, small but real, because you never knew with Jubal, that we wouldn't *have* to adjust. That somewhere along the way Jubal would figure out the new problem he was working on.

"I been studyin'," he had told me, before he went into the bubble again . . . still chanting his Hail Mary. When Jubal starts "studyin'," I prick up my ears. Not that I'll understand what he's studyin' about, but so I can take it to a physicist and see if there's anything useful in there. With Jubal's approval, of course; he knows he's way short in the practicality department.

"I been studyin' on it, and I got to wonderin' why we have to take so long to get to wherever it is we're goin'."

"Well . . . we can only go so fast. And we can't go faster than the speed of light. At least that's what you said."

"And it the truth, *cher*. But maybe we don't have to go no speed at all, and don't have to go nowheres at all. Maybe we can bring the somewheres to us."

"You've lost me."

"I been studyin' it since we got connected in the no-place place. We been there, you and me, and we know that everythin', it be in contact with everythin' else. We got tangled, like quantums. Didn't matter we were millions of miles apart. Wouldn't a mattered we been a billion light-years apart. We was touchin', see?"

"Mebbe." He had me doing his accent now.

"So I was wonderin', could we make a way to get from over *here* to over *there* without no time and no space. Mebbe we could make a sort of tunnel in the sky, pop right through that sucker, and save us a lot of time."

"That would be nice. Do you think you can do it?"

"I dunno, me. I'll study on it while I'm a-sleepin'. I think I do my best thinkin' while I'm sleepin' in the no-place place."

So there was really no telling but that the next time he woke up, Jubal might have a way to get us to the stars in an instant. I'm not holding my breath, but stranger things have happened around my husband.

MEANWHILE, WE WERE not out of contact with the folks back home, and wouldn't be for some years. Though the time lag is getting longer and longer . . .

Eventually the Doppler effect and the time dilation will make communication very interesting, but that's still a long way off. That's what happens as you approach the speed of light. The radio waves you're sending back to Mars get stretched out, and so do the ones coming at you. You start out broadcasting at a certain frequency but your message gets there on a lower one. Something to do with the red shift, I think. The engineers know how to cope with it, they say. Also, though our clocks on the ship will be running normally from our "frame of reference," if we compared them to clocks on Mars, they'd be running a lot slower. We won't notice a thing, but time will be stretching out.

I probably completely bumbled that explanation, but it gives you an idea.

So we still got news from back home. Most of it was bad. There were still people alive on Earth, perhaps millions of them, but we were in contact only by radio. Things were looking up on Mars, though. People were no longer living elbow to elbow, and the economy was thriving. They were entirely independent.

I just referred to Martians as "they," didn't I?

Well, it's true. I'll always have a soft spot in my heart for the planet of my birth, but I was no longer a Martian. I was a . . . what? A Roller? A Thunderite? I think of myself as a rolling stone. We're all rolling stones now.

How does it feel to be on your own? It feels pretty damn good, with a good man at my side.

And I still have a career. I write only for myself, but I perform in all the little clubs scattered around the interior. I've jammed with many other people, and we have some very talented musicians here. We have a famous trio, and we have a complete symphony orchestra, and everything in between. We have opera!

I send everything back to Mars, where Tina and Quinn elected to stay. I am still extremely popular, I'm still raking in the money at a fabulous rate, and Tina is distributing it all to charities as fast as I make it, minus her commission. It won't last, and I won't miss it, but it feels good to be making a difference, even this far away.

I'M SITTING IN a rocking chair of an evening on our back porch, which is over the big pond. Jubal is beside me, his hand resting on my belly. It's a warm night. It almost always is. Neither of us is wearing anything. My feet are up on the porch railing. I wiggle my toes. Hello, toes! I haven't seen you for months, when I'm standing up.

I look like I swallowed a friggin' pumpkin. You could drop a coin on my tummy and it would bounce halfway to the other side of the pond. My belly button is sticking out, and my breasts are full and a little sore. My back hurts, my ankles are swollen. I'm a week away from the Cesarean.

I've never been happier in my life.

We both have fishing lines hanging from cane poles propped on the porch railing. There are big, hungry catfish down there, and if we catch any, Jubal has promised to blacken up a mess of 'em. But neither of us much cares if we catch a fish.

Hard to believe this peaceful scene is hurtling outward from everything we've ever known at a speed I don't even like to think about, toward a destination still very much in doubt.

I know a story is not supposed to end this way, but my story is still a long ways from its end, I hope. Still, all those loose ends . . .

Did the crystals communicate with me? If they did, was it intentional, or just a side effect of being in the no-space they know like a fish knows water, and which is still largely mysterious to everyone but Jubal?

I don't know. Sorry.

What were the boojums? I don't know. Ask Lewis Carroll.

When we get to our new star, will we find the New Earth populated by people like us, or occupied by vast, slow, crystalline life-forms like Europans? Again, I don't know, but as Jubal pointed out, the crystals back home seem to only cause trouble every sixty million years or so, and only for a relatively short time. What are the chances we'd hit New Earth just as those crystals were doing their thing? The odds seemed pretty good for us, and if we do find a body like Europa with vast seas under thick ice, we'll damn well steer clear of it.

We now know two types of life. One is carbon-based, and much more vulnerable than we ever imagined. The other is crystalline, and totally alien to us. We never even managed to say howdy, as Jubal put it. Who knows what life-forms might be lurking beneath the clouds of Jupiter, or Saturn, or Neptune? We might never meet them, because we sure can't go down there to look.

If we're *lucky* we may never meet them. The last alien contact didn't go too well.

Who knows if creatures of billion-degree plasma might be frolicking in the center of the sun, like Jubal speculated? If they're there, I'm pretty sure we don't want to shake hands with them.

And what's the deal with my fainting episodes? I'm still having them, timed to some Jovian cycle, and we're a very long way from Europa. Will I still be having them when we're five light-years away? Twenty?

I don't know.

Why is Jubal the only person who can create a bubble maker, a Broussard Singularity? Is it because it's named after him?

Well . . . this time I'll share a little secret with you. Or part of it. Two days ago I was doing my mental concentration exercises. That's right, I was still doing them, trying to stare *through* some optical illusion Jubal thought might twist my brain in such a way that my brain could twist space, just a tad, just enough to make a pinch in space that could, in turn, fold space in a way that produced a squeezer bubble. I can't tell you what happened because I don't understand it myself, but suddenly it all fell into place. You know how you feel when you cross your eyes? Magnify that through the seventh or eighth dimension. Imagine crossing your third eye, your inner eye, falling into some Zen contemplative space—what is the sound of one hand clapping? How do you cross one eye?—where there is no space and no time . . . and then there it is. Floating above the picture you've been staring at, the most incredibly beautiful, incredibly minute, very frightening, tiny little whirlpool. An eddy in space.

Jubal nearly fainted. He did some things with some devices of his to trap it. I won't tell you what devices, or how he used them. Trade secret. I won't tell you what I was staring at. And I won't tell you if it takes a year of staring, half an hour a day, like I did, either, because I don't know, but I wouldn't tell you if I did know.

Did it really have to do with having been inside a black bubble? If it does, then there are many millions of people who might be able to do it now, given proper guidance. I don't think we're ready for that. Or did it have to be a black bubble in close proximity to the Europan crystals, such that one became "tangled" with Jubal's mind?

Don't know that, either.

Then there's probably the biggest question of all. Why didn't any of the old starships come back? We will probably find out, one of these days. Is it because of some new force we aren't aware of, some interstellar factor we're not taking into account? Dark matter? Dark energy? Something we haven't even postulated yet?

Is there some sort of malevolent Galactic Empire out of a bad science-fiction novel our ships fell afoul of? If so, why haven't they come for us?

Is it something even stranger? We know now that the universe is a stranger place than we had ever imagined. We've always known that man is a very small, very delicate animal. We need conditions within an extremely small set of parameters to survive in this hostile universe at all. If we can't find them on a planet like Earth, we have to re-create them on a planet like Mars, or in an artifact like *Rolling Thunder*. And now we know how easily those parameters can be upset on a planetary scale. We were learning about it even *before* the catastrophe, because what was global warming but Europan-style planetary engineering in slow motion?

Rolling Thunder is even more vulnerable. If Earth is a tiny grain of sand circling a pinpoint of light and heat, *Rolling Thunder* is a molecule rushing through spaces so vast and so hostile it doesn't bear imagining. When you think about it, it hardly seems we have a chance. We *are* fleeing, after all; this is not a triumphant voyage but a hasty retreat. Travis was right about that. We can't even kid ourselves that we put up a good fight. Stories of alien invasion aren't *supposed* to end that way, you know. In the end, we've always assumed humanity would triumph.

Aha! Water kills the alien creatures!

Thank God, we're saved, the aliens—Martians!—were killed by the common cold virus!

Didn't happen that way, not in this story, not in Podkayne's story.

So do we have a chance? I don't know, but I'll tell you what we *do* have.

We have Manny Garcia and Kelly Strickland, who with Travis and Jubal and two friends built and flew the first interplanetary ship to Mars and back.

We have Jim Redmond, my grand-père, Evangeline Redmond, my mother, and Elizabeth and Ray Strickland-Garcia, who with Travis entered the Red Zone right after the Big Wave and brought Gran out alive, and then Mom and Dad and Travis fought off a fleet of Black Ships and brought the Planet Earth to its knees.

We have the spirit of Betty Garcia, who held off looters and saved about a hundred survivors while waiting for Mom and Dad to get there.

We have Jubal Broussard, quite possibly the smartest living human, and Travis Broussard, possibly the gutsiest. Sometimes the most obnoxious.

I'll put that crew up against any Galactic Empire.

And we have thousands of people I haven't even met yet living and working in this big rock, and many thousands more hibernating.

I'm not worried.

KAHLUA HAS JUST jumped up and settled himself on my belly. He's staring suspiciously downward, where the babies—twin girls!—just tried to kick him off. These kids are either going to be black belts in karate or world-class dancers. I'll try to steer them toward dance.

Something's tugging on my line. I may have to land the damn thing. Blackened catfish à la Jubal sounds mighty good, but pulling on that line sounds a little too much like work. Life is so hard.

THERE IS A time for everything, a season for everything.

A time for traveling, a time for settling down. We've managed to do both at the same time.

I'm going to miss my home, the Red Planet. But now I'm between planets.

Now it's time for the stars.